CASE of the MISSING DICK

a fu chan mystery

by jUlie aNN cArvER

Published by

A division of d+2

Copyright 2013

Okay, in truth, some of my close friends agreed to let me name a few of the characters after them. They even liked the idea. I don't think they knew what they were getting into but these people have contributed to my life and this book in so many ways. All I can say is thank you for your encouragement and support.

"Ding-Dong! The Witch Is Dead" Copyright 1939 by Metro-Goldwyn-Meyer

Manufactured in the United States of America

Case of the Missing Dick
Fiction, Mystery

ISBN 978-1-58884-004-2

Chapter 1

Deadly Embrace

Richard Sooka awoke slowly, the pain and pressure in his gut forcing him to breathe shallow and quick. He tried to turn but was he held in place by some immovable force. His feet hurt, pinched into a painful position that he could not change. He wiggled his toes, glad to feel the sensation as they pressed against something cold and leathery. He heard that if you could move your toes it was a good sign that nothing was broken.

Spasms of lights blinked on and off but it took him a minute to realize that they were coming from inside his mind. The room was still dark. He tried to think. The last thing he remembered was going to bed and drifting peacefully to sleep. He dreamed he was scuba diving, floating weightless in a sea of alien creatures. Then this.

He moved his hand to his face to rub the sleep from his eyes. They felt funny, bound tightly inside some kind of glove. His hands were balled into fists and he couldn't unclench them. He wished he could see them in the darkness. He raised them to his cheek, brushing an itch he felt there.

He screamed. It was as if the glove were coated with sharp fragments of broken glass. It cut his face and he could taste the blood dripping past his lips. He worried about how big the gash on his cheek would be.

"Oh God," he moaned. "What's going on?"

There was no answer. God had deserted him.

He tried to move again, struggling with something unseen that kept him held tightly in place. He could tell that he was standing up, his calves ached with the effort and he longed for relief. He began to panic, his short breath becoming even shorter. He tried to use his forearm to wipe away an itch that was building near his ear. He let out another scream. There was a razor blade embedded in the gauntlet of the glove and he had just cut himself again. He wanted to cover the wound and stop the flow of blood but he didn't dare. What other damage might he do?

There was a whirring sound, something mechanical and pneumatic. He felt constricted, his lungs compressing until they could hold no air. His breath quickened again, lights in his brain telling him he needed oxygen. His sides hurt as something pressed against his ribs. He wanted to call on God again but he couldn't find the breath to speak. It came out as a whimper, hoarse and raspy as a dying breath.

"Help me."

Chapter 2

Money Problems

"Thank you, Mrs. Lee. I'm glad I could find your daughter. We were lucky."

Harry leaned forward, elbows on the desk, the phone pressed to his chin, his hands clasping his head. He did not accept praise easily. He knew he did a good thing, he just wished people wouldn't remind him of it.

"No. no, Mrs. Lee. You don't owe me anything," he said, his voice trailing off. The door in front of him opened and in walked a man twice as wide as he was tall, and this guy barely had room to get in. "I gotta go, Mrs. Lee," he said. "No, no. You don't owe me anything."

Fat Farnsworth cleared the door and stood aside, glaring at Harry as if he were dinner.

"Okay, Mrs. Lee. I'll settle for a plate of your special kway teow." Harry twisted in his chair. "Of course invite Sue. Thursday? Sure." He slowly pulled the receiver away from his cheek. Fat Farnsworth stood like a Marine, respectful and at attention. A small, squat man came through the door. He was wearing dark clothes, black pants with a black shirt covered with a black sport coat. When he smiled, his eyes looked black, as empty as promises on prom night.

Harry inched the phone towards the cradle. He could hear Mrs. Lee chirping away in the distance as he stood. "Gotta go, Mrs. Lee." He let the phone drop to the cradle.

"Good to see you, Fu," said the dark man.

"You, too," said Harry, extending his hand in greeting. The dark man looked at Harry's hand as if it were a wet garden hose.

"Really?" said the man. "Are you really glad to see me?"

Harry dropped his hand, his eyes moving towards the floor.

"You know what day this is, don't you?" said the man.

"The fifth," said Harry.

"What day?" asked the man, his face at an angle as he studied Harry through his left eye.

"The fifth," said Harry, a little louder and more sure this time.

The dark man stood erect, smiling and proud as if Harry had just passed his college board exam.

"So," he said. "You have anything for me?"

Harry began to sweat. Rent was due. He wondered why he ever took this deal. Binky was not only his landlord, he was a loan shark. Eight years on the police force should have taught him some common sense, but Harry was still trying to figure things out. It was time to back paddle.

"Not right now, Binky. Maybe by sunset? I got the rest of the day, don't I?"

The dark man nodded to Fat Farnsworth. Harry was suddenly pinned to the desk, his arm stretched behind his back. Fat Farnsworth leaned forward, pressing his weight on top of Harry. The desk creaked and Harry winced. Binky walked over calmly and removed the wallet from Harry's back pocket. He explored the contents, finding fifty dollars amid a slew of receipts and scraps of papers. He threw everything on the desk except for the money which he held up for Harry to see before folding it and placing in his pocket.

"Hey! That's my last fifty bucks," said Harry. Fat Farnsworth slammed his head into the desk.

Binky stepped back. "Then I'm sorry to hear that, Fu," he said. "I had hoped for more from you."

"That's all I got," said Harry.

Binky turned his back to him, talking to the wall and the empty doorway. "Didn't I just hear you refuse payment from a customer?" he asked.

"Come on, Binky. That was Mrs. Lee. I was helping an old friend. Sue went to school with us," he said. "Remember?"

"Still, Fu. This is not the talk of the entrepreneur to whom I rented this office."

Harry relaxed, the tension falling from his body. "You're right," he said.

Fat Farnsworth looked up. There was no more resistance in his prey. The dark man turned and nodded. Harry winced as Fat Farnsworth drove his elbow further into his back.

"What are we going to do about that, Fu?" said Binky, slow and clear. "Entrepreneurs are motivated, Fu. Give him some more motivation." Fat Farnsworth leaned forward and Harry groaned.

There was a noise at the door. Farnsworth and Binky lost focus on Harry and looked away. Harry twisted his head to see a big, blocky woman at the door. She had freckles and a close crop of red hair. Her arms and legs were pudgy, but there was muscle beneath her skin. She had a warm smile and clear blue eyes that sparkled like gems. It made him smile despite his predicament.

"I'm here about the job," said the woman. Silence. Everyone stared at her as if she had just asked them for directions to China. "The detective trainee job?" she said, trying to sound confident.

She considered herself a smart woman, but she often found herself in awkward situations. It seemed to be her lot in life, and this was one of those situations. A light came on. It was as if she saw the office for the first time. Harry pressed into the desk, an odd smile on his face. Fat Farnsworth bent on top of him, holding his arms as if they were lovers, and this small dark man staring at her with empty eyes that said she didn't belong here. "Is this a bad time?" she asked.

Harry spoke up. "You get this monkey off my back and you got the job."

The woman smiled, the gems in her eyes sparkling. Her hands came up to her chest, flexing as she slid through the doorway. Her legs stretched sideways into a fighter's stance as she moved towards the center of the room. Binky stepped back, the darkness in his eyes turning to terror. Fat Farnsworth released Harry, squaring off in front of her. Harry stood up, one arm rubbing his neck, the other his back.

The woman smiled at him. "Well, he's off you. Does this mean I get the job?" she asked.

"Not quite yet," said Fat Farnsworth. He leered at her as he moved between her and Harry.

"Look," said Harry, addressing the dark man. "We're old friends, you and I. We go way back, Binky. Give me a break here."

The beasts stared at each other like two junkyard dogs ready to pounce. The sparkling eyes were now hard diamonds, charged with electricity. She ran her fingers through her hair causing it to rankle. Farnsworth bared his teeth, his eyes narrow and observant. He rocked back and forth, pacing in front of her like a nervous cat.

Binky saw the danger. "Steady boy," he said. "Behave. The two of you. Go over there and become friends while I talk to my old buddy Harry here." The way he said it implied that they were not old friends. The animals didn't move but they appeared to be breathing slower. No foam at the mouth. He turned his attention to Harry. "Look, you see my point. I give you this place. Reasonable rent. No security deposit. I don't even ask for first and last month's rent up front. And how do you repay this favor from an *old friend*? You get a month behind."

"Give me a break, Binky. Please. Give me some time to build my business. I'm just getting started here. I haven't landed my big case yet."

"Big case?" asked Binky.

"The one that makes my name. You know. For Bogart it was finding that falcon. For Sherlock Holmes it was beating Moriarty. I need time to crack my big case. Make a name for myself in the business. You understand. I told you all this before."

"This doesn't help me get my money. I have bills too, you know." Binky seemed human for a moment, almost understanding. "Harry," he said. "If I let you get away with this nobody will respect me."

"Then tell them I paid you."

"It doesn't work that way, friend."

There were some grunts as Fat Farnsworth and the blocky woman reminded them they were still in the room.

"Give me a couple of days, Binky," he pleaded. "I got some skip traces I'm working for Lenny. I got a jealous woman wanting me to follow her husband. I got two cases of identity theft to work. I got a possible insurance fraud. You know how that works. I get in good with an insurance company and I'm on easy street. See? I got money coming."

Silence.

The dark man reached into his back pocket, pulling out a newspaper. He unfolded it carefully, holding it forward for Harry to clasp. The headlines were clear beneath the Seattle Times banner. Top Designer Kidnapped. Prize Dress Missing. A smaller headline below said Reward Offered.

Harry took the paper.

"I'll give you another day, Harry. Don't disappoint me." The dark man gave a sideways glance to Fat Farnsworth who continued to stare at the blocky woman.

"Maybe I'll get the chance to try you one day," said Farnsworth.

"I'd like that," said the woman.

The dark man snapped his fingers. Fat Farnsworth slowly moved towards the door.

"Good dog," said the woman.

The dark man glared at Fat Farnsworth, a signal for him to hurry it along. Then he turned to the woman. "Good luck working for this sap," he said. "Piece of advice: Get your money up front."

"Let me worry about that," said the woman.

The dark man nodded slowly, first to the woman then to Harry, then he turned and passed through the doorway. Fat Farnsworth scanned the room as if it were Christmas, a smile pasted as wide as his face. He slowly shut the door behind him.

Silence again. Awkward. The big woman looked at Harry. Her weight shifted from one foot to the other.

"So," she finally said. "Do I get the job?"

Chapter 3

The Big Squeeze

Richard Sooka could breathe again. He stayed focused, taking quick, shallow breaths, trying not to panic. He knew if he had another attack of spasms it may be his last. His sides ached and his legs began to tremor. Why was this happening to him?

Light flooded into the room and Richard closed his eyes tightly. They watered and he resisted the urge to wipe them, remembering the deadly gloves on his hands. He squeezed them shut hoping to push the tears away with his eyelids. Through blurred vision he began to see his surroundings.

He stood before a mirror, not more than a foot or two away from him. His cheek was wet with blood and an open gash dripped thick red streams down his neck. He was encased in some kind of strange garment, a corset of some kind that was mounted in a framework of metal and tethered with wires and tubes to a wall panel behind him. It was a ghastly pink color, all decorated with needless flourish and décolleté. He could have done such a better job with it. He was a world famous designer after all.

His face scrunched in displeasure. "Ghastly," he said.

There was a hiss from behind him, the sound of pneumatic pressure, gears and levers engaging. The corset wrapped itself tighter around Richard's waist.

"Aghhh," he groaned as his breath was pressed out of him. He couldn't inhale. His face flushed red with anguish, his eyes bulged. Just as he thought he was going to faint he started gasping, short staccato breaths that pulled every bit of air that he could into his lungs. He grew dizzy, his head teetering forward.

There was another hiss and the pressure on his lungs went away as the corset loosened. He continued to gasp uncontrollably, his body hyperventilating as he tried to catch his breath. He wanted to grab his throat but the gleaming razor blades in the gloves reminded him to keep still. He saw what had caused the scars on his cheek. The gloves were serrated on the back of his balled fists with holes like a cheese grater. There was also a design, glittery and glamorous, glistening like sequins, but made with sharp, broken pieces of glass. Razor blades were embedded in the gauntlets making his forearms just as deadly.

His breath slowed, almost to normal. He stared into the mirror, looking down at his feet. He was perched in a pair of impossibly high heels, worse than any sadomasochistic ballet boots he had ever seen. He didn't care that they matched the color of the corset perfectly. They were thigh length, yellow laces running up the sides, ending at the top in perfectly tied bows. Glittery pink stockings popped from the tops, attached to the corset with garters that hung beneath apron frills.

His crotch was left bare. The hair had been shaved clean and it tingled around his flaccid penis. He noticed a wire clipped beneath his foreskin, terminating at a panel on the wall behind him with the other wires and hoses connected to the corset. He looked at the odd looking curlers in his hair, more wires running to the panel behind him. His hair was wet. His mouth dropped, unable to voice what he was seeing. He thought of a prisoner strapped to the electric chair, wondering if he had been shaved for the same reason. He began to imagine what it would be like to have an electric charge run up your penis and out your skull.

He saw himself in the mirror. He screamed something primal, the sound of a trapped animal. He shook from side to side, swung his arms around like limp bags. He tried to stomp his feet. The corset held strong in its mounted framework. He started to sob. Emotions played across his face like clouds moving in a hurricane, a sampling of all the worst that could happen to a man. Fear, anger, futility, pain, hopelessness, anxiety. There was blood trickling down his cheek from a wound he couldn't even touch. More fear, images of death, despair.

On the other side of the mirror a man sat in the shadows. He watched Sooka, savoring every twitch, every tear, every bit of Richard's torment. He swiveled his chair around, reaching out to twist a nearby knob.

Richard looked away from the mirror. He couldn't stand seeing himself anymore. The mirror began to shimmer. His image faded before him, turning into a dark wall. The lights above him dimmed. He realized he was behind a wall of one way glass. Slowly, lights on the other side of the glass began to glisten. It revealed an office. He was elevated in a window behind a desk. The chair sat with its back to him, the drawer next to it open revealing a bank of switches, knobs, and levers. It was a nice office, rich and opulent, full of polished wood and leather. Thick carpet adorned the floor. On the opposite wall there was a door to one side and a large painting mounted in the center above an expensive couch and a reclining lounge chair.

He stared at the painting and thought he saw movement. Again he wanted to clear his eyes but he remembered the cheese graters on the back of his hands. What would it be like to rub your eyes with glass embedded sandpaper? He thought about it as he continued to stare at the painting.

Then he noticed that it wasn't a painting, it was a mirror, textured in a gold pattern that made it look like dark Italian marble. The movement continued, reflecting the swivel of the chair at the desk in front of him. As it turned, shadows crept across the face until it became clear who was behind all this. Richard drew a sharp breath and his eyes bulged.

"You recognize me," said a voice, clear and controlled with all the venom of a cobra poised for the strike.

"You!" gasped Richard, his voice coming out like a hasp shaving pieces of wood off a block. His breath became panicked again, short pumps of air that brought no relief.

"That's all you have to say?" said the voice. "You were never at a loss for words before, Richard. Or shall I call you Dick?"

Richard hated that name, hated being called that. "It's," gasp, pause, gasp, "Rich-ard," he said.

"No. It's Dick. Dick Sucker."

"Soo-ka," he replied, gasped in two syllables.

A hand reached for the bank of switches in the open drawer of the desk. The compression started again and Richard stopped breathing. His head slumped forward, his eyes pleading with his tormentor. The man in the shadows watched until he saw enough to satisfy him for now. He was toying with his prey and it promised to be a long night. Mustn't speed things along too quickly. He twisted a knob and the pressure stopped. He moved his hand away from the desk drawer.

"Don't worry, Dick. I'm not going to kill you without giving you a fighting chance," said the man.

"I'm..." He tried to continue but he couldn't breathe.

"Something to say?" said the man in the chair. "Here. Let me help you." The hand went back to the drawer and the panels behind Richard hissed again. There was relief as the pressure around his midsection went away. He fought to breathe again, sweet tasty air filling the deeper pockets of his lungs.

The man stared at Richard through the glass, a wry smile across his face. It was like seeing a tourist stare at a chimpanzee in the zoo.

After a long silence, Richard asked, "What do you want?"

The silence seemed to go on, and Richard asked again, "What do you want?"

The man drew a deep breath. "I thought it was obvious. I want you to die."

Richard's eyes watered again, tears blurring his vision, pouring out like a river of fear across the landscape of his life.

"First, I want you to know pain. Let's play a game I like to call Shock the Monkey." He touched a button in the drawer and Richard writhed in agony, his worst fears becoming reality. The electric current ran up his penis and out through his head. He could feel waves of tingling electricity wash across his body. His muscles jerked, his brain was on fire. He wanted to scream but his mouth would not move.

Richard's captor played with the voltage, adjusting it through a control in the desk drawer. He had another control that changed the current. He made careful observations of Richard's movements, as if he were a research scientist. He would jerk more with high current. There seemed to be an adjustment where the subject was docile, as if nothing were happening. Close observations of the eyes contradicted this, however.

Perhaps mental and somatic responses were reacting differently. Certainly the eyes reflected some kind of inner torment.

He flipped a switch. His experiments with electricity were over. He had learned over the years that too much electricity can fry his subjects, and after that they weren't much fun. Not at all.

He let Sooka recover for a minute. He walked over to the window for a closer look.

"Richard," he called through the glass.

Sooka lay limp, propped up by the garment and a series of braces.

"Richard!" Still no response. "Look, Richard. You've wet yourself, all over my nice floor. Now I have another mess to clean up."

Limp Richard moaned a little, then spittle poured out of his mouth.

"Well, if that's the way it's going to be, well, might as well get this over with and go back to work." He got up and went to a microwave on the other side of the room. He removed something from it and returned to the desk. He pulled a cool drink from a nearby dorm refrigerator and sat back in his chair.

Richard was aware of what was happening. He watched his tormentor's hand move towards a switch in the drawer of the desk. The hiss of pneumatics and the awful pressure began again. Richard tried to scream but his vocal chords needed air to function.

The world became black around him. Desperation set in. He clawed at his throat, oblivious to the flesh falling like Parmesan cheese at his feet, oblivious to the razor blades opening fresh wounds on his jaws, oblivious to the gleam in the dark man's eyes as he casually ate popcorn, staring transfixed at the only specimen in his private monkey house.

Chapter 4

Big Red

"You really want this job?" asked Harry.

The blocky woman smiled. "More than ever."

"How'd you hear about us?" asked Harry.

"Internet listing," she said.

"Oh, yeah," said Harry, mostly to himself. He had CraigsListed that two months ago and forgotten about it. He didn't think it would take this long to get someone, especially in this economy.

"So. Do I get the job?" she asked.

Harry looked into space for a minute. "Sure, yeah," he said. "I just got a few formalities." He began to rifle through the desk, moving between drawers and folders as he spoke. "I need certain information, like your name and social security number. For payroll and such."

"I wanted to ask about that," she said. "Salary, I mean."

Harry found what he was looking for. He held out a sheaf of papers for her, grabbing a pen from his desk. "We'll talk about that after you fill out this employment application."

She took the papers. Hesitant, but she took the papers.

"You can sit over there," he said, pointing to the spare desk at the other end of the office.

As she scuttled away he studied his office. He felt like an entrepreneur again. He had an office. Two desks, a couch, table, refrigerator, television, a VCR player, and two computers. Coffee maker, desk light, bookcase, window that looked out at an alley in Capitol Hill, not the best part of Seattle but not the worst. And now he had an employee. This has got to be what an entrepreneur feels like.

Up to his ass in bills.

The internet and cable were paid for. They weren't shutting off his land line and his cell phone was working. He had more going on at the office than his own apartment. Maybe that's why he spent so much time here. He had to make a go of this. What else was there for him?

He couldn't go back to the police force. That bridge was burned. Gotta move forward. Gotta pay the bills. He had that list of skip traces for Lenny, and the identity thefts. Might as well start there.

He was so absorbed in the computer work that he didn't hear the woman until she announced herself by clearing her throat. He looked up as she held out the completed application form. "Have a seat over there," said Harry, trying to stay focused. He was almost done with the identity thefts. Maybe the money would keep Binky and his trained pit bull at bay.

It must have been fifteen minutes before she cleared her throat again. Harry looked up. "Bathroom?" she asked.

"Down the hall. Here's the key," he said, handing her an obnoxiously large thing that reminded her of a cheap convenience store key ring. As if she'd walk off with it.

When she was gone he scanned the application. Rita Rockwell. Twenty five, some college, sports, knows boxing and kung fu. Current job: bouncer at a gay bar. He read on as she came back. She took a seat in an unsteady chair opposite the desk. She was pleased he was finally getting around to reading the application. He already told her she got the job, this was just a formality. She whispered to herself, Rita Rockwell, P.I. She smiled, hearing television theme music inside her head.

He stumbled on a few items. "What's this you wrote on experience? Clue? Charlie's Angels?"

She composed herself. "I was always the best in my neighborhood when it came to Clue. I could find Mr. Green or Miss Scarlet in no time. My friends eventually stopped playing with me because it was no fun. If there was a Clue Tournament or something I would have aced it for sure." Silence. "Clue champion of the world," she laughed.

"And Charlie's Angels?" asked Harry, not wanting to be denied the explanation.

"Good at that, too," she said. "Loved the old reruns on the Nostalgia Channel. Had the bad guy pegged by the second commercial."

"I see," said Harry.

"I always wanted to be Kate Jackson. She was the angel that got things done. Farrah Fawcett was eye candy and what did Jaclyn Smith do? Hell, she designs clothes for K-Mart now."

"Her clothes may be boring but be careful, Rita," said Harry. "We all eventually fall from grace."

"That's not the way I see it," she said.

"Explain," he said.

"I don't know about you but I'm moving up. I'm looking for grace. Nobody likes to fall."

Good answer, he thought. There was that sparkle in her eye, the gems he had seen when she first entered the office.

"Says here under additional training that you were in a band," said Harry.

"Yes," she answered. He stared at her in silence. "I played clarinet. Bothell High School Wind Ensemble and Marching Band. Go Cougars!" She pumped her hand up and down a few times like she was in pep squad.

"Oh," he said. "Clarinet, huh? You like Kenny G? He your favorite?"

"No," she said. "Woody Allen."

Harry put the application down on his desk, a little annoyed.

"Woody Allen plays great clarinet," she said. "Few people know…"

"How does this relate to detective work?" interrupted Harry.

"I just wanted you to know," she said. "In case you got any cases involving musical instruments. Missing Stradivariuses and such."

"I won't even ask about these other items," said Harry.

"Look, isn't this just a formality?" she asked. "You said I got the job. Shouldn't you be telling me about my first case?"

"Yeah, maybe I should." He looked on his desk, spying the newspaper Binky had left. The word REWARD stood out prominently. He read a little more, scanning words and phrases. Richard Sooka. Missing dress. Designer Derby. Fans need not worry says Producer Paul Briggs. We'll go forward with this season's contest as scheduled.

"Cold bastards these Hollywood types," said Harry aloud.

"Huh?" she asked.

"Never mind," he said.

"What about salary?" she asked.

Time to back paddle again. "Yes," he said. "We should discuss that."

"What does the job pay?" she asked.

"Detectives work by the case," he said. "You solve a case, you get paid."

"Oh," she said, somewhat disappointed.

"Don't worry. I'll train you," he said. "Being a detective is easy once you get the hang of it."

"What's a skip trace?" she asked.

"It's a term we private eyes use. It means locating a person."

"I can do that," she said.

"No doubt," he said. "So, are you willing to come on board as an apprentice? Work on a case by case basis."

"As long as you have work for me," she said. "What's my first case?"

Harry looked at the newspaper Binky had given him again. "Top case," he said. "Try you out on this." He handed her the newspaper. "You can have that desk over there. See what you make of this. Maybe you can get us some leads and find this missing dress."

She took the newspaper and went to the chair behind the desk, sitting in it as if he had told her it was the throne to England.

"Don't get too excited," he said. "See if you can come up with any clues. You're good at that, right?" he said.

"Clue," she said. "Yeah."

While she read the article, Harry went back to his computer. He finished his internet research in just under an hour, but he needed some help to close the loop. He looked at the clock on his computer screen. Almost lunch time and he had planned to see Lieutenant Bernard this morning. He printed out a few sheets of paper and gathered them up.

"Gotta go to the police station," he said.

"Can I come too?" she asked.

"Sure. If you wanna," he said. "Let's go."

She gathered up some papers as well. He looked surprised. "What have you got there?" he asked.

"My clues," she said. "Want to hear?"

He looked at the papers, a bundle of scribbles. She had been busy. His curiosity was peaked. "In the car," he said.

Harry wheeled the tired Volvo wagon around the corner. It let out a groan, the ball joints complaining like a ghost haunting an old mansion.

"Does it always sound like this?" she asked.

"No, he said. "Only when I make tight turns. So, what have you got, Rita?" He eyed the papers in her hands.

"Red," she said.

"What?" he asked.

"Red. I mean, you can call me Rita, but my friends call me Big Red."

"Big Red?" he asked. "How'd you get that name?"

"High school nickname," she said.

"Yeah," he said. "I got a number of those myself."

"Fu?" she asked.

He looked away, pretending to concentrate on his driving. "So, what do you have there, Nancy Drew?"

"Nancy Drew!" she said, excited. "I should have put that on the application. I love Nancy Drew. Of course, Emma Roberts totally screwed up the part, that's why it never made it to a sequel."

"Calm down," he said. "I'm glad you graduated from the Hollywood School of Crime Detectives. Makes you perfect for this case. Now, tell me what you have there."

She rifled through the papers. "What should I start with?"

"I don't know. Just brief me."

"We need to find this dress," she said.

"No shit, Sherlock." He turned to her as her mouth hung open. "And don't tell me you like Sherlock Holmes, too."

She stared down at the papers. "Well, I do," she said.

"Sorry," he said. She has a lot of enthusiasm. He didn't mean to hurt her feelings. "Go ahead. Continue with your briefing."

"There's this missing dress, see? It was designed by Richard Sooka. He's a famous designer but he's also a judge on that cable show Designer Derby. The dress was supposed to be auctioned off this coming weekend at a charity ball. Except he's missing and so is the dress."

Harry looked at her. She couldn't tell what he was thinking but wished she could. It's never good when your boss stares at you.

"There's a big reward for the dress," she said. "We find that dress and we're on easy street."

"Tell me something I don't know," he said. "Got any suspects?"

"A list of them," she said, swelling like a prize gamecock.

"Read them to me."

"Okay. Let's start with Sooka's ex-wife."

"He's married? I thought he was gay."

"Probably why he's divorced," she said. "I got the impression from the show that he liked men more than women."

"What makes you say that?" asked Harry.

"Didn't you watch the show?" she asked.

"Designer Derby? Yeah. I saw season one and two. Kinda lost interest in it after that."

"Huh? That show was great! What a concept. Take amateur designers and make them compete for a top prize worth over one hundred thousand dollars. And half the prizes are donated by the advertisers. Everyone's a winner."

"Yeah. Cheaper than hiring a single actor on a television series. Didn't those Friends get a million apiece for a half hour show? Sure makes the Derby sound like a bargain to me."

"You're right," she said. "Reality shows are much cheaper to shoot, too. That's what makes them so popular. Do you know the whole show is shot in less than a month?"

"What?" he said. "I thought it was ten to twelve weeks."

"That's how long it airs on television. They stretch it out in editing. Those designers are worn out by the end. Part of the drama is to stress them out. Haven't you noticed it's two or three days for every hour and a half of show?"

"Yeah, I guess so," he said. "Gotta stretch it out ten or twelve weeks for the ratings."

"Yeah," she said. "Do the math. Not only that, it's worth millions in product placement and endorsements. It built Sooka's career. He was a two bit purse designer before that. Now everything he touches turns to gold."

"Go figure," said Harry. "Hollywood!"

"Only thing better is sports," said Red. "Know how much a baseball player makes?"

"Let's not go there," said Harry.

"Okay," said Red. "Just tell me one thing. Since when did the size of your paycheck equal the size of your brain. I mean, I agree that some celebrities are smart and intelligent, but what makes them smarter than scientists or teachers?"

"Beats me," said Harry. "Okay, we're getting off track here. I agree we have to find the dress. What do you have?"

"Find Dick Sooka, we find the dress."

"Dick sucker?" He repeated it the way she said it.

"Sorry. Common street name for Richard Sooka," she said.

"Why that nickname?" he asked.

"Come on, you watched the show. Like I said, rumor has it he was gay. But there's another reason. Of all the judges he was the most caustic. Worse than Simon was on American Idol. He says the meanest things. Sometimes I just wanted to kill him."

Harry spoke in a low voice. "Maybe somebody already has," he said.

"If that's so, maybe I should cross him off my list of suspects," whispered Red. She took her pen and drew a small cross with a question mark next to Richard Sooka, the first name on her list.

"Don't scratch him off yet," said Harry. "I'd agree with you. He'd be my top suspect, not the ex-wife. He's the one who stands to gain the most from it."

"That's what I figured," she said. "Since the dress turned up missing, the news media is all over it. The show has lots of attention. The value of the dress has probably doubled, and his crappy designs are flying off the shelf. What a way to jump start your stagnant career."

"Why did you start with the ex-wife then?"

"I didn't think he had the guts to do it himself, so I figured he brought her in on it," she said. "Donna Pallatzio is her name. She was a model until he married her and made her a millionaire. I think they were married all of two months, yet she got half of everything he owned or ever will own."

"What?" remarked Harry. "How'd that work out? She must've had a good lawyer."

"Lawyers," she said, emphasizing the plural.

"How do you get half of everything someone will ever own?"

"Lawyers," she said, again emphasizing the plural. "Remember, they get half of everything she gets, so it's a mixed bag. Without the lawyers, though, she could have wound up with nothing. Like I said, the marriage only lasted a few months."

Harry thought for a while. "She must have had some juicy blackmail to get him to sign those divorce papers. Why else would Richard give up half of everything?"

"God, you're good," she said. "I never thought of that angle."

Harry smiled. "Got another question for you. If Dick Sucker was gay, why would he want a wife?"

"For exactly that reason," said Red. "Good cover. The fashion industry is quirky. I think most women want real men to design their clothes, not wussies."

"Wussies?"

"Sorry. Didn't mean the slur. Funny thing, a gay man will spot a wardrobe mistake quicker than another woman will. That's not a stereotype."

"I disagree," he said. "It's all about attraction. Gay men are just more attentive to how someone looks, male or female." He took a deep breath. "So we have Richard and his ex wife, what's her name again?"

"Donna Pallatzio. Next I have Heille Crumstein."

"The star of the show?"

"For the same reasons as Richard," she said.

"She's gay, has a vindictive ex-wife, and is a bad designer?"

Red laughed. "No, silly. But she has just as much to gain as Richard. She's not a designer, but she is Designer Derby. It's the sole source of her popularity. Without her, the show would not have a spokesperson. Fans wait every week to hear her say, "Sorry, you're off." You get the dramatic music, you see tears, Shakespeare couldn't have written it better. She's the Lady Macbeth of misery. Which brings me to my next suspect: Paul Briggs."

"Paul Briggs? Who's that?"

"The show's producer, of course. Don't you ever read the credits?"

"Not on television. They're written too small and pass too quickly on the screen. Besides, I'm a movie buff myself."

"Oh," she said. She looked down at her list.

"What's Paul's motive?" asked Harry.

"Free publicity, I'd think," she answered. "I imagine every time someone says 'Designer Derby' he gets a cut. People who never heard of the show will tune in just out of curiosity."

"Okay. Good," said Harry. "Who's next on your list?"

"There's Curran. He's the go-between who escorts away the designers who are voted off the show. Don't think he has the gall to do it, but I put him on my list anyway."

"That's okay for now," he said. "We start with a big list and narrow it down later."

"Okay," she said. She looked at the next name on her list. "Then there's Zanzibar O'Connell."

"Now who's he? The director?" asked Harry.

"Zanzibar is a woman," said Red. "Boy, you don't read the papers much either, do you?"

"Okay. Clue me."

"She was the model that Dick Sooka said was too fat to be on the show anymore. She was a size six for goodness sake but the jerk told the world she's too fat. Ruined her career. Do you remember now?"

"Seems like I saw something like that on the internet. Last year, wasn't it?" he asked, trying to place it. She nodded. "You're right about something, though. Richard had a lot of enemies."

"Which is why I include Carrie Rodriguez."

"The show's co-host?"

"She hated him as much as anyone else. Didn't you notice she always disagreed with him? They were like oil and water."

"Okay, okay," he said, growing impatient. "Got anyone on your list not associated with the show?"

"Sure, but I haven't finished my research," she said."I've got rival designers, Richard's jealous boyfriend..."

"Boyfriend? He had a boyfriend?" asked Harry.

"Not sure, but I'm checking," she said." Just an angle. I put it on the list after you came up with the blackmail theory." She looked down at her paper. "Then there's the Pink Mafia."

"Pink Mafia?"

Red looked stunned. "Pink Mafia. La Cosa Rosa?" She stared at Harry firmly, then rolled her eyes. "You don't know much about designer clothes and the fashion industry, do you?"

"I get all my clothes from the Goodwill," he said. "Cheaper that way."

"It shows," she said. "You'll have to take me shopping with you sometime. I shop there too. You can find some good stuff there. You just have to look."

"I usually just buy what fits."

"Uh huh," she said. "Anyway, the Pink Mafia is the fashion crime syndicate. How do you think foreign sweat shops get all the latest fashions?"

"They steal them?"

"Just the ones they don't license outright," she said smugly. "They're not crooks, but like all businesses they get tempted by shortcuts. That's where the Cosa Rosa comes in."

Harry thought she was grasping for straws. "Okay, what else you got?"

"The butler."

Harry looked at her. "Come on," he said in disbelief.

"Hey, you read enough crime novels. Gotta put the butler on the list, at least until we rule him out."

Harry laughed. "Next."

"Constance Wallington," she said. Harry looked blank. "The organizer of the charity event. She could have easily stolen or hidden the dress on purpose to drive the price up. Good media press, too. Now everyone in town, probably the whole country, knows about the auction. She should move it online to eBay. Get more money, I bet."

"So, you're saying this could all be a hoax," he said. "Constance could have just taken the dress, stashed it, and reported it missing."

"Wouldn't put it past her. She's not one of our noble rich."

"There are no noble rich," said Harry.

Red scowled. "I disagree. Bill and Melinda Gates, Oprah Winfrey, Jimmy Buffet, Larry Page and Sergey Brin..."

"Who are those last two?" interrupted Harry.

"Founders of Google. They have Google.org which gives away hundreds of thousands of dollars to charity."

Okay," said Harry. Name five more." Red was silent. "Don't kid yourself. The only reason rich people give away money is for the tax break. Especially when it's in their own best interest, like giving it to some politician so they can influence legislation that shifts the balance of power."

"What about the churches? You saying they're bad just because they donate money to politicians?"

"They're the worst," he said. "And the pundits are not much better. They're more interested in getting money than giving. Isn't there a Christian moral that says it's better to give than receive?"

"Yeah," said Red. "There's also one that says it's easier for a camel to pass through the eye of a needle than it is for a rich man to get into heaven."

"Heaven sounds like a nice place to be," said Harry. "Okay, let's move on, we're almost at the police station. Who else you got on your list?"

"Charlie Sheen. Mel Gibson."

Harry laughed. "Hollywood bad boys. Yeah, let's put Lindsay Lohan and Paris Hilton on that list. Maybe Martha Stewart. She spent time in the big house." Red grabbed her pen but Harry stopped her. "Just kidding," he said. "But when you continue your research, don't ignore disgruntled contestants. Everyone who was ever voted off the show is suspect too, especially ones with a grudge. I want them on your list."

She was scribbling now. Jotting notes and drawing arrows on the papers resting on her knees. Harry smiled. She certainly deserved an A-plus for effort. He doubted they could ever solve the case, but who knows? To him it was more like an exercise, like picking stocks and investing with paper money, tracking them to see what could have happened if you had any real money to play with.

She'd probably be good at skip traces, too. He'd have to train her, get her up to speed. There may be enough money in it for the two of them. May not satisfy her, but she'd have to come down to earth.

He couldn't remember Nancy Drew ever collecting a steady paycheck.

Chapter 5

Special Delivery

The driver sped away, Overlake Hospital fading behind him. Turning north onto Interstate 405 he headed towards his last destination. He glanced in the rear view mirror of the panel truck, the final package was secured to the floor.

In the monotony of the traffic he began to daydream. How do you get started in a career based on murder? It's not like he chose it, but he wanted to be famous. After trying other jobs he somehow fell into it as the best use of his talents, as the only path that would lead him to fame. His fame was certain now.

His brother wanted to be a race car driver at fourteen, something he knew in his heart. He probably would have been a good one if not for that accident. Speed kills, but it wasn't the speed that killed him, it was the lack of brakes.

"I knew at ten," he said aloud, talking to the box in the back. "Ten!"

It was in Larry's tree house. Larry was older and had outgrown the neighborhood kids, but that didn't stop everyone from using his tree house.

"Yes," he said to the box. "Larry's tree house. Alfred and I played there a lot, especially after Larry learned to drive and was never around much. Alfred was my best friend. Did I tell you that?"

The box remained silent.

"My best friend until he got that rabbit for his birthday." His voice dropped, bubbling anger. "A cute, white bunny. He brought it up to the tree house, flaunting over it. This went on for days. I tried to get him to think of other things, playing army, outdoor games, even chess or checkers but he would have none of it. All he thought of was that damned rabbit."

There was a police car in the median and he slowed down.

"I realized that Alfred no longer looked at me as his sole source of fun. That rabbit had replaced me as his favorite. I really had no choice but to kill that little bugger."

He scanned the mirrors. The cop remained still, stalking other prey.

"I was petting it softly," he said. "Just like Lenny in *Of Mice and Men*, but I knew what I was doing. Got the idea from that book and snapped its little neck. Ain't reading great?

"I threw the carcass in the river and told Alfred it must have run away. He was so dumb he never asked how it got out of its cage. I began to think that if he asked too many questions I would do the same to him.

"He didn't ask too many questions. I decided it was fun getting away with murder. I decided to up the stakes. I was the one who poisoned all those dogs on East Fifteenth Street. Remember them yapping all night long? Bothered the heck out of me."

He stared at the road ahead, traffic slowing as he approached a congested area.

"Wait! I was eight," he said. "It was much sooner. I was eight when I killed that rabbit. First grade maybe?" He smiled, nostalgia lighting his face. "First grade. Pretty traumatic for most kids, being separated from their mommy like that. Did you cry on your first day of school, Dick?"

The box remained silent.

"Me, I was glad to be away from her, out from under her monstrous control. The teacher tried to take mommy's place but I showed her. She had an exacto knife in her desk drawer. She took my favorite toy away, one of those little corrugated glass or plastic pictures that change when you tilt them at an angle. You know the ones that reveal two scenes depending on how you look at them. You ever have one of those?"

He moved the van in to the right lane. "Not too far now," he said. "I think she didn't like the fact that I looked at that little toy more than her. I was just fascinated how something could be two different things depending on how you looked at it."

Evergreen Hospital loomed in the distance, a giant complex of buildings that took up the entire side of a hill. "Sit tight," he said. "Almost there."

He took the exit ramp, merging into the thick traffic that always cluttered Totem Lakes. "This hospital's the best, Dick. At least that's what they say. Got your insurance card?"

He paused at the light, thinking while he waited for it to change.

"Of course that wasn't the first time I saw blood, you know. I cut myself by accident once. Stupid of me. Must have been four or five. I was fascinated. Cut myself again to see if it would happen again. Decided to see if anything else bled too. Rex, our dog, bled. So did Scraps the cat and did you know fish bleed?

"Meat doesn't bleed, not when it's frozen, but at one time there was blood in it. Maybe that's why I love the taste of a lightly grilled steak. Soft, chewy, slightly salty and metallic. You like steak, Dick?"

The light changed and he moved on. "Different meat tastes different. It doesn't all taste like chicken as they say. Did you know dog tastes like deer?"

He drove past the hospital offices, past the emergency room, winding through the maze of buildings towards the top of the hill. "Oh," he said, excited. "Did I tell you about the birthday party? We played lots of games. Brent kept winning, pin the tail on the donkey, bean bag toss, musical chairs. He had a small bag of prizes by the time we set up for the piñata.

"They blindfolded me but I could still see. I swung that bat right at old Brent's head." He chuckled. "He wasn't even looking. Cold cocked him good. I looked all innocent and sorry and no adult believed I would do such a thing on purpose."

At the top of the hill he turned the van onto a road leading to a small flat building. "Brent bled just like me," he said, coming to a stop. "Well, here we are, Dick. Your final resting place."

He reached into the back and loosened the restraints that held the package down. Then he grabbed the small box and got out of the van.

"Evergreen Hospice," he said, reading the sign on the door. He held the package up and whispered softly to it. "Might be a little late for you, Dick. Sorry."

He walked through the doors and up to the reception desk. An old lady sat there smiling. God bless the volunteers, he thought. He set the package on the desk and held up a clipboard. "Sign here," he said, sticking it in front of her face.

"What is it?" she asked.

"I don't know," he said. "Probably wine for some doctor's party. How should I know? Just sign," he smiled.

The old woman hesitantly took the clipboard and signed next to the X he pointed to with his finger.

She signed without reading. He took the clipboard away too quickly. He ripped off a sheet and handed it to her.

"Mind if I take a piece of candy?" he asked, his hand hovering over a bowl of wrapped chocolates on top of her desk.

She couldn't resist his smile. "Of course," she said sweetly.

"Thank you," he said. He turned and was gone before she had a chance to say anything else. The phone rang at the desk and she moved the package aside.

She didn't know it was him calling her, using the phone number he saw when he leaned over to take the chocolate.

"Is Doctor Johnson there?" he asked.

She sounded flustered. "I don't know," she said.

"Could you find out please? It's real important."

"Can I ask what it's about?" she said.

"Sorry. I can't tell you. HIPPA regulations, you know."

"Of course," she said. "Can you hold?" He saw her get up from the desk, the package lying unopened. It would be a while before she discovered it contained the severed head of Dick Sooka.

As he crossed the bridge back to Seattle, he threw the cell phone into Lake Washington. "Thanks for letting me use your phone, Dick," he said. "Guess you won't be needing it either."

Chapter 6

Cop Shop

"Hey Harry," said the receptionist. "Sure miss you around here."

Harry smiled. "How you doing, Nan? The boss in?"

"He's in a meeting. Should be over in a few minutes. Stick around. I'm sure I can keep you busy until he's done." She stood and leaned over the desk, her lips parted.

Harry ignored her with a nervous smile. She sat back down, threw her pen in the corner. Harry walked over and retrieved it. He tapped it in his hand a few times, then set it gently down on the corner of her desk.

"Honestly," she said. "Sometimes I think you don't like girls."

"But I do," said Harry. "I love women. Just waiting for the right one to come along."

Nan stretched her shoulders like a cat, then squirmed in her chair, looking all smug and rejected.

"You still married?" he asked.

"What's that got to do with anything?" she asked.

"Come on. You know I don't cross that line. Isn't there a commandment about adultery?"

"Who follows those old laws," she said.

"I do," he said flatly. He gave her a sisterly kiss on the cheek. "Gotta draw the line somewhere," he said. "Otherwise all society would go to hell in a handbasket."

"Where you been? Haven't you noticed we're halfway there?"

"Sorry," he said. "I see the glass half full. Ever heard of redemption?"

"I heard of it," she said. "Just don't believe in it."

"It's okay, Nan. I believe in you." He kissed her again.

The door opened and a parade came out. Some uniforms, followed by detectives in suits, and, like the end of all good parades, a Santa Claus. In this case, Lieutenant Matt Bernard, with a not-so-jolly look. He stopped at the door and the parade slowly moved on, some shuffling out the door, others dispersing into the field of desks outside Bernard's office. A small group stayed behind, huddled around a sharp dressed man.

Bernard turned and spotted Harry. His scowl became a grin.

"Harry," he blurted, extending a meaty hand. "Come to beg for your old job back?"

"Not quite, Matt," he said.

The sharp dressed member of the parade broke into the conversation, his hand smoothing the back of his hair as he spoke. "Probably looking for the number of your wife's seamstress."

"That's enough, Franklin," said Bernard.

"Oh. I know," said the suit. "He heard about the janitor cleaning out the women's locker room. He's here to pick up the leftover clothes. Lots of bras and panties. Lucky for you, Fu."

"I said that's enough," said Bernard.

"We did find a makeup case in your old desk. You can pick that up at lost and found."

Bernard opened his mouth. Red stepped in front of him like a wall. "Didn't you hear your boss. That's enough!"

Franklin squared his shoulders. "And what business is it of yours, sister?"

She leaned in close. "It's all my business. *Mister* Takanawa is my employer and if you say one more word, you'll be scraping your balls off the top of my shoe."

Harry smiled. Franklin was at a loss for words. Bernard just laughed. "Come on, Harry. Let's go in my office where we can chat in private." He turned to Red and Franklin, locked in a Chinese stare off. "I'll leave you two to get acquainted. Just go light on him sweetheart. The man doesn't have much in the way of balls. He's all mouth." He turned away, guiding Harry towards his office with gentle pats on the back. "So how the hell you doing? Detective business being good to you?"

"Geez, let me tell you, Matt..." The door closed.

There was an awkward silence. The remnants of the parade were gathered around them. Franklin seemed to be the only one not smiling.

"All right," he said. "Show's over. We got work to do, don't we?"

The crowd dispersed. Red continued to stare at Franklin.

"Look, maybe we got off on the wrong foot," he said. He stared nervously at her feet, regretting the way he said that. The metaphor was not lost on Red. "You know what I mean," he said. "Come over to my desk and I'll make it up to you. Got a fridge full of drinks."

She relaxed. "Got a diet Coke?"

"Yeah," he said. "Come on." They crossed the busy office to a desk in the far corner where he grabbed a couple of cans out of a small dorm refrigerator.

"Pretty far from windows and daylight," she said.

"I like it that way," he said. "Cops get shot through windows."

"Who would shoot a cop?" she asked.

"Haven't you read the papers lately? We're in an all out war here. Gangs, Russian mob, Tong warlords, meth heads, there's all kinds of weirdos out there. Cops are dropping faster than pins in a bowling alley."

"Maybe you're right," she said. "Seems I heard something about that."

He licked his hand, then stroked the hair on the back of his head. "Hazards of the job, sweetheart."

Red frowned. "Don't call me that."

"Okay, okay," he said. "Sorry. Old habit."

"I don't appreciate sexist remarks," she said.

"Okay, said I was sorry, didn't I?" He extended his hand and smiled. "Franklin Van Dorn, Detective Sergeant."

She thought about the saliva dipped hairball he held toward her, then she took it anyway. She had held grosser things. "You can call me Rita, but I also go by Red."

"You got quite a grip there," he said, pulling his hand back.

"Sorry," she said. "Old habit of mine."

"Where'd you get those muscles. Work out?"

"Speed bag, dead lifts, a little martial arts," she said. "I was State Woman's Boxing Champ in high school two years running.

"Good for you," said Van Dorn.

"That's why they call me Red. Big Red." She laughed. "One punch and I see Red. Some switch gets flipped inside me and I go berserk. Daddy says it's cause I have red hair. Feisty like my mother."

"I'd hate to meet your mother," he said.

Red frowned. "She's dead."

"Sorry," said Van Dorn.

"It's okay. She died when I was young. My dad raised me. Taught me everything I know about fighting. Except how to stop. Gets me in trouble sometimes."

"I can imagine," he said. "Tough losing a parent."

"Dad tried," she said. "He was good, but all broke up after mom died. He liked to get drunk and fight."

"Anger issues, huh?"

"You could say. I guess I took care of him as much as he took care of me. Maybe more."

They sipped their drinks, making slurping sounds together. Van Dorn changed the subject. "How long you been working for Fu?"

"You mean Harry?" she asked. "Mr. Takanawa?"

"Yeah. How long?"

"Just started," she said.

Franklin smiled. "Working on a big case?"

"Oh yeah," she said. "We're gonna find that missing dress."

Van Dorn laughed.

"What's so funny?" asked Red.

"Fu looking for a missing dress." He paused. Rita didn't seem to get the joke. "You don't know much about your boss, do you?"

"I checked him out before I applied for the job."

Van Dorn's smile widened. "You going to find this missing dress? Solve the Case of the Missing Dick?"

"What?" she asked.

"Missing Dick. You know, Richard Sooka. He's missing, too."

Red laughed. "Oh yeah. Missing Dick. I get it."

"What makes you think you can crack that case?" he asked. "Half the guys in this office are working that case."

"What makes you so sure you can solve it?" she asked.

"Look around," he said. "We got resources. Computers. Clues and leads. See those two guys leaving over there?" He pointed towards the door. One of the men nodded as he closed the door behind him. "They work for me. Top notch detectives headed out to do interviews."

"What kind of clues you got?" asked Red.

Van Dorn started to say something but stopped. "Sorry. I can't share that information with you. Have to get clearance from the Lieutenant."

"Harry's in there right now getting the gory details. Why not spare me the time? I'll share what we have."

He laughed, setting his can down to lick his hand. He stroked his hair. "What have you got that I need?"

"Suspect, list, motive. Working on clues."

"Pah," he said. "We got all that."

"Then let's compare lists."

"Told you," he said. I can't without the Lieutenant's approval."

"Okay. Make me wait until Harry briefs me. Don't listen to my clues and suspects." Van Dorn looked aside. She couldn't tell what he was thinking but he looked worried. "The pressure's on, isn't it?" she asked.

He shook his head. "Lieutenant's got every available man on the case. This one's a media nightmare. The public leans on the mayor, the mayor leans on the chief of police, he leans on the lieutenant and Bernard leans on us. Shit flows downhill."

"All the reason to collaborate," she said. "The sooner we solve this case the quicker all this goes away."

He seemed to consider it, and then said, "Now, why would I help Fu find his missing dress? He's a good detective. Let him find it on his own."

"I think you're a little jealous," she said.

"Of Fu?" He patted the back of his hair again, flattening it with his hand. "Come on."

"Why do people call him Fu?"

"How long you been working for your boss?"

"Told you I just started."

"Like I said, you don't know much about him, do you?"

She looked down. He was right. What did she know about him? Just what she read on the internet. She answered an ad on Craig's list, that was it.

"You know why he left the force?" he asked.

"Tired of it, I guess," she said. "Bullshit politics, Lieutenant leaning on everyone, daily grind. Maybe he decided he'd do better as a private detective."

He made a buzzer sound, like the kind you hear when you get the wrong answer on a television game show. "Annnk! None of the above. Care to try for two out of three?"

"Okay," she said. "Maybe he was tired of being a target for all those crazies you told me about."

"Wrong again," he said.

"All right," she said. "I give up. He wasn't kicked off the force, so why did he leave?"

Van Dorn smiled. "Get comfortable and let me fill you in. I know the real scoop on your boss."

Chapter 7

Saint Bernard

Lieutenant Bernard closed the door. "So, Harry. If you're not here to get your old job back, then what do you need?"

"Who says I need anything," he said.

"So this is a social visit?"

"Not exactly," he said.

Bernard sat down behind his cluttered desk. Harry stared out the window, the city spread behind it like some wild growth. For once it wasn't raining. Interstate Five snaked out from underneath it, cars crawling like ants towards some distant picnic over the hill. A ferry glided across Puget Sound, carrying more ants to the mound. Why do they do it? It's all about the money, isn't it? Doesn't matter who you work for. This city's filled with Binkies, all demanding their due.

"So, how is the detective business going?" asked Matt. "Working any big cases?"

"One big case, surrounded by a bunch of busy work that pays the bills," he said.

"I see," said Bernard. "What's the big case?"

"Same one you're probably working. The Sooka case."

Matt smiled and leaned back in his chair. "If anyone could crack that case it'd be you. That your assistant out there?"

"Red? Sorry, forgot to introduce you to her. My apprentice."

"She's good muscle. I would have enjoyed seeing her squash Van Dorn. Bastard's been way out of line since you left. He's gunning for my job. Actually thinks he has a shot at it."

"That would be sad," said Harry.

"You know it. He would run off every good man who worked under him. Wanna hear something even sadder? He could get it. Momma's got a lot of money, not that any of the Van Dorn's ever worked hard for it, but she knows a lot of players in this town. Contributed heavily to the Mayor's reelection fund last go around."

"That's what it takes," said Harry.

"Wish you would crack the case. They've been all over me downtown to make some progress. This designer show represents big money in this town. Not to mention the charity auction. They hardly film anything in Seattle any more. Hollywood's moved over the border to Vancouver. That's what we get for taxing the movie industry out of business here in Seattle."

"Got any leads?" asked Harry.

"Yeah, we questioned the usual suspects. Everyone associated with the show. Charity celebrities, jealous wives, where available. Your buddy out there interviewed Crumstein herself."

"Really?" said Harry.

"Yeah," said Bernard. "She called afterward. Found him disgusting. Said he kept rubbing his greasy hair and then wanted to touch her. She said not to send him around again."

Harry laughed. "Imagine that."

"Yeah. We got statements but no witnesses, no leads, and no place to go. Nearest I can figure is Sooka took off with the dress and went into hiding."

"What makes you say that?"

"Just a hunch," said Bernard. "That, and the value of the dress has tripled since it's been missing."

"You checked airplane flights? Ferry cameras? Private plane logs?" asked Harry.

"Yeah, yeah, yeah. Got Anderson working on that now," said Bernard.

"Traffic cameras? Border patrol?"

"Sooka's cars are all in Hollywood," said Bernard. "Sitting in his driveway."

"Maybe he had an accomplice?"

Bernard sighed. "You got any leads?" he asked Harry again.

"Yeah. Running them down."

"Getting anywhere?"

"Just started," said Harry. "Red, I mean Rita, she's working the case. Doing all the leg work. She's pretty clever."

"So, you came here to see what we had done, am I right?"

Harry nodded slowly.

Bernard laughed. "I know my men." He tapped his forehead with his finger. "Still got a detective's mind." He looked at Harry, his face scrunched in question. "But that's not all, is it Harry?"

Harry nodded.

"Okay then, what else do you want to know?" asked Bernard.

"I didn't come here just for this," said Harry. "Not completely. We just started talking about it and…"

"Then what'd you come here for?" interrupted Bernard.

"I need a favor." Bernard waited for Harry to speak. He watched Harry pull a sheaf of papers out of his pocket and slide them across the desk. Bernard picked them up and looked them over. "Skip traces?"

"They pay the bills."

Bernard dropped them on the desk like they were dead animals. "You can follow the usual procedure for these. Fill out the paperwork. We'll be glad to check these out and get back to you."

Harry lowered his voice. "I need these pretty quick, Matt." He stared at Bernard. "Today," he added.

"You that desperate, Harry?" There was no answer. "Hell, come back to work for me. I'll give you your old job back. You'll be one step away from my seat."

"Can't do it. Matt."

"So you gonna spend the rest of your life roaming the streets, playing lookout for jealous cheaters, tailing cons, and doing skip traces for Binky?"

Harry looked surprised.

"Yeah, I know who your landlord is. I was a detective once, you know."

"So give me a hand, Matt. Help me out."

"Fine. I'll help you out, but what are you going to do for me?"

"What do you want me to do?"

"Hell! Crack this Sooka case for me. Get the mayor off everyone's back. Find the missing dress. Collect the reward for God's sake. It's a win-win for everyone."

"Told you I was working the case. That wasn't all small talk."

Matt blew air, then looked at the pile of paper. He picked up the phone. "Nan. Send in Trish." He hung up the phone and faced Harry. "I don't understand you Takanawa. Ex Marine, decorated in the war. What makes you wanna..."

Harry cut him off as the door behind him opened. The young blonde caught their attention. She was well put together, both in style and frame, like a Sunday ad from Nordstrom's or Macy's come to life. Bernard stood up. "Trish, meet Harry Takanawa. Harry, Trish Wilder. She's an intern from U-dub putting her time in here."

Harry stood up. "Nice to meet you," he said.

Bernard got right to it. "Here's a pile of names. I need you to get on the system and see what you can find out for me. Use CrimeNet, DHS, Spartan Search, whatever you need. Then report back to me and me alone. These are important leads. I'm counting on you."

"Yes, sir," she said. She turned and left, the sound of her boots clicking on the floor.

"Nice outfit," said Harry.

Bernard shook his head.

"Thanks, Matt," said Harry.

"Not yet," said Bernard. "I was selfish. Now, we got that out of the way, if you're not coming back to work for me, this is the next best thing. You owe me one. Big time." Harry squirmed and Bernard sat back in his chair. "Maybe I like this arrangement better." He smiled. "Now, tell me how you gonna crack this case for me."

"I got my own intern," said Harry.

"Yeah. Rita."

"She's counting on me Matt. She's so gung ho. Really wants to be a detective."

"Maybe I'm talking to the wrong person then. I should be offering her your old job."

"Get her in here and see," said Harry.

Matt opened the door and glared into the room. "Looks like she's busy chatting to Van Dorn. Let me know what she gets out of him. He hasn't exactly been honest with me."

"Kid has trust issues, Lieutenant."

"Yeah. Nobody trusts him."

The phone rang and Matt picked it up, said a few words and went pale. He dropped the phone in the cradle.

"What?" asked Harry.

"Got a bigger problem than Sooka and missing dresses. I'm going to call my marker in right now. Favor for a favor. Most of my men are out combing the streets and I need your help. Harborview just called. Coroner just got a cut up torso delivered a couple of hours ago. Wants us to come take a look before he digs too deep into it."

Chapter 8

Hobbies

The dark man parked the van just out of sight of the cameras. It was an old hotel with obvious cameras, big and bulky, conspicuously mounted, not the modern fiber optic kind. He got out of the van and locked it, removing a plastic bag and a clipboard full of papers he had from his deliveries. He laughed at the gullibility of people, feeling superior to everyone in the world. The van was clean. All his packages had been scrubbed before loading. The police would learn nothing about him when they found it.

He stayed out of sight of the cameras, moving quickly to the street. He crossed to a gas station and waited for someone to come out of the bathroom. They graciously offered him the key but he declined. "Just give it back to the cashier," he said. "I'll only be a minute."

He took off the coveralls and removed his fake moustache and toupee. He had on a layer of padding, something he had devised to make him look fatter. Next came the rubber gloves and shoes. He took a fresh pair of shoes from a small shoulder satchel he had with him, along with a few other items. He put the clipboard, the toupee, the body padding, and the other things in it, then donned a cap and looked in the mirror. He put on a pair of sunglasses, hiding his eyes in darkness. He washed his hands and left the bathroom.

Someone was waiting outside. He let them in and walked two blocks where he came to a donation bin for a local thrift store. He put the coveralls inside and continued walking. Four more blocks and he came to another bin where he donated the shoes. Such a humanitarian.

The mall was a few more blocks. He went to the food court and had lunch, observing the streams of people. He passed judgment on them, commenting on the outfits he observed, some good, some bad. Overall he thought Seattle had no sense of fashion. Not like L.A or New York or even Washington D.C.

His appetite satisfied, he walked the mall until he came to a large, well stocked hobby shop. The clerk was friendly and helpful.

"Yes, we have those build your own robot kits. Very popular with the kids during science fair season."

"I need a big kit, one with at least four servos, cables, and motors.

"Over here," said the clerk, directing him towards the premium kits in the store.

He studied the box, flipping it over and reading the contents carefully. "I need something capable of generating 2.5 horsepower, enough to handle 250 foot pounds of torque."

The clerk was impressed. "You sure know your hobby specs. Must be a pretty big plane you're building. Plan on flying it in a windstorm?"

He smiled and handed the box back to the clerk. "I was hoping for a pretty decent drive speed," he said. "Something around 233 RPM's if you have it"

The clerk grabbed a stepladder and pulled a big box down off one of the higher shelves. "Will this do you?"

He studied the kit. It was something used to build small, durable robots, the type that can do battle, like on that old show Robot Wars. "Very nice," he said. "Do you have any with remote controls?"

"No," said the clerk. He directed him to another area of the store and showed him a model airplane remote control kit. He smiled. "If you buy this as well, you might be able to combine the two and get what you want."

"You've been very helpful," said the dark man. "One more thing. I need some balsa wood and dope, the kind you use to paint fabric that covers model airplane wings."

"Right over here," said the clerk, grabbing the items and carrying them to the checkout counter. "Anything else?"

"That'll do for now."

"Will that be cash or charge?"

He reached into his wallet, pulling out a wad of bills. "Cash please," he said. "And I need a receipt, too."

The clerk smiled. "These little projects can get expensive."

"Yes they can," he said. "I can't wait to get home and get started."

The clerk handed him the change. "Good luck. Have fun."

"Oh, I will. You can count on it."

Chapter 9

Fresh Meat

Harry stared down at the limbless torso. It looked like the head had been cut off with a hacksaw and there was ragged meat wherever an arm or leg should have been. Big Red and Lieutenant Bernard stared in fascination. Harry looked for a while and turned away.

He was back in the war. Ragged meat was everywhere, limbless torsos were part of doing business.

The humvee tooled down the street. He was excited to be on his first patrol, looking for action. He was the delivery boy, the one manning the fifty caliber guns in the turret, the best view in the house. It was exotic to him, the streets filled with strange people, all jabbering in a language that intrigued his ears. The dust and sand blasted his face. The dry air was far from the rain city he grew up in.

He scanned ahead and behind, part of a convoy passing through the small village. The whole place couldn't have been more than four or five blocks long. As they approached the end of town he could see brown, rocky mountains in the distance. He thought of Mt. Rainier and the purple majesty of the surrounding Cascades. He was a long way from home.

The road curved to the left as it wound out of town. There was a small group of houses on the right and then a wall. He saw the truck, a broken frame on wheels, behind it six men pushing. He thought they should stop and help them. He thought they needed a jump or something. They could easily push start it with the humvee. He just wanted to make friends with the villagers, show them Americans were not so bad.

Something tingled in the back of his neck. Panic followed his charitable thoughts as quickly as thunder follows lightning. The men behind the truck scattered as the momentum carried it forward. He looked for the driver but the seat was empty. The truck rolled towards the humvee in front of the convoy. There was gunfire behind him. He turned the big guns to face the noise. That's when the explosion happened.

He heard nothing from that moment on. Silence. He was in the dirt, laying on the ground with sand in his mouth. He thought, how did I get here? He spit, soundless, not even the resonance of vibration in his chest. It should at least sound like he was underwater. Shouldn't he at least be able to hear his own voice? He panicked, got up and started to run. There was smoke. He saw guns firing, bright sparks flying out of the barrels, but they made no sound. Someone was shouting at him. He made eye contact, saw them gesturing with their hands, their mouth forming the silent words, "Get down."

He tripped over something and fell, landing in the dust on his stomach. He pushed away, coming to his hands and knees like a crawling child. There was blood on his shirt. A lot of blood. There was a dead horse next to him.

Oh my God, it wasn't a horse. A man. A piece of a man. He screamed, his voice coming out silent again. He turned away. There was a limb beside him. An arm or a leg, he couldn't tell, it was just a piece of human flesh, red and ragged, bent and jointed in the middle. Nearby was another piece of meat, and another, and then another. Bodies twisted into impossible positions.

The smoke was clearing, the firefight was over, the enemy either retreated or dead. He stood up between patches of red in the bright, yellow sand. Meat was everywhere, like the floor of a slaughterhouse at the end of a busy shift. He bent over, trying to breathe. Someone touched his shoulder.

"You okay, Harry?" It was Red. She put an arm around his shoulder and pulled him close. It felt good. Human touch always feels good, especially when it's given honestly and freely. "First time you've seen a corpse?" she asked.

"That's not a corpse, Rita. It's a piece of meat."

"Where were you just now?" she asked.

He took a deep breath. "It's okay. I'm here now. Thanks."

"Okay, Boss," she replied.

"Let's go see what we have." They went back to the table and stood beside the Coroner. He was a young man to be doing work like this, not what they expected. His dark hair had flecks of grey, his face etched with worry lines. Harry wondered what horrors the man had seen in his lifetime. He didn't want to know. Bernard was asking him questions while Van Dorn and a few other detectives listened.

"... body parts turning up all over town," he said. "We're sure they belong to this torso. The leg turned up at Virginia Mason, an arm at U-Dub Medical Center. They sent them over and I immediately took a print off a finger. We're running it through the database now."

"What about the rest?" asked Bernard.

"No word yet. Would be nice, though. Especially if we had the head. Make it easy to ID. I'd like to see how it was removed. It looks like it was cut and burned. See this singed flesh? Almost like an electrical shock."

Bernard turned to Sommers, a young, lanky detective who stood behind him. "Get on the phone, Jason. Call every hospital in town. Start with the ones close by. Swedish, Group Health, then widen the search. See what you can find. See if any of them have received any body parts."

"Got it," he said. He stepped outside, pulled a cell phone and a small notebook from his pocket and got busy.

Detective Baily, another of Bernard's men, came in. "We checked out the story, Lieutenant. The torso was delivered to the cafeteria. Sick fuck even made the staff sign for it."

"What? And they didn't inspect the package?" asked Bernard.

"It was at the beginning of the lunch hour, busiest time of the day. Someone just signed for it and put it in the cooler. It was labeled: Fresh Meat, Keep refrigerated. They thought it was hamburger patties."

"Remind me not to have lunch here," remarked Van Dorn.

The Coroner's assistant came in, a young lady with blond hair that framed a sad face. Harry could tell she wouldn't last long in this job. She didn't have the temperament and she avoided looking at the torso. Her eyes were watery and her cheeks were streaked where her makeup had been smudged. She spoke with a tremor in her voice. "We got another arm on the way from Seattle Children's Hospital. They said it was delivered to the front desk in a flower box with a room number on it. It came wrapped in tissue paper and arranged with baby's breath."

"Was there a card?" asked Harry.

"I don't know," said the assistant.

"Thanks," said the Coroner. He could tell she was uneasy. It was time to get her out of here. "Why don't you get started on the paperwork, Kelly. I'll take the pictures if you begin the report. Leave the name blank. We may get a break and find out who this poor soul was."

Baily stepped back in the room for a moment. "Got another leg at Overlake, Lieutenant," he said.

"Good work," said Bernard. "Stay on it. See if you can find the head."

Red was staring at the torso. "There's no penis," she said.

Van Dorn laughed and turned to Harry. "Just like you," he said.

"Shut up," said Bernard. "You and Baily hit the road. Start making the rounds. Interview the witnesses. Somebody signed for these things at every one of these hospitals. I want a description of this nut. Stop by the station and grab an artist if you need one. I want a picture of this guy on the six o'clock news. Move it!"

"Okay," said Van Dorn. "If you're sure you don't need me here."

"I don't," said Bernard. "Baily can use his phone just as easy in the car. Call me if something important turns up. I want that head by the end of the day or I'll have yours!"

Van Dorn nodded. He sneered at Harry before motioning to Baily to follow him. The door slammed on the way out.

"Are you sure it's a man's torso?" asked Bernard. "Did you count the ribs?"

"Despite what the Bible leads you to believe, men and women have the same number of ribs."

"Twelve pairs," said Red.

"Correct," said the Coroner. "But look at the muscle. The flat chest, the broad shoulders. Find the head and I'll bet we see an Adam's apple."

"Harry, what do you make of this?" asked Red. She pointed to strange impressions running up and down the torso.

Harry laughed. "Look like the marks left from whalebone stays after wearing a corset all night."

Van Dorn came back in, noisily demanding everyone's attention. They all turned towards him, including the Coroner.

"I told you to get going," said Bernard.

"Yeah. Just thought you'd want to know. The fingerprint came back. It's definitely Sooka." He waited for a reply. With none coming he turned and left again.

The Coroner went back to examining the marks.

"Was Sooka a cross dresser, maybe?" asked Bernard.

"I wonder," said Red. "How do you work in women's clothes..." She caught herself. "I mean, in the women's fashion industry, and not be tempted?"

"That's a stereotype," said Harry. "Didn't expect that from you."

"You've seen Designer Derby," said Red. "Some of the boys take it too far. There's one that wore embellished jeans all the time. Another who tied a very feminine scarf around his neck."

"Doesn't mean they cross dress," said Harry. "Maybe they're doing it to stand out as designers. Make a statement. Look at Oscar de la Renta, Giorgio Armani, even Versace. They stay totally butch. Impeccable suits."

"Yeah," said Red. "So does Curran, the go between on the show. Yet every gay boy in the country wants to sleep with him."

"He's no Italian designer," said Harry. "Just a pimp for Heille Crumstein and her little panel of mean spirited critics."

"Gay boys dress pretty sharp," remarked Bernard. "Pay more attention to their clothes than a hetero." He thought of his own clothes, the rumpled blue suit, the tie not quite matching his off color khaki shirt. When was the last time he had them dry cleaned?

"Come on, Red," said Harry. "Curran dresses nice. It's his job on the show to comment on the designer's work in progress, but he's out of the closet. Does a lot of gay charity work. He's been spotted at the bars on Capitol Hill more than a few times. Look, there are some straight designers. If I had the talent I'd try it myself. Who wouldn't want to be surrounded by the most beautiful women in the world all day?"

Bernard smiled at the thought. Despite the circumstances, he had really enjoyed going to the Nordstrom's fashion show with his wife last month. She had picked out his clothes and it made a difference. He had a more pulled together look, and the women could tell that night. He felt and acted more charming and handsome. He wondered why he didn't dress up more often instead of wearing the first thing his hand grabbed when he reached in the closet in the morning.

The Coroner backed away. "You know, these marks would be consistent with a whale bone corset. There are signs the torso was compressed."

"Maybe Sooka wore a girdle because he was fat," said Bernard.

"He was overweight," said the Coroner. "But look at this. The torso is squeezed into an hourglass shape. These marks here on the chest definitely look like ones a corset would leave behind." He pointed to some other marks. "Look at these on the chest. They appear to be lines from a bra cup."

Red turned to the table behind her, staring closely at the dismembered leg. "And look at this. Imprints from garters. He was definitely wearing a corset or something like it when he died."

Bernard turned to Harry. "She's good."

Red smiled.

"Any traces of fabric on the body?" asked Harry.

"Nothing," said the Coroner. "He was naked when we got him. I imagine he was cleaned with a garden hose, just like you would an old car." He bent his head over the chest. "Look here." He indicated a pattern that was lost in the charred flesh near the neck. "This could be an imprint from a necklace of some kind."

Harry stood back, moving to the bottom of the table. "Looks like it was a pretty tight corset," he said. "Do you think he was squeezed to death?"

"Possible," said the Coroner. "The lungs are crushed and I found slight lesions in the lower ribs. But there is also the possibility that the killer did the damage when he cut the body up. I won't know until I dig in."

"Do you think Sooka put the corset on so he could wear the charity dress?" asked Harry.

"Maybe," said Bernard.

"Accidental death?" asked Red.

"If it was, then who cut him up and delivered the parts all over town?" asked Harry.

"And why do that?" asked Bernard.

"Certainly would add to the publicity," said Harry. "Bet that dress goes up another hundred thousand when this hits the news."

"Then maybe we should keep it out of the news," said Bernard.

"Well, guess this solves the case of the missing Dick," said Red. "So much for the reward."

The Lieutenant cleared his throat. "Not quite, Rita. As I see it, you and Takanawa still have a shot at it. The reward was for the return of the dress, not for finding Sooka."

Red lit up. "Hey, that's right."

"As if nobody cared for poor Richard Sooka," said Harry. "Human life is cheap."

"At least in Hollywood," said Red. "Here we are having this conversation again."

"It's a sad state of affairs," said Harry. "People are treated like chattel there. Commodities to be invested in and traded, then discarded when they get old and useless."

"They get paid pretty well to put up with it," said Red. "Sooka was worth at least thirty million."

"How do you know that?" asked Bernard.

"Looked it up on the internet when I was doing my research this morning. It was reported in the Wall Street Journal. He's also got a chain of stores with his name on the marquee. Overpriced bags and label clothes marked up way beyond their worth. No wonder he's debt free. He's capitalizing on his fame while he can, probably was getting ready for the Hollywood farewell. Shoot, I'll bet his stuff starts flying off the shelf. You think the dress went up, wait until the public hears there will be no more Richard Sooka originals."

"Rita, I had a thought," said Harry. "We should add Sooka's business partners to the list of suspects."

"I was getting to that before we left the office to go the police station," she said. "They're a little harder to research than celebrities."

The Coroner moved to the bottom of the torso and stared at it. He probed it with a pair of forceps he was holding in his hand, lifting the dead flesh and studying. "Did you ever catch that sicko that was raping women and cutting off their breasts?"

"The Greenlake Butcher? He's still at large," said Bernard. "Why. You think these are related?"

"Just wondering," said the Coroner. "I see some sick things in this job. I never get to see the part where justice is served."

"What's he talking about?" asked Red.

"Some time ago there was somebody going around Greenlake. Never got a description of the perp. All we found were the mutilated bodies of the victims"

"Mutilated?" asked Red. "How?"

"They were all women. All of them had breast implants. After stabbing them in the lower abdomen several times and slicing their throats, the killer would cut off their breasts and vaginal lips."

"Were those the murders I read about in the papers last February?" asked Red.

"That'd be about right," said the Coroner, still studying the torso.

"I don't remember hearing about any mutilations," she said.

"We try to keep that kind of stuff out of the papers," said Bernard. "Bad for tourism."

"And murder is not?"

"Murder is one thing," said Bernard. "But this kind of thing crosses the line."

"We need to keep this out of the paper too," said Harry.

The doors flung open behind them. Kelly, the Coroner's assistant, wheeled in a cart with a body bag containing a single round object on it. Her face was colorless, drained of blood. She looked down at the bag. "Evergreen just sent this over."

The Coroner opened the bag and carefully removed the severed remains of Richard Sooka's head. He studied it for a moment before placing it on the table at the top of the torso. "We have a match," he said.

Bernard thought he would be sick. Kelly left the room. Harry and Red moved closer for a look. The Coroner grabbed a camera and took pictures. The head stared back at them, eyes bulging, hair singed and burned, tongue sticking out and swollen like someone stuffed a giant maggot in his mouth. There were gashes on the cheeks, dried blood clotting the open wounds. His skin had been grated off in places revealing the muscle beneath. There was an agony about it, the face frozen in horror, a death mask of pain.

"I suspect the head was cut off with a tree saw," said the Coroner. "You know the kind that's like a hacksaw chain. These marks we thought were a necklace were actually a rope saw. Look at the face, the burn marks on the head, the serrated cheeks. I would surmise that Richard Sooka was tortured to death, made to wear the tool of his own dismemberment."

Chapter 10

Performance Review

Harry drove the old Volvo, keeping it exactly at fifty five. Any faster and it shimmied like an Egyptian belly dancer, any slower and it roamed the highway like a boat in the wind. "It was wrecked and rolled over once," said Harry. "But it still runs good."

"What happened?" asked Rita. She imagined high speed chases, gunfire, and a daring escape from bad guys.

"I was hauling a motorcycle inside a horse trailer. I should have used a better trailer, a smaller one, maybe a flat bed that was made for the job. I was arguing with my wife. I remember looking in the rear view mirror and seeing the horse trailer flip. I stopped arguing with my wife and told her to hang on. Next thing I knew we were upside down."

"How'd that happen?" she asked.

"The torque on the trailer hitch was enough to flip the car."

"What'd you do?"

"Couple of people helped me turn the car over. The horse trailer was totaled. I gave what was left of it to the farmer who came out to help me. It all happened right in front of his house. The car started okay so I drove it to the next town and rented a trailer, then came back for my wife and my bike."

"So, that's why it shakes?"

"Yeah. It's not the ball joints or the tires," he said. "The frame is bent."

"Can't help you there," said Rita. "It should be junked."

"I know. But it runs."

"Right, and you can't afford a replacement, can you?"

He nodded. "You did pretty good today, Rita," he said.

"Thanks, Harry. And thanks for giving me a ride to work. I hate to stop now. Things are just getting interesting, but I can't quit my night job."

"I understand that," said Harry. "We all got bills to pay. We can make a go of this. I'll show you how to do skip traces tomorrow and we'll work out a way you can get a cut for every one you do."

"Will I have to go to Bernard every time?" she asked.

Harry was embarrassed. "I was desperate and needed them done today. It's the fifth of the month and Binky wants his cash. I hate to ask Bernard for favors, but I'll show you the standard procedure used to get information from the cops, it just takes longer. Don't worry, I'll train you on all this."

"Bernard's a nice guy. Why did you quit?"

"I wanted to be a private detective. I thought I could help people more as a detective than as a cop. Police are hamstrung by policy and procedure, not to mention politics. As a private detective, those rules don't apply," he said.

"Oh." Red was quiet.

"Why?" asked Harry. "Did you hear something different?"

"Yeah," she said. "Not that it matters. I still want to work for you."

"What did you hear?" asked Harry.

Red remained quiet.

"Come on. Out with it," said Harry. "If we can't be honest with each other then we're gonna have problems. Come on, spit it out."

"Well, while you were meeting with Bernard, I was talking with Van Dorn. He didn't have nice things to say about you."

"Consider the source," said Harry. "Go on. What did he say?"

"He told me some cockamamie story about how you like to wear dresses. Said you got caught at a gay club one night during a police action. That true?"

Now Harry was silent. "No, not all of it. It was a restaurant and not a gay bar. What else did he say?"

"He said after that you weren't a very good detective. Said your career was ruined and you were ashamed to continue."

"Go on," said Harry. "I want to hear it all before I respond. Old detective's habit."

"He said Bernard tried to protect you. Said there were some kind of laws in place, anti-discrimination laws or something, that made it difficult to get rid of you. But you had become an embarrassment to the police. He said you wanted to start coming to work in drag, part of some plan you had to get a sex change operation that the city would have to pay for because of your medical benefits. Bernard was behind it but the other cops said they wouldn't work with you. They threatened to quit if you didn't resign."

"Anything else?" he asked.

"That's pretty much it. He said you were an ugly woman, too. Not that it matters," she said. "To me, anyway."

"Does it matter, Rita?" he asked.

"Nah. Not to me. Come on, I'm a lesbian myself," she said.

"Really?" said Harry. "I wouldn't have guessed."

"Why do you think I work at the Rose Hips? Best Les Bar in Seattle. Best drinks, especially the cosmos," she said. "I like fist fighting and cunnilingus and don't tell me any different."

Harry laughed. "You're okay, Rita."

"I know that," she said. "I had to get comfortable with who and what I am. I tried men. They were disastrous for me. Clumsy beasts who did nothing for my ego. Left me all bruised and battered inside, worse than any street fight I had ever survived. It's easier to treat the wounds you can see."

"Maybe you haven't met the right man," he said. "We're not all shit."

"Just most of you," she said. "Maybe I should correct myself. I'm more bi than full out lesbian. You're right. There is a difference. I'd give the right man another shot, I'm just tired of the bull crap." She looked away for a moment. "So, you really got caught in a dragnet?"

"That's a funny way of putting it," said Harry. "Again, consider the source, Rita. Van Dorn and I have a very adversarial relationship. Did he also tell you I got several commendations while on the force?"

Rita shook her head.

Harry continued. "Yeah, I thought not. He never mentions the good stuff except when he's talking about himself. I don't feel special. He talks down to everyone, even his own mother."

"I kind of figured that," said Red. "I'm sorry I jumped him in the police station. I have a low tolerance of verbal bullies. Comes from my childhood days."

"Bernard certainly seemed to enjoy it. I don't think he has a high opinion of Van Dorn either. Anyway, take whatever he tells you with a grain of salt and think for yourself. Guess I don't need to tell you that."

Traffic slowed ahead. Harry took the exit and guided the old Volvo down the off ramp. "I'm going to take the surface roads. Sometimes the interstate is jammed this time of day."

"Fine with me. No hurry. I appreciate you dropping me off at work," she said. "Gives me more time to hear your side of the story."

"Okay. Let me give you some background. I started cross dressing early in life. Don't know why, but it just happened. I can remember wanting to paint my nails as early as the first grade. Then I found a box of old clothes in the basement and tried them on one day. I thought they were my mother's or my sister's from when they were little girls. I liked it. Felt comfortable, and maybe that had something to do with it. Maybe wearing my mother's clothes was the next best thing to being held by her. I can't explain it. Been to therapy and my therapist can't explain it either, but she did try to help me accept that part of myself."

"Your disowned self?" said Rita. "That's what they call it. A part of yourself that you want to deny is there." She stared at Harry. "I've been to therapy, too, you know," she said smugly.

"Right," said Harry. "There's an old Chinese saying. To repress something is to give it great strength."

"Don't I know it," said Red. "But I'm not interested in why you cross dress. I just want to know why you quit the police force."

"Okay. Fair enough," said Harry. "I stayed in the closet forever. Never let a soul know about my little fetish. My therapist encouraged me to explore it more. She put me in touch with a transgender support group that meets weekly here in town. The group wasn't just for cross dressers. There were all types: transsexuals, pansexuals, neuters, metrosexuals, and everything in between."

"I get the picture," she said.

"Yeah, but it was not what I expected. Instead of helping me beat my habit, they encouraged it."

"That's what support groups do, Harry. They support you."

"Guess I was expecting something more like Alcoholics Anonymous," he said. "The transgender support group encouraged everyone to come dressed however you like. AA never encouraged me to come to a meeting drunk. I saw all types at the transgender meetings. I felt comfortable after a while and gradually started wearing women's clothes to meetings. It started with high heels and woman's jeans, then a bra under a guy's shirt. Finally I added a wig and it wasn't long before I went all out. One of the girls at the meeting introduced me to makeup."

"You didn't wear makeup before that?"

"No. I was in the closet. I was a full bore hetero guy who occasionally wore a skirt or a dress at home. No wig, nothing fancy."

"Okay, so go on."

"Some of the group members met regularly after the meetings at a Capitol Hill bar or restaurant or even a coffee shop. They changed the location a lot. Just an after meeting social. We went together and had coffee, drinks, a little food, and talked. Continued the work we did in the group. It was fun."

Harry waited at a stoplight. "As I continued to explore my cross dressing I became bolder," he said. "It was a safe environment, surrounded by other transgenders. It's no wonder I moved on from wearing women's underwear to more outward clothes. I felt more myself and more comfortable than ever. Then one night there was a police raid."

The light changed and he took off. "Like I said, we rotated places a lot. On this unlucky occasion we picked a restaurant the owner was using as a pot farm. It wasn't enough that he was growing it in the basement, but he was selling it over the counter."

"Why use a business?" asked Red. ""Isn't that crazy? To risk it all that way? Why didn't he just get a license to grow medical marijuana? Start a legal pea patch?"

"Because he was a stoner, Rita. Their minds don't think too clear," said Harry. "His reasoning came out later. He heard they were busting residential growers because of the amount of electricity they burned. Way above the limits for standard family living even if you had a dozen big screens going full time. But a business, well that's different. It was a restaurant, too. Not only did the smell of cooking hide the farm, but he vented it through the fume hood tied in with the stove. He used the carbon dioxide from his drink machine to enrich the air in his grow room. He even recycled food waste and coffee grounds into compost for his plants. Everything was packaged in food service supplies, aluminum foil and shrink wrap for freshness. When I went back over it in my mind I wondered how much take-out was actually packaged pot."

"How'd the cops get wise?" she asked.

"It was the State that tipped them off. He wasn't ordering as much food as he seemed to be selling. They thought he was evading taxes."

Red took it all in. "Sometimes I wonder why we don't legalize it and tax it. Do away with half the DEA and free the court system to deal with more heinous crimes. We'd probably cure the national debt in ten years at that rate, maybe sooner."

"You're not the first one to suggest that," he said. "So I was at this place the night it was raided. Police checked everyone's ID. Some got to go while others were brought in for questioning. Our group was taken downtown."

"Why didn't you just flash your badge?" she asked.

"I was embarrassed, especially how I was dressed. None of my group knew I was a cop. Besides, I had left it at home. It wouldn't have made a difference. They searched everyone, and two of the girls in our group had pot on them. One had a significant amount, I was surprised. They did seem to know the owner pretty well. You can guess the rest. Once I was identified, of course they let me go, but the news was all over the police station. I took a drug test and passed to waylay any suspicions but it was too late. The damage was done. Pictures of me started showing up in the locker room, on my desk, in the briefing room. Someone put lipstick and long hair on the picture of me in the lobby where I had gotten a citation. There was even a poster that I suspect Van Dorn had made. A picture of me in drag with the letters 'Wanted for fashion violations.' It just got ugly from there."

A car beeped behind them. Harry moved to the side and let them pass. "Van Dorn was telling you the truth when he said Bernard tried to protect me. There are laws against discrimination but I couldn't let him take a bullet for me. Higher ups agreed I was a good detective but also an embarrassment. In the end it became a hostile environment. I packed up everything feminine I ever owned and hid it in my closet. I swore I'd never do it again. Silly of me. I forgot what I learned in therapy. To this day I still fight with my disowned self."

Red put her arm around Harry. "I'd like to meet that disowned self sometime. She'd probably be a good friend. Someone happy who really cares about people. Someone worth knowing."

"I'm not sure Rita," said Harry. "She's a made up person. Artificial. Like a character in a movie."

"Larger than life," she said. "More real than most of the real people I know. Full of suffering and triumph and the best of what humanity has to offer, I would expect." Harry stopped the car. They had arrived at the Rose Hips bar.

"You exaggerate," said Harry. "But I like that about you. You have lots of imagination. You'll make a fine detective."

I am a fine detective," she said. "Present tense. I'm Trixie Belden, Kinsey Malone, Cagney and Lacey all rolled into one. I'm living the dream, Harry. Thanks to you."

"Working at a night club as a bouncer?" he asked.

"Keeps me in shape," she said.

"You got a positive answer for everything," he said.

"You bet. My philosophy on life," she said. "Unlike you, Harry, once I embraced my disowned self, I became larger than life. So full I burst at the seams. By the way, what is the name of your disowned self?"

"Haven't you figured that out yet Nancy Drew?" he asked. "It's Fu."

"Someday you'll have to tell me how you came by that name," said Rita. "But I got to get to work right now. Wanna come in for a drink?"

"Nah," said Harry. "Gotta deliver these skip traces to Lenny and pay my own bills."

"Okay," she said. "Some other time." She smiled and got out of the car. A big blocky redhead so full of life she towered over six feet tall. Harry drove off thinking how lucky he was to know her.

Chapter 11

Hard Times

Harry drove around the block three times looking for a parking place. He needed to see Lenny in the worst way. Binky and his trained dog would be back for another visit and he needed something to feed them. He knew he could've taken Fat Farnsworth, but that wasn't the way to deal with Binky. Harry needed all the friends he could get, and no matter what the circumstances, Binky was still his friend.

On the fourth time around he found a spot close to Lenny's place, Capitol Hill Pawn. He grabbed the envelope on the seat beside him and debated paying for parking. He jingled the small change in his pocket, decided it was cheap insurance. A ticket, or worse being booted, was a risk he could not afford. He pulled the change out and bought thirty four minutes of time.

Lenny was behind the counter dealing with a customer, someone hocking their kid's musical instrument.

"I bought this bass guitar in Vegas less than two months ago, now I find my kid's more interested in Guitar Hero than a real guitar."

"Yeah," said Lenny, stroking his long beard. He looked like a member of ZZ Topp except he didn't have gray hair yet, "Look behind me buddy. I have dozens of guitars. Can't give you more than thirty for it."

"But this is a brand new bass. New strings. Look I'll throw in the amp if you just give me fifty."

Lenny drew a deep breath. He opened the till of his register and stared into it. "Can't do it bub, things are tight everywhere."

"How about forty? Can you do forty?"

Lenny stared into the till. "You throwing in the amplifier and the patch chord, right?"

"Yeah," the man said. "The whole package."

Lenny reached in the till and pulled two twenties out. "All right, show me the goods." The man laid everything on the counter. Lenny looked it over, checked the chord for wear. "New strings?" he asked, twanging as his ear hovered over the guitar.

"Brand new," said the man.

"Got it in Vegas, you say?"

"I bought it with money I won. Had a lucky streak."

"The amp works, right? Or should I plug it in?"

"Go ahead. Brand new."

"Okay. We got a deal." He slid the money across the counter.

The man pocketed the money and smiled. "Thanks."

"Okay okay. Don't tell no one. Don't want people to know I've gone soft."

"I won't tell. Thanks." The man slid past Harry, anxious to get to the door before Lenny changed his mind. Lenny cleared the counter, put the amp on the floor behind him and hung the guitar from a hook on the wall.

"It's too late Lenny," said Harry. "Whole neighborhood knows you've already gone soft."

"Comes with old age, Harry. You'll see one day."

Harry held up a manila envelope. "Got your traces done."

"That was fast."

"Fast Harry. That's what they call me." He dropped the envelope on the counter. "Got anything left in the till for me?"

Lenny opened the register and stared into it again. "You want store credit maybe?"

"Normally I would, but I need cash in the worst way."

"Don't we all." Lenny grabbed a few bills from under the change drawer. He set them on the counter and picked up the manila envelope, opened it and inspected the contents.

Harry counted the cash. "A little short, aren't we?"

"So I'll owe you, Harry. Honestly, it's all I got right now."

Harry stuffed the bills in his pocket. "You're not the only one going soft, Lenny."

"I'm good for it, Harry. You know it. Maybe next Friday?"

"I know old friend. I just wish Binky would understand."

"Don't talk to me about that piece of shit. He's not my favorite person right now."

"Why?"

"Passed me some hot goods not too long ago. He knew it too. Told him I didn't care how far back we went, I'm not his fence. Just makes trouble for me."

"I hear you," said Harry.

"Look. I'll pay you as soon as I catch up with these deadbeats. Sooner if I get a break."

"It's okay, Lenny. I'll make it. Thanks for the business."

"I got one more, if you're willing to do it," he said. Harry nodded. Lenny went to a file cabinet and pulled out a piece of paper, made a photo copy, and handed it back to Harry.

Harry looked it over. "This one may take a little longer," he said.

"It's okay," said Lenny. "Time I got. It's money I'm short of."

"Okay. I'll try to be fast. The information is time sensitive. Sometimes these skippers move faster than the information highway. I'll get back to you soon."

Harry left the shop and walked to his car. He was about to slide his key into the lock when he sensed something behind him. He turned to face Fat Farnsworth. The big man leaned forward, pinning Harry against the car like an air safety bag filled with fat flesh.

"Where's your little red headed friend?" he asked. Sweat oozed off him, reeking of B.O. When combined with his breath, it gave him the air of sulfur-rich mud in a salt marsh.

"She likes you, fat boy," said Harry.

Farnsworth leaned into him harder, bending his back against the car. "I can break you like a stick."

"No, no, Farnsworth." It was Binky, of course. "We need him intact, well enough to work so he can pay the rent." Binky walked up to Harry and

Farnsworth backed off, but not before giving Harry a little jab. "Just remember, stick man. Snap. Snap."

"How much did Lenny give you?" asked Binky.

"Not enough," said Harry.

"It's okay. I'll take what you have as an installment."

Harry reached for his pocket but Farnsworth grabbed his wrists and pinned him back.

"Here, let me get that for you," said Binky. He reached in Harry's pocket and pulled out the money. He sniffed it like perfume. "Ahhh. Fresh from Lenny's counter," he said. He counted it. "You're short a significant amount by my accounting." He put the money in his coat pocket.

"Leave me something, will you Binky? I gotta eat."

"Entrepreneurs are supposed to be hungry, Fu. Gives them a business edge," said Binky. "Haven't you heard that?"

Harry stood silent.

"So what's your plan for coming up with the rest?" asked Binky.

"Lenny gave me some more work."

"And?"

"I'll find something. Give me some time."

"I'll give you another day."

"Thanks, Binky. You're a real sport."

"Don't mention it," said Binky. "Anything for an old friend."

"A saint, you are," said Harry. "Don't let anyone tell you different."

"I heard you and your new partner are working the Sooka case," he said. "I'm rooting for you Harry. I want you to solve it. Get your big break."

"Thanks, Binky. Got any clues for me? Any word on the street?"

"I haven't heard anything, but for you, Harry, I'll tap my sources." He looked at Farnsworth and they both turned their backs to Harry and walked away.

"Thanks, Binky. You're all heart." He didn't know if Binky heard him. It didn't really matter.

Lenny came out of his store. "I saw what happened, Harry. You okay?"

"Yeah. Could use a drink of water though. My mouth's kinda dry."

"Come back inside."

They went into the pawn shop where Lenny guided him into the back room and sat him down at a table. He brought him a glass of tap water filled with ice. The door buzzer rang in the shop alerting Lenny that he had a customer.

"Be right back," he said.

Harry took another drink, then went to the bathroom and splashed water on his face. He came out of the bathroom, heard the buzzer in Lenny's shop again, and felt like it was time to go. The shop was empty except for Lenny with a pile of new wares on the counter. He was staring into the register again.

"You're too soft Lenny. I told you that," said Harry.

"My wife says the same thing," he said. "She's tight, I'd let her work the counter but people have it figured out. They just come in when she's gone. The wait for Mister Softee, get their cash, and go next door to buy lottery tickets."

"Thanks for the water, Lenny. Be seeing you." Harry scanned the street through the window.

"Don't worry," said Lenny. "Binky left already. He's got other people to squeeze."

Harry started towards the door.

"Wait a minute." Lenny reached into the drawer and held up a twenty dollar bill for him. "Here you go, Harry. It ain't much but it'll buy you dinner."

Harry was reluctant, but broke. He took the money. "Thanks, Lenny. Appreciate it. You know I won't buy lottery tickets with it."

"I know," he said. "You'll give it to someone who needs it, some old lady or a friend who's down on their luck."

"Not tonight," said Harry. He felt his stomach rumble. "Dinner." He stepped outside in time to see a cop writing him a ticket. "Jesus, have a heart," he said, rushing to the car. "I paid. Didn't you see the sticker on the window?"

"Sorry. Time expired."

Harry looked at the sticker. "Less than ten minutes ago."

"It's still expired," said the cop.

"Can't you give me a break?" he asked. He thought about mentioning that he was a former cop but decided against it. Might make things worse. He may have heard of Harry, or worse, of Fu Chan, the Oriental transvestite. "Please, can you give me a break?" he asked.

There was no choice in the policeman's mind. The ticket had been written, pressed in quadruplicate on little paper with a number stamped in red at the top. It was his job to write up violators. He was lucky to have a job with so many people out of work. "Sorry. I already wrote the ticket. Can't tear it up." He ripped off one of the colored sheets and handed it to Harry, carefully avoiding eye contact. He turned his back to Harry and murmured, "Have a nice day."

Harry looked at the ticket. "Nothing like salt in an open wound," he thought. He stuck the ticket under his windshield wiper, felt his pocket for the twenty dollar bill. "Might as well go shopping," he said to himself. "At least I got a good parking spot. Right across the street from a grocery store."

Chapter 12

Santa's Little Workshop

The hobbyist looked at the items spread out on the table in his workshop. Surgical screws, small drill bits he had carefully milled to size, servos and motors from a build your own robot kit, Foley catheter, banded leather, glitter and fabric embellishments, lightweight wire framing, webbing, an old empty disposable lighter. He glanced at the clock on the wall, then picked up a hammer and smashed the lighter. He threw the plastic pieces in the trash and saved the upper part. He cut the band of leather to a carefully measured length, then shaped it into a circle and sewed the ends together. He cut bright pieces of fabric and covered the leather with small swatches.

Music played in the background. He was engrossed in his work, occasionally humming as he was drawn further into the project. Using a set of calipers, he measured tolerances and positioned the surgical screws exactly where he wanted. He attached servos and motors. Using the webbing he made a framework of metal and fabric, adding embellishments. It was creative, fun, and he enjoyed the work.

Hefting the project in his steady hands, he was pleased at how lightweight it all was. His smile widened, teeth bared between his thin lips. His eyes began to sparkle like bright lights reflected off the black side of a polished eight ball. He installed a trigger device in the framework, a piece of metal that folded over to make contact and activate the servo motor. He secured a small circuit board assembled with parts he purchased at a Radio Shack. He adjusted micro switches and rheostats using a jeweler's screwdriver, carefully monitoring a millisecond counter on a sports watch. One click in half a minute, another at ten minutes, and another at twenty minutes. Perfect. He tested it again, attached wires to the framework, and again marveled at the beauty and delicateness of the thing.

He filled the balloon of the Foley catheter with an amber liquid from a syringe, using a hemostat to clip it off when it was full. He weighed it on a scale. He tested the resiliency of the balloon, filled the syringe again and pumped more liquid into it. He tied the end off, removed the hemostat and checked it for leaks. He bounced it on the table. It rolled like a limp water balloon. He caught it in mid air as it rolled off the edge of the table. He was like a child with a new ball.

He used a piece of electrical tape to keep the trigger from activating. It was a safety device, pressed in place until he presented it to his next victim.

He hummed to the music playing in the background. He mounted the balloon on the framework and then turned his attention to the broken parts of the lighter. With tiny screws, he mounted it to the framework. He picked it up again, studying it like a sculpture, which it was. A one of a kind designer death, his trademark.

"Too bad all this workmanship will never be seen or appreciated," he said. "I'll have to hide it all beneath this glitter and fabric." He sewed swatches and embellishments and sequins, following some design from the twisted dregs of his mind. He stood back to admire his work. "Just a few more touches."

He added balls and wire and more glitz. More glue and glitter, fabric and pieces of leather. When he was finished he stood back, still humming to the music.

"My finest work," he said. "Nobody will be able to say I'm a bad designer."

He laughed, a clown without an audience sharing a joke that only he understood.

"Because nobody will be left."

Chapter 13

Sleepless in Seattle

There was gunfire and smoke, clouds so thick that Harry could not see. The gunfire continued. He heard bullets whiz past his ears as he dropped to the ground. Instead of solid earth, he landed in something soft and gushy. He turned and saw a headless corpse beside him. His foot was trapped underneath it and he tried to pull it free. He twisted, wiggling his toes at all angles but the corpse refused to release him. He screamed, grabbing the ground with his hands, trying to crawl away. The sand offered no traction and he desperately kicked his feet like a startled mule. He saw some large rocks ahead of him just out of reach. He stretched.

One foot broke free, the other caught on something. He turned on his back and reached down with his hands. Entrails wrapped around his ankle, tightening their grasp the more he struggled. His breath became short, gasping. He screamed again but there was no sound. He reached forward, looking for something to grab, something he could use to pull himself away.

Instead of rock he held an amputated leg. He threw it aside and reached again. This time it was a child's body, lifeless, but still warm and blood soaked. He reached again, tugging at the body of another blood soaked infant.

He awoke clawing at the sheets, the cold sweat of fear covering his skin. He smelled funny, acrid and rancid. His leg was wrapped tightly in a sheet, the corner still tucked under the mattress. His foot was trapped and held in place. The blankets were rolled around him, his hand clutching a pillow.

"Just a dream," he whispered. "Just a dream."

He unraveled himself from the tangle of bedding and went to the bathroom. He splashed water in his face and looked in the mirror.

"I thought I was free of these dreams." He looked into his eye. "Who do you think you're fooling, Harry? You can't escape your past." He looked down into the sink. "You'll always be a freaked out transvestite."

He started to cry. "Nightmares." The tears were uncontrollable. "Why couldn't I save them? Stupid truck. If I had just acted quicker. Shot those guys."

He felt weak. He went back in the bedroom and looked down at the mess that was his bed and decided to take a shower. The clock read five a.m. when he was finished. He was wide awake. "Might as well go to the office and get some work done."

"What work?" he asked himself.

"Lenny's skip trace maybe, but then I'd have nothing to show Red. Ah, I need the money. Damn Binky and his bulldog. Made a deal with the devil, I did. What made me think I could be a private eye? Bernard said he'd take me back. Anything's better than starving. Maybe it's not too late to ask Mrs. Lee for some money. Why did I help her find her daughter? Why didn't I take the money when she offered it? I'm such an idiot."

This dialog went on and on until he found himself slipping the key into the lock to the door of his office. It was still dark. He switched the light on and closed the door behind him. "Glad I left the car at home," he said. "Can't afford the gas anyway. Got a ticket to pay. Should I get Bernard's help? Ah, you can't fix a ticket like before. I'd just get him into trouble."

He turned the computer on and worked the skip trace. He didn't know how much time passed. The computer needed a small battery on the motherboard to fix the clock, another thing on his list of broken items. He thought about checking the naval observatory website but instead he got up and stretched his legs. It was daylight outside and he felt tired. He lay down on the couch in his office for a minute.

He was pulled out of sleep by rough hands. Pulled to a standing position. The hands twisted him around, his arms pressed flat against his back, facing Binky.

"It's okay, Farnsworth," said Binky in his calm but irritating voice. "You don't have to hold him up anymore. He can stand on his own two feet, can't you Fu?"

Harry was groggy but found his center of balance. "What the hell, Binky. What's this all about? Breaking in my office?"

"The door was unlocked," said Binky. "I knocked. This is a place of business, isn't it?"

"Yes."

"It's office hours, eleven o'clock by my watch," said Binky. "Seems like you were asleep on the job, Fu."

"I was resting," said Harry. "I had a rough night."

"So did I, but I'm here to take care of business, making my rounds collecting rent, my source of income. Speaking of which, you have something for me?"

"You got everything I had yesterday," said Harry

"Not true," said Binky. "You're holding out on me. I know you bought groceries after I left you last night."

"We all need to eat," said Harry.

"Yes, we do, don't we." Binky nodded gravely. "I thought you understood what I said. Didn't I tell you entrepreneurs were supposed to remain hungry? You didn't listen to me, did you?"

"Come on, Binky."

Binky reached into his pocket and pulled out an envelope. "I brought you something, Fu," he said to Harry.

"What is it?" Harry looked at the envelope as if it might contain Anthrax.

"It's okay," said Binky. "It's not an eviction notice, although I thought about it."

Harry took the envelope and opened it. "What's this," he said, scanning it. "A letter of reference for a job in the Jackson Federal Building?" he continued to scan. "... Security guard?" He closed the letter. "Why give me this?"

"I told you. I have your best interests at heart. You said you were hungry. I'm trying to point you towards work. Paying work. Granted it would take a few weeks before you get your first paycheck, but I know people there. I could get you processed and on the job by the end of the week. They even have night jobs for people like you who like to sleep during the day."

"I don't want to be a security guard, Binky."

"Sorry, Fu. I don't know anyone in the woman's clothing department at Nordstrom's. What else do you know? Any skills I can bank on?" he said. "Hey, I do know the manager of that tranny club up on Capitol Hill. Do you dance, Fu?"

"Knock it off, Binky. You know this is what I want to do."

"Yeah. You looked hard at work when Farnsworth and I came in today."

"I was taking a break. I've been here since five this morning working on another skip trace for Lenny."

"There you go again. Your network of business partners disheartens me, Fu," said Binky. "Lenny's another loser just like you. If he had better customer relations, he wouldn't need you to locate his deadbeats. His wife seems to understand that."

"Don't knock Lenny. The man's got a good heart," said Harry.

"But no money. Heart doesn't pay the rent or put food on the table, you know that. Come on, Fu. Be real. So what's it going to be? Security guard or exotic dancer?"

Harry stared at the ground. Binky smiled, shook his head knowingly.

"Can you give me another day, Binky?" asked Harry.

Binky's smile faded. "You ask a lot, Fu. You know, I have a mortgage to pay on this building. You think the bank has any heart? They're in foreclosure heaven."

"One more day, Binky. Please."

Binky took a deep breath and let it out with a long hiss. He looked at Fat Farnsworth who positioned himself behind Harry. A nod from Binky and Harry knew his arm would be twisted behind his back again.

"No one here to protect you today," said Farnsworth.

"Ah, yes," said Binky. "Your new employee. Just what you needed, Fu. Another mouth to feed."

"You'll get paid before she does, Binky. Or when she does. She's on commission and not salary."

"I see," he said. "I like her. She has a certain exuberance, and the good sense to not quit her day job, or night job in this case. Speaking of cases, do I hear you're looking into this missing dress thing? I hope you find it, but I'm not confident. I don't see you working hard on anything."

"Rita's on the case, Binky," he said. "We're putting serious effort into it."

"Good for you. Playing detective. Sounds like fun, but back to my problem, which is also your problem. I need rent to pay my mortgage. What are you going to do to help your old pal Binky?"

Harry looked at the ground.

"Okay, okay," said Binky. "Don't give me that wounded puppy look. I'm not going to throw you out into the streets. Remember, I came here to help you and, indirectly, me. I'll give you another day, provided you give me a decision by the end of the week. I don't care if it's security guard, exotic dancer, meter maid, or street cleaner. I just want some reassurance that you've got a source of income to pay the rent. Is that fair?"

Harry continued to stare at the ground. "Fair enough," he said.

"Okay then," said Binky. "But I still need to make a collection. Farnsworth, turn his pockets out."

Farnsworth bent Harry over the desk and emptied his pockets out onto the blotter. Binky picked up the wallet and went through it. "Where's the folding stuff, Fu? All I see here is a parking ticket."

"That's all I got, Binky."

"I'm disappointed. Maybe I should take a little insurance, like your computer. Wonder how much Lenny would give me for it?"

"Not the computer, Binky," said Harry. "I need that to do my work."

"Okay, then. Maybe your assistant's. She doesn't seem to be using it. It's a little older, but I'm sure I can get something for it."

Farnsworth released Harry, a grin on his face as he moved towards the computer. He bent over and was about to pull the plug when he heard, "If you want to use those fingers again, you'll take them off that computer."

They turned to see Big Red standing in the doorway.

Binky looked at his watch, then at Harry. "I like the office hours you two keep. Fu, I'd come work for you if this job paid anything. Is it her turn for the couch now that you're awake?"

Farnsworth positioned himself in front of Red, blocking her entrance into the office. "You want trouble, fatty?" she asked. "I can bend you over quicker than a queer in a gay whorehouse."

Binky laughed.

Harry couldn't help but smile. "Morning, Rita. Come on in," he said. "We were just having another discussion." He glared at Farnsworth who looked at Binky for instructions. One nod from the landlord and Farnsworth stepped aside and let Red enter the room.

"Same topic as yesterday?" she asked.

"Fu and I have an ongoing dialog about money. He's reassured me that I will be paid in full soon. We were just negotiating terms of payment and collateral holdings."

"I heard you from out in the hall," said Rita. "Look, we're on this case and you will get your money soon. First and last month's rent plus a deposit."

"So reassuring," said Binky. "We should all take payment in promises."

"It's a small price to pay to not see you or your bulldog every day," said Rita. "Tell me. When he shits, do you pick it up in a little plastic bag and dispose of it like a good pet owner?"

Farnsworth growled.

"Nice doggie," said Red. "Pull the leash in. I don't want to get bit."

Binky nodded at Farnsworth who stepped back. "I wish I had your faith in your employer," he said. "Unfortunately, I don't."

"So instead you deliver us ultimatums rather than news and clues?" said Red. "That your way of helping?"

"As I was explaining to Fu here, I need money too. I have a sizable mortgage payment of my own. Then there is the added cost of my management services. Collections are becoming more expensive. Time is money, my dear, and this is a daily meeting that I would rather not attend. I'm always disappointed when I leave."

Rita reached in her pocket and threw eighty dollars down on the desk. "Will this buy you off until the end of the week?" she asked.

Harry made a move but Binky snatched the cash quicker than a hurricane ripping shingles off an old house. "I see you're the kind of woman who puts their money where their mouth is. I like that. When you get sick of working for this deadbeat, come look me up."

"It won't come to that, I can assure you," said Red.

"You never know," said Binky. "Word is you might not be working at the Rose Hips much longer. Too violent with the customers, I hear."

"I'm a bouncer," she said. "It's part of my job."

"It's great that you do a thorough job, but the owner must be getting tired of paying those hospital bills. It's not good business when you break somebody's nose, especially when all they were looking for was a good time."

"Hey, that guy was out of line and had it coming."

"I don't want details," said Binky. "Just watch your back, sister. Don't want you to lose your job. He fanned the cash in front of his nose, then he put it in his pocket. He turned to Harry. "My arrangement stands with you. I need that assurance before the end of the week, Fu. Personally I think you'd make more money dancing than as a security guard, probably like the work better, but that's just my opinion."

Binky tipped his chin towards Farnsworth and then stared at Red for a long time. He finally turned away, taking a moment to smile at Harry. It was not a happy, good day smile. It was menacing, his teeth bared like rocks in a frozen winter stream. He winked, then turned and left the room.

Farnsworth smiled, a pale imitation of his boss, then he left as well. It just didn't have the same effect as Binky.

"Glad to see those two go," said Red. "Good morning, Harry."

"Is it still morning?" asked Harry. "You know, you didn't have to give Binky that cash."

"I did it to shut him up, but it didn't work. Dude can go on, can't he?"

"Binky is my problem, not yours Red," said Harry.

"Oh, con-traire, boss. If you go out of business, who's going to give me my big shot at being a private detective?"

"You could get a job anywhere, Rita, and you know it."

She looked away, moved towards her desk. "Not true, Harry," she said, her back to him. She remembered what Binky had said about what happened at the Rose Hips. "I have issues."

"Explain it to me," he said. "If you have issues, I need to know about them." He faced her back and spoke. "Look, I've told you a lot about me. And you're still here. Imagine that. So, you know a lot of my issues, what are yours?"

"You already know," she said.

"Anger issues?" he asked.

"Yes."

"That's it?"

"Don't belittle my issues!" she said.

"I'm not," he said. "It's not a big thing."

"It is to me," she said. "You heard Binky. I get mad. Real mad. That broken nose he mentioned is the end of a long list of things. Broken arms, broken legs. I once broke a girl's ring finger."

"That doesn't sound so bad," said Harry.

"It was the day before her wedding. She couldn't wear the ring."

"Oh," said Harry.

"See?" she said. "I have issues. Dangerous issues."

"It's okay, Red," said Harry. "I have issues. We all have issues."

"Maybe," she said. "But people don't get hurt when you cross dress."

Harry looked away, then went and sat behind his desk. "But they do. I break hearts. And don't say nobody gets hurt. I hurt Bernard, my mother, my ex-wife. Then there's me. I hurt myself more than anyone else."

Rita faced him and slowly walked towards him as he continued. "I'll be in a great relationship," he said. "Then she'll find out about... Well, it doesn't go well after that."

"What do you mean?" she asked.

"Women. Straight women, I mean, have a problem with it. I don't blame them. They're the ones who should look pretty, not me. I try to explain but they don't understand how I can be heterosexual and wear women's clothes at the same time. Sometimes they get vindictive, calling me all kinds of names. I don't make them feel right, not like women should feel when they're with a man."

"Women can be cruel," she said, putting her hand on his shoulder.

"Things will be going great. We'll sleep together and then she'll wonder why I have nightgowns on hand for her to wear or makeup and polish remover in my medicine cabinet or a bra that's not her size. At first they think it's another woman, and I let the lie go on sometimes. It's easier than the truth, but sooner or later the truth comes out."

"Truth is good, Harry. Nobody should have to live a lie. So you enjoy nice clothes. Big deal. Bernard's secretary didn't seem to have a problem with it yesterday. Does she know?"

"Nan? Of course. But she's married. I don't cheat like that."

"Kind of old fashioned, aren't you?"

"Hey, it's one of the commandments. It's like breaking the law. You start on one, next thing you know, you're breaking other laws, dishonoring your parents, stealing, coveting some neighbor's wife, slowly work your way up to killing."

"Killing?" said Red. "I would have thought the one about false idols would be at the top. Big sin, that one. Don't turn your back on God."

He nodded in agreement. "Man's law is one thing, but be careful about crossing the line with God," he said.

"Isn't it against the law to cross dress?" she asked.

"In some states. Not in Washington. Either way, I wouldn't go out in drag east of the Cascades."

"I never go further east than Issaquah. Sorry you feel bad about cross dressing. It's not a big deal to me. I'd like to see you in a dress sometime."

They smiled and there seemed to be no more issues. For the moment.

"Okay, can we talk business?" asked Red.

"If we must."

"First, what's the name of your detective agency?" she asked.

"Name," said Harry. I don't have one. It's just Harry Takanawa, Private Detective."

"Well, you need a name," said Red. "I was thinking last night, if this is a business and we want to make money, maybe we should run it as a business."

"Like charging Mrs. Lee for finding Sue Yen?"

"That's not what I'm talking about. We should always do a certain amount of pro bono work."

"Pro what?" he asked.

"Work for free. It's a legal term," she said. "I had some training. Worked for a lawyer once."

"I don't remember that on your resume," he said.

"I don't like to mention it. I had a few paralegal classes, and then went to work for this guy. He was a selfish bastard. I had to quit before I punched him out. He would have sued me and the ground I stood on the minute I touched him. I saw it coming. Don't get me wrong, there are good lawyers. He just wasn't one of them."

"Okay, so what's your plan for the business?" he asked.

"We should advertise. Get new business. Let people know what we can do for them."

"Advertising costs money," he said. "What'd you have in mind, ads in the penny saver?"

"Start with cheap," she said. "You found me through Craig's List. But before we advertise, we have to have an identity. A place where customers can go to find out more about us."

"Like a web site, maybe?" he asked.

"Great idea, Harry," she said. "I have a friend working on it right now."

"Oh. How much is that going to cost?" he asked.

"Freebie. This guy owes me a favor and I decided to call it in," she said. "You just need to decide what the public corporate name will be and what services you want to advertise."

"I still don't get it. How did I miss all this on your application?" he asked.

"I thought you were interested in me for my detective skills, not my business knowledge."

"Do you do accounting, too?" he asked.

"Some, not much," she said. "I know how to do payroll but that's as complex as it gets."

"Complicated enough," he said.

"It can be," she said. "Do you track your expenses?"

"It's all out of pocket for now," he said. "Should I start getting receipts from Binky?"

"It can wait until we formalize some of our business practices, but you should be keeping track of things."

The phone rang. It was Bernard. He was all business. "You seen the morning paper?" he asked.

"Matt," said Harry. "Good to hear from you, too."

"Cut to the chase, Harry. No time. There's a picture of the killer on page three. Artist's drawing. Every monkey in town is looking for this psycho. Things are heating up here and I need you on this."

"Got any new information?" he asked.

"Not to discuss on the phone. Come on down to the office when you get a chance."

"We're on our way, Matt." He hung up the phone. "Let's go, Rita. We have business to attend to. Real business."

Red rubbed her hands together and smacked her lips. "This is more like it," she said.

Chapter 14

Careful Preparations

The designer stepped back from his completed work. He admired his attention to details, the strip of leather ric rac he had painfully cut, the shaping of the brim, the clever opening at the top. It was truly one of his best designs, and his most deadly to date.

He looked inside at the mechanism one more time, the servos, the cables and motors, the balloon of liquid. Even more impressive was that he had done the work in a day, just like on Designer Derby.

"Wonder what Dick would say," he said aloud. He stood back and looked at the hat one more time before putting it inside the fancy hat box. He covered it with a piece of light fabric and put the lid on the box, tying it shut with a beautiful pink bow. "Someone's just going to love this little item," he said. He rotated the box and studied the presentation. He set the box aside and picked up the newspaper. On page three there was a crude pencil drawing next to the headlines, "Ghastly murder."

He read the article and chuckled. "Boy are they way off base," he said. "A suspect is wanted for questioning in a case involving a decapitation," he read. "He is described as a dark skinned Hispanic, black hair with a thick moustache, weighing approximately two hundred pounds." He hit the paper and laughed. "Police in this town are about as bright as a flashlight in a rainstorm." He wondered how much success they were having.

The fat suit had served him well, a pregnancy belly that he had modified from something found in a thrift store. All he had to do was reduce the breasts. Bought the brown pants and shirt in the same store. Tried it all on in the dressing room. The dark skin was easy. He used Dick's blood, smeared liberally on his skin as if it were cheap makeup. Risky, but he loved to play with blood. And the ruse had worked, that much was obvious.

His next disguise was equally thought out. He studied it one more time. It was all laid out on his sofa. Tight pants, close fitted shirt, cowboy boots with two inch heels. There was a blond wig with close cropped hair, something he had dyed and styled to perfection. Nothing like the long dark hair of the Mexican immigrant he had worn the day before. Instead of a moustache he had a Van Dyke beard to hide his features. He could leave his skin white and pasty, covering his eyes with contacts that changed them from pale blue to brown. .

He had a picture to go by, a man he had met at a bar three months ago. It was a one night stand, but it was all he needed. The man had taken him to his house. Before anything could happen he had an impression of his house and car keys. It was easy to convert the impressions to the real thing later, another little skill he had picked up along the way. It's all about training and education, whether you want to be a successful doctor, designer, or a killer.

He admired his package one more time, checked his watch, and decided to take an afternoon nap. After all, he had a long night ahead of him.

Chapter 15

Car Talk

Harry turned the corner, the old Volvo as always groaning with the effort.

"When you going to get those ball joints fixed?" asked Red.

"When I get time," said Harry.

"And money?"

"Yeah. And money."

"I'll help you," said Red.

"You know how to fix cars?" he asked.

"Just give me a Chilton's manual," she said.

"There's a ragged one on the back floorboards. You'll have to put some pieces together but it's all there. Well, mostly there. My big holdup is finding parts for this old clunker. It looks like crap but it still runs great."

"You keep saying that," said Red. "Are you telling me you wouldn't want a new car? Better place to live?"

"What better place to live than Seattle?" said Harry.

"It rains all the time. Winters are long and dark. It's cold," she said.

"People are warm. I like winter. Rain doesn't bother me," he said. "It's good for the plants. Makes them all green and lush."

"What are you going to do with the reward money?" she asked.

"What reward?"

"The money we'll get when we find the dress," she said.

Harry was quiet. "I don't know..." She looked so hopeful Harry didn't want to burst her bubble. What he meant to say was he didn't know if they would find the dress, but he couldn't bring himself to tell her that. He felt they had little or no chance of finding something that everyone was looking for, especially with the limited resources they had.

"I'm going to pay off my bills," she said. "Maybe buy my dad a nice present. He deserves it. Maybe get a breast reduction."

Harry had to laugh. "Breast reduction?" He looked at her chest.

"Don't you think these are too big?" she asked.

"No," said Harry. "They look average."

"I hate them," she said. "They've been a problem my whole life."

"I wouldn't say that," said Harry. "How can that be true? Your whole life? Did you have them when you were seven?"

"No. Eleven," she said. "Fourth grade. It was odd. Dad didn't know what to do. He talked to a neighbor lady, Mrs. Fitzgerald. She took me shopping for my first bra. All she could say over and over was, 'Good Lord'. When I put on the bra they just stood out like, well," she thrust her chest out. "Good Lord." She looked down. "Boys have been staring at me ever since."

Harry swerved. A horn sounded. He had been looking at her breasts and not the road. "Sorry," he said, regaining control of the car. He laughed.

"What's so funny?" She was hurt now. "I reveal my darkest secret and all you can do is laugh?"

"I was laughing at myself," he said.

She waited. "Well?"

Harry took a deep breath. "Why not?" he said, staring at the road ahead. "You already know the worst about me."

She waited.

"I've always wanted breasts. Wondered what it would be like to have them. Real ones, not plastic inserts or foam lined cups."

Red touched his arm. "Oh Harry."

He laughed again, and she joined him this time. "Well ain't this a stickler," she said. "They say it's true, a part of human nature, but we always want what other people have."

"It's why advertising and marketing work," said Harry. "Hey, let's change the subject. You said something about a web site?"

"Yep," she said. "Got my friend working on it, but he needs a little help. I need help."

"What?" he asked.

"I need to know what we're going to advertise, besides skip traces and missing persons."

"How about cheating spouses? We catch them on video," he said. "Lady asked me about it last week but she never gave me a retainer check. Don't do any surveillance without an agreement and a check up front."

"Good, good," she said. "What else do we do?"

"Stolen goods, identity theft, we basically do anything the police do, but won't."

"Won't?" she asked.

"Or can't, I should say. Police are underfunded and under resourced," he said. "They don't have time for everything people want them to do. Do you know there are police in this country who don't even respond to a stolen car or a burglary report anymore? They got bigger problems."

"Like what?" she asked. "Writing tickets?"

"Tickets create income, but yes. Think of what the highways would be like if police didn't enforce the traffic laws," he said. "It's part of every policeman's mission. Falls under public safety."

"Okay," she said. "Public safety. Traffic cops. Accident investigators. I get it."

"Look at the other things cops do," he said.

"Murder investigations?" she asked.

"Yeah, but I was thinking of legal actions, evictions, criminal arrests, prisoner escort, basic law enforcement."

"How about police escorts?" she added. "For funerals, visiting dignitaries and such."

"Yeah, that too," he said.

"And gang violence, drugs, industrial theft, homeland security," she said.

"All this is prioritized. Like marijuana is a low priority in Seattle, but the police are still concerned with crack and crystal meth, big deadly drugs."

"So," she said. "We would do all that? Harry Takanawa, Private Detective. We do everything the police do?"

"No," he said. "We can't. Some things are best left to the police."

"You're right," she said. "We should specialize, like all businesses. Find our niche. Pick the top five things we'd be good at, do a little marketing research, and target those things. Now, what would they be?"

The police station was just ahead. "Let's think about it some more and talk later," he said. "We're almost there."

Chapter 16

Papers

Bernard was ready for them this time. He met them at the door.

"What's this all about, Matt?" asked Harry.

"Got something for you." Bernard held out a sheaf of papers fastened together with paper clips. He removed some and handed them to Harry who took the papers and studied them.

"My license," he said.

"You've been approved. You're a licensed private detective now." He took the rest of the papers and gave them to Red. "So will you, Rita. Tentative, of course. Harry has some papers to sign to sponsor you, but if you fill out these forms we'll get the ball rolling."

She smiled like a five year old on Christmas morning.

"Why now?" asked Harry. "I filed this paperwork six months ago."

"We need you," said Bernard. "Isn't that how it always works?"

Harry stared at the official looking certificate, printed on thick cardstock, a number stamped in red at the bottom. He ran his fingers across the signature feeling the impression left from a pen.

Bernard turned towards Red. "You can sit down at that desk over there and fill out the forms while Harry and I talk," he said.

She left them and went to the empty desk he pointed at. Bernard led Harry into his office and shut the door.

Harry folded the paperwork and stuck it in his pocket. "Okay, what's up Matt?"

Bernard held out a manila envelope. "Got an offer for you," he said. "City wants to hire you as a contractor. I gotta warn you though. If you sign these papers, you'll be ineligible for the reward. Kind of a bird in hand offer. We'll guarantee a certain sum of money whether you perform or not. You'll be a contractor assigned to me."

"What if I don't sign?" he asked.

Bernard turned his back to Harry and stared out the window. "You'll be rogue, like every private dick in this city."

"Can I think about it?" asked Harry.

"Take all the time you need."

"What do you think I should do?" asked Harry.

"Don't ask me," said Bernard. "I have selfish reasons in mind. If you're rogue, you don't have to abide by our rules. You can go where you want, do what you need. If you do sign, you work for me. We have a contract with all the binding small print a contract can contain. The choice is yours."

Harry stuffed the papers back in the envelope then put it in his pocket. "What else did you call me down here for?" he asked.

"You're perceptive," said Bernard. "That's what I always like about you, Harry. Okay, I'll lay it out. We have a suspect in custody. Van Dorn is questioning him now."

"Van Dorn?" said Harry.

"I sent the bad cop in first. The suspect has a tight alibi. He's not coughing up anything."

"Does he have a lawyer?" asked Harry.

"He's an illegal alien," said Bernard. "They usually don't have lawyers, unless they're immigration lawyers."

Harry blew air. "So, immigration is not his problem, I assume."

"He fits the description of yesterday's delivery man. The van was found registered to a fruit picker up in Skagit County. His prints were all over the van, and there was blood on the floor. We're running tests now. He says the farm gave him the truck for his personal use. His wife will confirm it, he says."

"How'd this happen?" asked Harry.

"A towing company was about to pull the vehicle. They got a call about it parked in a hotel lot not far from Gateway Mall. Black and whites picked it up. It was on the suspicious vehicle list."

"And I'm here..."

"Because you're a potential contractor to the city. As such, and as your assigned point of contact, I want you to question the suspect. I want you to find out all you can, use that famous intuition of yours." He paused. "I need your help. I need Harry Takanawa on the case."

Harry reached over and touched Bernard on the arm. "I'm here, Matt. Let's see what we can find out."

Chapter 17

Good Cop

"I wouldn't do such a thing. Please, I have a wife and children. Why would I kill a man I don't even know?"

"That's what we're trying to find out," said Van Dorn. "And unless you cooperate, you won't see your wife and children again. You'll be lucky to see anybody again."

Harry had seen enough. He had been staring through the one way glass into the small, brightly lit room listening for some time now. Van Dorn's interrogation techniques left much to be desired. "All right, Matt," he said. "Time to send in the good cop."

Bernard nodded. A uniformed cop opened up the door and motioned for Van Dorn to leave. When Harry stepped into view, he sneered. Harry just smiled.

"What the..." said Van Dorn. Harry just pushed him aside and guided him out the door towards Bernard.

"Let a pro handle it now," said Bernard. He offered Van Dorn a chair next to Red. The uniform cop locked the door and they watched through the one way glass. Red leaned forward in her chair, observing Harry with deep interest.

"Sorry. We haven't met. I'm Harry Takanawa," he said. "I'm not a cop, I'm a contractor. Just trying to find out what's going on here. And your name is?"

The man looked into Harry's eyes and saw something different, something he hadn't seen in Van Dorn. He took an easy breath and extended a hand. "Hector Gonzales, fruit picker. Pleased to meet you."

Harry felt the grip of Hector's handshake, saw the sincerity in his eyes. He felt the warmth travel up his arm and into his heart. First impressions are the most important they say. This was just another human being in trouble. He looked at the man's hands, hard calloused paws that showed years of hard work. These were not the hands of a criminal.

"I just want the facts," said Harry.

"They say I killed a man." He started to cry. He lowered his head. "Now, why would I do such a thing?"

"I don't know," said Harry.

"I was with my wife, I tell you. We live in a trailer behind a barn. She will be worried about me." He looked at Harry. "Did they tell you I was with her when the *conios* say I was killing this man?"

"No," said Harry. "They didn't tell me anything. Nothing about your guilt or your innocence."

"I didn't do this." He wrapped his arms around his head. "And now they tell me I will be deported."

"I can't do anything about that," said Harry. "But I can tell them the truth. Your truth."

"I was home that day. It wasn't my day to work. They found my truck, the truck my boss lets me drive, in a parking lot in Seattle. Ah, *Dios mio*. I was doing so well. I began to think I would actually have a better life." He grabbed his head again. "Ay, the Gods are cruel indeed."

"We're put on Earth to learn," said Harry. "God tests us, like rats in a maze. If you are an honest man, as I believe, you will pass the test."

"They say I killed a man," said Hector. "What else do they say I do?"

"You tell me," said Harry.

"How can I tell you about something I did not do?"

"They say you are a farmer," said Harry.

"Yes. I pick the fruit when it is ripe," he said.

"Do you also butcher?"

"Of course," he said.

Behind the glass Van Dorn smiled. "Why didn't I think of asking that?"

"Shut up," said Bernard.

Hector continued. "I kill chickens all the time. My wife does not have the stomach for it, but once I am done she can prepare them well."

"Ever kill anything bigger?" asked Harry. "A cow perhaps?"

"I could never afford a cow," he said. "But once I helped a neighbor. It took many hours of work and he rewarded me with some meat and enough tripe to make a good menudo."

"Do you have the equipment and knives to butcher a cow?" asked Harry.

"No," he said. "I have only a small hand knife with a short blade. Good for cutting plants. The chickens, I snap their necks. There is less blood that way, and my wife, she cuts it up. She will use almost every part, including the feet."

"And you never butchered anything bigger?" asked Harry.

"Once I killed a dog," he said. "I was very hungry and the dog was skinny. I shared it with some other men. We cooked it over an open fire but it was greasy and tasted bad. We had no salt or seasoning. As I said, we were very hungry."

"And that's it?" asked Harry. "You kill anything else?"

"No," he said. "I swear it."

"They say you killed this man and cut him into pieces, just as you would a cow. They say you delivered these pieces to locations all over town in your truck. Tell me, why would you do this?"

"I am a happy man, until today. When my boss tell me my picture is in the paper, I am proud, but he is not. I found out why. He say I cause him trouble. Behind him are the police, and then my wife is crying and I am here."

"Yet, they found your truck and the keys."

"That is not true. How can it be? I have the keys. You check. They take everything from me before I am here, and they put it in an envelope. The keys are there, on a small ring with a medal of St. Christopher, and the key to my trailer."

"You live near Mount Vernon," said Harry, stating facts. "That's over an hour north of Seattle. What did you do yesterday?"

"I told the other man all these things already," said Hector.

"I'm new. This is the first time we've met or spoken. I need to hear your story again in your own words please."

"I didn't use the truck at all. I parked it at the boss's house behind the garage where I always do, where no one can see it. It's a nice truck, clean, a van we use to take fruit to the market. Behind the garage is a river. I went fishing. The Salmons are running and I like the change from chicken. Fish is good for you."

"Did you have any luck?"

"I fished all morning, maybe four hours, but I caught nothing. I admit I was not trying hard. I mostly sat beneath a tree and thought about my life. The harvest is over and there is no work. I thought about going down to California for the winter. I smoked a cigar and made a small fire to keep warm. I had been wading in the river to fish and I was cold and my pants were wet. I cannot afford good waders or boots. I even use an old pole from the garage, which is why I drove the truck there in the morning. I had to fix the reel first. The line was tangled and it needed grease on the moving parts. I think I didn't catch anything because I did not have the right lures or bait."

"Did you use the truck when you were finished?"

"No. I walked along the river bank until I came to a path that leads to my home. I was looking for a better place to fish. A lucky spot. I never returned to the garage."

"Did any of your neighbors see you? Can they verify that you were home that day?" asked Harry.

"I saw no one, not even my wife until I got home that evening. Many of the trailers are empty now that the harvest is over. Most of my friends have already gone to California where the season is longer and there is work there."

"Are you sure you're the only one with a set of keys to the truck?"

"I don't know. It's possible there are many sets of keys, but I don't know. The boss will know if you ask him."

Harry looked through the one way mirror, wondering if Van Dorn caught that comment. The action wasn't lost on Bernard. "You check that out?" asked the lieutenant.

Van Dorn shook his head. Bernard frowned and turned his attention back to staring through the glass.

"Did you ever give your keys to someone else?" asked Harry

"No, señor. The truck belongs to *el heffe*. I wouldn't do that."

"How long have you worked for the boss?" asked Harry.

"Since last summer."

"So, someone else may have had the keys to the truck before you?"

"*Si!* Many people. The boss, he lets only his trusted people use the truck." He grabbed his head. "And now I have betrayed that trust."

"No you haven't, Hector. I will go to your boss and explain things. Together we'll talk to your wife. If you were there all day, it will be proven. I believe there is no way you could have driven all the way to Seattle, killed a man, made these gruesome deliveries, and then found your way home in a reasonable time."

"Then why won't they let me go?" he asked.

"Because you are here illegally," said Harry. "You know I can only address the murder charge. I cannot help you with these other things. Shall I contact an immigration lawyer for you?"

"Si, yes," he said. He understood Harry's limitations as much as Harry understood his.

"Sometimes we just have bad luck, Hector," said Harry. "I will tell them that I believe you didn't kill this man. As to the other things..."

Hector was excited. He rose and shook Harry's hand despite the restrictions of the handcuffs. "Thank you señor," he said. Then he sat back down. "It is not my place, but can I ask something else?"

"What, Hector?"

"My wife. Can you tell her not to worry? Can you see her and tell her that you know the truth now. She's just scared, as afraid as I am."

Harry didn't know if he could keep that promise, but he knew what to do. "I will try," he said. "Do you have her phone number?"

Hector asked for a pen and Harry gave him one from his pocket. Hector scribbled a number down on a scrap of paper torn from a notebook on the table. "This is a neighbor and…" He scribbled some more. "This is my address. I will be grateful."

"It's okay," said Harry. "I'll do what I can." He nodded towards the one way glass and the door behind him opened. The uniform came in and stood beside Hector. "Time to go," said Harry. "Good luck, Hector. I will contact your wife and get her statement. The truth will be known."

"Thank you." He looked hopeful for a man in his situation, a lot better than after Van Dorn interviewed him.

Harry left and met the others in the observation room. He watched the uniform chain and escort the prisoner through another door in the opposite side of the room. Harry watched him through the one way glass, wondering who felt sadder, him or Hector. "He didn't do it," he said to Bernard.

"Let me show you the videos," said Van Dorn. "I have the surveillance tapes from Evergreen and Seattle Children's Hospital. They say otherwise."

"I don't care what you have," said Harry. He didn't do it. Can't you see that Franklin? Aren't you a good judge of character?"

Van Dorn looked at Bernard. "Come on, chief. Who you going to believe here? Looks like case closed to me. Let's get the mayor on the phone and wrap this up."

"I'm not so sure," said Harry. "I'd say the killer is still at large."

Chapter 18

What Happened the Rest of the Day

Somebody asked what happened the rest of the day. Nothing really. You didn't miss a thing. Just keep reading.

Chapter 19

The Heart Cave

"Ah, what a day," said Harry, not to anyone in particular. He closed the door to his tiny apartment, a deadbolt, two locks and a chain, all it takes to make a man feel safe these days. He didn't feel like much of a man. How much ridicule can a man take and not stand up for himself?

"Don't answer that, Harry," he said out loud.

"I should get a pet," he said. "At least I won't sound like I'm crazy."

He went to the cabinet, moving the soup cans and bags of rice aside. Back behind the beans he found it, a clean bottle of Stoli 100, begging him to open it.

He took a glass out of the next cabinet, filled it with ice, and put a squirt in it from a plastic lime he took from the door of his refrigerator. He put the glass next to the bottle. He stared at the dishes in the sink for a long time, reached in his pocket and pulled out a small coin. Turning it over, he read, "God grant me the serenity..." He put the coin in his pocket and continued from memory. "To accept the things I cannot change..." He stared into the glass of ice. "The courage to change the things I can..." He looked at the bottle again, shook his head slowly. Then he put it back, hiding it once again behind the beans, rice, soup, and other meager stores in the cabinet.

"What am I doing? What have I gotten into?" He shut the cabinet door, filled the rest of the glass with tap water, stirred it with his finger and took a drink. He finished the serenity prayer. "And the wisdom to know the difference."

His phone beeped. He noticed a voice mail on it, picked it up and punched a couple of buttons. Binky's voice came on, sounding like chalk against a blackboard. "Hey, Harry. How's your investigation coming along? I hear you and Red are really working hard on this case, but I still need my money. Come see me after Lenny pays you. Don't make me track you down like yesterday or I'll send Farnsworth over for a visit. Oh, yeah. Checked with my buddies. The security guard job is a go. This ain't the mall, buddy. This is cushy, full time work watching government offices. Think about it. Let me know. Either way, I'll see you soon."

Harry put the phone down on the table and went to the bedroom. He lay back in the bed staring at the ceiling with its broken plaster and yellowed paint. He could smell his sheets, now in need of serious laundering.

"God knows what else lives in this apartment with me," he said aloud.

He took a shower, the warm water trickling over his body, falling like a flood off a mountain into the bathtub under him. He stared at the hairs on his arm. He hated them. They grew in places he never expected them to. That was the problem. The older he got, the more hair grew on his body. If only it would grow where he wanted it, but no. This was in small, ugly patches on his forearms, his legs, and his ass, thick like pond scum in July. Asians were supposed to be hairless and smooth skinned. Must have a white devil somewhere in the woodpile, he thought.

He turned the water off, stepped out of the tub, grabbed a towel and dried. He had an epilator in the medicine chest, a small device that ripped the hair out by the roots. He turned it on, tiny wheels spinning to snatch the hairs on his arms as he passed it back and forth over his skin. He looked over his shoulder, running it across his butt, wincing as the machine did its work.

"It's cheaper than waxing," he said to himself in the mirror. "And it hurts about the same."

When he was done he turned it off, taking a moment to clean the hairs caught between the rubber wheels on the head of the device. He put it back in the cabinet and removed a bottle of lotion, spreading it across his sore spots.

He went to the bedroom and opened the dresser drawers, looking for something to wear. Unsatisfied, he went to the closet and rifled through the hangers, nothing but slacks, button down shirts, and sport coats. He looked down at a laundry pile on the floor of the closet, some well worn shoes scattered among the dirty clothes. An old suitcase sat in the far corner in the darkness behind everything.

He paused for a moment, starting at the suitcase. He reached for it, hesitating at first, then with deadly conviction. He took it out and laid it on the bed, unzipping it slowly, carefully, as if he were diffusing a bomb. He threw back the cover of the suitcase revealing carefully folded clothes, high heels, bras and panties. He ran his fingers over the soft fabric of a black skirt, a gentle sigh escaping his mouth.

He knew every article that was in the suitcase. It was packed tight, compartmentalized like a jewelry box. He reached down and touched the silky fabric of a pair of panties, then fondled the lace of an elegant brassiere lying beside it.

What kind of woman will I be tonight? Out on the town? Exercise girl? Day wear? Shopping? Office attire? They were all there – the many faces of Fu Chan, the exotic Asian transvestite. It didn't matter what he chose, he wasn't going out in public. After all his bad experiences, the cost of his job on the police force, the therapy, the pain he caused others, this was something he only did alone anymore.

He decided to go with basic black, always in style in Seattle. Maybe it was even the norm. Black pencil skirt, black choker neck top with eye catching cutouts. Women put as much effort into building an outfit as an engineer puts into constructing a skyscraper. His mind worked backwards, designing the right foundation for the final look. Shapewear with enhanced cups and padded buttocks, long black tights and heels. He wondered if he should start by painting his toenails.

He dressed leisurely, layering the clothes gently as if building an expensive decoupage. In this manner he moved slowly towards the final illusion. Inside his mind a dormant part of him stirred, becoming as strong and as automatic as breathing. He posed in front of the mirror, his hips and breasts bursting with latex and foam. He pulled on the skirt, zipping it in the back and centering it perfectly. He put the top on tenderly, pulling at it until it hung in just the manner his eye demanded.

Then the heels. He slipped his stocking feet into the black, leather pumps like he was loading a gun. Careful, gentle, deadly. Amazing the effect of a simple arch of the foot on the hips, the stride, and the attitude. He walked around, getting used to them again, comfortable. He felt good again, as relaxed as a smoker after the first drag of a cigarette.

It wasn't long before he was staring at himself in the mirror. "All dressed up with no place to go," he said.

He decided to change a few elements. He went back to his closet and reached up to a high shelf where he took down a large shoebox. He exchanged the pumps for a pair of boots that he had in the box, then he removed the makeup bag from the suitcase and went into the bathroom. He reached for a pair of tweezers, plucking the hairs from between his eyebrows. Then he began to apply makeup. Satisfied with his effort, he took a small jewelry box from the suitcase and chose a few trinkets. Last came the wig, dark brown hair that cascaded off his shoulders and down his back. When he came out, he stood before the mirror again.

"Perfect," he said. He was indistinguishable from any other woman out on the town in Seattle tonight. He had on leather boots, three and a half inch heels curving his feet into a feminine arch. Dark hose ran up his legs, disappearing underneath the black, silky skirt. Beneath it black shapewear molded his body, foam breasts and padded butt adding curves where there were none.

The short sleeved top accented his bare arms. He ran his fingers across them, glad he had taken the time to use the epilator. His lips were accented in pink, his cheeks flushed with slight color. "Too much makeup?" he asked his reflection in the mirror.

He walked across the room, relishing the click of his heels on the floor. The girdle held him tight in its grip the way Harry liked being held. Earrings scraped across his cheeks as he moved his head. The feeling only made him move his head more. He went back to the mirror, smiling at his reflection. He practiced a few dance moves to music he heard in his head. Then he stopped. "You look silly," he said.

"What's wrong with me?" he asked Fu in the mirror. "Why do I enjoy this so much?"

He found himself in front of the kitchen cabinet again, moving aside the beans and cans to reach for the bottle.

His hand stopped in mid motion, his eyes looked down at the counter. He filled his glass with water and another squirt from the plastic lime. He downed it quickly, as if it were a real shot of alcohol, slamming the glass on the countertop. He leaned forward, both hands on the counter, staring at the empty glass. He looked up and shut the cabinet door.

"Why do I judge myself by society's standards?" he asked. "I know I'm different." He went to the mirror to continue the conversation with himself. "Come on, Harry, you have this dialog all the time. You may have some strange habits but you're a good man. You'll make some woman a wonderful wife one day."

Wife? Is that what he wanted? He wasn't a woman. He didn't want to be a woman. He was one hundred percent hetero. There was just this one teensy problem.

There was a sound behind him, a faint hiss. He turned and saw a newspaper had been slipped under his door. He picked it up and opened the door. The hall was empty. He ran to the stairwell and heard footsteps disappearing down the stairs. "Hey!" he yelled. He looked over the railing and saw a thick, hairy hand gripping the banister as it descended. He started to follow, hearing the dainty click of his own heels. The heavy steps moved quicker and he heard the door to the street open and slam shut. He had barely gone one flight down.

"Damn these heels," he said.

He heard someone behind him say, "They're cute."

He turned to walk back up the stairs and faced a blond woman. "Oh," she said. Her smile turned to astonishment. Horror, maybe. Something disturbing, Harry couldn't tell. "Didn't recognize you," she said, coming down the stairs. She passed him, walking a little quicker, trying not to look at him and laugh.

"I'm not a monster," he said.

"Honey, I don't know what you are," she said, continuing down and out of sight. He went up the stairs, the sound of his high heels in concert with hers. He went back to his apartment and shut the door. He dropped the newspaper on the counter and went to the mirror. He looked hard, trying to determine what gave him away. Then he saw it, a wisp of his hair coming out from under the wig. It wasn't centered right, either. And he had spoken aloud, damning the high heels in a man's voice.

He straightened the wig, adjusting a Velcro band at the back of the head for a tight fit. He tucked his hair out of sight and pinned it in place with bobby pins. He tugged at it, confident it would stay in place. He started talking in a high, girlish voice, experimenting with different sounds. He brushed his hair and made adjustments to his makeup.

"Much better," said Fu Chan, her gentle voice coming out like a mother's kiss. He was poised before the mirror; knees bent, one foot on tip toe the other flat and angled on the floor. It made his hips look curvy where there were no real curves. Feminine grace is all about illusion.

He looked away from his reflection and saw the paper on the counter in the mirror. He turned and snatched it up, sat down on a chair and opened it up. It was two days old, the same paper Binky had left in his office when he challenged him to solve the case. This one was marked up. Words were circled on the page. Designer Derby, ninth season, missing dress, Carrie Rodriguez, Richard Sooka, Heille Crumstein. He followed the article down to "continued on page three."

As he opened the pages something fell out. It was a page from a magazine, an article about Zanzibar O'Connell, a model that Richard Sooka described as "Too fat to wear his designer dress." The response from Heille Crumstein was circled. "I agree with Richard," she said. "O'Connell no longer projects the image we want to portray. We're replacing her next season with a smaller model."

He put the pages aside and continued scanning the paper. There were more circled words. "Heille could not be reached for comment. She remains in town, sequestered in her Mercer Island mansion. She plans on leaving this weekend with her long term friend Carrie Rodriguez for the relative safety of Beverly Hills." He picked up a pencil and circled that last fact.

His mind went into overtime, facts sifting into finer detail like flour through a colander. One of his facts wasn't true, he knew it. Which one? He scanned the circled items in the newspaper and he saw it. Of course! Bernard said she was afraid and leaving tomorrow. "Oh my God," he said. "I know who the next victim is."

He looked at the paper again. It made sense. "The killer could be there now. Should I call Bernard? Hell, it's after seven, the cops are all home." He looked in the mirror. "No time to change," he said.

He grabbed a purse from on the counter and threw his cell phone and wallet in it. Then he grabbed a woman's trench coat from the dark side of his closet. He took the keys off the table and was out the door as fast as his heels could carry him.

Chapter 20

Hot Head

When Paul got home from work, he took a shower and had a light dinner. Afterwards he felt sleepy and he laid on the bed to rest. He wanted to catch a short cat nap so he would be awake when his favorite show came on tonight. Instead he would sleep all night, courtesy of a drug introduced into his food, something hidden by the taste of rich spices.

He wouldn't miss his car. He would never know that someone had borrowed it. He didn't even know that the man who used his car had been in his apartment all along, waiting for Paul to close his eyes. A small injection and Paul would sleep all night with no memory of what he did.

The killer left Paul's apartment and locked the door behind him, stopping at the mirror to check his disguise. Except for the clothes, he was a twin of the man asleep in the bedroom. A neighbor saw him leave the apartment and waved to him.

"What's in the box?" she asked.

He just shrugged and moved on, an 'I don't know' kind of motion. He smiled and waved as he went past her, indicating he was in a hurry.

He got in Paul's car, pulling out of the driveway and heading towards Mercer Island. It was still early. Plenty of time to finish his task and be home at a reasonable hour.

A short jaunt east on I-90 and he was on the island, travelling across hilly roads to a gate that made the victim feel safe. He got out of the car and pressed the red button on a speaker beside the gate.

"Paul Hendrix to see Heille Crumstein. I have her things from the show," he said.

A tinny voice answered through the speaker. "Come around back. The delivery entrance is right at the next road. Follow the fence line to the gate. It's open."

He obeyed the instructions and pulled through the open gate. A plain clothes guard met him as he got out of the car.

"Getting dark early," said the imposter, trying to make conversation.

"What's in the package?" asked the guard.

"Miss Crumstein's hat," he said, carefully opening the box to let the guard take a peek.

"That's some bonnet," he said.

"Probably costs more than you and I make in a year," said the substitute Paul.

"No doubt," said the guard.

"You going to be around to let me out? I'm only going to be a few minutes. The studio wants her to try it on before I go."

"I'm on my way out," said the guard. "Joe's the night guy. He's over there in the control room." He pointed towards a door on the side of a nearby building the size of a small house. "I'll leave the gate open for you."

"Okay. Thanks," said fake Paul. "I need a place to fix the hat. The designer was adamant about the presentation. Said it would ruin her attitude if it wasn't just right."

"Know what you mean," said the guard. "Heille's a temperamental bitch. Just see Joe in the control room. He'll fix you up. Good night."

He watched the guard walk towards a line of parked cars where he got into an old pickup truck and drove off. He carried the open box into the control room. An old man sat before a bank of television monitors casting a dull glow across the dimly lit room. "I need to fix this up before I give it to Miss Crumstein," said the substitute.

"Table over there you can use," said the old man.

The killer set the box down and began carefully packaging the hat again. He saw the plain clothes guard drive off. "Ted's left the gate open for you," said the old man.

"He said he would. I'll shut it when I go. I'll only be a few minutes."

"Okay," said the old man. "Heille's on the first floor in the study working at her desk. I'll announce you," he said, picking up a phone.

The killer heard the old man speak a few words then set the phone down. "Follow the path outside the door to the main house." He pointed to a map of the house and property he had on the desk in front of him. The killer looked over his shoulder as the guard ran his finger along the route. "The side door is open. Down the hall and to the right you'll find the study," he said, his finger tracing the way along the floor plan of the main building.

"Thanks, Joe," said the killer, driving a syringe into the old man's neck. "You've been a great help." He held the guard's head, carefully letting it down on the desk in front of the monitors. "Have a nice nap," he said, stroking the old man's hair gently as if he were nursing a patient in an old folk's home. He saw a video tape recorder. He stopped the machine and removed the security tape. He studied the guard's desk and found the main power chord that came out the bottom and led to the wall. There was no plug to pull, it was wired directly into an electrical box. He looked around and found a panel box with some breaker switches. They were well marked and he flipped the one that was labeled Main Control Room. "Lights out," he said. An emergency light came on. He picked up the hat box and headed towards the house, stopping to throw the security tape in the front seat of Paul's car.

The door was open, just as the old man had said. He found the study with no problem. Heille ignored him as he expected. She had little tolerance for the army of people who worked for her and served her every need. He was just another of them. He cleared his throat. She didn't look up, just stared into her computer screen. He waited patiently, cleared his throat again.

She looked up, irritated, fire in her eyes. How dare he interrupt the work of the great Heille Crumstein. "What is it?" she asked.

"Sorry. Throat dry. Need a glass of water."

"On the way out," she said. "Just set whatever you have on the chair over there."

"Studio asked me to stay until you tried it on," he said.

"What is it?" she asked.

"A designer hat," he said. "They want your take on it."

"Bring it here," she said.

He set the box down on the desk. He was right about presentation; she was delighted by it. She undid the bow, smiling as the ribbon fell beside the box. She opened the top and looked inside, her eyes widening as her mouth shaped into a little "o". He smiled too, but she was fixated on the hat.

"What have we here?" she said, her voice now filled with overbearing sweetness. He smiled, his cheeks puffing slightly. He knew her venom was still there. Like a vicious animal she could turn on him at any minute. But this time it was she who was being drawn in for the kill.

She pulled the hat out carefully, studying it. She liked the ric rac, the interesting drape and fold of the fabric, the dangles and the wire-supported balls at the top. "It's beautiful," she said.

He clapped his hands together, glee rising inside him. "The color matches your eyes," he said.

"So it does," she said.

"What do you think?" he asked. "The designer would love to hear your thoughts."

"Tell her I'm amazed. The detailing is superb. It's light and airy, not earthbound despite the size. It's fabricated with such flair." She rotated it in her hands. "I've never seen anything like it. Similar, maybe. I love these balloon like things. What are they?"

"Try it on," he urged her. "Can I take a picture of you wearing it on my cell phone camera?"

"Of course," she said. He held his phone up in readiness. She struck a pose, a perfect model, and she gently placed the hat on her head. She smiled and he snapped the picture.

There was a whirring sound and she said, "Oh, it's animated too." The servos were at work turning small screws attached to the fabric covered steel headband. She felt a pinch as the screws worked their way through her scalp, then pain as they drove into her skull. Her mouth turned down and he snapped another picture.

Her hands went up, trying to remove the hat, but it was held tight by four surgical screws. He hoped he had measured correctly, just enough to pass through the skull and not break the meninges, the membranes that cover the brain. He stepped closer and snapped another picture. He checked his watch and set the timer.

She opened her mouth to scream and he moved forward, stuffing a handkerchief in her mouth and easing her back into the chair. He took the thick ribbon and tied her with it. She stared into his eyes as he shushed her. "Be quiet," he said. "You'll want to hear what I say."

Her eyes watered, overflowing with pain until the tears streamed down her cheeks. Her muffled breaths and moans escaped the handkerchief. She was pleading with him but it was his turn to be indifferent.

"When you quiet down I'll be here, ready to talk." He looked at his watch. "But you're wasting your time. I, on the other hand, have plenty of time."

She moaned, trying to quiet her breath. A trickle of blood streamed down from her forehead, dripping onto her blouse.

"A shame to ruin that, dear," he said. "A designer original, isn't it?"

She nodded.

He stared at her. "You're right about the hat, though. It's perfect for you. You and that hat are one now. In case you haven't figured it out, it's not coming off."

Her breath became panicked.

"You don't remember me, do you?"

She shook her head.

"Sooka didn't either, not until I reminded him." He pulled off the fake van dyke and the blonde wig and stuffed them in his pocket.

She tried desperately to think. Who was he? She thought her salvation lay in recognition, but she was wrong. He turned his head from side to side, giving her a good look at his profile. He waited some more before trying some hints. "Season two," he said. Her eyes still had a blank look. He was disappointed. "I was off early. You and Sooka were cruel, uncaring, but you are who you are. Any clues yet?"

She shook her head. Panic betrayed her, fear welling inside.

"I'm still a designer, you know. I made that hat myself." He manipulated his phone, and then held it out so she could see herself in the hat. It was the second picture he took. She was gleeful and happy. "You saw something familiar in the hat. Almost had it figured out, didn't you?"

She said nothing. He looked at his watch again. "Well, my name's unimportant. Let's move on. As you can see, I didn't let your sarcasm discourage me from being a designer. Humiliated on national television! You hurt my family as well. They were watching. It was seven seasons ago. They think I committed suicide, the price of failure, and I have never seen them again. I have no regrets. In a way I did commit suicide. I died that day, killed by you and your little pack of wolves. What power made you a judge of human life?"

He looked into her eyes. She was begging again.

"I died inside and I was reborn. I embarked on a new career with a new identity. I brought all my talents of the past together into a unique understanding of myself. I invented a new name for myself."

The pain was unbearable, a headache that made it difficult for her to concentrate. "Oh, I'm still a designer, but now I design... death."

She cried, her breath becoming quick and panicked.

"Careful," he said. "Breathe easy. Calm down. I told Sooka that but he didn't listen to me. I watched him breathe his last breath. It's horrible to suffocate, you know. Air is the one thing we can't do without. You can live for three weeks without food, three days without water, but only three minutes without air." He looked at his watch again. "I'm sorry, time is running short."

Heille began to panic again, choking on the handkerchief.

"Calm down, I said. Don't worry, I'm not going to squeeze the life out of you like I did Sooka. I've designed something much better for you. A designer death, delivered to you personally by me, Dr. Couture."

There was a beep from the hat and the little Foley catheter balloons burst, dousing Heille in fluid. It smelled bad, like petroleum. The recognition came late for her as the lighter kicked in, a small spark. The hat burst into flames.

"They burn witches, don't they," he said.

Chapter 21

J-Dog

Harry took the first exit off I-90 to Mercer Island. It felt funny driving the old Volvo in high heel boots. It was a man's car demanding a man's attention. He didn't know how the old girl would react to a woman at the helm; probably just as confused as he was. He was nervous about driving around in drag, especially on Mercer Island, home to some of the richest, most powerful people in the world. The streets looked dark and foreboding, the houses set back far from the road behind walls and fences scanned constantly by security cameras. How did the killer hope to get past these controls and checkpoints. How did Harry?

He should have changed, at least his shoes, but there was really no time. If his hunch was correct, the next victim may already be dead and his chance to thwart the killer gone. If he was wrong, no harm done. He may be ridiculed later, called Fu and humiliated publicly, but Harry thought it was a small price to pay for saving someone's life. He had to trust his instincts. Something inside told him he was doing the right thing.

There was a blue light behind him followed by the short whelp of a police car siren.

"Oh, crap," he said. He pulled the car over. He forgot about the Mercer Island cops, known for checking out every strange car or vehicle that wandered onto their turf. They reportedly had a database of people who had legitimate business on the island. He heard a voice announce, "Stay in your vehicle, please." A uniform stepped out of the driver's side of the car about a half a minute later. He knew his license plate was being scanned for a cross check.

The uniform had one of those long, heavy security flashlights that take a bunch of batteries and can be used as a club in a close fight. He shined the beam into the car, lighting up the back seat, the passenger seat, and finally Harry's face.

"License and registration, Ma'am," said the cop.

Harry reached for the purse on the passenger seat. "Slowly, please," said the cop.

The passenger door to the cop car opened and another uniform approached the car. He nodded to his partner who continued to keep his light shining in Harry's face. Harry opened the purse and the light moved to the handbag. Harry didn't have anything but a wallet and a cell phone, maybe a lipstick and a pen. He opened the wallet under the cop's scrutiny, pulled out the license and handed it to the uniform.

"Registration, too, please," he said. Harry reached towards the glove compartment. "Hold it," said the cop. "Says here your name is Harry Takanawa and you're a thirty year old man."

"Yes. That's correct," said Harry.

"Harry Takanawa?" said the cop's partner. "From the Seattle force?"

"Yes," said Harry reluctantly.

"Fu?" he said. "Fu Chan? The Oriental Yentl?"

"That's me," said Harry in a low voice.

"It's me," said the partner. "Joe Smitters. J-Dog. You remember me?" The partner leaned over and stared into the window. "You look...hot," he said. "Never saw you like this. I would've pegged you for a real woman."

Harry laughed. J-Dog. He remembered the street cop who tried to cross the fence and move from a flatfoot on bike patrol to a detective. Van Dorn had killed the deal. He was on Joe's review panel. Instead of getting a tough guy with street smarts they got an old bureaucrat, one of Van Dorn's regular fan club members.

"Harry, meet my partner John Herc, but we just call him Hercules," said Joe.

"Pleased," said Harry.

Hercules lowered his flashlight. "Uh, charmed, I'm sure." He nervously handed Harry back his license.

Harry turned to Joe. "J-Dog. What are you doing on the Mercer Island force?"

"Got tired of peddling a bike. Kept looking for an opening, then this came up. It's much easier going up and down hills in a car," said Joe. "So, it's true what they say about you. You like women's clothes."

"True that," said Harry.

Hercules laughed. "So, you really know this tranny?" he asked Joe.

"He's cool. Best detective on the force. He's the one who solved the Armstead case," said Joe. "Also saved Shirley O'Conner's life."

"O'Conner?" asked Hercules. "The one wounded in that big gun battle in Seattle last year?"

"The same," said J-Dog. "He even took out a couple of the gang down that started that mess. Bunch of meth-heads who declared war on the Seattle cops. Shirley was shot and lying on the pavement in open ground. Fu here came out from behind his safe cover and dragged Shirley off the field of battle. Took a bullet in the leg himself."

"It was a flesh wound," said Harry.

"Ha! Dirty Harry. That's what they should have called you."

"No, seriously," said Harry. "The bullet just grazed me, didn't even penetrate the skin."

"Look, Harry," said Joe. "I don't care what you do in your time off, you're okay in my book."

"Thanks, J," he said. "I appreciate that."

"What are you doing here on the island?" asked Joe.

"I went private," he said. "Here checking out a lead."

"Undercover?" he asked.

"No," said Harry. "Not really. I was on my way out tonight when I got a tip that something bad was about to go down."

"You need help?" asked Joe. "What's the address?"

"Crumstein's house," he said. "You heard what they did to Richard Sooka. I think someone's going after Heille now."

"Let's roll. She's on our watch list. We'll check it out with you," said Hercules. "Follow us. I know exactly where it is."

They got back in the car and turned off the blue lights. Harry put the old car in gear and pulled in behind them. A short ride over hilly terrain and they found themselves in front of an iron gate. The cop car backed up and stopped beside the old Volvo. J-Dog spoke through the open window. "We got another call, Harry, but we spoke with Heille's security."

"You have their number?" he asked.

"We have everyone's number on Mercer Island," he said.

"Figures," said Harry.

"They said to go around to the back gate. It's the next right, down the long road. Follow it until you come to a gate on the right. We'll look you up when we're done."

"Okay, thanks guys," said Harry.

"Good seeing you again, Harry," said Joe. "Glad you're on the Sooka case. I know it will get solved."

"Thanks for the vote of confidence," he said. "See you around, J-Dog."

"Yeah." The car drove off. Harry followed the directions around the corner and down the long dark road. He could see Lake Washington through an opening in the trees somewhere at the end of the road. An old pickup truck approached him head on and he had to pull to the side to let it pass. The man was friendly and waved as the truck squeezed by.

Harry stopped at the gate. It was open but he waited. There were two cars in the driveway, an old battered compact car and a modern looking red sedan. He saw the small voice box with the red button on it. He parked the car off to the side, then he got out and pushed the button.

"I'm here," he said. "Harry Takanawa to see Ms. Crumstein."

There was no answer. He waited, then something tingled inside him, a second sense. He pushed the button again. No answer. The tingling wouldn't go away. It seemed to get worse as he walked through the open gate. He scanned from side to side, looking for any signs of activity. He tried to locate the security cameras. No alarms sounded, no bright lights came on. He saw the house in the distance, unpretentious, a simple structure that melted into the landscape as if it were a part of everything around it. There were lights on and he saw shadows and movement in a window on the far right bottom. There was a small dark building on the right, a sign that read "security" on the door. He went over and knocked on the door, announcing himself.

When there was no answer, he opened the door. There was an old man in uniform asleep at the desk, his head bent over in front of a bank of monitors. A bright light shone down from behind him casting shadows across the desk.

"Hey!" shouted Harry. "Wake up."

The old man didn't move. Harry went up beside him and shook his shoulder. "Hey, old man," he said.

The old man was breathing deep. Air from his mouth fluttered a piece of paper that was weighted down by his head. Harry looked up and noticed the monitors were off. Then he saw that the bright light was emergency lighting. He picked up the phone to dial 911 but the line was dead. He wished J-Dog and Hercules were here. He debated going back to the car to get his cell phone from the purse he'd left on the front seat.

He saw that the power was off. He went to the panel and jiggled a few switches and circuit breakers. The emergency lighting clicked off and the monitors flashed on. The middle monitor displayed two people talking, one sitting in a chair wearing an odd looking hat, their backs to the camera. The other was a man who appeared to be taking pictures with a cell phone. The man kept talking and laughing. Then he stopped laughing and pulled off his beard, a short van dyke style and a wig, and put them in his pocket.

A shiver went up Harry's spine. He noticed things he hadn't seen before. The man's smile was sinister, the thin lips curling at the edges, a line of white teeth bared like a snarling wolf. He bobbed up and down, like a barnyard rooster, his body jerking with confidence. There was lettering in the corner of the screen, the word "study" in bold white, then the image jumped to another room, a dark screen with the words "guest bedroom 1" in the corner. He tried the phone but it was still dead. There was a floor plan of the house on a table. He looked it over, figuring he could go to the window of the study and eavesdrop from outside. With that in mind, he left the security shack and headed towards the big house.

It was dark outside. His high heels clicked on the stone path even though he tried to remain silent. He stepped off the path in front of the house moving closer towards the window. The high heels sunk deep into the ground and he wobbled to regain his footing. He thought about taking the boots off. They were getting ruined in the dirt anyway.

There were shadows from the window, lights flickering. The light blared in his face and he remained motionless.

Through the window he saw the man talking to Heille Crumstein, his eyes alight with glee. He was bald with dark brown eyes. His ears curved outward at the top, away from his head like a wolf. His skin was white and pasty, the teeth even whiter. How much whitener does it take to get them that clean? How much effort and discipline? He studied the face, the thin lips and lack of distinct features making him look anonymous and ordinary. It was the way he smiled that was disturbing; it was like watching the devil on holiday.

He was talking. Harry inched closer, straining to hear what he was saying.

Suddenly the hat burst into flames and Heille started screaming. She reached for the hat, trying to remove the insidious thing but it was screwed into her skull. She beat her head with her hands and all of a sudden her sleeves were on fire. She twisted in the chair, the smell of burnt hair and flesh beginning to fill the room. She reached for the curtains and fire shot up the wall.

Couture was smiling again, snapping pictures with his cell phone. Harry didn't know what to do, it all happened so quickly. The fire had started instantaneously with no time to react. He picked up a brick and threw it at the window, but there were iron bars blocking him. The flames were everywhere at once. He looked around for a garden hose, anything.

Inside Couture watched the room catch fire. He took it all in, a culmination of days of effort. Then he noticed something. The firelight illuminated a face in the window. He stared at her, an Oriental beauty. He loved the way mascara accented Asian eyes, the way her long, dark hair hugged her boyish face. They made eye contact for a moment, and then she disappeared.

Heille had long since stopped screaming. The Killer admired his handiwork, another perfect designer death, delivered in person by Doctor Couture. He snapped one more picture on his cell phone. The smoke alarm went off, chirping and screaming louder than Heille did. The flaming corpse fell forward across the desk. Paper caught fire, blackening the corners as it was consumed by flames. The computer keyboard melted, distorting in the heat. The flaming skull looked at Couture with hollow eyes. He could see the metal framework of the hat, the band screwed in place, servo cables twisted about her head like an amusement park roller coaster. Her clothes were black, her skin gently charred like a grilled steak. He drooled, sniffing the delightful scent of death by fire.

Now, where did that Asian beauty go?

Chapter 22

The Great Escape

The killer left the house through the front door, leaving it open. The fire drew air into the house, demanding oxygen to feed itself. He looked left towards the window of the study. The Asian woman was gone, but he saw the flames through the window. A fist came at him from the left, out of the darkness and into his peripheral vision. Couture ducked but he felt the hand glance across his skin. It was electric, exciting, like a first date. He faced the Asian woman. She looked all angry and scared at once, her feet planted on the ground, her eyes full of dragon fire.

"What have we here?" asked Couture.

"The end of your madness," she said, her arm rearing back for another strike.

His eyes sparkled. He loved a challenge. "If you like fists, I have no problem hitting a woman."

Harry balled his hand up and Couture blocked the punch easily, swung sideways at her midsection. She bent, twisting her body to avoid his thrust. He smiled again. "I like you," he said. "Are you as quick in bed?"

Harry tried another punch, hard to keep his balance in the boots. He couldn't maintain a fighting stance. He needed a flat even surface and the sidewalk in front of the house was narrow. He tried not to slip off in the dirt where he knew he would be at a real disadvantage. He crouched into a slight squat, using his legs as springs to add force to his punch. He thrust forward, like a defensive tackle pushing off the line. Couture sidestepped and pushed him into the dirt. The killer took out his cell phone and snapped a picture of Harry.

Flames crackled behind them. The glass in the window exploded and a funnel of fire poured through the open window. Couture dropped, rolling away from the flames. He came to his feet quickly, running away from the Asian woman. He could hear sirens in the distance, the approach of fire trucks and heroes.

"Mission accomplished," he yelled. He turned his back to the fire, his mind calculating his escape route. The exit road would be blocked by the approaching fire trucks. Time to abandon the car he had stolen. He ran around the side of the house towards the back, down towards the waterfront dock on Lake Washington.

Harry got up and ran after him, his heels clicking across the pavement as he pursued Couture.

The dock was ahead. Couture ran down the planks with ease. Harry thought if he could just catch up to him he could tackle him. At least throw a body block against him. Help was on its way. The sirens were getting louder. He imagined them coming down the long dirt road towards the burning house.

Couture saw a kayak on the end of the dock, heard the Asian woman step on to the other end behind him. Her heels clicked on the wood. He turned and looked at her, light from the fire flickering in the windows of the house behind her, her silhouette getting larger as she drew nearer. He would have to deal with her.

Harry's heel caught between two boards. It snapped off at the bottom and he stumbled forward, one foot suddenly longer than the other. His ankle twisted slightly and he fell. As he hit the dock his wig shifted and lay sideways across his face.

Couture was on him quickly. Harry looked up to see the killer standing over him. He tingled, fear creeping over him like a million dancing spiders.

"Ho ho!" he said. "What have we here?" Couture reached down and ripped the wig off Harry's head. "Peek a boo, I see you!"

Harry started to move but Couture kicked him in the side. He reached down and grabbed Harry by the necklace, lifting his head off the dock as his fist accelerated towards Harry's head. There was a soft, meaty thud and Harry was cold cocked. Couture let him slip from his hand and drop back to the dock.

He snapped another picture of Harry, kicked his face until it lay sideways and snapped a profile. The sirens were near now, he could hear shouts in the distance. No time to finish this. He turned and ran to the end of the dock, dropping the kayak off the side. He slid into the seat and grabbed the paddle off the dock.

It was a new moon on Lake Washington. Houses dotted the shoreline, their lights reflecting off the water. Couture paddled the kayak silently, skillfully, maneuvering it away from the chaos on the shore. He paddled hard, away from the flames and the excitement behind him. He could hear the sirens, the shouts, sounds of breaking glass and the crackle of the fire. As he paddled further away his night vision began to kick in. He scanned the horizon for lights and landmarks. The wind blew towards him across Lake Washington and he angled the kayak to correct his course.

"Stupid of me," he said. "I'm getting too comfortable with myself. Why did I take off my disguise? That witch didn't even recognize me. It was for nothing."

He dipped the paddles rhythmically and the bonfire faded behind him. He took the toupee and fake beard out of his pocket and held it out over the side. He found a fishing weight and a piece of line attached to it in the bottom of the kayak. He tied it to the wig and beard and dropped it overboard.

His mind raced as he struggled to capture the details. He hadn't planned on the house catching fire, but that was something he could deal with. Everything was going well until he encountered the Asian woman. Asian transvestite, he corrected himself. Who was she? I mean he? Where did she come from? What was her connection to Crumstein?

It was hard for him to think of her as a he. First impressions are hard to overcome, and he had met the tranny and come to think of him as a woman. She was beautiful and exotic. He focused on the details as he paddled, fixing her face in his mind. The dark lips, deep (were they brown?) eyes, the black hair.

How tall was she? Hard to tell with the high heels. She was definitely shorter than he was, and allowing for the heels, maybe five nine or five ten. He shouldn't discount the heels, they had been his salvation. If she hadn't tripped on the dock, he might never have turned the situation to his advantage.

He had a longer reach than her, that was apparent from the fight. She was strong, well trained too. She moved like a ninja, graceful and fast, almost an equal match for him. He would have to think about their next encounter, devise some kind of advantage. She may not be wearing heels next time.

"Make no mistake. There will be a next encounter. Soon, I hope," he laughed, putting more effort into his paddling. He couldn't wait to get to his lair where he could download and analyze the pictures he took of her.

He heard a helicopter in the distance and quickened his strokes. He wondered if they had radar or night vision on board. Damn these Homeland Security grants that equipped the local police. Nine eleven had truly changed everything. He was glad the kayak was black. He picked up the pace and began paddling with more vigor.

He saw the shoreline up ahead. There was a long dock extending into the lake and he paddled towards it, positioning the kayak under it to rest and catch his breath. He scanned for the helicopter, any sign of a police boat or activity.

He heard footsteps coming down the dock, people talking.

"Wonder what's happening over there?" asked a man, pointing across the lake.

"Who cares?" came a woman's voice. "It's cold and windy out here."

"Don't you want to see?" he asked. "Here. Check it out through these binoculars." He handed her the field glasses.

She took a cursory look. "I can't see anything," she said, handing him back the glasses.

"Look at the spotlight from the helicopter," he said, holding the binoculars out for her. "See that woman lying on the dock? Looks like something's wrong with her."

She looked again. "All I see is a fire. It reminds me it's cold out here." She handed him back the glasses. "Let's go inside."

"In a minute," he said, taking them from her to look again. "Looks like Christmas over there with all the flashing lights."

"Uh huh," she said. "I'm going inside. You coming?"

"In a minute," he said.

"Okay," she said. The sound of her footsteps echoed down the dock.

He stared through the glasses. A chill gust of wind blew and Couture held onto a wooden strut under the dock to steady the kayak. He heard the man shiver, then the sound of his footsteps running after her. "Hey, wait for me," he called. "It's cold."

"That's what I said," she answered.

He waited a few minutes until the coast was clear, then he paddled out from under the dock following the shoreline south. He kept low, studying each dock in case there were other people out trying to satisfy their curiosity. The woman was right. It was cold.

He saw a familiar sight ahead, his own dock. He pulled up next to it, stepping out of the kayak and onto the rickety planks. His pants caught on a nail and he cursed. He twisted and sat, heard a ripping sound over the lapping of the water. Using a paddle, he pushed the boat away as hard as he could. He set it down on the dock and stood up, watching the kayak drift out towards the center of the lake. The wind finally caught it and he fought the cold to watch a little longer as it was carried away.

"Safe," he thought, laughing to himself.

In the luxury of the moment he thought about the murder, Heille in flames, the sound of her terror. If she hadn't grabbed the curtains, the house would have never caught fire. What a nice bonus! He wondered who would get the insurance money since the witch had no next of kin. Probably her producer. They'd find some way to make money off this turn of events.

He smiled as he savored her death. Another designer original worthy of the great Dr. Couture. Revenge is not best served cold. If that was true, why did he have this warm feeling inside? Light and happy, like a little kid at Christmas. He turned and looked across the lake. He couldn't see the fire and he imagined it was dying. The couple was right, the flashing lights had made it look like Christmas, the helicopter overhead shining like a star to guide the wise men to the manger.

And he had been the angel in this drama, albeit the angel of death. No one would ever know that. All the evidence of his designer death probably evaporated in the fire. An investigator might find evidence of the hat, maybe raise a lot of questions, but in the end he had outsmarted them.

Only one problem: the transvestite. She had seen him, seen his face, and seen him commit murder. He would have to deal with her, the sooner the better.

Then, a stroke of brilliance, a flash of insight!

Thoughts bubbled inside his head, an idea he had a few months ago, a designer death he had first envisioned for Carrie Rodriguez, but then changed his mind. He had all the components; everything he needed to complete his design was already in his workshop. It wouldn't take long to prepare it. And it would be a designer death fit for a transvestite.

He was full of adrenaline from the escape, awake and clear. Might as well finish the design.

He looked across the lake again, feeling satisfied. Sooka, Crumstein, two down, one to go. He breathed a sign of satisfaction. Deep in his mind he was the star of his own version of Designer Derby and he had just passed a difficult challenge. In this home version of the show he was also the judge and he patted himself on the back for his cleverness and his ingenuity. He well deserved to go to the next round. Almost there...

"Wait!" His mind uncovered a twist in the plot, the mainstay of reality television. Sorry to disappoint you, Doctor. Not one to go: two. You must add the transvestite to the list.

He could hardly contain his excitement. He loved a challenge, and he prided himself on being able to rise to the occasion. He turned towards the house, heading for the secret room beneath the free standing four car garage, whistling a tune from an old movie.

There was bounce in his stride and a smile on his face, a feeling that everything would be all right. He sang out loud, joy spewing from his mouth like a thousand birds of paradise.

"Ding dong, the witch is dead, the wicked witch, the wicked witch. Ding dong the wicked witch is dead..."

Chapter 23

He Who Fights and Runs Away

Harry awoke, and although the lids were shut he still saw lights in front of his eyes. There were lights flashing behind them, too. He felt like some kind of cartoon character watching planets and stars circle his head. He opened his eyes, becoming aware of the hard planked wood beneath him. There was bright light all around him and he was center stage, the main act in a big show. He shook his head, feeling dizzy and nauseous. His face hurt where Couture had punched him. He saw his wig lying beside him, noticed he was wearing boots with tights and a black skirt.

Did I fall?

The bright spotlight swept across the dock and over him again.

Is that spotlight for me? Am I supposed to dance and follow it?

Then he remembered where he was. He sat up, his hands resting against the wooden dock. He saw the house on fire in front of him, heard the sound of firefighters shouting instructions, high pressure hoses and generators running at full throttle. He picked up his wig and pressed it against his cheek where it hurt.

The spotlight passed over him again and he saw the helicopter circling overhead. He was nervous and he put the wig on, centering it by memory. He hastily pressed a few bobby pins in place and combed it flat with his hand. The light passed over him again and he was overcome with the urge to escape. He got up and nearly fell, then remembered his right boot had a broken heel. He limped down the dock, moving quickly towards the property line and as far away from the burning house as he could get. He followed a fence that ran perpendicular to the beach. He stayed hidden underneath a canopy of trees as he worked his way through the shadows. The helicopter spotlight lost sight of him and moved away, scanning the shoreline for activity.

He came to his car, the old trusty Volvo was parked in the perfect getaway spot. The fire trucks had come in the main entrance, choking the driveway with emergency vehicles. He had parked outside the gate at the employee and delivery entrance near the security shack. He fired up the old car and headed down the long, side road that led to the street and freedom. He could still hear the helicopter overhead and waited to be targeted by the spotlight but it never happened. An ambulance approached and he pulled to the side. Once it had passed he accelerated, moving quickly onto the street and back towards the I-90 bridge that would carry him towards Seattle and the safety of his apartment.

Back in Capitol Hill he found a parking spot easily this time, one of those places with confusing signs. You can read them two or three times and still not know if you can park there without getting a ticket. This one said "No parking end in place 8AM-5PM M-F delivery only." Signs like that were all over Seattle. He got out of the car, self conscious about how he was dressed. He stood out as he limped down the block in the broken heels. A band of kids heckled him, calling him names. He didn't look or feel like much of a woman anymore. It didn't matter. He was disappointed in himself. Once again he had failed.

He limped up the stairs, the sound of his heels echoing like an old horse down a cobblestone road. There was nobody around, no woman to make him feel insecure or inadequate, no bullies to pick on him. Just him alone in the stairwell. He was tired and his head started to spin. He had to stop a few times to catch his breath.

He was angry and disappointed in himself. Once in his apartment he practically ripped the clothes off his body, throwing them on the floor in a pile in front of his closet. He took off everything but the panties. He picked up the boots and looked at the broken heel, then threw them in the trash. He put on a robe and realized how tired he was.

There was nothing in the refrigerator but a bottle of ice water and some condiments. It wasn't real bottled water, just a plastic bottle he refilled over and over with tap water so he'd have something cold to drink. Experts say not to do that, some kind of danger from contamination or bacteria, but he did it anyway. He took a drink of water then pressed the cold bottle against his cheek for a minute.

He opened the cabinet and saw a box of saltine crackers. Somewhere behind the dried rice the bottle of Stoli Vodka called to him. He answered, taking it out of the cabinet and setting it on the counter. He stared at it a minute, then took another drink of water and reached for the crackers. He ate a few before opening a jar of peanut butter to spread on them. He poured himself a glass of water and sat down at the kitchen table making peanut butter cracker sandwiches and eating them one at a time.

The next thing he knew he was in bed. There was a knock at the door that quickly became a pounding.

"Harry! Harry!" said a voice, an old woman calling his name.

Then there was a softer, younger voice. "Harry?" The doorknob twisted and he heard the squeak of his hinges. He covered himself with the robe and got up, meeting them halfway to the door. It was Mrs. Lee and Sue.

"Harry!" the old woman said excitedly. "Where were you tonight? You supposed to come by. I make your favorite. Kway teow." She pulled the top off a sealed storage bowl and Harry caught a whiff of something exotic. She waved it in front of his nose and set it on the counter next to the stove. She got a good look at him in the bright light. "Hey, what's up with you?" she asked. "You no look so good."

"He's hurt, Mom," said Sue.

"You right," said Mrs. Lee. "Come, you lie down and I fix." She directed him towards the couch but he staggered towards the bedroom. Sue pulled down the sheets and he laid back in the bed. Mrs. Lee pulled the robe open and began to examine him. Sue looked down at the lump of his penis pressing outward from underneath the panties. She looked away and went back to the kitchen. She began to clean up the mess from the peanut butter and crackers when her mother called. "Sue! You come now."

She ran to the bedroom. "He hurt. You clean him up while I go get medicine," said Mrs. Lee. Sue got a pot from the kitchen and filled it with hot water. Harry heard Mrs. Lee opening cupboards, the sound of his microwave, running water and ice cracking. Sue came back with a dishrag wrapped around ice. She wiped his cheek and pressed the cold cloth against it. "Hold this while I clean you up a bit."

It felt good. The cloth absorbed the pain. He pressed his hand hard against his cheek, trying to force the swelling down. It was a stupid thing to do. It just made him ache more.

Mrs. Lee brought in a cup of hot tea. "You drink," she said, thrusting it in front of his face. Harry sat up and let the warm cup rest against his face before taking a drink. "I have to run home. Get big medicine. I only carry around tea and a few simple things. You wait. Sue take care of you until I get back." She turned and left, stopping to say something to Sue. Then he heard the front door slam shut.

Sue came back in with a pot of water that she set near the bottom of the bed. The washcloth floated in it like a lotus on a still pond. He looked at her. She was seven years his junior, thin and beautiful, tall for an Asian woman, like a model. She sat down on the edge of the bed and took the cup from Harry's hand. She adjusted the pillow and placed her hand gently on the back of his head, elevating it enough to rest his lips on the edge of the tea cup. "Here, drink," she said, her voice falling like a soft rain on his ears.

It tasted good, some kind of herbal concoction. He could feel the warm liquid running down his throat and into his belly. He took another sip and Sue moved the cup away and set it on the night stand beside his bed. She turned to the pot of water, gently squeezing the rag out over it and cleaning the wounds on his body.

"What happened to you?" she asked.

"I tripped and fell," he said.

"Right," she said. "Your face tells a different story. Let me ask you, When you fell, whose fist did you hit on the way down?"

He looked surprised.

"It's okay. I know what it feels like to be hit," she said. She looked off into the distance for a minute, a window into her past where she huddled in a corner while someone swung at her with angry fists. She looked back down at his chest, dabbing the sweat and grime from his body. "I meant to thank you for finding me Harry. I was lost," she said.

"No you weren't," he said. "You just needed a ride home."

"How'd you know I was in Tacoma?" she asked.

"Can't tell you my trade secrets," he said. "I may need them to find you again."

"I was involved with the wrong man," she said. "Tom had me trapped there in some kind of spell."

"That's what your mother said."

"She may call it a spell, but it was just drugs." She continued to clean him while she spoke, stopping occasionally to elevate his head for a sip of tea. "Tom smoked something that smelled funny, I never knew what it was and I never asked him. He made me try it, I didn't want to but he kept pestering me. I guess my curiosity got the best of me. I did and soon I was smoking it with him. A lot. It made me very unproductive, uncaring about myself and the world in general. I knew it was changing me. I wanted to quit but somehow I couldn't. And I was afraid to leave him, afraid he would hurt me, afraid I would lose the drugs and the feeling they gave me."

She dipped the cloth in the pot and squeezed the water out of it, rubbing it gently across his skin. "Then you showed up. You were amazing. The way you decked him with that sucker punch. Then when you stood over him and told him we were going. I saw him reach for the knife and I guess you did too. Next thing he's screaming like an animal, I never heard a man make that kind of noise. Like hearing a dog hit by a car. Then he was crying like a pathetic, spoiled child. He won't be using that hand for a while." She kissed him gently and noticed he had makeup on. She rinsed the cloth and started to wipe it off his face. "Then the way you threatened him. God, I never saw that side of you. He had fear in his eye, and I knew I was free of him and you were too. I knew he wouldn't bother either of us ever again." She stopped and stared into his eyes.

"You changed my life, Harry," she said. "Did I tell you I'm back in nursing? The school let me back into the program."

"You're a good student, Sue," he said. "You'll make a fine nurse."

She wiped more makeup off his face, glanced down at his panties. "You're a handsome man," she said. "Why do you want to be all girly girl?" she asked.

"I don't know," he said. "Just something I like to do."

"You come see me when you feel better," she said. "I'll make you forget all about wearing dresses."

It was as if she had pulled thoughts right out of his mind. "I'd like to see you try," he said.

"Oh," she said, stopping to kiss him gently on his sore cheek. "I'll do more than try." His lips started to quiver and he wanted to kiss her back. "Not now," she said. "Momma will be back soon. I know how she is, got sixth sense about me. We'd just get started and then she'd come in and ruin it all." She stood up. "There, your face is all clean," she said. She put the washcloth in the pot and took it to the kitchen, set it in the sink, and then came back. She saw the pile of clothes in the corner by his closet and she reached down and picked them up. "These tights are ruined," she said. "You'll have to throw them away." She folded the skirt, inspecting it for damage. There was a rip in the blouse as well. She folded it too and put them gently on his dresser.

"You'll be okay when Momma gets back," she said. "She's an herbalist. Old school from China. My uncle once told me she's a witch."

Harry cringed at the word, his body tensing like the hiss of an angry cat. Witch. It was what Couture called Heille.

"Oh, don't worry," she said. "She's a good witch. The kind that helps people. She'll fix you up right."

They heard the front door open again, the squeak of the old hinges. "I back," said Mrs. Lee. She went straight to the kitchen, rinsed the pot and the washcloth that Sue had used to clean Harry. She took some powders out of her purse, small bottles and such, and mixed them into the water. She went in the bedroom and began dabbing them over different places on Harry's body. She took several acupuncture needles from out of a small, folded kit that was in her pocket. She pressed them into his body, working her magic.

Sue went to the kitchen and prepared him a plate of food consisting of rice and kway teow. She made him another cup of tea by reusing her mother's tea ball from the first cup. She came in the bedroom and pulled up a chair to sit beside him. She fed him forkfuls one at a time while her mother continued to tend to him.

"You eat," said Mrs. Lee. She shook her head negatively. "Too bad it not fresh. Tastes much better when crunchy. That's why I bring it over tonight. Eat! You need it."

She was right. With each bite Harry felt strength returning to his body. He had forgotten the other advantage of a good fighter: healthy nutrition.

Harry was suddenly tired. "He needs rest now," said Mrs. Lee. She took the pot of herbs to the kitchen and washed it out then came back to collect her acupuncture needles. "You be okay now," she said. She turned to her daughter. "Sue, you put up food. He have enough." She turned to Harry while Sue left the room. "I leave you rest of kway teow. You bring back bowl when you come to my house for dinner next week. We try again. Nothing like fresh kway teow."

Sue put the food away and cleaned the mess. She saw the boots and took them out of the trash. They looked expensive, almost new and not worn at all. She studied the broken heel and laid them on the table. Mrs. Lee came in and began to gather her herbs off the kitchen counter. She saw the bottle of Stoli on the counter. "He no need this," she said. "Bad for spirit. Bad for health." She put the bottle of Vodka in her purse.

Sue smiled and went back to the bedroom. "Good night Harry. I'll lock the front door on my way out" she said, turning the light off. He was already asleep. She stopped to pick the boots up off the table before she left with her mother.

Chapter 24

Got to Be a Morning After

Harry went to Bernard's office as soon as he woke. He was glad he had managed to slip away from the Crumstein place before he got caught up in police procedure. He didn't want to stick around dressed as he was and answer a bunch of questions. He'd have to deal with it sooner or later though, and Bernard was always a good starting point.

As he made his way towards the Lieutenant's office he passed Van Dorn leading a man away in handcuffs. He had close cropped blond hair, a van dyke beard, and he was whining.

"You're going down," said Van Dorn. "We got your car, a witness, and we placed you at the scene. Dumb shit, you even left the security tape you stole on your front seat." He saw Harry standing off to the side and smirked. "You can go home, Fu," he said. "The professionals are hard at work here. The Sooka case is as good as closed."

"Did you find the dress?" asked Harry. Van Dorn said nothing. "Did you find the murder weapon that did in Sooka? Got the saw used to cut him up? Blood samples?"

Van Dorn licked his hand and stroked the back of his head. Harry went over to the handcuffed man and yanked his beard. "Ow," said the man.

"He didn't do it," said Harry. "You got the wrong man."

"That's what I said," replied the real Paul Hendrix. Harry moved on. "Hey, come back," shouted Paul, trying to get Van Dorn to make the connection. Harry continued towards Bernard's office, shouts getting louder behind him. "He believes me," said Hendrix. "See. I didn't do it."

"We'll see," said Van Dorn. "Move on." He pushed him down the hall and through a door.

Bernard was on the phone when Harry found him. He cut the conversation short and hung up the handset. "About time you showed up," said Bernard.

"What's up?" asked Harry.

Bernard narrowed his eyes, "Don't get cute on me. I know you were at the Crumstein place last night. Right before all hell broke loose."

"Who me?" asked Harry.

"Mercer Island P.D. had you on the scene at nine twenty. Said they escorted you there. Now what the hell happened after that?"

Harry drew a deep breath.

"Out with it!" said Bernard. "I know you. You get this innocent look every time you're guilty. For years I worked with you. I know your ways like one of my own. Now talk."

Harry looked away, stared at a blank wall. "I saw him, Matt."

"What? Saw who?"

"I saw the killer. Fought with him." He dropped his head into his hands. "He killed her, Matt. Burned her to death." His hands hid the beginnings of tears.

"No shit," said Bernard.

"It wasn't the guy Van Dorn has in custody," said Harry. He lifted his head up, wiped his eyes on his sleeve.

"I don't know. We found his car at the scene. Night guard ID'd him. Said he slipped him a Mickey and took the security tape. Found the tape on the front seat of his car. Sure looked like him."

"Doesn't this sound familiar? Come on, Matt. Look at the guy's m.o. He picks an innocent person, disguises himself as them, steals their car, and then makes sure he's seen."

"Okay. I'm listening," said Bernard. "What you say so far may fit. Now tell me something new."

Harry looked off, closed his eyes. He was outside the house again looking in the window. He visualized the killer. "He has brown eyes, bald, about six feet tall. His ears stick out slightly. He's strong, his reach was longer than mine. I tried my best moves and he wiggled free. He knows judo or karate, maybe tai kwon do. Some kind of oriental fighting style." He concentrated now, but all he could see were flames. He gasped.

Bernard was beside him, his hand on his shoulder. "It's okay," Matt said. He had a bottled water in his hand and he gave it to Harry. "Have a drink."

He unscrewed the cap and took a long gulp. "He just burned her, Matt."

"With what? Kerosene?"

"No, worse. She went up like a Fourth of July barbeque grill. Poof. Had to be something like starter fluid."

"Napalm maybe?"

"I don't know. I was outside looking in the window when it happened. I went for a garden hose but it was too late. I tell you, Matt. She just burst into flames. Spontaneous combustion." Harry's back bent. He put the water bottle on Matt's desk. "Poof," he said, his hands coming together to make a soft explosion followed by a puff of air. "She started flailing around. Caught the curtains on fire. That's when he spotted me... He wasn't afraid of me, came after me. Thought it was fun. It didn't even bother him to hit a woman."

"What? He hit a woman?"

Harry had been seeing it in his mind. The words came out automatically. "Did I tell you I was... undercover?"

"No," said Bernard. "I missed that fact."

Harry was ashamed. "I could've taken him if I hadn't been wearing high heels."

Bernard laughed, then composed himself. "Sorry," he said. "Now I know why you didn't stick around and make a statement. I wasn't laughing at you. I just found it funny that both you and the killer were in disguise."

Harry reached for the bottle and took another drink of water. "Look, Matt. I don't want to meet this guy again. He's dangerous. Arrogant and fearless. Smart and well trained."

"Sounds like a young cop I knew once," said Bernard.

"That cop doesn't exist anymore," said Harry.

"I know. He's a tough, fearless, arrogant private detective now."

"You left out drag queen," said Harry.

"I don't care about that," said Bernard. "We're all a lot of different things. But I don't need a drag queen right now. If I did, I'd come see you, you're probably a damn good one. Right now I need a detective, a damn good one. Isn't that what you're supposed to be?"

"Why can't I be both?"

"That was last night, this is morning," said Bernard. "Come on, Harry. Why you being so hard on yourself all of a sudden? What's eating you?"

"He saw me Matt. If the house wasn't on fire, if the fire trucks weren't there, I think he would have killed me."

"All the more reason to get out there and find this guy," said Bernard. "But before you do, you owe me something."

"What's that?" asked Harry.

"A report."

Harry frowned.

"Look you can either write me a report and I'll send it over to Mercer Island P.D., or you can go over there and tell them what you just told me. Either way, someone's getting a statement. Standard procedure, you know that."

"I'd rather it was you getting my report," said Harry.

"I figured that," he said. "Now go park yourself down at a computer out there and start writing."

Harry stood and started to leave. "Can you do me a favor, Matt?"

"What is it?" He looked toward Harry's hand, expecting another skip trace, but it was empty.

"Let that kid go. The one Van Dorn is hounding. Let him go before Franklin does some damage. He's no more guilty than that Mexican fruit picker."

"Okay," said Bernard. He picked up the phone and called interrogation, then spoke into the phone. "Van Dorn is down there talking to a suspect, blond guy with a beard." Pause. "Yes, tell him to get a statement and let the kid go." Pause. "No, just tell him not to leave town." Pause. "The kid, you idiot, not Van Dorn." He hung up the phone. "God these rookies get dumber all the time." He looked at Harry. "There. Satisfied?"

"Thanks."

"You better be right about this. Now get me a report so I have something to back that up. There are people around here beginning to think Van Dorn got it right."

It took Harry most of the morning and part of the afternoon to finish the report. He went to Bernard's office when he was done but the Lieutenant was gone. He left the report on his desk and wandered off. He went down the hallway past the interrogation rooms. He came to an open door, a small, empty observation room crowded with chairs. The room was dark and inviting, a dim glow from the adjacent interrogation room escaping through the one way glass. He went in and sat alone in the room staring through the glass at the Spartan features of the empty room. He'd asked a lot of people questions in rooms like this. He always felt safer on this side of the glass.

The darkness felt good. He needed time to think, time to slip out of his funk. His cheek was beginning to throb and he needed more aspirin. He ran his hand gently over the swollen lump, a tear coming to his eye.

He had watched her die. He lowered his head, staring at the floor. He had never witnessed a murder firsthand.

Not true. In the war he had seen death visited on the unsuspecting over and over. But that was war where murder is sanctioned in the name of victory. The enemy was faceless, and the cause was just. What was just about this? What possible evil had Haille Crumstein and Richard Sooka done to deserve this? If he knew the answer to that he might have another clue about this killer.

Could he have saved her? Could he have saved those men from death by an exploding truck? Could he save anybody, even himself?

The door flung open and the bright light from the hall silhouetted a tall figure standing in the doorway. The head moved back and forth, scanning the dark room. "Harry?" he heard a voice say.

It was an effort to speak but he recognized the voice. "I'm here Rita."

"Somebody said they saw you come in here." She reached for the light switch and flipped it on. Harry squinted, wincing with the pain of a sleeper waking to a loud alarm clock. She saw his reaction and turned it off, plunging the room back into darkness. She had a fix on him and she slowly groped her way to the chair next to him. "You okay?" she asked. She put her arm around him. "I read your report, the one you left on Bernard's desk."

He shuddered, holding back the tears. Undignified for a man to cry, despite the therapeutic value. He didn't want her to see him cry.

"It's okay," she said. She was silent for a while. "Whatcha doing here?" she asked.

"Thinking," he said.

"Great," she said, full of Big Red enthusiasm, her voice as excited as a game day fan at the Super Bowl. "I have too. I think I have this thing figured out."

Harry drew a deep breath, trying to shake free of his emotional quicksand. Maybe, like being in quicksand, all he had to do was sit quiet and calm until someone came to rescue him. Why shouldn't it be Red? He was used to being the hero, though, and not the victim. It's quicksand, just stay quiet and listen, a voice inside him said.

He heard the rustle of papers. "Mind if I turn the light back on?" she asked.

"What have you got there?" he asked.

"I think I have the answer," she said.

He was doubtful, but it was hard to squelch her excitement. "Go ahead. Turn the light on. Show me what you have."

She flipped the switch and he winced again. He wiped his face with his shirt sleeve and looked up. She held out a bunch of photos, some of them grainy, as if they were printed out from tiny internet photos. "Recognize any of these?" she asked.

He looked. "What is this?"

"A suspect book, my list, or whatever you call it," she said.

"It's called a photo lineup" he said. "Just like the ones done in person, except with pictures. Who are these people?"

"Never mind for now," she said. "Just look over the pictures. Here's a pen. I want you to put an 'X' over the ones you definitely think aren't the killer, and circle the ones you think may be."

Harry had never been on the receiving end of a photo ID. How many times had he put another victim through this process? What she said made sense though. It was a tried and true police technique. He took the photos, some printed four or nine to a page, some full face shots, some even group photos. He looked them over and began.

She watched him draw 'X's over some of the photos instantly. On the group photos he just drew an X over the faces. She would have removed the obvious ones, but left them all in. She suspected some of these photos were seven or eight years old. A person could change a lot in that amount of time.

Harry continued to scan. "Where did you say you got these?" he asked.

"Later," she replied. "Just do what I ask."

He knew the procedure. Over half of them had been eliminated already. He studied the rest, the X's coming more slowly now. Soon seventy five percent were gone. He put the pictures down and rubbed his eyes.

"It was dark last night," he said. "I can't be sure."

"You fought with him," she said. "You were as close to him as anybody could get. And you're a trained cop. You're supposed to have uncanny powers of observation." She paused. "You're the best shot we have."

He went back to looking. More X's. "Why are these women in here?" he asked. "We know he's a man."

She scrunched her face up at him. "Anything is possible, as if you didn't know."

"Oh," he said. He got it without her having to say it. He went back to scanning.

A few more X's, then he set the pictures down and stood up. He stretched, yawning as he extended his arms. There was a table in the back of the room. He laid the remaining pictures out, gathering up the pages where all the suspects had been eliminated and putting them aside. He stood over them, finally circling one, then another.

Rita smiled and stood back, giving him room to pace in front of the table. Two more X's and an O. It was like a kid's game with much higher stakes.

In the end there were seven circles spread across five sheets of paper, one the only O in a group photo. "This is as far as I go for now," he said.

"Okay," she said. "Let's take a break. Want a cup of coffee? I'm buying."

She stuffed all but the five pages in a manila envelope she had and paper clipped them together. There was a coffee shop right across the street. Hell, there was a coffee shop right across the street everywhere in Seattle.

"How do you take it?" she asked as they stood in line.

"Americano," he said.

"That's rather bland," she said.

"It's the cheapest," he said.

"Splurge," she said. "We're one step away from finding that dress and claiming the reward."

He laughed. He was going to say "Right" but then he changed his mind. "I'll have a latte," he said.

She ordered the coffee, smiled at Harry, and daydreamed while she waited. She had been working hard, trying to solve this puzzle, Nancy Drew on steroids. Wait. Nancy Drew would never take steroids, and neither would Rita Rockwell. Okay, she was more like Nancy Drew in overdrive. Working hard, exciting work, interesting work, nothing like being a bouncer in a club. She had it going now. Meeting police, Lt. Bernard, coroners, interrogations, did I mention decapitated corpses and missing penises? Eat your freaking heart out Nancy Drew. Make way for Rita Rockwell. Yeah, that's it! She was two hundred and fifty pounds of Nancy Drew, packed full of brains and barroom brawn.

"You know I never thanked you, Rita," said Harry.

"For what?" she asked.

"Getting Binky off my back. You know, giving him that money yesterday. I'll pay you back when I get a chance."

"It's okay, Harry. We're in this together." She handed him the pictures. "Go grab that table over there and give these another look. I'll wait for the coffee."

He went to the table and looked at his selections. There were a few photos that didn't have any markings and he studied them carefully. He kept looking for distinguishing features but nothing stood out. He wished he had more to go on, like height and body size. The killer had a frail look that couldn't be captured in a face shot. He tried to think.

He had funny ears, he remembered. They bowed out at the top, kind of like a wolf. He looked again at the photos, wishing they were professional police photos, head on and profile of each suspect. Instead they were black and white photos downloaded off the internet. He closed his eyes to think. The killer had dark eyes. He saw them in his mind, reflected in the bright firelight. There was no fear in his face, no remorse. Harry was just a little bug that had gotten in his way.

He cursed himself again. Damn high heels. I don't ever want to cross dress again.

Red brought the coffee. Harry took a sip. It had been a long time since he had tasted a good cup of coffee. Not in his budget anymore. He looked up and she was smiling. She always seemed to be smiling. She smiled when she fought Fat Farnsworth, but it was a different smile, different even when she had threatened Van Dorn. But it was always a smile. Whatever her anger issues, she hid them well.

"Any luck," she asked.

"This is the best I can do," he said.

"Great," she said. "Thanks."

"For what?" he asked. "I still haven't ID'd the perp."

"No," she said. "But eight is a lot less than a hundred and twenty seven. I'll consider these unmarked ones possibilities, too." She took the photos from him and put them with the others in the manila envelope.

"Mind telling me what this is about?" he asked.

"Just a theory. Let me do a little more research and then I'll explain," she said.

"Don't you want to let your partner in on it? You know, detectives work better when they bounce things off each other."

"I may be wrong," she said. "Just let me check my facts."

"I'm always here for you," said Harry.

"Thanks," said Rita. "That goes for me too. It felt good to hear you call me that, too. Did you mean it?"

"What?" he said. "What did I call you?"

"Partner."

It had been automatic. How had he come to think of her as his partner after only a few days of working with her? She had all the qualities he would want in a partner and they were in this together. Till death they do part. He mulled over the words. Till death you do part. The words sound much more real when you have a killer after you.

He took a sip of coffee, a small luxury at this moment of his life. He was beyond thoughts of killers, partners, and men like Binky.

Binky was still there, though, circling like a shark through murky water. What a sense of humor, too. Exotic dancer or security guard. He and Binky had been childhood friends. There was a depth to their friendship that few others understood. Harry knew Binky really had his best interests at heart. In his own twisted way, Binky believed in him.

He had to crack this case. Show the world that Harry Takanawa was not a lost cause.

He was staring at the coffee cup when Rita interrupted him.

"Deep in thought?" she said.

"I guess so," said Harry.

"Bernard said you were roughed up pretty bad. You have a scar on your face and that cheek looks like it's going to be swollen for a while."

"I think I got it when I went down. Sucker cold cocked me Rita. I went down like a sack of rice falling off a truck."

"I could teach you to fight," she said.

"Wouldn't have made a difference." He cursed the high heels again. "He definitely had the advantage." He took another sip of coffee.

"I almost forgot," she said. "Bernard told me to tell you they found an abandoned kayak on Lake Washington. He said you'd be interested to hear that."

Harry perked up. "Where?"

"I don't know exactly," said Rita. "Somewhere on Mercer Island."

Harry's mind kicked into gear. Whether he liked it or not, he thought like a detective twenty four seven when he worked a case. "I need to know where," he said. "And what did the kayak look like? Was it black?"

"Bernard knows. He said some old lady reported it this morning. She thought we should be looking for someone who fell out of the canoe and drowned on the lake."

"We should be so lucky," he said. He drained the rest of his coffee as a light flashed in his brain. "Although. This may be the clue we've been looking for."

"Howso?" asked Red.

"You're working on the who, I'm trying to answer the where. Finished your coffee yet?"

"I can take it with me. Why? You ready to get back to work?"

"It's the only way I see out of this funk," he said. "Work your way out."

"Then what are we waiting for?"

Chapter 25

Doctor in the House

Dr. Couture, as he liked to call himself, woke up about mid morning rested and serene. The wind had died down and the water laid flat across Lake Washington. He had coffee with dry toast as he looked out the window of his waterfront home. It was shaping up to be a nice day.

It wasn't really his house. It belonged to his boss who was continually away. Someone who spent his whole life working for things he never had the time to enjoy. He was just the caretaker. Still, it gave Couture plenty of time and opportunity to make the modifications to the property to create his secret room.

He had started by trying to dig out the crawl space under the house, but the building inspector stopped him. Bureaucrats wanting him to pay for permits and environmental statements and expensive modifications to bring it up to modern code, even though the house was built over forty years ago. Then FEMA weighed in and said something about the house being in a floodplain, said it would cost him an arm and a leg to insure it under the National Flood Insurance Program. They said the garage was an outbuilding and not part of the insured package. They told him to insure the house and move the cars to higher ground if there was ever a flood.

That's what gave him the idea. The garage was a mechanic's dream. It had a pit built in it, the kind where you could walk down a short staircase and work under a car while you were standing up, kind of like those quick change oil places have. Nice.

It was easy to dig it out. He hired some day labor immigrants who stood outside Home Depot looking for work. No permits, no hassles, all done in secret. He thought about killing them when it was done, burying their bodies under the concrete floor like the pharaohs buried their servants as a reward for building their burial chambers. He decided it was not worth the effort and he let them go. Very magnanimous of him, he thought.

In the end he had the perfect hideout. A false wall in the pit under the garage slid sideways leading into a secret room. It was fairly large, about twenty feet wide by thirty feet long, paneled and carpeted. He wired it himself. He prided himself as being able to learn and do anything, to learn anything he put his mind to.

Medicine was one of his other special interests, a passion developed in childhood. How many animals had he patiently dissected, and then later, a few humans? He wondered what he could have done with his life had he taken more formal training. He took a few pre med classes and even though he didn't have a certificate of any kind he still called himself Doctor, such was his arrogance.

Self taught, just like Abraham Lincoln. It was rough, harvesting his own cadavers when he needed them. Hard work, almost as much work as cutting them apart. He didn't worry too much about getting it wrong, it was all experimental science, and there's always something fresh to harness out there.

The doctor in him was needed again. He went to the internet, reviewing medical journals and papers. He studied the procedure he had in mind carefully. He thought he might practice on another victim but decided against it. He thought about all the possible problems he could have performing an operation in his crude facility. It was just a large shower with a floor drain but it would do. It was the same place he used to cut up Richard Sooka after he had died.

Sterile technique? Yes, he would do is best, but what did it matter? The tranny would be dead before the infection set in. And that was the goal after all.

But what a death! She should be honored. Another designer death, custom delivered by Dr. Couture.

Now where did I leave my surgical instruments?

Chapter 26

GIS

Bernard was in the squad room when Harry caught up with him. The lieutenant stared at a map that was part of a wall display of Seattle. He wished it was all of King County.

"What's the skinny on that abandoned canoe that was reported?" he asked Matt.

"Huh?" He had derailed the lieutenant's train of thought. "Ask your buddy Van Dorn," said Bernard. "He took the call."

"Oh." You could hear the disappointment in Harry's voice. "Where is he now?"

"Probably celebrating," he said. "Killer's locked up downstairs and Franklin said he's an inch away from a confession."

"And you believe him?"

Bernard laughed. "About as much as you do."

"Didn't the kid go free? I heard you call someone before I went across the street with Red."

"I was overruled," said Bernard. "They're not letting him go."

"Who's not letting him go?"

"Gotta give Van Dorn his minute of fame," said Bernard. "He plans on going public in an hour. Got a press conference all lined up."

"And you authorized this?"

"I did not," he said. "Little prick went over my head straight to the mayor. Chief said let him go. I'm just waiting to see the show. Stick around."

"Can't," said Harry. "I'm checking out an idea about the abandoned kayak."

"I read your report," said Bernard. "I haven't showed it to anyone. Next time Mercer Island asks I'll fax them a copy, otherwise I'm going to sit on it. Either way I got my butt covered. Somebody's right, you, Van Dorn, Rita, maybe even me. I'm turning it over and over in my mind just like you guys. I'm just as anxious to see Van Dorn's next move as I am to see your next move."

"Okay. Here's my next move. Who do I talk to about the kayak?"

"Ask Sommers," he said. "Jason may know. He was with Franklin when he got the call."

Harry walked down the hall to the main office. Jason Sommers was on the phone. Van Dorn was nowhere in sight. Harry went over to Franklin's desk and sat down, indicating he wanted to talk. Sommers smiled and held his hand up, giving him the signal to sit tight and wait."

Harry scanned the desk while Sommers finished his call. Van Dorn was messy. There were candy wrappers and balled up wads of paper, empty coffee cups lined up like parking cones, stains on the desk and crumbs of pastry scattered like volcanic debris. He got up and went to another desk.

Sommers was done and hung up the phone. "How ya doin' Harry," he said.

"Could be better," said Harry.

"Looks like someone messed your face up real good," he said.

Harry's hand went to the scar. "Yeah," he said. "You win some..." He let the rest trail off.

"Whatcha need?" asked Sommers.

"Bernard said you or maybe Van Dorn took a call about a lost kayak?"

"Van Dorn took the call. Wrote down the contact info and told me to follow up on it. He had bigger things to do." Sommers started to grin. "He let me know all about it, too. 'Got bigger things than lost kayaks, Jason.' He said it just like that." The grin turned to a chuckle. Harry could only imagine what Van Dorn must have sounded like. He was sure that Sommers heard enough. "I was about to call and follow up," said Sommers.

"Mind if I take it?" asked Harry.

"Lost kayak? Sure." Sommers sifted through the piles of paper and notes on his desk. He handed Harry a post-it note with a name and a phone number on it. The word 'kayak' scribbled sideways on it. "Here ya go."

"Thanks." Harry dialed the number, then hung up the phone abruptly. "What is this, a misprint?" he asked, pointing to the name on the paper. "I-N-G-R. Are we missing a few vowels?"

"That's the name," said Sommers. "It's pronounced Eeen-grrr. It's Swedish."

"I get that from the last name," said Harry. "Swenson." He nodded, acknowledging Jason's help. "Thanks." He tried the number again.

"Hallo," said a voice on the other end.

"Mrs. Swenson?" he asked.

"Ya, dis is eeen-grrr," she said.

"My name's Harry Takanawa. I'm assisting the Seattle police. I'm following up on a kayak that washed up on the beach."

"Oh, ya," she said. "Did they find that poor soul who fell out of it? Did they drown?"

She sounded worried. Harry softened his voice. "Oh, no ma'am. Nobody drowned. The kayak broke loose from a dock nearby. It happened during that fire last night."

"Ya, I saw that fire," she said.

Harry regretted mentioning the fire. He could hear the worry again. "It's okay. The fire department put it out. Nobody was hurt and the whole house didn't burn down."

"Lucky us," she said. "The wind, she was a-blowing last night. Coulda caught the whole woods on fire. I don't live too far from that house. Maybe a couple of miles south. Thank goodness the wind was blowing off the lake," she said.

"Yes, it was." Harry remembered the wind blasting in his face as he chased the killer down the dock.

"What I don't understand," said Mrs. Swenson, "is how that kayak blew onto my beach. If it came from the house on fire it would have blown right back to the shore. Woulda never come this far south. That's what made me think there was some poor lost soul out there."

The lights in Harry's brain flickered again. "What did you say your address was?" he asked. "For the record."

She repeated it for him.

Sommers heard him. He stood over Harry, handing him an official police report form. "Might as well fill this out while you're conducting the interview."

Harry frowned. He nodded, picked up a pen and started to scribble. "Was there anybody near your house last night? Did anyone beach the kayak there on purpose?"

"I don't think so. Thor would have let me know if there was somebody there."

"Thor? Your husband?"

"No. My German shepherd. I'm surprised he doesn't smell you talking to me over the phone, otherwise he'd be barking."

There was a woof in the background.

"Oh shut up," she said. "I wasn't calling you when I said your name." He could hear the dog whimper and he imagined her petting him gently.

"What color was it?" he asked.

"It was black all the way around. Usually they're a different color on the bottom. It was kind of an ugly little boat."

"Are you sure nobody was there last night?" he asked.

"I went down there and looked myself." Her voice became childish, like she was talking to a baby. "Yes. You went too. Me and Thor." Harry heard another whimper. "Ya, we looked around there good, Mister," she said to Harry. "Ours were the only footprints on the beach. It's what made me think that somebody drowned. It's why I called you guys and reported it."

"Thank you ma'am."

"You can come down here and check for yourself if you want. You sound like a nice young man," she said.

The comment took Harry by surprise. He felt his cheeks flush, then throb.

"Yes, ma'am," he said. "Thank you, but that won't be necessary. Your word is good enough for me."

"Don't worry about Thor," she said. "He barks a lot but he's never bitten anybody."

"Like I said, ma'am, that won't be necessary. You've been most helpful. Thank you." He hung up, not too quickly he hoped, just before Mrs. Swenson, Eeen-grrr, got in another word.

He looked out the window, deep in thought for a minute.

Sommers was on the phone again. He covered the mouthpiece and said to Harry, "The form? The job isn't done until the paperwork is." He smiled and went back to his phone conversation.

Harry's left brain filled out the form, a familiar task to him, while his right brain began to intuit and sift facts. It took him about ten minutes to complete it. He wondered why this wasn't on the computer like most other routine forms. When he was finished he was glad. He went to the copy machine and made a copy for himself. It had all the information he needed.

He left the blank for investigating officer empty on purpose. He laid it on the desk in front of Sommers, pointed to the blank and smiled. He raised two fingers to his forehead and gave him the Boy Scout salute.

He walked out the door and back to the squad room where Bernard was still staring at a map. At least it was a different map this time.

"Hey, Matt?" said Harry. "Hate to interrupt you, but do you have a GIS department?"

Chapter 27

Sweet Water

"Yeah we got GIS," said Bernard. "You mean Geographical Information Systems, right? The map guys? I can't keep up with all the acronyms these days."

"Yes," said Harry. "Can I use them? I mean, I'm a contractor, sort of, working for you, and … well, I got an idea and I need GIS. Can you help me?"

"Sure, use 'em all you want."

"Thanks." Harry turned to leave.

Bernard called after him. "You'll have to go to County. They're not in this building anymore."

"County?" asked Harry.

"Yeah. They consolidated services across the County last month. Saves the taxpayers millions they tell me. Frees up money for other things."

"Like hiring more parking enforcement."

Bernard laughed, then squinted his eyes. "You get another parking ticket?"

Harry looked to the side, over Matt's right shoulder. "Yeah," he said.

"Give me the damn thing," he said. Harry hesitated. "Come on. Fork it over."

Harry opened his wallet and took out the ticket. It did not escape Bernard's eye that it was the only thing in his wallet. Matt took the ticket, scribbled something on it and stuck it in his pocket.

"Thanks," said Harry, looking him in the eye. Bernard smiled and Harry felt a strange mix of emotions. His eyes started to water like he was going to cry, but then he laughed along with Bernard, and a faint pressure passed over his heart.

"You're lucky," said Bernard. "I'm in a good mood."

"What's got you so happy?" asked Harry.

"Television," he said. He pointed to the TV constantly on in the situation room. "I'm waiting for Van Dorn's live press conference. Pull up a chair. I'll buy you a cup of coffee."

"Thanks Matt, but Red just bought me one. Wouldn't say no to a glass of water, though."

Bernard's smile widened. "Pull up a chair, I'll be right back."

Harry sat down while Bernard wandered off. Matt was a good friend. Harry never knew what Matt really thought about his cross dressing, but then he had never asked. He'd rather fill in the blank with his own perceptions, something like shame and disrespect, a feeling that always emerged when he thought about it. He imagined he had let Bernard and himself down in some big way, even though he knew Matt respected him. Harry tried to think of his own admirable traits but his mind didn't work that way. Maybe it did at one time, but not today and not at this minute. He had disowned too much of himself. Besides, hubris was a trait best left to men like Couture and Van Dorn.

Matt came back with two bottled waters. He gave Harry one and unscrewed the top from the other. He took a deep drink. "Sweet water," he said, sitting down.

"No coffee?" asked Harry. He tipped the bottle up and let the water cascade down his throat.

"I agreed with your choice. Water is better for your health, especially this water."

"Why's that?"

"I got it from Van Dorn's refrigerator."

Harry laughed and took another drink. "Sweet water," he said.

"You're partner's in there banging the keyboards. What's she working on?" asked Matt.

"She's playing Clue," said Harry. "She's good at it. Actually put it on her resume."

Bernard laughed out loud. "No shit?"

"She just led me through a photo lineup across the street like she'd been doing it her whole life."

Matt nodded in respect.

"You don't really think Van Dorn got this case solved, do you?" asked Harry. "You believe me about this madman I saw last night?"

"I don't believe anything until I see the evidence."

"What's Van Dorn got on this guy?" asked Harry.

"Vehicle found at the scene. Neighbors saw him leave with a big, odd shaped box, one lady actually spoke to him. Said he blew her off, seemed to be in a hurry. Guard at Crumstein's house saw him less than an hour later with a box that matched that description. One of a kind box, nothing common about it. We found the security tape from the guard shack in his car. When we played it we found images of him coming through the gate with the box. We found his fingerprints all over the car. Found no fingerprints in the house because of the fire. The guy has no alibi, he claims he was asleep at his apartment all night. If that's true, he goes to sleep pretty early by normal standards. Enough evidence for you? Open and shut case if you ask Van Dorn."

Harry laughed. "He's mad, you know."

"Who? The killer or Van Dorn?"

"Both of them actually," laughed Harry. "But in different ways."

"The killer, he's mad, like in crazy mad. Van Dorn is just angry type mad," said Bernard. "Hates my guts. That's why he did an end run around me and the Captain, straight to the Mayor."

"You left out his Mom," said Harry.

"Huh?" said Bernard.

"His mother," said Harry. "Van Dorn went around you, then the Captain, straight to his Mom who went straight to the Mayor."

"Yeah," said Bernard. "That's probably just like it happened."

"Now, now," said Harry. "What's Van Dorn got against you? What's there to hate about you, Matt?"

"Oh, he's mad because he's acting," said Bernard. "He's had your old job ever since you left, something else I think his Mother arranged."

"I'd agree with that," said Harry. "She can be pretty influential."

"So they gave him the title, temporary I mind you, of Acting Head Detective. He's been acting ever since."

Harry's shoulders bent forward. "It's been almost two years since I've been gone!"

"They left it up to me to make it permanent," he said. "I guess I never agreed with them. There's better men for the job." He looked in Harry's eyes. "Sometimes I think enough time's gone by since your retirement to come back. I don't know. Maybe that's just an old man's foolish dream. I like working with you, Harry."

Harry was uncomfortable and shifted the focus back to Van Dorn. "So that's why he went to the Mayor."

"I knew what he was doing. I let him go. Give a man enough rope."

Harry's face twisted into a wry smile. "You old devil," he said. "How'd you find out what he was up to?"

"Hey," said Bernard, tapping his head with his forefinger. "I'm a detective."

The monitor flashed and the screen went dark blue with white lettering that read, "Special Report". An announcer came on to say, "We interrupt this program for a special Channel 11 news report." The profile of a newswoman filled the screen. "Hi, I'm Marjorie Fullerton with Channel 11 news room City Watch. This just announced," she said. "Seattle police have in custody a man believed to be the killer of cast members of Designer Derby. Paul Hendrix, a local worker hired as a courier for the crew, may have been disgruntled over the conditions of his work. Police say he was underpaid and overworked by the group that manages the show and this may have contributed to his aggression. I'm here with Mayor Allright and Lead Detective on the case, Franklin Van Dorn.

The image of the Mayor filled the screen. "In line with our goals to make Seattle a safe place to live, we have captured the Derby Killer, as he has come to be known. The charity dress has not been found but police feel like it is within their grasp. Here with more details with the arrest is Detective Van Dorn."

The Mayor stepped back and Van Dorn took the podium. "We apprehended the suspect after midnight last night at his apartment, sleeping as if he had done nothing. Meanwhile police found his vehicle at the crime scene. His fingerprints were all over the car. We believe he set the fire in Crumstein's house after he murdered her to hide the evidence."

The newswoman nodded and turned to the camera. "I hear it's a grisly scene at Heille's burned mansion on Mercer Island. A charred corpse tangled in what appeared to be a desk lamp."

Van Dorn smiled and licked his hand, then pressed the back of his hair flat. "He escaped us by stealing a kayak. An abandoned kayak was found this morning less than two miles from where he set fire to her house. We apprehended him at his home shortly after that, so his escape attempt was for nothing. Once the fire inspectors are finished looking over the scene and pronounce it safe, we'll be able to go in and finish up our investigation."

"Here is a picture taken by one of your Channel 11 City Watch Team." The screen went blank for a minute, then cut back to Marjorie Fullerton, her name plastered across the bottom of the screen in case you forgot it. "We're sorry. What you should have seen was a picture taken through the window of the mansion, the last we'll see of Heille Crumstein, her remains tangled in a macabre sculpture of death."

Everyone was quiet for a moment. The Mayor smiled.

"But I guess you won't see that right now. Meanwhile Lead Detective Van Dorn, do you have anything else you can tell us?"

Van Dorn licked his hand and stroked the back of his head. Then he said, "We got him locked up. Interrogators are still questioning..."

His image flashed away, replaced by something that looked like it was taken with a wet cell phone camera. It was shot through a window and overlaid with the reflection of one of the Channel 11 City Watch Team holding a cell phone. If you looked hard enough you could barely make out a brown blob in a pile of dust and fire debris, maybe it was a tabby cat, a big brown one, but nothing like what Marjorie Fullerton promised.

"There's that image," said Marjorie. "That blob in the lower right is her head slumped over a melted computer keyboard." The image flashed away. "And you can get that off our website later after this interview." She nodded to Van Dorn, who thought she was flirting with him.

"We're trying to determine where he might have hidden the charity dress," said Van Dorn.

Marjorie interrupted him. "That dress has more than doubled in value since it's been missing and it's now reported to be worth over seven hundred thousand dollars, maybe even a million."

"We're charging him with murder right now. We think he acted alone, but we haven't ruled out the possibility that he has an accomplice."

"Tell us how you cracked this case, Lead Detective Van Dorn," she said.

"Acting," said Bernard.

"Hard detective work," said Van Dorn, licking his hand and patting the back of his head. "We questioned a lot of suspects in connection with the Sooka slaying. Crime Scene Investigation produced the evidence we needed to confirm we had the right man and we acted quickly to remove this threat from circulation. The Mayor backed us up and provided us the police resources to make the arrest. We feel like this nightmare is over for now and the people of Seattle have nothing to fear anymore."

"Yes," said Marjorie. "Carrie Rodriguez will certainly sleep sounder tonight thanks to the work of you and your team. Any other comments, Mr. Mayor?" She stuck the microphone in Allright's face.

"Maybe now everything can get back to normal," said the Mayor. "I hear the charity ball we've been waiting for has already been rescheduled. My wife and I have tickets and were looking forward to it. It's just a short matter of time before Detective Van Dorn and his team discover its whereabouts and recover the dress, bringing an end to this nightmare."

"Thank you Mayor Allright, and thank you Detective Van Dorn." She turned to the camera. "This is Marjorie Fullerton for Channel 11 City Watch Team news."

Bernard turned to Harry. "You feel any safer?"

Harry shook his head. "Not really." A deeper truth hit him though, the reason why he didn't feel safe. The killer was still at large and they had seen each other's face. Couture even had cell phone pictures of him. All Harry had was a rough memory of what the killer looked like. They had to find this guy before...

Before what? Before he killed again? Was it Carrie Rodriguez, or was it Harry Takanawa he was worried about?

"What about going to County?" asked Harry. Bernard looked puzzled. "GIS?" he reminded him.

Bernard laughed. "Things aren't like they used to be," he said. "It used to be simple, now it's pretty complicated. Last week I went down to County GIS just to get a few sector maps made. You have to fill out a form, get it approved, then they put it in a queue after they first ask you how soon you need it. Oh, we're very busy, Lieutenant Bernard, maybe late this afternoon, tomorrow by COB for sure. But I need it for the morning briefing, I say. They tell me a story about needing lead time for production, whatever the hell that is. It was a lot different when I could go downstairs and tap Ron Langhelm on the shoulder and get something done quick." Harry looked as if Bernard had told him all holiday leave was cancelled. He changed his tone, trying to sound more hopeful. "You can go down to County and lay paper at the feet of the Gods of GIS if you want, but I have another idea."

"What's that?" asked Harry.

"It's called Google Earth."

They went to Matt's office where he pulled up the popular program on his computer. "Lookee here, GIS without the paperwork."

"So you can make your own sector maps now?" asked Harry.

Bernard frowned. "Not quite. And I can't print out those big maps, the ones that make you look good in an official police briefing. But it's quick. Now what do you need?"

Harry reached in his pocket and looked at the police report he had written up about the abandoned kayak. He read the address to Bernard who punched it into the computer. The software zoomed right over the house that Ingr Swenson lived in. He saw the rock beach behind the house where she probably found the empty kayak this morning. All that was missing was Thor the German Shepard.

Harry looked closer at the image. He though he spotted a dog lying in the back yard. This Google stuff was good.

"Can you mark that spot?" asked Harry.

"Sure," said Bernard. He added a placeholder and put a giant blue stickpin right in the center of the house. "Can you move it down to the beach behind the house?" asked Harry.

"No problem," said Bernard. The stickpin moved to the beach.

"Now," said Harry. "Where's the Crumstein place?"

"Got the address right here," said Bernard. He shuffled through some papers on his desk and produced the address. He entered it into the computer and soon there was a big yellow stickpin on the house where Harry had met the killer last night. He even saw the dock behind the house. He looked for signs of a kayak on it but didn't see anything.

"Yes, that's it," said Harry. "That's the house all right. There's the long driveway and the security building where I found the old man unconscious last night." He pointed to the screen. "And there's the dock behind the house. This is the place all right. Now zoom out."

Harry studied the two pins on the map. "Any way to tell how far apart they are?" he asked.

Matt used some Google magic to measure the distance. "About one point eight miles."

"Okay," said Harry. "I need one more piece of information," he said. "Any way to tell the wind direction last night? I knew it was blasting in my face as I ran down that dock, but I need something scientific."

"NOAA makes all those observations," said Bernard. Harry watched him work. For an old guy Bernard was pretty agile with a computer. He did a little internet research and produced a whole set of statistics and tables for Harry. "What time?" he asked. "Sand Point observatory puts out data every ten minutes. They're on the west side of Lake Washington."

"Let's see, allowing him time to paddle across the lake, ditch the canoe, I'd say nine, maybe ten o'clock."

"Nearest I can figure is the wind was clocking out of the northwest at about 300 degrees. It was pretty steady at 17 to 25 miles per hour most of the night." Matt's face lit up. "Hey! I can see where you're headed with this," he said.

"Okay," said Harry. "Then complete the picture for me."

Matt worked the keys like a pro. He hit the print button and left the office for a minute.

"Had to go down the hall to the big printer. Eleven by seventeen is the biggest I could get this." He laid the map down on the desk. He had drawn a line at 300 degrees heading northwest from the point where the kayak was found at Ingr Swenson's. The line stretched all the way across

Lake Washington. Harry pointed to the area where it intersected the shore. "This is probably where he got out of the kayak, somewhere along this shoreline. Can you get me a blow up of that area?"

Matt did some magic again, left the office and came back with a detailed print of the neighborhood. "I know this area," he said. "Lots of residential houses."

"Think there would be any value to canvassing the area?" asked Harry. "See if somebody saw something last night?"

"Good idea," said Bernard. "Except for one thing."

"What's that?" asked Harry.

"Now that Van Dorn has this case all wrapped up, I don't have any resources I can assign to it."

"You may not," said Harry. "But I do. What is it you said to me a few days ago? I don't work for you, so I'm not bound by the rules you have to play by."

"Something like that," said Bernard.

"I think I might head over there and take a look." He scooped up the maps and started to go. Matt followed him out of the office. Red was still sitting in front of the computer, licking her lips like she was eating the best meal in town. "Find anything, Rita?" he asked.

"I'm close, Harry," she said. "Just need a little more time."

"Okay," he said. "I'm going to check out a lead."

She looked up, excited. "Do you want me to go with you?" she asked.

"No," said Harry. "What you're doing is more important. We need to know who this guy is. You know Clue, Rita. Gotta find three things. Who, where, and with what. You're working on who. I'm working on where."

"That still leaves one thing, Harry," she said. "What."

"We already know what," said Harry. "He kills with all kind of creepy things. This isn't Mr. Green in the Conservatory with the pipe wrench. I'm not trying to find out where he committed these murders, I'm trying to figure out where he's hiding. He's holing up somewhere, a secret lair or something, and that's where I'm headed to check things out. Maybe I'll get lucky."

"What if he sees you first?" said Red.

"Like I said, maybe I'll get lucky. He only knows what I look like as a woman, and I had a thick layer of face paint on last night. Maybe I'll catch him off guard and take him by surprise."

"You said he was a better fighter than you were," said Bernard.

"Don't worry," said Harry. "I have a plan."

"Everybody has a plan until you get punched in the face," said Bernard.

"That's good," said Harry. "Can I quote you on that?"

"Can't take credit for that one. Mike Tyson said it."

Chapter 28

Gotcha

Harry drove the old Volvo to Rainier Valley, a neighborhood southeast of downtown Seattle that bordered the western side of Lake Washington. It was directly opposite Mercer Island. If his theory was correct, the killer had at least gone ashore somewhere here, then abandoned the kayak and set it adrift. He had a deeper suspicion though, that he lived in this neighborhood. He went over the facts in his mind.

The kayak had been abandoned, blown from the other side of the lake to Ingr's beach. Taking in the wind direction, set at 300 degrees north-northwest, did not lead directly across the lake from the fire. If all he wanted to do was escape, then why didn't he follow the quickest route? Why cross the lake and exit at a point almost a mile and a quarter south of the opposite shoreline? He'd be out in the open on the lake, a sitting duck all that time. Why did he risk it?

The answer, Harry hoped, was that the killer lived in this neighborhood, somewhere within walking distance of where the wind line drawn from Ingr's house crossed the shoreline in Rainier Valley.

He thought that was a good starting point. Maybe he'd get lucky, find another Ingr Swenson who had seen someone come ashore, maybe seen him push the kayak back out into the lake where the wind would catch it. If he walked the beach he might find signs of a landing, a place where someone had dragged the kayak ashore, footprints leading off to somewhere, maybe the impression of a paddle blade where the killer had steadied himself in the uneven sand. Darkness does not hide footprints.

He studied the printout of the map Bernard had made for him. The streets were labeled and he easily cross referenced his location. He got as close as he could to the wind line on the map.

It was a quiet neighborhood. The road, sloping gently towards the lake, was made of large poured concrete squares typical of the time this neighborhood was built. He parked the car near a high line of hedges and got out. He decided to work his way north first, figuring the wind wasn't the only factor and maybe the prevailing current on the lake helped push the kayak further south.

The street led to a flat area on the beach. He walked around trying to move his way up the shoreline. The beach was rocky with patches of soft sand. His feet sunk in the mud in places and the bottom of his pants collected dirt. There were occasional clumps of trees and thick brush that made it impossible to pass through some areas. He had to double back to the road and try to work his way around them.

He came to a dock with a man standing on top of it, looking down at Harry with more anger than curiosity. "Hey," he yelled. "You!"

Harry stopped. "Huh?"

The man towered over him from the dock, staring at him like he was some kind of insect at his feet. "This is private property," he said.

"Sorry," said Harry. "I thought the beach belonged to everybody, especially the tidal zone."

"Don't be a wise ass," said the man. "Get out of here or I'll call the police."

"Actually, I'm working with the Seattle police. Investigating a case."

"Oh, really," said the man. "That's your story?"

"Yes, I'm looking for clues," said Harry. "We believe an escaped felon came ashore in the area last night in a stolen kayak. Did you happen to see anything?"

"I didn't see anything, mister," said the man. "Now get off my property."

"Sorry," said Harry. He took a step forward but the man shouted.

"Hey! Back the way you came," he said, pointing south.

"I'm just going up the beach."

"The other way you are. Back the way you came."

"Why?" asked Harry. "I'm just going over there."

"What," said the man. "So you can trespass on my neighbor's property? Get out of here now! I mean it."

"Thank you for your help," said Harry. He turned and walked away, feeling the man's penetrating gaze on the back of his neck.

He came to a street and turned to look back. The man was still standing on the dock glaring at Harry.

It took the wind out of him. It was starting to get dark anyway, time to shift tactics. He decided he'd canvas a few houses and ask people if they had seen anything. He outlined the interview in his mind, beginning by introducing himself as a private detective working for the Seattle police. Then he would ask for the information.

Pretty much how it went for a while. Nobody saw anything. It was a cold and windy night and most people had stayed indoors. He kept trying.

He came to the house that belonged to the man on the dock. He recognized it above the low hedges and could see the dock in the back yard. It was a big, pretentious house, a large boat on a trailer in a long driveway, two cars, both expensive imports, perfect manicured lawn no doubt maintained by an army of immigrants to lord over. He avoided thinking about the old stereotype but he couldn't help it. Yeah, yeah. What's the difference between an expensive import and a porcupine? One of them has pricks on the inside. Just like this house, I guess. He kept walking.

What makes some rich people so unhappy, he thought. Fear maybe. Fear that someone will take it all away. Silly, especially when you consider that you lose it all in the end anyway. Death eventually robs us of everything we ever owned. Only our deeds and our actions remain. That's why it's important to lead a good life.

Harry wondered if the killer lived in one of these houses. Just a hunch. He had to have money to indulge in a hobby built around murder. He makes designer deaths, not a cheap thing judging by what Harry had seen. These little gee-gaws and devices had to cost him something. Not to mention the time. Now, what kind of day job would a murderer have?

Harry continued down the row of houses. He decided to try a few more and then quit for the day. The interviews were short.

"Too cold."

"Stayed in."

"Didn't see anything."

It was already dark and he was getting tired. He was ready to go home and rest. His calves ached from walking in the soft sand and the rock rubble on the beach. They ached from walking in the broken heels the night before. Different muscles. His cheek throbbed. He thought about stopping to see Mrs. Lee on the way home and asking her for some more herbs. They seemed to be helping.

The old style rural mailbox had no name on it. The place looked familiar to him but he couldn't place it. He wondered if he had been here sometime in the past, maybe on police business. He went up and rang the doorbell.

He waited about a half a minute and rang it again. He was about to leave when heard a speaker on the wall next to the door. "Be with you in a moment," it said. He waited, staring out at the yard in the dimming light. This home was not as well maintained as some of the others. Must be an older person living here, they don't have the money or energy for home maintenance. Would also explain why they were taking so long to answer the door. It was probably okay to have a messy lawn. It was hidden from the street behind a fence and a line of shrubs.

He heard the door open behind him. He turned, a smile on his face, about to deliver his speech.

"You!" he said, staring into the eyes of the killer.

"Gotcha," said Couture. A hand clamped over his mouth. He felt a damp, cold rag against his face, smelled a peculiar yet familiar chemical. He struggled but it was too late. The world around him faded to black.

Chapter 29

Designer Challenge #3

Shortly before Harry got there, Couture once again managed to win his own personal Designer Derby. In record time he had assembled his latest designer death, a creation fit for the Asian beauty. This had been more fun and more challenging than the corset he designed for Dick or the hat he had made for Heille. This was a whole piece of work, art, something special he had done just for her. It was a lot of work. It involved alterations, modifications to both body and fabric.

In truth he had cheated. It was based on the design he had in mind for Carrie Rodriguez. He had all the materials on hand. He had gathered them in Greenlake a long time ago when he started planning his revenge against the stars of Designer Derby, back when he was doing research. He did some thinking on this one. You couldn't say that he wasn't creative.

"I spent more on this challenge than any other," he said to himself. "Why? She's just going to die in the end."

He toyed with some spring coiled devices, tested the remote control that activated them. He picked up the garment he had made and began to stroke it gently. He smelled it. He had used a hint of perfume to scent it, enough to deaden the industrial smells from the work on his modifications.

"Speaking of modifications," he said to himself, "The garment isn't all that will need some cutting to fit right." He picked up a printout from a medical paper he had gotten off the internet. He had been planning this for some time. He had read about this operation in detail, but it never hurt to read it again.

He thought about his first surgeries, long before he was a doctor. Well, he wasn't a real doctor, but he had enough brains and talent to take pre-med classes at U-Dub. He could have gone farther, maybe all the way through to graduation if not for his mother and Designer Derby.

He sighed, looking up from the paper. "There are better things to think of," he said. "My first surgeries..."

He reminisced about his youth. He was in the sixth grade. He had already grown bored with killing and dissecting dead animals. He watched the medical channel a lot. The series on burn victims was interesting. Did you know that burns to over fifty percent of your body are fatal? The skin gets infected and you die. He thought about the kittens he had shaved and burned in various places and ways. Afterwards he tried to nurse them back to health, applying layers of harvested skin from another live animal, some layered with petroleum jelly mixed with everything from diesel fuel to squeezings from a neighbor's aloe plant.

Sure, I'll take the whole litter, he had told the old woman. She was hesitant and he had to make up a story. They're not just for me. My friends and I all want kittens. We got a clubhouse where we meet. The kittens will all be friends just like us. He smiled that innocent kid look he had come to use so often. She seemed relieved and he knew he had done her a favor by taking them off her hands. She gave him all seven and he took them home in a big box. Nobody saw him. His hospital wasn't very sterile and his survival rate was horrible, but he was learning. He really knew how to play doctor.

After kitty burn ward he moved on to mice, the mainstay of medical research. With a small investment at a pet store and a few cages he'd bought at a garage sale he had an endless supply of patients. Well, not endless. He finally killed them all, growing bored with tending to their needs. But what fun he had! Amputations, birth defects, implants made of rubber erasers and marbles, and his experiments with making a mouse that was part male, part female. Sadly, the best he wound up with was a weird, Siamese twin looking thing that he killed after a few days, but he liked taking two mice and sewing them together in different ways.

Once he had even made a human Medusa, legendary sister of the Gorgons. He must have been twenty or so. He had sedated a woman whom he considered evil. She continually had a scowl on her face and she was unhappy with everyone and everything. She had yelled at him once, for no reason he could determine. She was just evil like that.

He took her on a Sunday morning, knocking her out with some sleeping pills he had stolen. He had a bunch of snakes he got from a distant friend's neighbor who kept them as pets. He played with them a while, feeding them live mice and watching them grow. He experimented with Nembutal as a way of anesthetizing them. Amazing what drugs you can buy on the black market. After all his preparation he finally made notes and planned his surgery.

When the woman awoke she was tied to a wheelchair facing a mirror. She was gagged and she had a terrible headache. Her hair had been shaved. She had over a dozen snakes sewn into her head. He had made slits in her scalp and inserted the snakes into them, sewing them in place once they were positioned. All but two of the snakes recovered, the ones that didn't survive hung limp from her head. The rest hissed angrily as they tried to work their way free. He never forgot the look of terror she had when she discovered what he had done. After a while they began to fight, biting each other and her as they became agitated. She eventually died, he couldn't figure out from what, but he concluded that he would need more research before he attempted to make another Medusa. In the end, he turned her into bait and used her to catch crabs, but it had been one of his greatest projects to date.

Maybe that's what made him turn to sewing as a second passion. Garments didn't squirm as much, and you could take them out in public and show them to your friends, unlike his science lab creations. When his mother learned of his interest she taught him everything she knew. She hadn't sewn in years, but she was good. She learned at her great grandmother's knee dating all the way back to the time when she was a little girl. GG, as great grandmother was called, well, GG was a master. She could make the most intricate designs and do things with fabric that would baffle the modern clothing industry. She knew the sewing secrets from a bygone age when most women made their own clothes. Bones and stays. Hooks. Darting. Folds and perfect pleats, GG could do it all. Momma had the clothes to prove it, things she made for her when she was a little girl, stored in big airtight plastic bags in an old cedar chest.

"Why'd you have to leave me, Momma," he said out loud. His eyes watered as he fell further into the past. Tears of a killer, the only chink in his armor.

He put the surgical paper he was reading aside and looked at the clothes he had designed. He put them on the dressmaker dummy, imagining he was dressing his little Asian beauty. He added a scarf when he was done, adjusting it to the perfect drape. He wondered what he should do to her hair. Yes, she must have hair. Long, flowing hair, not that cheap wig she had on last night. Maybe hair extensions. It had been years since he had done them, a skill he picked up at the hairstyling academy. Might be good to stay in practice, and he still had that drawer full of human hair he had harvested back in Greenlake.

There was a picture pasted to the dressmaker dummy's face, a download from his cell phone camera of his Asian beauty. A little fuzzy at this level of enlargement, but it completed his fantasy. Around the dummy and on the floor lay scraps of paper, the remains of other pictures he had of her. The same cell phone copies, but they had all been cut or altered. On one he had drawn a beard and a moustache, on another different hair. One was just a face, the eyes holes cut out, red circles on the cheeks, like some China mask found as wall décor in an Oriental restaurant. There were a few prints of the profile he took, tattoo designs drawn across the neck. He thought of all the things he would do when he possessed her.

A buzzer sounded. He went to the desk and punched a few keys on his laptop. It brought up the web cam he had installed to monitor the front door.

Oh my God. It was her! Fate had brought her to his doorstep. He grabbed one of his prints off the floor and compared it to the screen. He blocked the long hair off with his thumbs focusing on the face. It was her, looking different than the last time he had seen her, but it was her. She had short hair and a button down shirt on, dark wrinkled slacks with dirt on the cuffs. And those shoes, they would have to go.

But it was her. Right down to the swollen cheek where he had punched her.

"I'm so sorry," he said.

The buzzer sounded again. He tapped a button and spoke, his voice transmitting to the speaker next to the front door. "Be with you in a moment," he said.

He went to his shelf of chemicals, trying to decide what he should use. Ah, good old chloroform.

Calm, calm, he told himself. No need to get excited. No need to make mistakes. He grabbed a rag and the scarf from around the dressmaker dummy. If she put up too much of a struggle he could wrap it around her neck and use it to choke her until she was unconscious.

He was out of his lair and inside the main house quickly, two feet above the ground the whole way. He looked through the peephole. She had the back of her head to him. Yes, we'll have to do something about that short hair too.

He wet the rag with chloroform and set the bottle down on a nearby table, then braced himself. He yanked the door open and pounced on her.

"You," she said.

"Gotcha," he said, clamping his arm around her in a headlock as he pressed the rag into her face. He pulled her inside as he felt her weaken.

She fell into his arms like a lover at midnight, collapsing towards the floor where he gently laid her on the carpet.

"Sleep well, my dear," he said as he bound her with the scarf. "Rest. I have big plans for you."

Chapter 30

The Killer is Born

Red had been in the office all morning. She sat in the chair at her desk in the run down detective office. She looked at the old desk that Harry used and felt emptiness inside her that she couldn't describe. It wasn't much of a desk, an old metal monstrosity that looked like it came from a Government office in the fifties. The left bottom drawer was bent and stuck out a little. The blotter on top was ripped in places and covered with doodles and scribbling. It hid an even less aesthetic desktop filled with scratches, stains, and peeling Formica. There was a fold out desk calendar that looked like an insurance salesman giveaway, small with sheets the size of post it notes denoting the numbered days of the week, Sundays and Holidays printed in red. He had a beige monitor to the left of center, stained, warped, and melted from years of heat escaping the vents along the top. It probably put out enough radiation to keep Harry sterile for years. The keyboard had debris, dust bunnies, and bits of food stuck around the keys, layered in like mortar between bricks in an old house.

It was quiet. She tried to stay focused on her research on the internet. She had a name and a face thanks to Harry's identification, just couldn't connect it with much of a history, let alone a location, which was the ultimate goal. Four out of five of Harry's suspects had been found. She managed to eliminate the impossible and narrowed it down to one remaining name: Carol Huntington. She kept digging but came up empty handed again and again. Her eyes were getting tired from staring at screens all day.

It was too quiet. Even a visit from Binky might break the silence.

"Be careful what you wish for, Rita," she said to herself.

She looked at the clock. It was almost four. All day and still no Harry. The final word wasn't in on how she really felt about him, their relationship was still too new. She had respect for him, he was a decorated police officer and a veteran of one of our country's many wars. She watched the way he dealt with people. His pursuit of the facts was admirable and he was a good detective. He was honest, even when it came to his personal faults and weaknesses.

When it came down to it, though, he was her partner. He used the word himself. That title came with certain responsibilities, even if they aren't designated in writing. It's one of a long list of titles that carry a social onus: bridesmaid, godfather, BFF, designated driver. She was worried about him. In the end she couldn't really explain her feelings, but knew she had to act on them or they would continue circle around her like the dark cloud of a tornado. She looked up a number on the internet then picked up the phone and dialed it.

She didn't want the automated answerbot asking her a series of questions in a droning voice. "To report a robbery, press 4... To report a suspicious person, press..." She hit the pound key, star, O, anything that might interrupt the voice and get her to a live human.

Something worked, a woman's voice finally came on. "Seattle P.D., what can I do for you?" she asked.

"Lieutenant Bernard, please," she said.

There were some clicking sounds on the telephone. She didn't know whether to hang up and dial again or just hold on and hope for the best. She wished she had Bernard's direct number and didn't have to go through all this.

She stared at Harry's desk again. There was a stack of VCR tapes sitting on the desk, and a VCR player across the room connected to an old pre-HD TV. Harry was definitely in the dark ages.

The line clicked again. "Bernard."

"Lieutenant Bernard, this is Rita Rockwell, Harry's Partner. You know, Big Red."

"What's up?" he asked.

"Have you seen Harry today?" she asked. "Has he been to your office?"

"No. Why? Is he on his way?"

"No. Not that I know of. I just haven't seen him all day."

"He stays busy," said Bernard. "He might be working something else. Day before yesterday I gave him a stack of skip-traces we ran for him. Maybe he's out making a delivery."

"Okay, thanks," she said. "Just let me know if you see him. And can I get your direct number?"

"Sure," he said. He told her and she wrote it down on a piece of paper. She could enter into her cell phone later.

Bernard changed the subject. "I haven't found anything on that name you gave me yesterday," he said. "It's like Carol Huntington doesn't exist."

"He's listed on the website as a past contestant in Designer Derby," said Red. "It's where I got the picture. Harry identified him in my lineup. Why can't we find him?"

"I don't know," he said.

"How does someone slip through the system these days?" she asked. "I would have expected something to turn up. Parking ticket, license, hospital report, something."

"There are people who have no electronic footprint, Rita. They live off the grid."

"I get that" she said. "Yet this guy was on television seven years ago. I tried to contact the show and get his application but they said they purge those records a year after the show is aired."

"You think Carol Huntington was an alias? A made up name?"

"Hadn't considered that," she said. "So how do we find his real name?"

"Carol Huntington could be his real name. Or he could have another name. I'm just saying, consider the facts, Rita."

"Yeah, thanks," she said. "You've given me something to think about."

"You did good," he said. Bernard could hear her smile over the phone. "Harry told me you ran that photo lineup like an old pro."

She was flattered. "I read a lot of mysteries, watch a lot of crime shows when I'm not working." She could hear noise in the background, Bernard mumbling.

"I gotta go, Rita," he said. "Don't worry about Harry. He'll turn up soon. Just stay on task. Remember, we're not looking for a killer, we're looking for a dress. Get me the dress, I'll see you and Harry get the reward." He hung up.

She went back to her research. There wasn't much on the show's website about the past seasons, it was all about new. The main page said the show was on hiatus while they retool, but viewers could still buy copies of past season shows. There was a plethora of other advertising, everything from face cream to underwear. Big flashing banners about buying anything, including items from the very last original Richard Sooka collection ever to be created. The site hadn't been updated past then. There was still a message from Heille Crumstein promising loyal fans that she would find a good replacement for Richard. "We're considering Simian now that he's free of his contract from American Pin-up Star."

But no past biography for Carol Huntington.

She got up and paced the room. Quiet. Empty chair. Now what did Bernard say? Skip traces. Maybe she should call Lenny.

She tried to think, but all she knew was Lenny's first name, not even a last name. Harry had never told her where she could find him and she never went with him when he visited Lenny. She looked down.

On the blotter in the middle of the scribbles she saw the number. The word Lenny, a box drawn around it for emphasis, and the number at the bottom of that box. She picked up the phone and dialed.

"Capitol Hill Pawn," came the voice.

"Lenny? Is that you?" asked Red.

"Whozzis?" he said.

"It's Rita. I'm looking for Harry."

"Rita who?"

"I work with him over at the detective agency," she said. "The skip traces?"

"Oh, yeah," he said. "You can bring that last batch over. I got two more for you. And I have some money to pay on my bill."

"Thanks," she said. "Didn't Harry come by last night? Thought he had them ready for you."

"Haven't seen Harry in a few days," he said.

"Okay, she said. She didn't know Lenny's relationship to Harry, but she saw no need to worry him. "Thanks," she said.

"Hey," said Lenny. "So you coming over? Like I said, I got two more traces I need."

"What do you do with all these traces, Lenny?"

Lenny became hostile. "I told Harry and I'll tell you. Don't ask. You start asking questions and I'll take my business elsewhere. You want the work, or not?" He took her silence as a yes. "Okay, then. When you coming over?"

Red knew there was more to it than that. "Harry's the best, isn't he Lenny? He's certainly got the best sources of information."

Lenny backed off. "There are other guys just as good." There was a pause. "Harry's usually the quickest."

"Maybe because he's hungry, Lenny," said Red.

"I know he is," said Lenny. "That's why I give him the business. Now you coming over or not?"

"Let me catch up with Harry first," she said. "Then I'll get back to you."

"Okay," said Lenny. She hung up. She looked at the pile of old VCR tapes on the desk. She started reading the titles. They weren't movies like she thought they were, the labels said they were recordings of Designer Derby.

She was excited. It was a random assortment of videos but she narrowed it down quickly. Several of them were season two and she fumbled about, feeding them in an out of the old VCR player. She finally found what she was looking for.

It was the first show of season two where they introduce the designers that will compete. She freeze framed the image on the screen when it came to the suspect. "He looks so young," she said. "How frail and skinny."

The image on the screen was almost sickly, anorexic. His chest was concave and his legs were like sticks. Carol dressed snappy, though. A glittery scarf seemed to be his signature piece, worn around his neck the same way women wear them, looped and not wrapped. He had hair, thin and splotchy. What was he trying to do by gelling it up like that? He wore an earring in the right ear. Didn't that used to mean something? He looked tat free, but you never know what people hide beneath their clothes. The camera pulled away and a voice came on as she pressed the play button.

A voice told the tale she could not find on the internet. "Carol Huntington learned to sew in Junior High at his mother's feet. And she learned from her Great Grandmother, affectionately known as GG."

The scene jumped to one of the competitors. "Isn't Carol a girl's name?"

"That's what I thought," said another.

A woman corrected them. "It's German, actually. I think it means manly or strong."

Carol's shoulders and head filled the screen, his arms crossed on his chest as he spoke. "GG had skills. My mother passed on knowledge and a tradition that spans six generations of Huntingtons." The camera zoomed in as he waved. "I love you mom!" It cut to a picture of a woman in a beauty pageant. "This is Miss Olympic Peninsula," he said. "I designed that dress. Many folks said she won that contest because of that dress." The image cut to another still shot of a beauty queen. "This is Miss Coulee Dam. This outfit won her the evening gown competition hands down and was written up in Northwest Fashion Quarterly as one of the best to come out of the five state area." The scene shifted to an interview with Miss Coulee Dam. It had been a few years since she had appeared in the dress. Let's just say that her cup wasn't the only thing that runneth over.

Then there was another shot of Carol. "I want to show everyone that a world class designer can come from Mount Vernon, Washington."

Red paused the video. She found a piece of paper and a pen. She wrote down Carol Huntington at the top. Then places of residence and a line under it. Her first entry was Mount Vernon. In another column she wrote Miss Coulee Dam and Miss Olympic Peninsula. She pressed play.

The show droned on. She watched a little more, fast forwarding and moving randomly through the tape. Carol lasted at least half the season. His designs were solid and he seemed to be popular with the judges. She kept watching and moving forward. Occasionally she jotted notes and clues on her paper, organizing them under little columns. She was looking for the ending, the point when Carol finally got voted off the show. She had to fast forward through several shows.

She found it. Carol was up on the stage with two other designers. The judges were giving their comments. Richard Sooka sat back in his chair, overflowing the sides with his bulk. He had lost weight as he aged, sometime in the last seven years, probably for his health. In the middle was Heille Crumstein, looking pale with eye shadow so dark it made her look like an albino raccoon. Her lips were double lined, almost clown like if you considered the proportions, painted with the color of a canker sore about to burst. Her hairstyle was curled and styled, the type that tried to look natural but was impossible to archive without a lot of styling gel.

Then there was Carrie Rodriguez, looking smug, her long, straight hair falling perfectly around her. Her lips were thin, and her lipstick made them look like a slashmark made across a wrong answer on a mid-term exam paper. She leaned forward, trying to show cleavage like a hooker trolling at a cocktail party. She had a pretentious laugh to go along with it. It was irritating the way she laughed at all of Richard's stupid comments.

Sooka was speaking. "Your design looks like a seagull evacuated on a burlap sack. Is that your color scheme? It just makes your model look fat."

"And what were you thinking with that hat?" asked Heille. "Those dangling baubles make her look like a walking planetarium."

"I wanted to say a mobile hanging over a child's crib," said Sooka.

Carrie Rodriguez laughed, bobbing her head and flipping her hair like a high school diva. All she was missing was the drink in her hand. "I like the baubles," she said.

"The only thing good about them is they draw attention away from her hips," said Sooka. Carrie laughed again. Damn irritating. It was hard to tell who was she mocking, Richard Sooka or Carol Huntington. "That dress screams, wear me if you want to look fat," said Sooka.

"She needs a corset," said Crumstein. "This garment is more like a trash bag that you'd wear to cover yourself in an emergency rainstorm."

"Yes," said Richard. "The only positive thing I can say is: Thank God it's not a collection."

"I disagree," said Carrie. "I think it's the model. If only she had bigger breasts. It might give more shape to the garment."

"You say that," said Sooka. "Because you have no breasts."

"Don't get personal," said Carrie.

"But it's true, Carrie," said Sooka. "Just stating a fact."

Carrie laughed, squeezing her arms together to accentuate her breasts. There still wasn't as much cleavage as she imagined. "What about these, Richard."

Richard looked away. "Well, what I'm saying is, would you wear this outfit Carrie?"

She laughed. "If I had bigger breasts maybe." They went on like that, the three of them, pummeling Carol Huntington with their blunt words. Painful to watch. It was Heille Crunstein that delivered the fatal blow. She stood, a stern look in her eyes, all determination and judgment. "Either way you cut it, Carol," she paused for effect. "We're sorry. You're off."

Sooka nodded. "Yes. Thanks for trying. Sorry you're such a disappointment to your mother."

Red paused the tape on that final look on Carol Huntington's face. There had been quick cuts to his reactions as the panel of judges made their comments. Red studied his changing facial expressions, trying to read the mind behind them. She turned the sound off. Amazing what you can see without the noise. She stopped the tape several times, wishing she had a way to print them out. To her it was becoming obvious, the evidence passing before her eyes at sixty frames per second.

She saw the clouds of emotion pass over Carol Huntington's face. First there was pain as the comments fell on his ears like a thunderstorm on a wedding. His eyes began to contort. You could see his face twitch and the bright reflection of studio lights as tears formed in his eyes.

This passed to anger. His jawbone stiffened and his lower lip jutted slightly. His eyes widened and she froze that image, studying it for a while.

This was the birth of a killer. The way Carol looked at Dick Sooka was scary. Hell, after the things he said, Red wanted to kill him, but not the way Carol Huntington did. There was a crazed look in his eye, something menacing. The pain was gone, the tears had stopped. He had gone from frail designer to beast in a matter of minutes. His chest was puffed, no longer sunken. He stopped twitching, his stance became firm, his legs steady and sure. His jaw hardened, and the tears changed to fire.

She let the tape roll and play out the rest of the drama. He was a different person altogether. You could see his mind working. The clouds had passed to resolve. He accepted Heille's final "You're off," as if the decision were nothing, as if she were an ant who crossed his path and stood screaming before him. It didn't matter at all. He didn't hear her.

Heille came over to him for the final hug before his walk of shame. His lips were pressed together and he glared at her. It was not a warm embrace. The cameras followed him backstage where the other designers tried to comfort him. He avoided their touch. He mumbled something. Red stopped the tape and played it over three times, listening intently. "I don't want your pity," is what she thought she heard. Curran stepped through a door, the door to another world, the final exit from Designer Derby. He greeted Carol with the sympathy of a mortician, taking his hand like he was a dear friend and drawing him out the door.

She heard him mumble again. She repeated the tape trick, straining to hear what he said. She didn't catch the words, but the demeanor was obvious.

As he walked through the door he turned and looked back at everybody. Red had seen similar faces, they were in the news every day. Tortured prisoners, hostages, condemned souls defiant to the end. The face of the dead and dying inside. The face of the radical, the human bomb that has just walked into a crowded marketplace.

A killer was born.

Chapter 31

Recovery Room

The Asian beauty had been asleep a long time. Couture finished his work while she napped, making modifications to both her and the garment. He used morphine suppositories to sedate her, much better than chloroform, one of the many drugs he had stolen from patients when he volunteered to help out at the nursing home. She felt no pain. He was in and out with all three of his procedures done in less than an hour. Afterwards he checked on her regularly throughout the day, giving her time to recover. He fixed himself a hearty meal of fresh ribs with all the fixings, a reward for his success. He checked on her again, added a fresh liter of water to her IV, and lay down on a couch next to her. They both slept.

His dreams were happy, the kind that come from a full stomach and a good day's work. He awoke rested, made some coffee and did a few chores. Then he turned his attention towards her.

"Wake up, wake up," he said, his voice sounding to Harry like the calling of the Lorelei from a distant shoreline.

Harry had been asleep for a whole day. He felt groggy, as if he were seeing the world from the bottom of a swimming pool. Now, where am I? He went to rub the fog from his eyes but he couldn't move his hands.

"You've been restrained," said the voice, nearer now, and not so benign. "For your own safety. You've just come through a delicate surgery."

He tried to move other parts of his body. They wouldn't move either.

"Drink this," said the voice. "You need nourishment."

"What is it?" Harry asked, but it came out more like, "Wuh ish ih?"

"A protein smoothie. It will feel good on your throat."

His throat was dry. He accepted the bent straw, guided gently to his lips by the hand of the stranger.

"Wuh hap-pened?" he said.

"You'll be okay. Just finish your drink. I'll have you up and moving in no time," said the voice.

Harry drank. There was something familiar about that voice.

"The secret is to move around after the operation. Get back on your feet in a hurry. That's the HMO theory. Get them out of the high paid hotel room. It actually turns out to be good for you."

Harry had another sip. It was cool, thick liquid and he could feel it run all the way down his throat to his stomach. How long had it been since he had eaten?

Couture watched the Asian beauty feed. The way her cheeks moved and her throat rippled as she sucked. He held his hand on the back of her neck to prop her up. "Good, good," he said. "You're appetite is returning."

Something familiar about that voice.

"Drink it all and then you can rest again," he said.

Harry sucked it down. He blinked his eyes but the fog hadn't lifted yet. He drank some more until he heard the cup drain. The straw made gurgling sounds as he sucked air bubbles in from the bottom.

Couture pulled the cup away and put it aside. "I need to check my work," he said. He pulled back the sheet and looked. He adjusted the laces and stays on the modified surgical garment. He admired the way it looked on her. He might have started this challenge with a coarse, practical surgical garment, but he had turned it into a fashion statement. He had covered it with soft satin in places, pink and black, with ruffles and bows that flared out at the hips. There were garters with attached white stockings, and her crotch was laid bare.

After all, why hide some of his best work?

He ran his hand across Harry's crotch, down to the underside between his cheeks. Harry felt a moment of discomfort as another morphine suppository was pushed inside him.

"You'll be okay," said the voice. "How do you feel?"

Harry didn't know. He was too numb to feel anything. He tried to talk, moving his hands as he did. He felt the limits of his restraints. He couldn't touch his sides, and his legs were restrained, spread eagled and tied to the bottom corners of his bed. He felt some other things, bandages across his body, sore spots that, if he thought about it, would draw focus to pain he didn't want to feel.

Surgery? What had been done to him?

"You'll be able to move around tomorrow," said the voice. "I promise."

Couture stroked Harry's hair, as if he were petting a small animal, reassuring and trusting, but Harry felt neither.

He was confused and didn't know what to feel. His body felt different. His hair felt different. He didn't remember his hair being that long. Each stroke of Couture's hand tugged at the roots. The hair felt natural, not like the insulated, artificial world of wigs he was used to.

"Rest, my sweet Asian beauty," said the voice. "I have great plans for you."

She would be asleep soon, thought Couture. He had put her through a lot. She needed more time to recover, and he needed time to finish the garment. He had not installed the deadliest components, the ones that would take her life away at the push of a button.

A button he controlled.

He tucked her in, then went to his workshop and gathered the final pieces of the garment, the pieces that would complete a designer death so perfect, he shuddered with pleasure.

She would be ready to die when he was through with her. Death would be a welcome release. He thought of the perfect torture. It was always more fun to torture people instead of animals.

And the fun was just beginning.

Chapter 32

Office Blues

A night and a day went by with no sign of Harry. The next day at the detective office was even worse than the day before. Red got up from her desk and wandered around. She was pacing as she sorted through things in her mind. Where could Harry be? She had so much to tell him. She had the suspect narrowed down to one, but she didn't know what to do next. Harry would know. She waited for him to show up at the office, moving all nervous, like a spider in a frying pan.

If she were home, she would be hitting her speed bag. Maybe lifting weights or exercising, something to work off this nervous energy. She tried to do some yoga poses. Someone had told her to study yoga, that it would help her grow calm and control her anger. She could hold a pose for about ten seconds before getting bored. And when the teacher had everyone in the class breathe deep and say Ommmmm, well that was when Rita really wanted to hit something.

Yoga isn't for everyone.

She went back to pacing, thinking as she walked back and forth between the furniture, stopping occasionally to stare at one thing or another in the run down detective office. Harry saw the tools of an entrepreneur: gleaming desks, computers connected to the internet, coffee maker, refrigerator, television and VCR player. Rita saw the reality. There was a picture on the wall of a painted vase of flowers, the kind you would get at a hotel art sale. There was a ceramic oriental lucky cat on a narrow table in the corner, a stack of dusty, worn magazines lying beside it. There were some business cards in a little holder. She picked one up. They were the kind you designed and printed on special sheets of paper purchased from an office supply store. You print ten at a time and tear them from a single piece of paper. The edges of the card were rough and ragged where the perforation was poorly torn from the sheet. She put it back in the dusty holder.

There was an extra chair next to the table. It didn't match any other chair in the office. It was a one-piece molded fiberglass and metal thing, a refugee from an airport renovation project. She sat in it for a moment. It wobbled and she saw that one of the legs was weak. The screws needed tightening and it was in danger of falling apart. She looked around for a screwdriver, a knife, something she could use, but she couldn't find anything to do the job.

She came back to Harry's desk. She looked at the old desk and felt empty inside. She couldn't describe it. Her feelings had intensified since yesterday. She tried to sort through it, tried to see if it was only her selfish yearnings for employment as a detective. No. There was something about Harry she liked. He showed her his insides. He seemed to trust her and hold no secrets. He had a take me or leave me, this is what I am kind of attitude. He owned up to the truth. There is a lot to be said for that.

Her chest heaved and her eyes watered. She didn't know why. "Harry, where are you now? I'm worried," she said.

The phone rang. She picked it up.

"Harry?" she asked.

"Yeah," said the voice.

"Doesn't sound like you, Harry," she said.

"No," said the voice. "I'm looking for Harry. Harry Takanawa."

"I'm looking for him too," she said.

"Rita? That you?" It was Lieutenant Bernard.

"Yes, It's me," she said. "Didn't recognize you."

"Still no word?" he asked.

"No. Not here," she said. "Haven't seen him all day. You have anything?"

"Nothing. I'm worried too, Rita. I couldn't file a missing person report, you have to wait at least forty eight hours for that, so I did the next best thing. I reported his car stolen. I'm hoping one of our patrols spot it somewhere. Descriptions are out on it now."

"Anything I can do?" she asked.

"Just sit tight," said Bernard. "Call me if he shows up." He thought he heard her sob. "Hey, hey, stop that," he said. "Harry's a big boy. He can take care of himself."

"He could be lying dead somewhere," she said.

"Or he could be on a stake out somewhere. Think of better possibilities than death, Rita," he said. "You have to."

Bernard knew what she needed. A task. A good detective is only happy when they're flexing their noggin. He needed to give her something to do besides sitting around the office worrying about Harry. "How about the charity dress? Any leads on that?"

"Find Carol Huntington for me. If we find him, we find the dress." And maybe Harry, too, she thought.

"I told you. We got nothing, Rita. It's like Carol Huntington doesn't exist."

"You think Harry found him?" asked Rita.

"It's possible," said Bernard. "Last thing he did was go out looking."

"Where?"

"You know, that Google map I made for him," he said. "Here let me open it up. The program saves everything you do." She heard him typing on the keyboard in the background.

"I thought Van Dorn had this case cracked. I saw an article in the news this morning about how there haven't been any more murders. And Carrie Rodriguez is safe in Beverly Hills. Do you think Franklin is right? Or do you think the killer is still out there?"

"My money's with you and Harry," he said. "Two days of interrogation and Van Dorn has yet to pull anything solid out of this guy. The evidence team took his apartment apart and didn't find a thing. He looks clean to me."

"Where did he say he was during the Sooka murder?" she asked.

"Same place as when Crumstein was murdered. Asleep in his bed."

"This guy sleeps a lot," she said. "So no alibi. You think maybe Van Dorn is right?"

"Told you my money's on you and Harry," he said. She heard a beating sound, a keyboard being slammed.

"I'm eMailing you that map right now," he said. It was time to be firm with her. Get her out of the office and on task. "Now, don't get me wrong. We may have a murder suspect in custody, but we still have a missing dress out there worth a lot of money. Like I told Harry, the reward is for the return of the dress, not for solving a murder. Van Dorn's latest theory is that Paul Hendrix sold the dress and hid the money. Seattle PD feels it will turn up on eBay soon. They're not putting any more resources into this. Case closed as far as the Mayor's concerned. Anything else is bad for tourism."

She checked her eMail. "I got your map," she said. "Give me a minute to open it up and take a look."

Matt's detective brain was still working. "Maybe the killer went to L.A.," he said. "He could be down there now stalking Carrie Rodriguez." He blew a hiss of air. "At least he's out of my jurisdiction."

"What are you saying?"

"Old habit," said Bernard. "My brain never stops working. I'm still processing evidence and facts. I'm wondering why there haven't been any murders in two days."

"This is an interesting map," she said. "Do you mind explaining it to me?"

Matt filled her in on the details, told her what Harry was thinking. "He said he was going to comb the area where that line crosses the beach in Rainier Valley. Look for signs of a landing where the murderer came ashore. Harry had a hunch the killer lived in that neighborhood."

It was like electricity. Now Rita's brain was going. "Maybe I could go down and take a look myself. Do you think there would still be evidence of that landing two days later?"

"I don't know," said Bernard. "Harry also said he might do some door to door interviews. Someone might have seen something. That what you're thinking of doing?"

"Maybe," she said. Anything was better than going stir crazy in an office. "What do you think?"

"I don't know, but following Harry's footsteps might not be a bad idea." She liked it, the mere thought of following in Harry's footsteps. It's what an apprentice should be doing.

"Sounds like a plan," she said.

"I don't want to hear about it," he said. "You're private so you can do what you want. We haven't finished processing your license application but as his employee, you're covered under Harry's banner. That doesn't mean you can be reckless."

"Yes, sir," said Red.

"I'll back you up as far as I can but it would be easier if you produced some results."

"I want the reward as bad as you."

"Look, Rita, if you decide to do this I want you to do me a favor," he said.

"What's that?"

Matt sighed. "Harry went in there without a plan, and now he's missing. I have a better idea. Call me every hour, give me a report and your location. If I don't hear from you, I'll know something's up. If I don't hear anything for a while, then I'll start calling you. What's your number?"

He had called on the office land line, so it was easy. She told him and he dialed it from his cell phone. She answered and stored it to her phone.

"Now call me back and see if it works."

She followed his instructions, heard his phone ringing. "It worked."

"Okay," he said. "Contact me when you get there. Every hour," he emphasized. "Understand?"

"Matt," she said. When she said his name he could hear the worry in it. It came out tiny, a small version of Rita Rockwell asking her Daddy if everything was okay. It was the sound of a deer in the headlights.

"What is it?" he said, sounding soft and comforting.

She replied in a coarse whisper. "I can think of another reason there haven't been any murders."

Bernard waited.

"The killer is busy with other things."

Chapter 33

Borg Implants

He finished his work while the Asian beauty napped, installing the final modifications to the garment. He used another morphine suppository. He woke her only to feed her and she had slept almost two days now. Time for physical therapy.

"Sleepyhead," he said, softly, lovingly. He might as well been waking his wife on their honeymoon.

Harry groaned. His hands went up, but he found them still restrained to the bed. He felt like he'd been kicked in the chest and his groin ached. "Where am I?"

"With me," he said.

The drugs were starting to wear off. Couture was running out of them. It was all the recovery he could afford for Harry. What would it matter soon? He would probably tire of his victim as easily as he tired of his poor, tortured animals. Then...

"Wake up," said Couture. "Time to learn, time to play."

What was he saying? Harry had no idea. "What happened? Who are you?" he asked. Something familiar about that voice.

"You just had surgery. I'm your Doctor," he said. "Don't you remember? Come, come, sit up for me and I'll explain everything. He moved behind Harry, helping prop him up on some pillows. Harry's head tilted down, looking at his chest. He saw pink satin and ruffles and bows. And something else, cleavage.

Couture saw her staring at her new breasts.

"What did you do to me?" asked Harry.

"Do you really want to know?" taunted Couture.

Harry nodded. Of course he wanted to know.

"Tell you what," said the killer. "You do something for me, and I'll do something for you. Sort of a tit for tat."

"What do you want?" asked Harry.

"I want you to get some exercise. Okay?" he said. "You need to move about. It's not good for you to lie here like a lump."

"You're my doctor?"

"Doctor Couture," he said. "Your physician." He added, "Also your executioner."

Those words had a cold, sobering effect. His mind was starting to clear. Harry knew the truth, recognized the killer. He was trapped in Couture's game. He should play dumb, pretend he's weak from the drugs, and wait for the killer to make a mistake.

"What kind of surgery did I have?"

"You waste your questions," said Couture. "You ask the obvious. Why, breast implants, of course."

Harry shuddered. His hands strained at the limits of the restraints.

"Stop, stop. As your doctor I have to warn you. Don't struggle; you'll just ruin your new breasts. Maybe break something else. Open up a suture, cause some bleeding. You wouldn't want that. I wouldn't want that."

Couture moved his hand to her hair, stroking her gently. He moved his hand to the back of her neck, applying a slight touch, feeling the underside of her scalp. His other hand stroked the side of her cheek, moving gently towards her shoulder. She shuddered. His Asian beauty. His to do with as he pleased. And in the end, oh God he couldn't wait, but patience. Patience. First we must have a little fun.

He was torturing small animals again.

Harry knew what fear was. He was back in the war. He had been briefed, they all had. If captured by the enemy, build a persona, a shell to hide behind. Expect to be tortured. The shell can collapse, but you will survive. He heard about all kinds of insidious tortures the enemy was known to use. The one that made him cringe was where they put a glass rod up your urethra, drive it right up the center of your penis as far as they can. If you don't talk or do whatever they say, or sometimes just for fun, they would break the glass.

Fear. It ran through him, overtaking him, coming out of him like sweat on a hot afternoon. Couture saw it, drank it in. Animals squirm and whine, but they don't show fear, not like a human. Animals don't really process what's happening to them like humans, the brain of an animal does not have the capacity to imagine as much as a human can.

She seemed to settle down, become less agitated. "Good," said Couture. "Now be nice. I'm going to take you to the exercise room. He pulled back the sheet and Harry got a good look at himself. He was dressed in a pink, corset-like garment with accents of black and glitter. Pink straps with bows ran over his shoulders. His legs were bare, smooth and hairless. He felt something funny in his crotch, but he couldn't see beneath the flounce across his hips. Then there was the cleavage, disturbing to see. It was like having a fantasy come true that was best left a fantasy. As much as he liked to play dress up and imagine what it would be like, he would never have done this to himself.

He was sweating fear again, imagining the glass rod. He'd seen what this madman designed for Heille.

What has he designed for me?

Harry couldn't see that he had on a thick dog collar, the kind you would find on a prize French poodle, all sequins and glitter. Couture grabbed a leash from shelf and clipped it to the ring in the collar. He moved to the wrist cuffs and released them one at a time, attaching them to two heavy duty rings he had built into the garment on each side. He gently helped Harry to his feet.

Harry was woozy at first, dizzy. It was the drugs and the effect of being bedridden. He felt gravity on his breasts, heavy mounds of flesh pulling downward on his chest. The garment was stiff, heavy like canvas, holding everything tightly in place like an iron maiden, firm, form fitting and shaped. Except it didn't feel like canvas. It was soft and satiny.

"Try not to move your midsection too much. You might break something loose."

"What?" asked Harry.

"I removed a few ribs. I got the idea while I was digging around in your chest. I thought it would give you a little more shape if I took out a few lower ribs."

"You took my ribs?" said Harry. Sweat. Fear. But also anger. The persona was emerging, the shield that would insulate him from the torture. The fear belonged to the shell. Inside, he was anger. It lay beneath the shell, and he must keep it there. Mustn't let the doctor see it. Give him the fear, and you keep the rest.

Couture led him by the leash. Harry felt groggy. It was painful to walk. His breasts hurt. He wanted to scratch them but his hands were held tightly at his sides. The restraints locked him in like a prisoner in transport. He wasn't going anywhere.

"By the way," said Couture. "They were delicious. And I do love barbeque ribs."

Fear. Anger. A desire to laugh at the insanity of it all. How do I separate these emotions?

Couture pulled aside a curtain that was around the bed. He led him to the other side of the room. The floor was concrete and he appeared to be in a garage. There was a car parked over a pit that a mechanic would use to work on the underside. They went to the other side of the car and down a small flight of stairs. There was a wooden panel that Couture pushed aside. It led to a hidden room, an office, lush with carpet, wood and a big desk at one end. There was a table and a treadmill beside it. Couture led him to the treadmill and secured him to the railings, transferring the wrist cuffs one at a time. He tied the leash to the front of the machine just beyond the control panel. He turned the machine on slow and Harry began to walk. It felt so different, like he had never walked before. His breasts jiggled, he watched the fleshy part bounce as it poured out of the top of the bra. He felt long hair gracing his shoulders. His center of gravity was different and the stiff garment kept him from moving in a natural style. Harry didn't smile. He didn't frown. He tried not to acknowledge anything. He just focused on walking.

Couture pulled the chair away from behind the expensive desk. He sat down, watching his Asian beauty walk. "You can go barefoot for now, but later on we'll have to make some adjustments. You need to practice walking in high heels a little more, but let's try this for starters." He smiled. He took out his cell phone and took a picture of his Asian beauty. She was a perfect model to work with, just like on Designer Derby. What would Dick and Heille say about his work now?

The sound of the treadmill entered into his daydream. The room was quiet except for that. He watched her walk, studying every movement of her body. Her little painted toenails, pink with black tips and a dab of sparkle to match the outfit. The makeup was superb, her dark outlined Asian eyes adding a bit of mystery, a bit of helplessness. Her skin was smooth, rubbed with luxurious oils, like an expensive spa treatment. There was a scent, feminine and heavy, permeating the air, mixing with the fear and sweat. Couture reached over and turned the speed up a little, almost a normal pace. He was proud of the work he had done to her.

"Now, to answer some of your questions," said the killer. "After you answer some of mine." He launched right into it. "How long have you known about me?"

Harry thought about it. Thought about the glass rod. What do you reveal, what do you withhold? How much truth can you afford? What will the enemy do with you when they have extracted everything they want to know?

"Not long," said Harry. "Since the night I ran into you at the Crumstein place."

"When you saw me kill her." He stated it like a fact. "You were watching through the window. You saw me remove my disguise. How much more did you see?"

"Nothing else," mumbled Harry.

"I'm not so sure," said Couture, his voice quiet, coming out at the pace of her steps on the treadmill, mechanical and rhythmic. "What did you think of her death?"

"You burned her alive. What did you dump on her to make her go up in flames like that? Kerosene?"

He didn't answer. There was a long pause of silence. "You didn't know about the hat," said Couture. Another statement of fact. "I wish you could have seen it. It was complicated, just like your little get up. Just as deadly. She put it on," his hands went to the side of his head, motioning as he spoke. His face winced, a caricature of hers when she felt the pain in her scalp. "Tiny little rotors turned and drove surgical screws into her head. The hat and her were one, joined together like rats. I used a timer, I didn't want to mess with a button. There was no point in torturing her like I did Sooka. She was not a complex animal, not worth keeping around." His fingers suddenly opened, like lawn sprinklers on a golf course. "Poof, the tiny decorations burst around her head, Fourth of July fireworks. So pretty. Her hair caught fire first. It flared, demanding oxygen. The flames suffocated her. A merciful part of the design, but truthfully I didn't want to hear her screams. I just wanted to watch my little kitten burn to death."

Harry knew fear again. What had Couture done to him? The glass rod was already in him. Nothing he could do about that. There might still be a chance for him, if only his imagination would stop filling in the unknowns. What monstrous death lay within the garment he was wearing?

It was as if Couture knew what he was thinking. "Yes, I gave you implants, took some liberties with other body parts. I contemplated slicing your Achilles tendons." He leaned in close. "I thought of many things for you, my dear. You want to know more about your implants?"

Harry let the fear shine through, but at the core he was curious.

"They came from a woman in Greenlake, a generous donor," he said. "One of several sets of implants I harvested for my medical research. The woman also donated the basis of the garment you are wearing. I tracked her from the doctor's office to her home. Did you know that many phones have GPS technology? Makes it too easy to stalk. Like hunting with modern weapons, artificial scents and long distance scopes. In the end, though, I like things close and personal don't you?" he asked.

Harry nodded slowly. Agree with him. Whatever you say.

"She had long hair, like you. I'm not sure if she was your blood type, but I did clean the implants well. I wouldn't give you dirty implants. I wanted them bigger, figured you might too, but you'll have to settle for a C cup. That's all she had in stock. Anything larger would have been too powerful." He laughed, like it was a private joke. Harry looked over at him. He was holding two breast implants. He turned and put them down on the desk. "Used breast implants, do you think there's a market for them? Like well worn jeans that have been broken in?"

Harry didn't answer. "How are you holding up? Getting tired yet? Let's step it up, then we'll do a cool down." He adjusted the treadmill controls slightly, a little faster than a normal walking pace.

"How did you kill Sooka?" Harry asked. Keep him talking.

"That's right, you weren't here." Couture walked over to the other side of the room and stood behind the desk. A light came on behind him inside a display case built into the wall, like a department store window all framed and curtained. "With this," said Couture. It was a corset, mounted on some kind of framework, a number of hoses and cables led off the side to a panel on the wall behind it. Couture animated it by pressing buttons. It compressed, small and tiny, about the size of a fruit bowl, then it grew, back to normal size. "Dick was a big man. He needed some restraining."

"You squeezed him to death?" asked Harry.

"Like a bug. You wouldn't believe what I had to do to get it clean again back there. Richard was always such a mess." He changed the subject. "How did you find me here?"

Harry hesitated.

"You'd better answer my questions," said the killer. He held up a remote control device that had been sitting on the desk. It had several knobs but only one red button. His thumb hovered over the button. "Don't make me show you what this button does."

"What does it do?" asked Harry.

"How did you find me?" he asked.

"Just got lucky. I've been looking for you since you murdered Sooka."

Couture smiled again. "A fan of my work?" he said. "How nice. And now that you've found me? What now?"

"I don't know," said Harry. "I guess you're calling the shots."

"Yes," he said. "I am. How perceptive of you. We're going to get along just fine I can see."

"What have you done to me?" asked Harry.

Couture reached over and turned the knob up a little bit on the treadmill. Harry paced a little faster.

"Fair enough. You've answered my questions." Couture grinned, and Harry looked away. "As you can see, I've made your dreams come true. I've given you breasts. I wish they could have been bigger, I told you that. But they're big enough for the job." He laughed, another private joke. "Besides, anything larger is just too unnatural, too artificial looking, don't you think?"

Harry agreed. What else could he do but keep the villain talking. Every second gave him a chance at more life, a chance to figure a way out of this situation. The shell of a persona was doing its job, feeding Couture with fear, but deep inside his brain was working overtime. Harry used his police training and studied everything in the office, his mind taking in every detail.

"Your breast implants are very special, made just for you. Before I tell you more, though, another question. What's your relation to Crumstein?"

"Nothing," said Harry.

"Then what were you doing at her house two nights ago?"

"Acting on a tip, a hunch."

"Are you a policeman?"

"No," said Harry.

"What are you then?"

Harry was quiet. Couture held up the remote control, his finger hovering over the button.

"I'm a detective," said Harry.

"And there's no one else looking for me?"

"I wasn't looking for you, I was looking for the dress."

"The dress," said Couture. His eyes scanned a nearby wall. The dress was in a large picture frame, mounted like a prize on the wall. Harry turned and saw it behind him. Why hadn't he noticed it before? "If you're nice, maybe I'll let you try it on. You'd like a new dress, wouldn't you?"

"I don't think it would fit," said Harry.

"You're probably right," he said. "Not that you're too fat, it's just that it was designed for a much smaller woman. A model, maybe size three? You're a what? Eight? Ten?"

"Something like that," said Harry.

"Don't you like the outfit I designed for you?"

"A little over the top," said Harry.

"Befitting a drag queen," said Couture.

"I'm not a drag queen," said Harry.

Couture agreed. "No you're not, my Asian beauty," he said. "But I thought you would appreciate the feminine touches. I put a lot of work into this outfit." He moved beside Harry. "See how carefully I integrated this receiving antenna into the corsetry? It meshes with the natural boning."

Receiving antenna?

"I see you have some idea of what I could have done," he said. "You probably have a vague idea that the button on this remote control I hold and the outfit you are wearing are interrelated." He paused for effect, leaning his head close to Harry's ear, whispering. "They are."

"What did you do?" asked Harry.

Couture pointed to the tips of Harry's breasts. "This surgical bra has been fitted with an incendiary device. A small amount of explosive. Hardly enough to fire a kids cap pistol. I could explode it in the palm of my hand and barely get a burn mark. But you, on the other hand, well. An explosion of that size so close to your breasts could be fatal."

"What do you mean?" asked Harry.

"It's designed to deliver the charge subcutaneously," he said. "Sorry. Medical talk. Beneath the skin. The charge will go off about three or four centimeters below your skin, about dead center of your breasts. Dead center of your breast implants."

"What did you do?" asked Harry

"I altered the breast implants slightly. I removed the silicone and replaced it with a special mixture," he said.

Harry felt fear like he never had before. His voice became a whisper, the persona that held the fear spoke. "What did you do?" he asked.

"It's your designer death, my dear. Like Sooka and Crumstein, you have become something special to me."

He didn't ask the question again. He didn't want to beg anymore.

Couture smelled the fear, took in the scent of it. Sooka had that fear, he had extracted vast amounts of it from Dick Sooka. So different than torturing a woman, and the Asian beauty was all woman to him. She was shaped like a woman, she walked like a woman, she exuded fear like a woman.

Couture laughed. "Haven't you figured it out?" He laughed louder. "You are a little dense, but not that stupid. Don't pretend with me." Couture bobbed his head, as if Harry would get it any minute. Finally he shook his head in disappointment, a frown across his face.

"I replaced the silicone with high grade liquid explosive. I've given you explosive breast implants."

Chapter 34

William Binkley

Red set the phone down. She printed out the map Bernard had given her and studied it closely. The streets were labeled and she could see the aerial view of the houses. She went to the Seattle Metro trip planner web page. She could catch a bus that would take her to within a tenth of a mile of the Rainier Valley beach where she guessed Harry had started his search. She printed out the bus itinerary.

There was a knock at the door. Before she could answer it she heard the doorknob turn and the squeak of the hinge. Fat Farnsworth took up the whole doorway. He smiled at Red and stepped inside, making way for the main attraction.

"How are we doing today," said Binky, his voice as inviting as a bed bug infestation. "Is the manager around?"

"He's not in," said Red.

"Any idea when he will be?" asked Binky.

"Do you have an appointment?" asked Red.

Binky laughed, the cackle of a jester at a funeral. Farnsworth moved into position and Red stood up.

"Now, now, Farnsworth," said Binky. "She was just making a little joke. Weren't you, my dear?"

"I am not your deer," she said.

Binky sneered. "No, you're not. Your boss and I have a business matter to discuss, some debts to settle."

"I told you he's not in," said Red.

"He hasn't skipped town on me, has he?" he asked.

"He should be so lucky."

"He promised he'd give me a decision by today."

Red was concerned now. Was Harry about to be evicted? "What kind of decision?"

"That business is between him and me," said Binky. "However, since you are his partner, if you want to help settle any of his debts, I would be glad to take your payment."

"I don't have time to play your game, Binky," she said. "I'm on my way out."

"Ah, cracking the big case, I see," he said. "Or is this another skip trace?"

"You don't have to be sarcastic," she said.

"It's my best trait," he said.

"Whoever told you that was lying to you." She made a move to go around him but Farnsworth stepped in the way.

"You haven't been dismissed," he said.

"Don't push it Binky," she said. "I'm not Harry. You're not going to bend me over a desk."

"Who says?" said Farnsworth.

Binky went over and sat down in Harry's chair. "Where are you off to in such a hurry?"

She was exasperated with them both. "To find him," she said. "He really is missing."

Binky sat up straight. "Missing?"

"Two days now," she said. "I have a lead on where he went." She indicated the maps in her hands.

"Then we might have a common goal," said Binky. "You know I want to find him, too."

"So you can squeeze him for money? I thought you were his friend."

"I *am* his friend," he said forcefully.

"Then why don't you act like it," she said.

He couldn't answer.

The phone rang. Rita picked it up.

"Good," said Bernard. "Glad I caught you before you left. They found Harry's car."

"Where?" she asked. He told her. "That's very close to where I was headed. Maybe I'll take a look at it when I get there."

"Too late," said Bernard. "I reported it stolen. It's being towed, on the way to the yard already."

"The fact that it was there tells us he did go to Rainer Valley," she said.

"And he never left. At least not in his car," he said.

"I'm going down there," she said.

"Remember what I told you," said Bernard. "Call me. Every hour, starting when you get there."

She hung up the phone and made for the door. Farnsworth blocked her way again.

He didn't know what hit him.

Oh, sorry. He did know. Red made some kind of move he had never seen. She squatted a few feet away in front of him and pulled up both fists as she uncoiled her legs, amplifying the impact. She hit him square in the stomach and he doubled over trying to catch his breath. He started choking. Binky came out of his chair. She stood beside Farnsworth and pushed him out of the way. He fell over, wincing in pain.

"Wait," said Binky.

"If I hurry I can still make the bus," she said.

"I'll give you a ride," said Binky.

"Not if you're going to pester him for money," she said.

Binky moved towards her. Something changed. She heard sincerity in his voice. "I won't." He clamped his hand on her arm and she looked like she would chop it off with a meat cleaver if she had one. He adjusted his grip from a forceful squeeze to gentle retainer. "At least give me an opportunity to explain myself," he said.

"You don't have to explain yourself to me," she said.

"But I do," he said. "You were right about me. I really haven't been a good friend to Harry lately. Let me give you a ride. Where do you need to go?"

She showed him the map. He snapped his fingers. "Lock up and join us downstairs when you're ready, Farnsworth. We'll be in the car."

The fat man twisted on the floor, looking up at them. He nodded, still wincing.

"You have a key to this place?" she asked.

"I have keys to all my properties," he said, guiding her through the door. "Do you have a key?"

"No," she said. "The place was open when I got here this morning."

"Let me get you one," he said.

Soon they were on the road, Farnsworth being a little too quiet. Red sat in the back seat of the car with Binky. It was hard to think of him as a friend, but at least he was helping her.

"Just how long have you and Harry been friends?" she asked.

"Since the second grade," he said. "We grew up in the same neighborhood. It wasn't the best part of town. Both our families were poor."

"I didn't get a silver spoon either," she said.

"Where did you grow up?" he asked.

"Tacoma, mostly" she said. "North side of town, not far from the rail yard. Used to play there a lot when I was a kid. Pretty dangerous."

Binky snickered. "Harry and I played cops and robbers a lot when we were kids."

"Let me guess," said Red. "You were the robber."

Binky looked offended. "We were usually both cops," he said. "One day we'd be Starsky and Hutch, then Riggs and Murtaugh, and every now and then Butch Cassidy and the Sundance Kid. Either way we'd both be heroes. It sure beat playing Stick Quiz."

"Stick quiz?" she asked.

"That's what a lot of the other kids in the neighborhood played. You never played?" he asked. "It's where they ask you a question, and if you get it wrong, they hit you with a stick."

She reared her head back, looked at him funny.

"Harry was good at it," he said. "One of the best. He's always been smart."

They drove in silence for a while.

"Why do they call you Binky?" she asked. "How'd you get that name?"

"My real name is William Binkley. Bill Binkley. Somehow it got shortened to Binky along the way."

"Why did you come to see him today? What kind of decision did you force on Harry?" she asked.

"Not a very pretty one," he said.

He was quiet, introspective. Then he spoke. "I told him if he couldn't make it as a private detective, he should at least get a job to pay his rent."

"I have a job," she said.

"I know," he said. "I pointed out that virtue to Harry."

"Did he take you seriously?"

"He should," said Binky. "I used my influence to line up two possible jobs for him."

"Wow," she said. "Where?"

Binky was quiet again. "One was security guard at the Jackson building."

"Security guard?" she said. "You really think he'd be interested in that?"

Binky was quiet. "His other choice was exotic dancer at the Flamingo Club up on the Hill."

"That quasi-tranny club?"

"They were really interested in him when I talked to them," he said. "Said they'd try him out. I thought it would be easy money for him."

"Does Harry know how to dance?"

"Sure, he does," said Binky. "He's one of the best belly dancers I know."

"Belly dancer?" There was still a lot she didn't know about her boss.

"Ask him some time," said Binky. "He's been doing it a long time. I was with him when he had his navel pierced."

"Harry has his navel pierced?"

"He said it hurt more than getting shot in the war."

Red didn't know what to make of that.

"Believe me, I've been helping him."

Rita didn't believe him. "How have you been helping him?"

"I got him the Designer Derby tapes," he said. "Left them in his office. Did he even scan them for clues?"

"I don't know if he did," she said. "But I did."

"Did you find them useful?"

She wanted to tell him she did, but something stopped her. It was Binky, after all. "They were useful. They helped a little."

"And the clue I had slipped under Harry's door?"

"I didn't know about that," she said.

"Word on the street was Crumstein was the next target," he said. He didn't want to tell her how he knew. It was all a matter of odds. People will gamble on anything, and if there was a profit to be made in giving odds on who was next to die, well...

Binky was a businessman.

The car came to a stop on a quiet street. "We're here," said Farnsworth. "This is where you said his car was."

"I don't see it," said Red. "Tow truck must have already picked it up."

"The lake's down that street," said Binky. "Farnsworth, pull down there. I think there's a park there." The faithful chauffeur and humbled bodyguard obeyed. Farnsworth parked and Binky reached around her and opened the door for Red on her side.

Red looked at her map. "You're not coming?" she asked.

"This is as far as we go," he said. "Good luck finding him."

She stepped out of the car.

"It will be dark soon," said Binky. "Better get going."

Chapter 35

The Walk of Shame

Couture let her sleep for a long time. She had done well. He had taken her out on the treadmill twice today already but it was time to kick it up a notch. He had been busy again while she slept.

He loved watching her sleep, although he suspected at times that she was awake and pretending. It didn't matter, he had his way with her. He had touched up her makeup, even drew a tattoo design on her shoulder with a fine point magic marker. He considered burning it into her skin with a soldering iron, but he liked the touch of her smooth skin. He combed and stroked her hair, and then he added a few finishing touches.

He woke her up when it was time for the treadmill again. He fed her a little yogurt and some oatmeal, and had her drink milk. He wished he had breast milk. It would have been a nice touch.

He went through the routine, handcuffed her and helped her stand up. Harry looked down. He had on white stockings that ended in strappy high heels. They had locking ankle straps. Harry didn't know what to say.

Couture saw the surprise on her face. "Delightful," was all he said. He led Harry to the treadmill. "I've made another modification to the treadmill, something to motivate you," he said. "I'm just like that, always trying to improve things."

Harry looked down. He saw something he had to step over as he climbed onto the treadmill from the back. Couture stopped him. The villain pointed down at Harry's feet. He backed him up a bit and bent him down in the stiff garment so he could see what it was. It was a row of sharp knife-edged blades, all pointed towards the front of the machine, soon to be pointed at Harry's ankles.

"I got the idea from the parking garage. I remembered seeing a warning sign that said, "Do not back up, severe tire damage can occur." He tugged on Harry's leash and wrapped it around the bar in the front of the machine, pulling Harry like he was being loaded in a horse trailer. He hooked him as usual, transferring his wrists from the rings on the garment one at a time to rails on the treadmill. He let Harry stand there for a minute. He just wanted to admire his Asian beauty. Harry stood like a natural woman in the heels, one knee bent, his hip out. Couture saw it as the beginnings of submission, but only the beginnings. First there must be more torture. He smiled and turned on the machine. Slow again, like last time, then he began ramping up the speed.

Harry's sides ached and his breath was shallow. His feet pinched in the tight shoes. His ankles hurt where the locking straps circled them. And there was the constant thought of the knives behind his ankles. Some tire damage could definitely occur.

Couture watched her walk from his comfortable office chair. Harry saw the remote control on the desk nearby. Couture followed her eye to the remote, smiling as he saw the fear erupt, oozing out her body like molten lava. He picked it up, toyed with it, his finger hovering over the button. He studied her reactions, then set it down again. Mustn't play with fire, he thought. It might get out of control. It's all about control.

Harry looked away from all this, staring forward, walking. Expecting the end to come at any minute. Couture turned the treadmill up a bit.

"You can't ever remove that outfit," he said. "It was made for you."

Harry looked forward, the persona of fear shielding his anger. He bit his lower lip.

"It has a trigger device. Any attempt to move it away from your body will trigger the explosion." He paused, picking up the remote for a minute. "If I touch this button, it will trigger the device. If you don't do what I want, I will trigger the device. Do you understand? Don't try to take off the outfit. I want you to stay alive, probably as much as you do."

Fear. It pooled at her feet, like she was wading through a pond full of scum water. Couture could feel it, her steps slow and heavy. She should have boots on, like the first time he met her. Still she needed practice walking in heels. He was doing her a favor, training her like this. What else could he do with her? How else could he make her a better woman?

The heels were beginning to hurt Harry. His feet moved gingerly, like a man with frostbite about to lose his toes. Couture smiled. Women say high heels are torture. Let's just see.

He leaned back in his chair, listening to the lulling sound of the treadmill, beginning to daydream again. He thought of many games he could play with her. He could chain her to the wall, his own personal lap dancer, his to command at any time. He could sew things to her body, maybe Dick Sooka's penis, sitting in a jar in a small refrigerator nearby. She'd be a real freak show then. He wanted to sew her anus shut and see how long before she fell apart. That would be fun. He tried that on an animal once, but never on a human. The animal just got more and more lethargic. He wondered what would happen to a human.

Then there was the ultimate pleasure. He hadn't imagined what sex with her would be like. He found it interesting, but he was not homosexual despite what people thought of him. He understood cross dressers. They usually weren't homosexuals either, but they do raise interesting possibilities. He shouldn't have done that third operation, the one that altered her crotch. Seemed like a good idea at the time. Sex with her would be difficult now, but not impossible, at least not by definition in certain states.

Yes, he was enjoying his daydreams.

Harry continued to walk onward, watching different emotions play across his interior. As they came up he sorted them like cards, some for the outside shield he had created, some for the inner Harry filled with anger and resentment. He came to shame. Why would he feel that? Because he was dressed like this? Because he had allowed himself to be captured? Because he had no one to blame but himself? Shame. He could almost cry, but he didn't want to give Couture that gift. Not yet. Maybe it would be a good strategy to use later, another trick to keep the nervous finger away from the red button.

He felt all the shame he had ever felt about his cross dressing, wearing an outfit he could not remove, slave to a controlling madman, every step possibly his last. What if the device went off by accident? Had Couture built in any safeguards? Probably not.

He stared forward, the sound of the treadmill humming softly. He didn't want to look at Couture, he suspected he was masturbating from the sounds he heard behind him.

The walk of shame continued, each step filled with fear and humiliation. And now, hopelessness. The spirits of the people in his life circled his mind. Binky, Lenny, even Franklin Van Dorn. Who could rescue him? Sue Yen?

She and Mrs. Lee already had. They nursed him to health after his last encounter with Couture.

Bernard?

Bernard didn't even know where he was. How long had Harry been prisoner in this house? How long had he been recovering? Was anybody even looking for him?

Red?

He reminded himself to use her real name. Rita? He didn't even tell her where he was going. Some partner. She would be disappointed with him the most.

The hopelessness showed on his face and Couture fed upon it like a starving beggar. Huge heaping portions served up by the shell that hid the real Harry Takanawa.

All Harry could do for now was continue the walk of shame.

Chapter 36

Trail of Tears

Red got out of the car and Binky drove off. She called Bernard, reported her location and checked the time. She walked down to the beach and began working her way north along the shoreline. It was Bernard's suggestion and she agreed with him.

It was rough walking on the beach, there were either stones beneath her feet or soft sand to sink in. She came to roadblocks, clumps of bushes and shrubs, little estuaries of creeks to ford, and deposits of logs and driftwood to cross. She just plowed through it all, scanning the beach for any sign of anything. Her footprints, by and large, were the only ones she saw on the beach.

She passed the roadblocks and a long stretch of beach opened up before her. She walked beneath docks and past large waterfront homes. The water lapped gently at the shoreline and she focused her eyes there, looking for indentations in the sand. She was so focused there she didn't see the man standing high on his dock glaring down at her.

He made sure she noticed him. "Hey you," he yelled. "Get off my property."

"I'm not on your property," she said. "I'm on the beach."

"I own the beach, too," he said. "Now get off my property before I call the cops."

Red noticed a neighbor had come outside of the house next door. The man acknowledged him, "Hello Fred," he said.

"Bill," said the neighbor. Fred didn't intervene, just observed what was happening.

"Okay, Missy," said the man. "Turn around and get out of here now before I call the cops."

It was his tone of voice that set her off. "Call the freakin' cops," she blurted. She held up her cell phone. "I'll even dial them for you."

"I'll call my lawyer," he threatened.

She balled her hands into fists. "Cops, lawyers, bring 'em on. I'll take them all."

"So," he said. "You want to fight?"

Red bit her tongue. God, she could use a good fight right now. Work off some of this nervous energy. "You want me to come up there? Or you coming down here?" she asked.

"Look, Missy," he started again. She hated the way he said it. So demeaning. He needs to be taught a lesson in manners. She took a step closer, her hands beginning to clench.

"Stop right there," he said. She stopped, then took another step. "Right there," he demanded.

"What are you going to do about it?" she said. She took another step. She thought she saw the neighbor laugh.

"I've run off people like you before," he said. "I had to chase a bum off two days ago. You people are always trying to cross my line. You don't belong here, now get out."

"Two days ago?" She seethed with disbelief, her voice skeptical. "Describe him," she demanded.

"Little Asian piece of crap. Shabby pants, rumpled shirt. At least he left when I told him to, which is more than I can say for you. Now don't cause trouble or I *will* call the cops." He emphasized the word "will".

"I am the cops," she said.

"Little Asian crap tried that same line on me two days ago. It won't work," he said.

"Did you ever think he may really be the cops?" she asked.

"Like you?" he asked. "Hah! Show me your badge."

Red didn't have a badge, but she did have issues with this man. She debated calling Bernard, calling his bluff.

"Don't make me come down there," he said.

Another lame threat like that and I'm taking him out, thought Red. She looked aside. The neighbor was definitely smiling. She looked back at the man, imagining what he would look like with a bloody nose. He was asking for it.

No, Red, she said to herself. What would Bernard think of her? What would Harry? Violence is supposed to be a last resort. Still, she had issues with this man. Think, Red! Don't hit.

"Look, Mister. Just because you own a piece of land, don't go thinking you own people, too."

He had no retort for that. His mouth hung open and he fumbled for words. Bested him without raising a fist, she thought. She smiled at him, irritating, phony, and pretentious, just like he was. She walked proudly across his beach ignoring him. He continued to shout things, obscenities, threats, but it didn't matter anymore. He was behind her now.

She smiled. She found out that Harry had come this way two days ago. Bernard was right. She was on his trail.

She went back to the task at hand, scanning for signs of a kayak landing. Harry must have seen something. She kept walking. The beach narrowed and soon she had to jump up on a bulkhead that protected a row of houses from the lake. A dog began barking at her, running towards her. She smiled and reached out to it. She was good with animals.

"Come on, boy," she said. The dog stopped barking and approached her cautiously. She reached out and pet it, tussling the dog's hair. "You're too cute to fight, aren't you boy. No, we don't want to fight." The dog whimpered. She stood up and looked down the narrow strip of beach that rested against the bottom of the bulkhead, wondering if it was worth continuing. Even if there had been a landing, the tide would have covered up the signs of it. She checked the time and dialed Bernard.

"Been an hour," she said.

"How's it going?" asked Bernard.

"Nothing so far," she said.

"Where are you?" he asked.

She pulled the map out of her pocket, looking at the lay of the land and the shapes of the houses on the imagery on the map. She told him an approximate location. She debated telling him about the altercation with the neighbor, then decided it was important. She left out the part about her wanting to knock him senseless.

"You were right about one thing. He did come this way," she said.

Bernard was excited, hopeful. "Okay," he said. "Keep at it. Check in with me in another hour."

She hung up the phone and continued walking. The dog followed her like a faithful friend. She enjoyed the company and she spoke to him. "I should try making friends more often," she said to the dog. He seemed to agree. "Lots of things bark at first, but maybe they can be turned into a friendship." She wondered if there was any way to turn the angry man on the dock into a friend. She reached down and pet the dog, holding his jaw in her hands, looking at him as she spoke. "Animals are so much better than humans."

She sat down on the bulkhead to rest, staring out at the water. The dog licked her softly. She looked at the docks around her, one had an expensive boat at the end, another a gazebo filled with comfortable chairs and a barbeque grill. Another was bare except for a paddle.

Something clicked in her brain. A paddle. But no boat. She got up and walked out on the dock, moving in for a closer look. The dog followed her, curious about her actions. She picked up the paddle and studied it. It was a black double ended paddle, the kind used in kayaks. She looked at the house at the end of the dock. There was no boat on the shore, no boat pulled up on the bulkhead. She decided to check out the house.

At the end of the dock the dog whimpered. He refused to go any further. She started to move closer towards the house and he barked. She urged him to come, but he wouldn't follow her. "What are you trying to tell me, boy," she said. The dog only whimpered. "Okay, just be quiet. You can wait for me here."

The dog understood her. "Stay," she said. He barked, a small rough bark, but she reassured him. "Stay," she said firmly. He whimpered again. No need to tell him twice. He smelled something.

She approached the house cautiously, looking for signs of the kayak. It was quiet. She walked between a detached garage and the house. She looked in the garage and saw a few cars but no boat. One car was parked over an oil pit, but there was no way to get a boat under that. She moved towards the house and looked inside a window. There was no activity. She walked around it and moved towards the front door. She was going to peek in another window. "This is stupid," she said. "Why don't I just knock on the front door like a normal person?"

She stood in front of it, her hand poised to rap on the door.

Chapter 37

I See Red

Harry continued walking on the treadmill, refusing to look anywhere but straight ahead, staring at a wall. Couture had finished doing whatever he was doing. Harry didn't want to know. He was creepy enough without adding pervert to his list of accomplishments.

A buzzer sounded. Couture went to the desk and punched a few keys on his laptop. It brought up the web cam he had installed to monitor the front door. Harry couldn't see the screen. Couture tapped a button and said, "Be with you in a moment."

Couture turned the computer towards him. Harry thought he saw Red for a moment, but he couldn't be sure. He buried all sense of recognition deep inside himself, allowing only the shield of fear to remain. Hope didn't seem to belong to him anymore. Couture stared at him, looking at something, looking for signs of something. Harry continued to stare at the wall in front of him.

Please ignore me. I'm not here.

"Look over here," said Couture, pointing to the computer screen. It was an image of Harry walking on the treadmill. Harry looked away from the wall, quick darting glances trying to figure out where the camera was located. He finally figured out that Couture had simply pointed the built in webcam on the computer towards him. "Now be good," he said. "I'll be watching you. Any tricks and..." He picked up the remote control, his finger wiggling above the red button.

"Please shut this thing off," said Harry.

Couture was angry. He slammed the remote control down on the desk. "Don't tell me what to do," he said. "You need your practice. You know that. You just keep walking. I'll get back to you in a minute." He left the room.

There was a dog outside, the same dog Couture had been trying to lure into his grasp for weeks. He swore he would kill that dog one day. He didn't know why, but the animal bugged him. "I'll deal with you later, too," he said to the dog. He took a step towards the animal and it turned and ran.

Couture went into the house through the back door. He picked up a remote and turned the television on in the main room. It showed an image of Harry on the treadmill. The Asian beauty was frowning, her face in distress. It appeared painful to walk in the heels. It made Couture smile, knowing he had a lot to do with it.

The doorbell rang again. "Coming, coming," he shouted. "Hold your horses."

He opened the door.

Chapter 38

The Big Fight

Rita stood at the door waiting patiently. The house had signs of slight disrepair. She could see weeds in the flower bed, paint peeling off the outside walls, stains on the windows and bare wood where the front door was worn. She imagined the roof full of leaves, the drain spouts clogged with debris.

The door opened and she stared in disbelief at the face. It was older, the hair was gone from the top. There were lines etched in the cheeks and the forehead crevasses were deeper. She had seen that face transition from contestant to killer in a matter of minutes on a video tape only yesterday.

She was shocked. "Carol Huntington," she said. Plain, not questioning, a statement of fact. His face changed to surprise.

He slammed the door in her face. She pounded against it. It suddenly opened again and he reached out and pulled her into the house. He kicked the door shut with his foot and clamped his arm around her neck in a choke hold. She felt a damp rag across her face, the smell of chloroform.

She knew how to break a choke hold. It was almost instinctive. Her hand wedged between her neck and his arm. He was strong, pushing the rag into her face. She opened her lips and took it into her mouth along with his fingers and bit down.

He winced and let her go. She spit the rag out and twisted away from him, facing him in full fighting stance. She took deep breaths, trying to shake the dizziness aside. He backed off, nursing his fingers with his other hand, angry now. She had awakened the beast in him. He glared at her. His eyes held death and violence and she felt a pang of fear in her chest, but also excitement.

She didn't show it. Never show an animal any fear. "So, you wanna fight?" she said.

"Who are you?" he asked.

"You take another swing at me and you'll find out."

He loved a challenge. He circled around her and she pivoted until her back was to the dining room, a large hutch behind her. It was filled with glass and crystal, flatware and metal goblets. He lowered his head and barreled into her, pushing her back into the glass doors of the hutch. She twisted slightly, grabbing a hold of his shirt. They both crashed into it.

There was the sound of wood smashing and glass breaking. Red felt the back of her head hit something hard and sharp. She let go of him and he fell to the floor, rolling through the debris. He was quick, rolling up and into a standing position. He grunted, the sound of a boar getting ready to charge, then he was on her, grabbing her by the collar, ready to beat her head up and down against the hutch.

She dropped her head, wiggling lower into her jacket. His hands slipped off her collar as she twisted to one side. He tried to push back against her but she had regained her stance. She was stronger than he expected. She taunted him. "I heard you liked to hit girls," she said.

"Who told you that?" he asked.

She ignored him. "Bring it on," she said. "There's two things I like: fist fighting and cunnilingus. As a big pussy, you qualify for both." She pummeled him with her fists.

He stepped back, trying to avoid her. After an opening he fought back, his long reach connecting with her face. She felt his blows and started to reel.

He tried a kick but she saw it coming. "You even kick like a girl," she said as she deflected his foot. He lost his balance and fell across a low table. She pounced on top of him and the table broke beneath them, one leg of it snapping off. They rolled across the floor together through glass and debris, neither relinquishing their grip on the other. They hit a wall and began to roll back in the other direction towards the broken table, picking up pieces of glass and splinters of wood in their clothing. As she passed over him she brought her knee up, catching him in the crotch. She heard him grunt as her knee connected with his groin on every roll. Ugh! Oof!

He butted her with her his forehead and she let go. Now he grabbed her, his grip tightening on her arm. She saw the broken leg of the table and picked it up. She swatted him with it. She heard him cry out and he let go. She stood up, preparing to kick him again. He moved sideways, rolling like a sagebrush down a hill. Suddenly he was on his feet and facing her.

Whap, whap. The sound of meat being tenderized. They traded blows but neither seemed to gain the advantage. Fists, feet, and technique, they came at each other with everything from championship karate to free style street brawling. Whap. More blows. Grunts. The action slowed. They voiced threats and feeble attempts at humor as they both stalled for time to catch their breath.

The fight moved to the living room where Red caught a glimpse of the wall mounted television. She saw Harry on the treadmill.

Carol saw signs of recognition in her face. "You know her?" he asked. "You know my Asian beauty?"

"What have you done to him? And what's that he's wearing?" she asked.

He laughed. "Do you like it?" he asked.

"I need to look at it up close to make the call," she said. "Why don't you take me to see it?"

He laughed. "Sure," he said. "Just let me get that rag full of chloroform over your mouth and I'll take you right away."

She laughed back at him. "I got a better idea. Why don't you just take me there now? Avoid the part where I beat the crap out of you until you confess everything and blubber like a sobbing little girl."

She struck a nerve. "Nobody makes fun of me like that!"

He hit her again with renewed effort. He picked up a snack table and pinned her against the wall with it. She winced, feeling trapped, her arms wedged at her side beneath the legs of the table. While he held the table he couldn't take a poke at her, but neither could she. She tried kicking until she connected with something. She finally hit his knee. He dropped the table and stepped back. She was free.

She didn't waste any time retaliating. She pummeled him with her fists, so much they began to hurt. They felt like they had swollen to the size and weight of watermelons. She was breathing heavy, dipping from side to side to present a moving target. Every now and then she would duck down and deliver a blow below the belt. To add insult, she laughed as she did it. "You must not have any balls left," she said. "Feels like I'm tapping on a panty liner down there."

This girl was something special, he thought. She fought professionally, like a policewoman or a soldier. She was well trained. He needed to even things up a bit. He picked up a heavy statue made of granite and heaved it at her. She ducked and it hit a picture on the wall behind her. More broken glass, and now a hole in the wall.

Rita saw a broom leaning in the corner. She picked it up and swung it at him. He used a karate chop and broke it in half. She threw things at him, anything she could find, umbrellas, fruit, a candlestick holder, even a decorative snow globe of the Seattle Space Needle, but he kept coming.

"My mother made sure I knew how to fight," he said. "She was afraid I would be picked on at school. Thought I needed some 'manning up', boy-type activities. She sent me to boxing lessons, judo, and later karate. I've been practicing a lot in the last seven years. You don't stand a chance."

Red feared he was right. She reminded herself again: Don't show the beast any fear. He came towards her slowly, catching his breath, a trickle of blood dripping down the side of his cheek. She calculated her options. The best fighters know when it's time for a defensive move, maybe even time to run. If she could get to a safe place she could contact Bernard, come back with reinforcements. That would be the smart thing to do.

She saw Harry in the television monitor. He was limping; she could see he was in pain. The look in his eye, it was haunting, full of despair. She wondered what was going through his mind. She looked at Couture, the arrogance and fire flashed in his eyes. She wanted more than ever to put that fire out.

Running away was suddenly not an option. The situation demanded a rescue. No telling what this madman would do if she left Harry alone with him now. Still, a phone call to Bernard wouldn't hurt. She made careful observations and calculated her odds.

He stood between her and the front door. She saw an open door off the kitchen leading to an attached garage. She inched towards the door as Couture approached her. He saw what she was trying to do and lunged at her, all fists and fury.

They exchanged blows. Red was in her element, just like her father taught her. Punch, punch, jab, punch. Uppercut to the chin and a few straight shots to the face. Her hands were really beginning to hurt now. It was hard to keep them balled into fists.

Couture had stamina. He wasn't doing so bad. He toyed with her. He delivered a punch, then reached out and squeezed her tit. It caught her off guard and he laughed.

Big Red. She didn't get that name by accident. The periphery of her vision blurred but her eyes stayed focused. It was as if she were suddenly wearing red sunglasses. Instead of retreating she took a step forward and let loose with a punch to his face. There was no cracking sound but Couture started to bleed. His hand went to his nose. It was covered with blood when he pulled it away.

"You bitch," he said.

She turned and ran for the door to the garage. She threw a kitchen chair at his feet and bolted through the door. She tried to slam it closed behind her but he rammed it like a tank. She saw a bag full of golf clubs. She kicked it over in front of him as she pulled one out. She swung it at him but he ducked, stumbling over the clubs. He went down to the floor, struggling inside a pile a golf clubs. She saw his confusion and took the opportunity. She turned and raised the club over her head, swinging it down on him. He twisted and instead of hitting his head it came down on his side. She raised the club again. Before she could hit him, he grabbed a putter and used it like a hook, working it behind the heel of her foot and pulling on it. She fell over backwards and he lunged on top of her. They rolled on the floor again, muffled grunts and sounds of pain filling the garage.

It was a big garage, three car, connecting, built on to the side of the house. It was different from the free standing one that hid his lair. There was a boat on a trailer next to the wall and a brightly polished black Lexus beside it. She managed to push him off and roll to a standing position. She ran between the boat and the Lexus, cover on both sides now, a narrow alley to defend. She held the club out in front of her.

Couture picked up a hammer, a big roofing hammer with a thick leather strap attached to the handle, something you could wrap around your wrist. In case you dropped the hammer it wouldn't go anywhere. He looped it around his wrist and swung the hammer over his head like a mace, swinging it to build momentum. He cut loose.

Red ducked, feeling a breeze pass near her cheek. The hammer smashed into the boat hull. Red looked at the hole, the head of the hammer hanging just inside. She reached for it with her free hand. He picked up a golf club off the floor and hit her on the wrist. They started to spar with the clubs, fencing like two opponents in a duel. There was no style, just raw, brutal blows. Suddenly Couture had two clubs, one in each hand. He pushed against her chest with one, knocking her backwards while he swung the other in front of her face. He tapped her again in the chest and she fell backwards. Her leg caught on the fender of the boat trailer and she stumbled into the Lexus. She rolled to her left across the car, barely avoiding another blow with a club. It smashed into the car.

"That's gonna cost," she said, staring at the dent in the car.

He smiled, sinister, like a wolf about to feed on a lamb. "You're the one who's gonna pay." He swung again.

She ducked, moving backwards. The radio antenna was up on the car. She broke it off and began whipping him with it. It struck him on the cheek and he screamed. A welt appeared and his bloody hand went to his face.

She turned and saw the side door to the garage that led to the outside. She ran. She rounded the back of the car and turned, steps away from freedom.

Couture tracked her, plotting a collision course right at her. He hit her broadside like a defensive lineman. She went down, her head striking the corner of a car battery that was on the floor. He grabbed her and turned her over.

She was already dizzy, but the last thing she remembered was seeing him above her, victorious, his face staring down at her in contempt. He was soaked with blood from the nose down. It spread like an alluvial fan across his shirt. His teeth were bared, white and angry, blood raining off his face like a broken lawn sprinkler.

"Lights out," he said. His fist came down at her, over and over like a jackhammer busting open fresh pavement. She raised her fists but it was no use. Blackness began to surround her like ink from a frightened squid as she slipped into unconsciousness.

Chapter 39

The Doctor is In

Red lay unconscious on the floor of the garage. Couture stared at her, his anger seething like a locker full of wet TNT. Blood dripped from his nose and fell on her quiet body. He turned and looked at his reflection in a mirror on the wall. He saw the welts on his face, marks from her blows, and the blood spreading across his chest. He picked up a shop rag and pressed it against his nose, the smell of garage floor oil making him pull it away and throw it at her. He stood next to Red and kicked her, screaming at the top of his lungs. "Who's the better fighter now?" He spit on her, a wad of bloody spittle landing on her neck.

There was no sound from her, no groans or muffled agony. It was not satisfying. "Who are you?" he asked her. He pulled a wallet from her back pocket, a puzzle emerging as he explored the contents. There was very little to go on, a driver's license said her name was Rita J. Rockwell. He placed the address at somewhere in Capitol Hill. No employment badge, no business cards, a coupon for discounts on tampons, who is this bitch? "She even knew my name, too. Nobody calls me Carol anymore." He rifled through a bunch of folded receipts nestled between four one-dollar bills.

"What else do you know?" he said to her. "You big.. whatever," In his mind, a question arose. Just how big was the biggest thing he ever tortured? She was at least the size of four or five dogs. How much did that pony weigh, the one he tried to cut the ligaments on? He looked at Red again, studying her dimensions. She's probably one and a half Dick Sookas maybe?

"That gives me an idea," he said. He went to get the chloroform and a wheelchair, singing some little ditty he made up. It went something like

"Fat little hooker. You're fat like Sooka, and the Doctor, he has what you need…"

She was still unconscious when he returned, but he gave her a dose of chloroform anyway. She was heavy, but he managed to get her into the wheelchair. He wiped his bloody nose on her shirt, then cleaned up a bit in a large sink that was in the corner of the garage. He checked outside for signs of activity, nosy neighbors, irritating dogs, and curious spectators on passing boats. He pushed her through the side door and outside to the nearby service garage.

He wheeled her to a sink inside the detached garage above the secret lair. He used a spray hose attached to the faucet to clean her off. Water trickled across her, running towards a floor drain inside the garage. He pulled her clothes off, studying her body. He pushed back her head and gave her a kiss. The kiss of death. "You taste like bad Chinese food," he said to her. "With too much MSG."

He took off his shirt and cleaned himself a bit more, then dried off with a fresh towel that was next to the sink. He changed his pants donning some cotton scrubs and a shirt from a locker in the shop. The doctor was in.

He wheeled her to the steps next to the oil pit that led to his lair. He tilted the chair, dropping her body down the steps. She tumbled, new bruises finding places to grow, Rita fell in a heap at the bottom of the stairs.

"Oops," he said, laughing to himself. He treated the wheelchair with much more dignity, folding it up and carefully bringing it down the stairs. He stepped on top of her body and set the chair up on the other side of her, working her back into it for the final journey into his lair.

He had made Sooka's deathtrap a little too big. Dick had fooled him and lost some weight. It seemed better designed for someone her size.

One thing he had done right in his design was make sure it constricted to an impossibly small sized waist. He was good at working with canvas covered satin, the material could withstand the pressure of a body that's sixty percent water. The chain metal design in the horizontal stays helped, pulled tight by pneumatic pressure. All he had to do was hook it up to the system that was already installed in the expensive hobby man's garage. He felt so creative and clever.

Dick couldn't resist that kind of pressure. He remembered Dick at the moment of death. The corset had squeezed the life out of him. His eyes bulged, blood started coming out his ears, he heard ribs cracking and the last air hiss out of his lungs. Dick tried to breathe, you could see his eyes pleading, begging for another taste of air. He seemed to stay alive for a long time, but it was probably less than a minute. Pure agony and torture, but so satisfying to know that he had deprived Dick of any way of speaking. You need air to talk and he had silenced that horrible voice forever. Dick trembled like an epileptic, the whole corset apparatus shook with the effort, and then he was silent. It was glorious, and like a kid who yearned for his favorite candy, Couture wanted to taste it again.

He patted her on the shoulder like an invalid grandma, pitying her. "Don't worry, the doctor is here."

He opened the secret panel and wheeled her into the room, singing an old song.

"There's gonna be a party tonight, a party tonight, till dawn…"

Chapter 40

Don't Drive Me Crazy, I'm Close Enough to Walk

Harry walked on the treadmill. It was all he could do for now. Couture had fixed it so he could not lift himself off the machine and rest his feet. He had to keep walking. The cuffs were just short enough to force him to keep his hands at his sides. If he didn't keep walking he would fall helplessly to the floor and be pushed backwards by the moving walkway, right into the tire shredder.

Just like George Jetson taking his dog out for a walk. If George fell, it was a two hundred and eighty floor drop. Assuming, of course, the Sky Pad Apartments where the Jetsons lived was two hundred and eighty floors high. A fall like that could be fatal. How fatal would it be to fall on this treadmill?

Harry's feet hurt, he kept shifting his style of walking to move different muscles. He had to go to the bathroom and he still couldn't see his crotch, but something felt funny down there. The urge to urinate came and went. His calves ached and his toes cried for mercy from the straps of the high heeled sandals. They were definitely designed for good looks and had nothing to do with comfort. He cursed the fashion industry. He was as much a victim of the fashionistas as he was a victim of Couture.

Harry was descending into madness. Few torture victims escape from it. Couture thought he had designed the ultimate torture for his Asian beauty. Harry was beginning to see the genius in it. He stared at his new breasts, unable to touch them, unable to explore Couture's handiwork. The insanity of what the madman had done to him. Harry considered some of his options. He wondered if he had the courage to take a knife to his own body and remove the explosives.

And what did he do to my crotch?

He plodded on, trying to avoid these thoughts. He thought about a time he went hiking on Mt. Rainier with some friends on the Wonderland Trail. It was beautiful, the experience of a lifetime, but he could remember parts of the trip being pure drudgery. One foot in front of the next, always uphill, an endless incline towards the heavens. By God the view was worth it: beautiful on both sides and every way you looked. He tried to remember that day.

But it was hard to ignore his present fate. His body complained, toes screaming for release, ankles rubbed raw and red by tight straps, and his calve muscles trembled with effort. Each step an effort. The inside of his head began to pound like the galley drum of a Roman warship. He thought of Ben Hur, the beat of a slave master driving the oarsmen, the rhythm of a condemned man. Keep moving, severe tire damage if you back up. He tried his old boot camp routines from his days of basic training. Something to keep him going. He could remember marching all day to a cadence. It had a way of making a tedious task easy. He just had to change the words. Instead of "left, right, left, right," he said "heel, toe, heel, toe." One step ahead of the knife blades.

The torture was working.

He was surprised to notice he was wiggling his butt. How long have I been doing that? It seemed to make things easier. His balance and his ability to walk in the heels were definitely improving. He still couldn't tell what he was wearing, but it felt very feminine. It triggered a lot of responses in him. The garment reshaped his body, aided by Couture's sick surgical experiments.

Wonder what my ribs tasted like? Did he have them with barbeque sauce? Carolina or Texas style? They probably tasted something like dog.

He looked down at his breasts, held in place by the altered surgical garment, sitting like too much cleavage on a shelf. They wiggled like Aunt Patty's jello dessert. They were outlined in dark ruffles attached to bright pink cups. He wanted to see more but his neck was held in place by the dog collar and the leash. It didn't leave him much range of motion. He looked at himself like he was watching an old time horror movie, the ones made before the days of special effects and cinema gore. His imagination filled in a lot of what his eyes did not see.

Harry was descending into madness.

He wanted to scratch his cheek. His ear itched something fierce. He tugged at the hand cuffs, the jingle of hard metal chain echoing through the underground lair. He wanted to cry. He saw himself on the laptop monitor on the desk. It was so far away he could see movement but not details. His breasts hurt, his sides ached where the ribs had been ripped from him, and why did his crotch feel funny?

He saw the remote control near the laptop. Couture had not taken it with him. Harry wondered how much explosive he carried in his breasts. How big were they? Maybe a half to a pound of explosive in each breast. What did Couture fill them with? What would an explosion that close to his heart do?

The curtain of fear closed around Harry.

Keep walking.

The door opened behind him and Harry heard Couture struggling with something. He heard huffing and puffing, grunts and the sounds of straining metal. What was he doing?

Couture took a break, moved towards his Asian beauty, his treasure of the moment. Her face looked tortured, pained. Her legs moved gingerly, she stepped carefully, one foot in front of the other. Her hips were swaying, and when he looked deep in her eye, he could see the pain. If he looked long enough, he could see the fear. She wouldn't look at him, she tried to ignore him. Good. She was learning. The best torture is not of the body, but of the mind.

And I have given you both, my dear. I've given you my best. I want to torture you at every level I can.

Harry stared straight ahead. He felt Couture's eyes crawl across his body. They lingered on his breasts, leered at his ass. The beast did not touch him, thank god, but Harry could feel his breath.

Couture turned off the machine. He went to the desk and opened a drawer. A new apparatus. He unhooked his Asian beauty's hands and placed them in the apparatus. It looked like it was made out of golf club covers, hard leather socks that rendered Harry's hands useless. He ran a double chain through the rings on the garment and hooked her to the wall with a lock. There was a lounge chair for her to sit in with enough length to make it comfortable. She was a like a Doberman on a choke chain in a small yard.

Couture pet her gently, stroking her long hair. He even spoke to her like a dog. "Be a good girl, now. Stay!" he said. He jerked the leash for effect, pulling her closer. He whispered to her, low and harsh, like a dark promise. "You rest up for now. I'll have a need for you later." He kissed her on her leather clad hand. "Just because I don't spend time with you doesn't mean I've stopped loving you."

Harry cringed.

He had given Couture a good serving of fear. Was it enough to satisfy him? Just get away from me now. Please. Don't you have something else to do?

If only his imagination would not keep filling in the details.

Harry laid still. He closed his eyes. Maybe Couture would be gone when he opened them again. The doctor turned and went back to what he was doing. Harry listened to him fumble with something.

What else could he do? He was afraid. Death stalked him.

Couture seemed to be occupied with another project. There might be an opportunity to escape here. What would he would do to Couture if he were free? He imagined strangling him with the choke chain, just like Princess Leah did to Jabba the Hutt. Maybe bludgeoning him with something, a rock or a piece of furniture. Inside Harry's mind he raged against his captor, but outward he was powerless. He couldn't even scratch his cheek if he wanted to. He felt like crying but couldn't. These were new emotions, tearing at his heart as if it had already exploded.

How could I let someone do this to me? I'm so worthless. Doomed to die. A garment I can't remove without exploding. I'm just a scared little girl.

Just what Couture wanted him to be.

The scared little girl had a name.

They called her Fu.

Chapter 41

The New Dick

Couture wheeled Red to the corner of his showcase. He pulled the curtains closed, hiding the display case from the office. Like a temperamental window dresser, he would reveal his masterpiece to the world when he was ready.

He wrapped a strap around her body and attached it to a power winch that rode on a rail along the top of the showcase. Perfect for lifting engine blocks and unconscious victims. It was the same kind of strap the Coast Guard used when they pluck people from an angry sea. He proceeded to mount his latest specimen in the pneumatic corset of death. A big overweight redhead, trying out for the role of the new Dick Sooka.

"You know things about me," he said to her. "Know things about the show. You and I are going to have an interesting chat when you wake up." He started to truss her up into the garment. He worked hard at it, opening it to its limits to squeeze her into it. It took a little time, and he didn't bother with all the details like he did with Richard Sooka. No pretty stockings and tight laced high heeled boots. Just the corset.

She deserved this fate, she had really let herself go over the years. Her breasts were huge, they overflowed the top of the cups. She was so much fatter than Sooka. How could she have ever hoped to fight him and win? How much fat can a person carry? It really didn't matter. This would be the final garment the bitch would ever wear. He stood her up on the stand, a giant mount for a life sized Barbie doll. It had clamps that attached to the garment. He used the overhead winch to position her perfectly, lining up the brace and connecting the pneumatic hoses. He began the tedious task of lacing it shut.

He put the sinister gloves on her hands, the ones that balled her hands into little useless fists. But it was the outside of the glove he liked the most, the side with the mounted razor blades and the sharp glass, glued like glitter in a deadly design.

He checked the restraints. He didn't want this one to get loose. This one was dangerous.

He would squeeze her for information, then when he was done with her, he would squeeze her to death.

"At least you won't die a size twenty four, baby. I'll get you down to a good size six, maybe even a girlish three," he said. "The last Dick to wear this garment thought size six was too fat. He ruined some girl's career over that. Said it one day, like all the crap that comes out of his mouth. He says it just to draw attention to himself."

He stood back from his work. "You look fine. We're not going to bother with shoes, but I do believe we need some makeup."

He left her mounted in his display case and went to the desk in the office on the other side of the window. He looked over at his Asian beauty. She was asleep. Soon it will be time to walk the dog again. Then teach her a few new tricks.

He took a makeup case out from under the desk and went back into the display to finish his model. He turned the lights on bright, viewing her from different angles, trying to decide what to do. "I know," he said. "Let's go with fat lady glamorous." He started with blue eye shadow, lots of it. "Wish I had a paint roller, honey. Sure would make my job easy."

He went on and on, insulting her, pretending he was Dick Sooka handing out criticism like everyone wanted some and couldn't get enough.

"You know how to make love to a fat girl?" he asked her.

"Roll her in flour and look for the wet spot."

He laughed at his own joke. Why not? It was his party.

He gave her clownish lips, outlined and red, the complete wrong color for her complexion, but he did it anyway. He thought he should dye her hair blue; old lady blue. It was all totally wrong for the pink corset, but he had to give new Dick something to talk about. "The show must go on," he said.

Red hung there like a stuffed animal at some little girl's tea party. Inanimate, limp, totally at the whim of the hostess.

He finished the makeup. Something she said that he remembered. "What were the two things you liked?" he asked her. "One of them was fist fighting. Well, we've had enough of that for today. Fist fighting and... cunnilingus!"

"Oh God, I've just had the best idea! Let's give the little fat girl everything she wants."

Chapter 42

If a Phone Rings and Nobody Is There to Hear It, Does It Make a Sound?

Above the lair in the corner of the garage and beneath a pile of bloody clothes, inside the pocket of Red's pants, a cell phone began to ring. It rang eight times, then sent the caller to the message box. There was a pause and the phone rang eight more times. Then eight more times.

Even though it was muffled by the clothes, it was still loud enough to echo off the concrete walls of the garage.

No human heard it.

A curious dog outside peaked its ears at the sound, but it went no closer. It was the smell of blood that marked the territory. It wasn't an inviting smell of blood either. Not like a steak or a butcher shop treat. This was something foul and rancid.

The phone rang again, eight rings.

On the other end, the nervous caller set his phone down. Maybe if he waited a while there might be different results. Maybe the cell phone was out of power, it was a common problem. It would explain why he only got the message box when he called. Maybe she was someplace that didn't get reception. That would explain it, too. Maybe she dropped her cell phone.

He dialed again. Eight rings.

It was Sunday night. He called dispatch.

"Bernard here. Anyone available for resource support tonight?"

There was a pause. "Can't help you Matt."

"You can't spare one friggin' unit?"

"No can do. Everyone's got festival duty."

Bernard cursed. Seattle had one kind or another of a festival every weekend. They were always pulling units to monitor the crowd. Need someone to direct traffic, someone to close gates, someone to watch for the pickpockets. His favorite was hempfest, a god-dammed festival dedicated to marijuana. Hippies so bold they would shamelessly light up reefers in front of the cops.

He was about to give up. "Wait," said the voice on the phone. "I got a potential green flag. Someone might be available in an hour and a half. Want me to send them your way?"

"I would appreciate that," said Matt. He gave dispatch his address. "Give me a courtesy call when they're on their way. Thanks."

Matt hung up the phone. He had resources an hour and a half away. Better than nothing. Now he needed a plan. It was his turn to play Clue. He pulled out the map he had of Rainier Valley, staring at the red line crossing the shore. There was an X on a street where Harry's car had been found. He marked the spot where Rita had called him when she started her search. She mentioned the neighbor with the high dock, a beach beneath it. He stared at the map, his mind calculating times. On foot, how long before the encounter with the man on the dock? Let's see, when was Red's next call supposed to be? They both must have disappeared about here. Focus on this area.

So many houses. Where do I start?

He went to his computer so he could study the imagery in more detail.

"There must be a better way to do this," he said.

He stopped for a moment. "Maybe there is," he said. He punched in the address of a web site he had recently visited.

Chapter 43

Dance Fever

"Perfect," said the killer. Couture was finally finished with the fat girl. He was pleased with the results. Not his best work, but not bad for something he came up with on the fly. "All that's left now is to wait until you wake up."

He studied her closely as he spoke to her. "You hold a lot of secrets," he whispered. "You knew where I lived. You called me by name when I answered the door." He stroked her body, pressing his thumb down hard on top of one of her bruises. "I haven't used that name in years. How do you know these things?" He pushed open an eyelid, peering into her lifeless eyes. He felt the bumps on the back of her head. He took out a magic marker and drew a smiley face on the exposed part of her left breast. "I can't wait for you to wake up." He stepped back. "I can't wait to squeeze you for information."

He laughed and walked down the short steps that led back to the office. He shut the wall panel that hid the entrance to Red's prison. He opened the curtains and left the light on in the display case, Rita all lit up and propped up like a mannequin. Her hair was teased and her makeup was comically overdone. "Later," he said to her.

He turned and saw his Asian Beauty, his favorite creation. He had outdone himself on this challenge. He had taken an ugly surgical garment and made it into a magnificent piece of wearable art. He had even altered the model to fit the garment, assuring a perfect fit and look. "A unique solution to the problem," he said, continuing to study her. "I'm light years ahead of my time. This is what beauty will be in the future, where people are altered just as easily as garments."

The breast implants were genius, he thought. He worked the calculations carefully, long ago when he first had the idea. How many grams of material would you need to create an explosion capable of taking out the heart? How much can be contained by the ribcage? Do you add the material to the top, bottom, or middle of the implant? How do you ensure detonation? Can fail safe mechanisms be put in place?

Men like Couture put a lot into their work. Just research the Nazi death camps in World War Two. Engineered for perfect efficiency, designed by minds considered educated and smart. The only thing these men had over Couture was the sheer massive volume of killing on record. In that sense, Doctor Couture was an artist, designing his deaths one person at a time. Perhaps even the Nazis would admit he was in a class all his own.

She was perfect in every way that he imagined. He went to her side and stood over her, admiring his handiwork. She slept quietly in the chair, breathing like a child. He decided not to disturb her.

She must be close to the point where she will do anything for me, he thought.

He had seen it many times in his victims. They all come to submission in the end. They're fun for a while after that point, but he usually tired of them quickly once he had broken them. He would grow anxious to create their deaths, execute his experiments and analyze the outcomes.

"I would like to spend more time with you but I have other things to do," he said to his sleeping beauty. "The house is a mess and I'm hungry after fighting with the fat girl, not to mention all this work." He looked at his prisoners one more time. He took the remote control for the implant detonators and put it in the top drawer of his desk. He closed the drawer that contained the controls for the corset and locked the desk. He surveyed his rumpus room one more time and went to the house.

Red awoke a short time later. She was standing up, held in place by something stiff and heavy. She couldn't move. Her hands were held tightly in some kind of gloves. She started to scratch her nose.

"Stop," she heard someone shout, a muffled sound from another room. "Stop," they yelled again. "Don't scratch yourself."

Red stopped. "Harry?" she asked. "Is that you?"

"Yes," he yelled. He had been in a shallow sleep and something woke him. From behind the glass in the display case it sounded to Red like he was a million miles away. "Stay still," he said.

She laughed. "I can't do much else," she said. "I'm kind of pinned in here."

"Those gloves have glass on them," he said.

She held them up in front of her. "And razor blades, too," she said. "What about you? Where are you? I can't see you."

"I'm all trussed up and chained to the wall." Harry rattled his chains enough for Red to hear.

Red thrashed about in the corset. She was pinned in tight but she thought she felt it give a little. She tried again. It was hot under the lights and the exertion made her breathe heavy with the effort. The corset restricted her and she felt out of breath.

"Suckers, both of us," she said, catching her breath. "At least I didn't go down without a fight. Damn it was a good one too. Nothing like a fight for your life to add a little spunk to things. How about you?"

She didn't hear an answer right away. "He got me with the chloroform," he finally said.

"He tried that on me," she said. "He wasn't expecting me to put up a fight. I caught him by surprise and broke his choke hold. Then we fought like wild bobcats. Golf clubs, hammers, hell, I threw a rock statue at him. Guess it didn't make a difference in the end, though. Here I am."

Rita studied her trap. She could see herself reflected in the mirrored glass in front of her, but she couldn't see into the office where Harry was. She looked at the outfit, studied the boning, the shape of the corset. She rocked back and forth, seeing if the framework around the corset moved at all. She looked for any way out. She saw the cables leading to a panel behind her. High pressure hoses like you see in tire shops and garages. The corset looked well made, thick and heavy. A good bit of the metal support built around her was just to hold the weight of it in place.

Then it hit her. Facts sifting through her mind until they dumped all at once, paying out like an old style slot machine in Vegas. "Harry?" she asked nervously.

"Yeah?" he answered.

"I think I'm in trouble."

"I think we're both in trouble," he said.

"No. Seriously," she said. There was a tremor in her voice when she spoke now. Harry heard it, falling on his ears like a cry for help. "I think I'm wearing a dead man's clothes." She sighed deep. "I think I'm wearing the last outfit Dick Sooka wore."

Harry realized it too now. It made sense. Sooka had been squeezed to death.

"I don't like this, Harry," she said.

"Neither do I, Rita." He pulled against his chains. He went to the wall and studied the clamps. They were U-bolts, cast into the wall, probably tied to the reinforced steel inside the concrete. The chain was heavy, the kind you would use to tow a car. The collar was locked on with a thick padlock.

"What did he do to you?" she asked.

It boggled Harry's mind to think about it. "Exploding breast implants," he said.

"What?" she said. "Did he cut you open?"

"He calls himself Doctor Couture," he said.

"He's really Carol Huntington, disgruntled contestant from season two of Designer Derby."

"How'd you figure that out?" he asked.

"With your help. I worked my list of suspects. You identified him in the lineup. I did a little cross check and some more research. Then I actually saw the show where he cracked. He turned into a killer before a whole nation of viewers. Don't know why anyone didn't put it together before now."

In the living room of the main house, Couture was busy cleaning. He straightened up the television and turned it on to see if it worked. It was still set up to monitor the lair from the laptop on his desk. When the picture finally came on he could see them both talking to each other. The fat girl did nothing, but the Asian beauty was acting feisty. Pulling against her chain and pacing like a Doberman. Perhaps he had been wrong about the point of submission. He couldn't hear what they were saying. The monitor didn't transmit voice like the one on the porch. He started to leave when he heard a knock at the door.

It was the neighbor. He opened the door a little, blocking the view to the living room with his body. "I heard some noise here," she said. "Wondering if there was any trouble." She craned her neck to the side to try to see around him and into the house. He moved to block her view.

"I had a bunch of workmen here earlier doing some renovations," he said. He was always good at coming up with a lie in a hurry. "Maybe that's what you heard."

"Sounded like a bar room brawl," she said.

"The men were yelling at each other, fighting over something," he said. "That's what you get when you pick up labor in the Home Depot parking lot."

It made sense to her. She would never use spot labor like that. "Always hire a licensed contractor," she said.

"I'm regretting that I didn't," he said. "Now, if you'll excuse me, I have to clean up after them."

"A licensed contractor always cleans up after himself," she said. "My husband was a contractor for forty two years and he always cleaned up after himself. He used to say that you can charge thirty percent more if you stack the lumber and sweep up every night."

He tried to close the door but the woman ranted on. "Do you think I can get him to clean up around the house?" she said. "Hell, no. I'm his slave until the day he dies. One of us retired but I'm still a licensed housewife."

"Look," interrupted Couture. "I have to get back to my work. Maybe another time?"

"Yeah, sure," she said as the door closed in her face. She heard him lock it and move away from the door. She started to peek in the window, but the curtains closed in her face. She shook her head and headed back towards the street and her own side of the fence.

Couture was out the back door and down the stairs before she hit the end of the driveway. He was angry. He stormed into the lair and shouted in Harry's face. "What did you tell her?" he demanded.

Harry cringed. He pulled back into a little ball, folding in on himself like a child. Adrenaline. Fear. He was a scared little girl again.

"Leave him alone," yelled Red.

Couture adjusted the lighting so Red could see out of her prison. He went to the desk and unlocked it. He opened the desk drawer with the controls for the corset. He took out the radio detonator for the implants and put it on the desk. He looked at them both.

"One of you will watch the other die," he said. "This much I will promise you." He paced the room, his head swiveling back and forth between them. "I don't know which one yet. That remains to be seen. It all depends on you." He stopped pacing and stood before Red. "Let's start with this. Who are you?"

"Screw you," she said.

Couture laughed. "You're pretty feisty for someone in your predicament," he said. "Yep. Pretty feisty. And I don't understand that. I really don't. You know what I'm capable of." He walked over to the desk drawer and stood before the controls for the corset. "Do you need a little demonstration?"

He saw the fear in her eye. She was silent, compliant. No demonstration necessary, for now.

"Okay. We'll save that for later," he said. "So. Who are you?"

"My name is Rita, but they call me Big Red," she said. She should have left it at that, but the belligerent lesbian in her filtered to the surface. "Let's be friends," she said. "Come on up here and shake hands with me." She held her razor blade and glass hand gloves out for him to grab.

He snickered. "Feisty," he said. He pushed a button in the desk drawer. Rita cried out, a short whelp like a wounded lap dog. Her face bulged and she couldn't breathe. He stared at her. He loved the observation part. She couldn't speak but she had so much to say to him, so much to ask. Breath is the one thing we cannot live without for long.

"I watched Sooka die the same way," said the killer. "He was fat like you, did I tell you that? This device was made for people like him and you."

She looked like she wanted to say something.

"My mother was fat, too. She had a corset like this when I was young. I used to help her get into it sometimes. She wore it on special occasions. It always seemed like the effort to put it on and wear it was far more than the effort it took to diet, but she didn't see it that way."

The agony began to read on her face. The pain. How empty her lungs must feel. To be denied something so simple.

"You look a lot like her. The clownish makeup, the teased hair, the billowing flesh pushing out everywhere. The corset cannot contain it all. How much fat does a person need?"

She had no answer, or if she did, she could not voice it.

"How far will fat compress?" he asked. "How long before it pushes against the organs, the lungs, the heart, the intestines? I watched Dick closely. I kept waiting to see what would happen first. What would break? The ribs? Maybe the internal organs would be crushed. I wondered which organs would survive and which would not. Or would everything inside be squeezed out through his anus or his mouth like a big, broken tube of toothpaste. I cut him up for the autopsy, but then I remembered that I electrocuted him too. It biased the results."

She tried to grunt, to make any movement in her chest. She began to see stars around her, bright lights inside her brain. Her head started to bob and fall forward.

"That's why I will watch you with great interest." He looked her up and down. "Big Red won't be so big anymore."

Harry couldn't take it any longer. He began to scream, his voice high pitched, crying like a girl.

Couture adjusted the controls, loosening the corset. Red gasped for air. The killer turned his attention to his other victim. He grabbed the chain and pulled her by the collar to the center of the room. He went back to the controls in the desk drawer. His hand hovered over the knobs as if deciding what tortures to inflict next.

Red flinched, unaware of what was happening. Harry screamed again and Couture laughed.

"Quiet, my beauty," he said to her. "I was only turning on the music." His hand moved and music began to play. Deep, seductive music, the kind found in topless nightclubs across America. "I want you to dance," he said to Harry. "Dance for me."

Harry didn't know what to do.

"Don't be shy. Dance for me," he said.

Harry began to move but Couture didn't approve. "No, no," he said. "This is not what I want. You know what I want."

Harry didn't get it, but old triggers were firing inside him. This is what Binky wanted him to do. Perform at some transvestite bar up on Capitol Hill. Dance for the tourists. It sounds so innocent. He moved a little, wiggled and bounced. The killer scowled.

"That's not what I want," he said. "Come on. Let's see you work hard, baby."

Harry started to gyrate, his hips moved in a circle. The shame he felt made him tingle in a way he couldn't explain. Couture goaded him, then picked up the remote control and pointed to the button. "Don't make me ask again. Dance for your life, sweetheart."

Harry knew how to dance, he even enjoyed it, but Couture had taken something beautiful and innocent and made it all ugly. Harry didn't have much of a choice. He started slowly, moving his hips in an Egyptian figure eight, trying to clear his head of everything. He remembered when he first went to a belly dance class. He had a strange urge to try it, back when his therapist told him to experiment with himself. He was the only man in a room full of beautiful women. The women were all shapes and sizes, but somehow belly dancing made them all feel exotic and slim and beautiful. He liked that aspect of the class. He wondered what they thought of him. The teacher was so understanding, accepting him for what he wanted to do, allowing him, like a child, to learn and play through dancing. Eventually she taught him to dance both like a man and like a woman.

He found that he liked it. There was no shame for a man to like belly dancing, either as a spectator or as a dancer. There was even a history of it. In Turkey, he learned, men would cross dress. Cultural conventions and Muslim rules kept women from showing certain body parts in public, but it was okay for a man. He didn't understand why catching a glimpse of a woman's belly button would be such a crime, but it seems all societies have their rules for what defines a harlot. Not all men dressed as women. There were also men who danced as men, troupes of Egyptians who were cane dancers, a hybrid of belly dancing that used stick props for movement and emphasis. His teacher taught him all of these things.

He closed his eyes and he was back in the classroom with his old teacher, the great Mellilah. He started to dance one of her choreographies he had practiced with her, straining to get it perfect.

Couture was fascinated. She was full of surprises, this Asian beauty. He adjusted the music to something more appropriate, middle eastern, four beats with an Arabic twang.

Something was still missing. He could see it easily. He stopped the music. In the quiet he heard Red gasping behind him. It was disgusting and distracting. He adjusted the controls and loosened the corset, allowing her to breathe easier. Then he went over to the Asian beauty and removed the hard, leather socks that kept her from using her hands. He stroked her fingers, stopping to admire her pink fingernails. He unlocked the cuffs and removed one hand from the side restraint that attached to the waist of his outfit.

"First, a warning," he said. "Don't disappoint me. I'm doing this for you." He unlocked the other hand. "How could you hope to be graceful and willow without the use of your hands? I know you are capable of so much more in your dance. I want you to show me."

He adjusted a desk light so it illuminated Harry. He sat down behind the desk and held up the remote control. "Remember what I said, my dear. I hold all the cards." He wiggled the remote. "Don't disappoint me."

He turned the music on again and Harry began to gyrate. Harry closed his eyes. He wanted to scream but he thought of his teacher and how she taught him grace and movement, how to dance in time to the music, how to taqseem and transition to different steps. His arms moved slowly, two fingers together at all times, just as she taught him. The hands told a story, wavy hands that offset the moves his body was making. Head slides and shimmies, Saidi and gwazi. With his hands free he moved much more gracefully, more enticing.

Couture drooled.

Harry kept his eyes closed, focusing on the dance and the music.

There is no shame in what I do.

There is no shame.

Chapter 44

The Birth of Fu Chan

Harry was ten. Third grade. He found a box of girl's clothes in the cellar of the house. He didn't know who they belonged to but he tried them on for fun.

It was hard to button the dress up in the back, but he managed. He didn't think his hands could contort to that position, and he had to twist the fabric around a bit, but he did it. There was a pair of panties with ruffles to go with it, a little girl's party outfit. Maybe it was her Easter outfit. There were socks and little mary jane shoes too, a little big for him but they still fit. He couldn't resist it. Finally there was a cute hat, a bonnet with a ribbon circling the brim. It matched the trim on the dress.

They felt good. He enjoyed wearing them and didn't want to take them off, but something inside gave him the feeling of guilty pleasures. He knew he was doing something wrong. Boys do not wear dresses, and they're definitely not supposed to enjoy it.

He took the clothes off and put them away. He went back to playing cops and robbers with Binky. Then on a quiet day not soon after, he found himself in the basement again staring into the box of clothes. The forbidden fruit.

He dug deeper into the box, determined to try something different this time. There was a long dress, formal, red, with an oriental collar and black trim. Next to it was some strange, exotic underwear, bra cups with rubber inserts pinned in place. Long stockings that attached to garters that hung from a corset. He put it all on. The only shoes in the box were the mary janes but they worked with the outfit.

One thing was missing. There wasn't a mirror in the basement. He couldn't see what he looked like when he was all done. His curiosity got the best of him and he decided to go upstairs and sneak a look at himself.

Nobody was home. He went into his mother's room and stood before the mirror. She had makeup sitting on her dresser. He dared to use it, marking his lips with a tube of lipstick. It was all he could do, all he wanted to do. He didn't know much about makeup or how to use it. He turned to go back down to the basement and saw Binky standing in the hallway.

"I came over to see if you wanted to play," he said. "But I see you're busy."

Harry didn't know what to say. Fear and shame overcame him and his insides turned like a basket full of clothes in a front loading washer.

Then Binky laughed. "You look pretty dorky," he said. "But if that's what you want to wear to play, it's okay with me."

Binky took away all Harry's fear and guilt with those words, but he didn't stop there.

"Just don't make me play those stupid girl games. I'm not playing house, or school, or even jump rope."

"Okay," said Harry.

"In fact, we keep playing detective, except you're a girl detective now. Fu Chan. The smartest detective of them all. Fu Chan. Daughter of the great Charlie Chan." Binky began to make up a history for Fu.

"Charlie Chan is sick of his stupid sons. Number One and Number Two can't figure their way out of Chinese handcuffs without Daddy's help. The real family genius is with his number one daughter, Fu Chan. She is one smart little cookie."

"Why Fu? Why that name?"

"It sounds exotic," said Binky. "Great name for a detective. You'll see. Let's go Fu."

Harry was afraid to go outside but Binky encouraged him. Harry didn't know why he did. Maybe because it had stopped raining and he wanted to get out of the house. Maybe he was curious what other people would say. In hindsight, it was a stupid idea, but what did he know. He was just a kid.

Two boys saw them. They threw rocks. Binky threw one back but they teased him. "Sticking up for your girlfriend, Binkley?" Harry picked up a rock and threw it back. It hit one of the kids in the ear. A trickle of blood touched his cheek and the kid went screaming home for his mom. Fu Chan definitely knew how to throw a rock.

A group of girls invited them to play, but Harry and Binky knew they had other motives. They giggled too much and they smiled like cats before a plate of fresh mice.

In the playground, a mother hid her child's eyes as if Harry was the Gorgon herself. Don't look, you'll turn to stone. "You should be ashamed of yourself," she said to Harry.

"Why?" he asked.

She had nothing useful to tell him. "Go ask your mother if you don't know why."

They kept playing Fu Chan. She grew larger every time they played. She was smart, a double doctorate in criminal psychology, one from Shanghai University, one from California State. Binky would pretend he was the brawny one of the duo, the tough detective who would use his fists to combat evil. Fu Chan was the smart one, the one who dug up clues and produced evidence. They would be running through an alley and suddenly Fu would spy something, drop to one knee and pick up a shiny rock. "Look," she'd say. "We're on the right trail. The Tong Warlord must have dropped this precious gem when he came this way. The secret entrance to his lair must be down this alley." And off they would go.

Sometimes they would sit on the porch, pretending they were flying to Egypt or China or Tierra del Fuego. The bad guys often ended up being a stick or a bottle or bricks or anything they could find to line up and punch until it fell over. In absence of that, a street sign worked real good, but they never seemed to fall over.

On days that he couldn't play with Binky, Harry was taking lessons from the girls. They accepted him as their latest plaything, and Harry knew the terms. Inside he knew they were laughing at him, but he didn't mind. They taught him things he wanted to learn, like how to cheer, how to dance, and how to behave like a little lady. This usually went on until Binky showed up and drew Fu Chan away and into greater adventures than tea parties and cheerleading practice.

Fu became a ninja. She could do deathly moves that started like cheerleading routines and ended up in backflips and kung fu kicks like you never saw. Harry invented them and then practiced until he got them right. At least Binky was impressed. Of course, it helped that he could dress the part. The girls had thoughtfully supplied him with a cheerleader outfit.

They solved crime after crime. Recovered jade statues, infiltrated secret societies, and eluded dangerous villains. Sometimes Binky liked to be Charlie Chan, sometimes Wo Fong, an oriental genius. Every now and then he would be a bad guy, someone to play against Fu. They had a game that was something like hide and seek where Fu had to find and catch the evil villain before he destroyed the world and everyone in it. In the end they would chase each other through streets and turn the long days of summer into memories powerful enough to cement a friendship forever.

Then one day Harry went to the basement and the box was gone. As he turned to leave, his mother stood at the top of the steps. "So, this is what you've been up to," she said. "I have to hear this from the neighbors? My little boy's a pansy?"

Suddenly his life was filled with shame. His innocence was gone, lost under the angry glare of his mother's eye. "What would possess you to do such a thing?" she asked.

He had no answer. All he could come up with was, "It was fun."

"Fun!?" His mother didn't understand. "Wait here," she said, parking him on the couch while she disappeared into her bedroom. She returned with a dress, a rather drab one she pulled from the collection. "Put it on," she said, holding it out for him.

"I don't want to," he said.

She slapped him. "Put it on," she demanded. "I want to see what you look like."

Harry didn't want to. As much as he enjoyed wearing the clothes, it had now turned ugly and shameful. She slapped him again and threw the dress in his face. She ripped the shirt off his back. "Put it on," she screamed.

Harry slipped into the dress. It hung on him like a baggy potato sack. His mother started to cry.

"I'm sorry," said Harry. He didn't know why, but he knew he had made his mother cry. She looked at him through tear filled eyes and then ran for her bedroom. He heard the door slam. He stayed there on the couch for a long time wondering what to do. Finally, he took the dress off and threw it in the garbage. He put on his own clothes and went to his room. He could hear his mother crying next door and soon he began to cry himself.

She came back out and screamed at him again. "Did I say you could take your dress off?" She hit him again. He was surprised by her anger.

"I'm sorry," he said.

"You better be sorry," she yelled. It just made him cry more. "Tomorrow I'm taking you to talk with Father Michaels. He'll tell you what's wrong with this picture."

"What is wrong?" Harry asked. "I'm just playing. It's like Halloween."

"Halloween is one thing, but what you're doing is immoral."

"Why?" he asked. "I wasn't hurting anyone."

"Father Michaels will explain it to you." She started to cry again. "Just wait until your father gets back from the war. He'll explain it to you."

Harry never got his explanation. His father died in that war. They didn't even send his body back, just a picture of it in a coffin. The enemy stole the body before they could ship it home. Who steals a human body?

It was a long time before Harry put on a dress again. The days of Fu Chan were over for now. His mother had successfully killed her by keeping a constant eye on her boy for any irregularities. No shame in this house. She vowed not to have a bene-boy for son.

It never stopped the neighbors from talking.

He made her proud when he joined the Marines on his eighteenth birthday. She thought he did it because his dad had been in the Marines, that he had finally grown up and become a man. But the truth was, he did it because he needed to get away from home.

Chapter 45

Headed for Trouble

Bernard opened the door and greeted the two uniforms. "Glad you guys could make it. This won't take long."

"I'm Jackson," said the shorter of the two. He was still bigger than Bernard, besting the lieutenant by at least a foot. "This is my partner Roberson. We call him Robernaut." The Robernaut stood behind Jackson, his head bent slightly so he wouldn't hit it on the hanging lamp over Bernard's entrance.

"Thanks for coming," said Bernard. "Give me a second and I'll be right with you." He had everything he needed in a small pile on the dining room table. Maps, cell phone, GPS, computer with mobile internet, bottle of water, gun and holster. When he got outside the guys were in the car waiting. Bernard got in the back.

"What's this all about, Lieutenant?"

"Nothing," said Bernard. "At least I hope it's nothing."

"Could you at least give us a briefing?"

"Okay," he said. "But drive. Head towards Rainier Valley. I'll explain on the way." He had a printout of the Google map. He handed it to Robernaut who was riding shotgun in the front seat. "See this pin here?"

The Robernaut nodded his big, blond head. Even inside the police car his head scraped the roof lining.

"Get us to that spot. I'll brief you after I get my equipment set up back here." Bernard turned on the GPS, set the cell phone beside him on the seat, took a sip of water, and strapped on his shoulder holster and gun. He opened the computer and it came out of hibernation. He bent over and studied the screen. Jackson watched him in the rear view mirror.

"You're getting pretty amped up for nothing, Lieutenant."

"I just like to be prepared for anything," he said.

"Should I turn on the lights?"

"If you need to," said Bernard. "But I want to go in quiet when we get there."

"Mind letting us in on the story?" asked Robernaut.

Bernard took another drink of the water and cleared his throat.

"It may be nothing," he said. "But then again." Bernard took another sip of water. His throat was dry, his head ached, and he itched all over. Something didn't feel right to him. "I have a detective that was working a case. Last reported at this location we're headed. He disappeared two days ago. So I sent someone after them earlier today and now I've lost touch with them, too."

"That doesn't sound good," said Robernaut.

There was a logjam of cars ahead. Jackson hit the lights and whooped the siren. The logjam trembled a bit but it didn't move much. The siren whooped again, Jackson angling the car against the grain of the traffic. They cleared a path and he hit the accelerator.

"Let's get this over with," he said. He whipped the car down the street, edging cautiously through the intersections. He loved driving fast with the blue lights blazing.

"Like I said, this may be nothing." Bernard took another sip of water. The bottle was almost empty and he still felt dry. "The second detective I sent was supposed to call me every hour, and they were, but then the calls stopped coming. I'm just a little concerned."

"Cool," said Robernaut. "We'll check it out. What's your plan?"

Jackson dropped the accelerator another quarter inch and the car jumped into overdrive. He passed slow moving cars and bounced through several intersections.

"Slow down a little," said Bernard. "I'm getting thrown around back here."

Jackson turned the lights off. "You take all the fun out of it Lieutenant."

He drained the bottle of water and tossed it on the seat beside him. He stared at the screen on the laptop. "We're not far now, but I want to get there in one piece," he said.

He dialed Rita's number again, listening as it rolled to the message box.

"I just hope we find somebody next to the phone when we get there."

Chapter 46

The Little Black Dress

Couture put his Asian beauty back on the treadmill and locked her hands to the railing. It was time for more stress testing.

"Maybe later you can dance for me again," he said. "The way you move, I bet you make a hell of a lap dancer." He licked his lips.

Harry cringed.

The treadmill started.

Couture disappeared outside for a moment.

"Harry," said Rita.

"What is it?" he asked. He was breathing hard and having trouble talking. Couture had set the treadmill a little fast.

"Look on the wall," said Rita.

Harry turned his head. "It's a framed dress with a little plaque. I can't quite read it."

"No, no," she said. "That's the dress. That's THE dress."

"The designer dress? The quarter million dollar dress?"

"Three quarters of a million," she said.

"It's a simple black dress," he said.

"With a Richard Sooka label sewn inside."

"It's a simple black dress," he said again.

"No it's not. Look at that asymmetric stitching, the subtle ruffle," she said. "Don't you know anything?"

Harry still didn't get it. It was a simple black dress. "I may like to wear dresses but it's obvious I'm no fashion expert."

"Harry?" There was that quiver in her voice again.

"Yes, Rita."

"What are we going to do? He's got us."

"It looks that way," said Harry.

"Do we have a plan?"

"I don't think so," he said.

"Bernard was monitoring my location when I went looking for you. I called him every hour to check in. He said if he didn't hear from me in two hours, he would come looking for me."

"That's something to hope for," said Harry.

"Except he doesn't know where we are."

Couture came back in. He had a large, plastic storage bin, the stackable kind that can hold a lot of stuff. He put in inside the room with Red. "Got a little surprise for you, sweetheart," he said. "Another experiment I've designed."

He opened the top of the container and quickly stepped out of the room. He turned the lights up and shut the door behind him. He put a piece of masking tape over the bottom of the door, covering the small space between it and the floor. He looked at his Asian beauty and could tell she was curious. He smiled and took a seat before the window in the chair behind his desk.

The container had flies in it, thousands of flies. Red could hear them. They were slow to leave the container, but they began to emerge, anxious to spread their wings. The hot lights above called them out.

"I know what you're thinking," said Couture. "Where do you get so many flies?" He paused, but there was no answer. "You don't think I just went out and bought these? Excuse me, Mister Pet Store Owner. I need a thousand flies to feed my frogs."

He saw her wince. It must stink in there. The lights were making it hot and the flies were getting agitated. He could see them landing on her body. Crawling. Stopping. Rubbing their little hands together. Crawling. How long before she would go mad? How long before she made the choice to use the deadly gloves and scratch herself?

"I see a lot of flies in there. I really didn't know how many I would get," said Couture. "I raised them myself from little baby maggots. I gave them some fresh meat to feed on, a piece of Dick Sooka himself. You should be honored to be in his presence, even if it is only a small piece of him."

Rita began to retch.

He watched a fly crawl across her vagina. It went over her labia, stopping close to her clitoris. It rubbed its little hands together. "Sweet as molasses," he said. "Shoo fly pie."

Rita gagged. Her arms waved, fanning a breeze, but it was no use. It was like standing in a rainstorm without an umbrella, no matter what motions you make, you still get wet.

"I have a bug bomb ready to gas them any moment. You can start talking at any time. When I've heard enough, I'll get rid of the fly problem. Okay?"

The flies were everywhere. They landed on her nose, on her arms, on her face, on her legs. One crawled down in between her cleavage.

And it stank, the smell of week old Sooka heavy in the air. She felt ill.

The flies were dense, buzzing in her ears. They explored her like ants at a picnic. She swatted at them. She knew what would happen if she touched herself anywhere. Blood. That would only attract more flies. Maybe they would lay eggs and produce maggots. Rita's mind began to run away with thoughts of horror.

"You have nothing to say to me?" he asked. Rita gagged and spit. "Nothing you want to tell me?"

She could hardly hear him. The buzzing sound was all around her, the flies became her world, a world without Harry, without Couture, without end. She screamed, sucking in flies as she opened her mouth and inhaled.

Couture pressed a button in the desk drawer. Red gasped as the corset shrunk around her. Silence. Harry could tell she wanted to scream but she couldn't. She had no air. He struggled, the treadmill rattled. His chain jingled and Couture heard it. He turned to Harry and held up the remote control, his finger moved over the button like it was in a thumb war.

"Stay!" he said.

Harry stopped struggling. He was reaching the point where he didn't care. He felt like a prize winning beagle, maybe a French poodle, a trained show dog Couture could be proud of owning.

"Good girl," he said. He put the remote control back on the desk.

Harry wondered how big the explosion would be. Would it be enough to take out Couture? What if he held the killer in his arms and pressed the button himself? Would it be enough?

Red was in trouble. Her head bowed forward. She gasped. Harry could see her from the treadmill. There were so many flies he couldn't believe it. Swarms of them. They were all over the window of the display case, all over the walls, and all over Red. She flicked her head, shrugging the flies off. They hovered a few seconds, then found new places to land. One crawled up her nose and got stuck. Harry couldn't imagine what it felt like, not even having enough breath to snort and get rid of it.

"Did you have something to say to me?" asked Couture. "You can call me Carol if you like. I haven't used it in a long time." He looked off into the wall, somewhere into his past.

"My mother named me that. My father argued against it, even begged her not to do it, but it was too late. When the doctors asked what name to put on the birth certificate, she said it. It was her grandfather's name from the old country, somewhat of a family tradition." He heaved a sigh. "I wonder if the old bastard got teased as much as I did in school. Wonder if that was another..." He spit the words out like poison: "Family tradition."

Couture opened another desk drawer. He took out a portrait of his mother and held it up. Red looked almost like her. The comical makeup, the pudgy face, the overdone, pouty lips that he had painted on her. "My mother was fat," he said. "She tried to make me fat. She made a lot of cakes and sweets. Fudge, homemade ice cream, pudding. Her idea of a diet dessert was jello with nuts, lots of whipped cream, and a pile of maraschino cherries on top."

He looked at Red, thinking of his mother. He seemed almost indifferent as he adjusted the corset and allowed her to breathe again. He was deep in thought about his own life.

"I was fat, up until the sixth or seventh grade. That's when I started sports. I didn't know I was fat until a parent told me. You're not only fat, she said, but you also have a girl's name." He sighed. "Stuff like that hurts. It sticks with you."

Red was still catching her breath. She tried to say something but it kept coming out in huffs, whispered one word at a time. A fly crawled into her mouth when she inhaled and she started choking. The killer laughed. Red spit several times, then threw up.

"Please stop it," yelled Harry. "Please!"

Couture ignored him. Harry continued to beg. Rita's eyes rolled in her head, her eyelids flickered, trying to keep the flies away from her eyeballs. Her hands flailed about, brushing the air around her.

Harry screamed.

Couture slammed the picture of his mother down on the desk. The frame broke and the glass cracked across her face. He stood up, staring down at it, horrified. "There!" he screamed. "See what you made me do?" He looked at Harry.

Now Harry tried to ignore him. Couture went to the front of the treadmill and stood there. He moved his head to wherever Harry turned. They could not help but make eye contact.

Couture saw the fear in his victim's eyes. "You scream for me to do something, then when you have my attention you ignore me," he said. "Just like a woman." He grabbed her head and kept her from turning away, looking right into her eyes. "Well, here I am, sweetheart. Wanna play?"

Harry sunk down deeper into himself. The words settled uneasily on him. He didn't want to play, but somebody did. Someone who would enjoy coming out to play. A larger than life villain deserves a larger than life adversary, someone who might even be able to put him in his place.

Or die trying.

"Yes, I want to play," said Fu, the cleverest, most wily detective the noble Chan family had ever seen.

Chapter 47

When Your Disowned Self Knocks on the Door of Your Sanity, By All Means Let Them In

That's a long title for a chapter in a book, but it does a good job of putting into words exactly what happens next in the story. It's hard to explain without coming off like split personalities, the ghost of Hamlet's father, or some kind of invisible friend you talk to when you need one. Let's get it correct. Fu Chan was none of these. She was a disowned part of Harry Takanawa, something that was always there. Without Harry, there would be no Fu Chan, for they were one in the same.

Fu was knocking on the door of Harry's sanity, begging to be heard. She was Harry's secret self. His disowned self. And thanks to Couture, they were on a collision course towards each other.

For Harry, the journey was a descent into madness. Tortured, his body altered, invaded, the threat of death by the killer, the odd costume, it all twisted him in a troublesome way. Harry liked being able to take the dress off when he was done playing. That didn't seem to be part of Couture's game.

While Harry's journey was a descent, for Fu, it was a climb up from the depths. Buried for years beneath piles of psychological bandages and broken dreams, she was still there waiting to heal, waiting like East and West Berlin for the day the walls would one day come down. Reunification. As Harry grew weaker, she grew stronger. Harry didn't realize it, but he had already become her in body. She knew how to walk in heels, how to shake, move, and use this new body. Fu Chan had a plan. She had confidence, born from the knowledge that she was the hero, that right would always overcome might, and that evil would fail miserably in the end. She was, after all, more clever than this villain, and capable of more than Harry could muster under the circumstances. She knew how to look for an enemy's weakness and exploit it.

But first she had to overcome the barriers that Harry had cemented in place over the course of his lifetime.

What follows is a conversation, for this is the best way to represent it. And isn't it through conversation that we really get to know one another?

The whole conversation takes place inside Harry's head, parts of it unheard by him, and certainly never by anyone outside his own mind. It was more like something he felt, an argument that ended in acceptance and a nod of his head to a power he could no longer ignore. The conversation could even have taken place in a matter of seconds, the gist of it rising like the sun over the horizon, waiting for the Earth to tilt and spill light where there was once darkness. It could even have been spread out over the two days Couture had tortured him. The human mind does not measure time like we do. For the unconscious part, the ninety percent we don't use, time has a different meaning altogether.

"You need me Harry," said Fu.

The marine in him had been his strong voice, his voice of reason and survival. Harry the Marine remembered the rules of torture, the tricks the enemy would use, and how to survive. It was the person his mother and father most wanted him to be, and so the voice was loud and demanding.

"You can't live without me," he said. "Seems like you need me."

"You're right," she said.

"I'm always right," he said.

"Do you have to be?" she asked.

After a long pause, "No."

"I know you want to kill him. Hold that thought," she said. "Listen to me. I have a better idea."

"How can I trust you?"

"You have to trust me. Don't you trust yourself?"

"Do I?"

"I'm you Harry."

"No, you're not."

"But I am, Harry. I'm your disowned self. Remember me?"

Harry had known that all along. He had been afraid to admit it. "Fu?"

"Yes."

"Fu Chan?"

"Yes. We can survive this. You know we can. We can win."

"How can we win?" asked Harry.

"If you listen to me. Do what I say."

"Since when did you get all this hope?"

"It's our hope, Harry. Not mine, not yours. It's always been ours. We are each other, and there's hope enough for the both of us."

"I don't need you Fu," said Harry.

"Why are you so ashamed of me?" she asked.

"Momma told me to be. So did the priest. It's unnatural," said Harry. "I'm a sick person."

"You're not sick, Harry. When you were little, it was okay. It was innocent fun. At what point did Fu become bad?"

"When other people said it was," said Harry. "I scared parents and little kids."

"You didn't scare any little kids, their parents did," said Fu. "Normally, this is nothing, Harry. Kids play dress up. They pretend to be all kinds of things. They all go through this phase and they usually grow out of it. But because somebody made a big deal out of it when you were young, well, it's stuck in your life."

"What you say makes some sense," he said.

"I'm here, Harry, whether you own me or not."

Fu emerged from the darkness of Harry's interior. She was battered, beaten and hurt. Bruises across her face, a black eye. She walked with a limp.

"You look horrible," said Harry. "Did he do this to you? Did Couture abuse you?"

"No, Harry," she said. "You did."

Harry didn't know what to say. It's hard to dispute the truth, just as hard as it is to hide it again once it's known.

He started to cry. It was Fu who put her arm around him. The weak comforting the strong, as it sometimes is. How could he be so cruel to himself? He was ready to defend Fu from anyone. But how can you protect yourself against the damage you do toward yourself?

"Be your authentic self, Harry. People can tell when you're lying, even if it's only to yourself."

"I'm not honest with myself," he admitted.

"You're more trusting of others than you are of yourself," she said.

"I scare myself," he said. "Sometimes I don't know who to trust."

"If you can't trust yourself, who can you trust?" she said. "Trust comes over time."

"How can I trust you?" he asked.

"When will you learn?" she said. "You have no choice. You can't lie to me. I will always know."

"Everyone hated Fu Chan," said Harry.

"That's a lie. You didn't, Harry. You loved being me."

"I did," he said. "I loved being you." Harry began to realize that you can't lie to yourself. He understood, and with that came acceptance. "What should we do?"

"Give Couture what he wants."

"What's that?"

"You know. You've always known. Fu is all he sees. Give me to him."

"Give in to him?"

"Don't resist," she said. "He wants the scared little girl. As long as you're that scared little girl, you stay alive. You have to continue to hide the real Harry from him."

"That's what I thought I was doing," he said. "Hiding behind you."

"A time is coming when we will need all our cunning and strength. Yours and mine," she said. "Let me take the burden for a while. Stop thinking and let me play. Let yourself play."

"What do you mean?"

"We have skills together. It is our strength."

"We do?"

"Remember our feminine wiles and our cunning, Harry? Remember them?"

Harry began to think. Fu Chan was larger than life, a fantastic woman born of intense yearnings. She was an expert detective, clever, passionate, and a ninja cheerleader. How had he ever disowned something so strong?

He hadn't. Fu had been there all along. The Chinese have a saying. To suppress something is to give it great strength. And Fu was very strong right now.

And so the self and the disowned self approached each other, and seeing that they were one, both part of the same thing, there was nothing else to do except surrender. Fu Chan would always be Harry, and yet could never be Harry.

Harry, on the other hand, could be Fu Chan any time he wanted. All he had to do was surrender.

There was really no other choice.

At that point, Harry slowly dissolved into the background. He was a child again. No worries. He and Binky were playing games and he was Fu Chan, the greatest detective in the world.

Chapter 48

Better Dead than Red

Red squirmed inside the deadly corset. She gasped for air and her lungs ached for relief. The flies circled around her in an angry tornado. They landed on the vomit she had extruded on herself. The smell of rotten Sooka made her swoon. Even when she could breathe, it gagged her.

She rocked back and forth, side to side, trying to rip the bolts out of the floor. She thought if she could just yank the hoses and wires out of the wall, somehow break away, break the connection, maybe she would be okay. As long as Couture had his attention on Harry she would try, but if the killer figured out what she was up to it could be her last gambit.

She wondered how Harry was doing. She could see Couture talking to him, standing close to the treadmill.

"So you want to play?" said Couture. He was all about his Asian beauty. His hand stroked her cheek. "I'm busy," he said. "But I will make time for you." She licked his hand like a dog and he loved it. Submission of the best order. He had won. "I like it when you distract me," he said. "But I told you I'd make time for you later."

He turned around to watch Red. She stopped rocking and went back to flicking her head and waving her arms. She still had not scratched herself. He had thought she would give in by this point. It was not what he predicted for this experiment. "Next time I should try mosquitoes or horse flies," he said, nodding his head in assurance.

He turned his attention back to Fu. Without a word he increased the speed of the treadmill.

"Something to keep you busy," he said as he adjusted the controls. The treadmill churned and she began to trot. Her face looked pained. The strap lines on the high heel sandals began to chafe and her leg muscles ached. Her sides hurt where her ribs had been taken. He turned it up a little more. He sat in the chair and watched her for a while. He could see the point of submission in her, the one he had been waiting for. The pained look on her face told him she had enough.

It hurt to walk, but Fu knew that every minute the killer watched her was a minute his attention was away from Red. It was obvious what Rita was trying to do. It was a good plan, and she just might be strong enough to pull the whole contraption down.

The heels pinched, but not enough to complain. She knew how to walk in heels. "We like wearing heels," she said to herself. It was true, so what was different now? She always felt sexy in heels. She let herself go and began to wiggle, her rear swaying as she pumped her feet across the treadmill. It felt better, more natural. Couture watched with interest. She glanced sideways at him and smiled. The killer smiled back.

Wiles. One of Fu Chan's best assets. Make him feel at ease. Make him think his torture and programming were working. Come closer, my enemy, she thought, her smile genuine. Fu Chan will make you a promise she will keep. It ends tonight. Between you and me, I make you a promise. One of us will see the other die.

Fu Chan began to assess the situation with the mind of a top detective. It was a cheaply made treadmill, the railings were not as sturdy as she originally thought. It looked like they were made of rolled aluminum, the flimsy stuff that bent when it was put under too much stress. The railing didn't even appear to be fastened to the machine very well. Most of the strength came from the plastic dashboard that held all the controls, and even that looked cheap. She could probably break it in two with a karate chop. How did these facts escape Harry?

Maybe it was the chain that she wore. It was formidable, thick linked chain that was heavy and confining. Maybe that was all Harry saw. No way that chain would break, but the aluminum supports on the treadmill were another thing.

Fu Chan was thinking, calculating, planning. My prison is a sham, she thought. It's true. We create our own boundaries and limitations. Harry may be limited, but Fu Chan is not.

Couture still had his back to Red, unaware that she was shaking back and forth, rocking the corset and the gantry that held her in place. Fu could see her partner trying to find a way out of her own trap. Looks like they both had a plan in the making. The time for action was drawing near.

There was a loud creak as Red pushed against the framework that held her in place. Couture turned in horror. He could see bolts sticking up out of the floor, their heads pried loose by the rocking motion. She was ruining his creation. He panicked, went to the desk and touched a button inside the drawer. Red let out a gasp and stopped moving. The corset squeezed harder than it ever had.

"You force me into a decision I didn't want to make yet," he said. "I can't have you rolling around here like some kind of loose cannon."

Fu saw Rita in pain and something broke inside her. She thought of a time when Harry was driving the old Volvo, an abject lesson in torque. Her mind began to race. Behind her, the knives pointed at her heels. Forward seemed the way to go. She started running, ninja cheerleader style.

She vaulted over the top of the dashboard controls in front of her and did a mid air horizontal twist. She pulled her hands in close to her body. The torque flipped the treadmill over like it was a Volvo hauling a motorcycle on a horse trailer. In the process the handrail came loose and broke in half. She slid her right hand down the aluminum tube and off the end, freeing one hand.

Couture heard the noise, turned and saw what had happened. He reached for the remote control and picked it up, his thumb going for the red button.

Fu saw a rock on a nearby table, a geode that was an office decoration. She picked it up and heaved it at the villain. It hit him in the wrist and he dropped the detonator. It fell to the desk with a clunk. Fu twisted again, dragging a piece of framework from the treadmill behind her.

Couture stretched across the desk, reaching for the remote. Fu swung her arm about. The framework warped, bending as she yanked it with all the strength she could muster. It broke free from the bottom and hit

Couture in the side, knocking him off balance. A piece of tubing cut into his lip and he began to bleed. She dove forward, her arm extended, ready to scoop up the remote.

Couture picked up the piece of broken tubing and hit her across the arm. She let out a yelp.

"You're not afraid of me anymore," he said. "Usually my victims just oblige me and die."

"You're not the first one to try to kill Fu Chan," she said.

"Fu Chan?" he said.

"I'm not a scared little girl anymore," she said. "I'm Fu Chan, and I'm more than your equal."

Couture wiped the blood away from his lip and laughed, amused by this new turn of events. His victims often went nuts in the end. "This is more like it," he said. "I've been torturing you hoping to see this woman again. She is worthy of me. Not this wimpy man who was so easily overpowered on my doorstep."

"Be careful, Couture," said Fu. "Wimpy man heard that." She spun her hand sideways and the remaining piece of treadmill dropped free. She stepped forward, delivering a series of blows to his face. Fu had all of Harry's knowledge and skills to draw upon, including his training in hand to hand combat when he was a Marine.

Couture reached into the desk drawer and picked up a surgical knife. He sliced the air in front of her face. It made a sound as it cut the wind close to her cheek. Whoosh. Whoosh. Fu ducked and he switched from a side to side motion to up and down. He stepped towards her, the knife now slicing in an x pattern in front of him. Fu twisted again and stepped back. The scalpel came down on her shoulder, cutting the strap of her outfit. It nicked her shoulder but she didn't bleed.

"I'm afraid that may be a fatal stab, my dear," he said. "Did I neglect to tell you that I installed a manual detonator on your outfit as well?"

Manual detonator! Her brain lit up. No time for fear, Fu, she said to herself. Stay on task. Rita needs you.

Couture could see her confusion. "The timer has been activated. You have less than five minutes to live."

Her mind went through the possibilities. If this was the end, then she would take him with her.

He became playful, like he had the upper hand. He tapped her on the hip, slapped her on the side of the head. He laughed, taunting her. The knife sliced in front of her again and she stepped back, nearly tripping over pieces of the broken treadmill.

Something told her that he was worried. His moves were becoming more impulsive and less controlled, acts of a desperate man. "Bullshit," she said. "You're bluffing. I can tell when you're lying. There is no manual detonator."

"How do you know?" he asked. "How do you know for sure?"

She didn't, but there wasn't any other choice for Fu Chan. This was a fight to the death.

Chapter 49

The Calvary Arrive

"Take a left up here," said Bernard. "I think we have it."

"How do you know where to go?" asked Robernaut.

"I got a tag on the cell phone," said Bernard.

"What do you mean?" he asked.

"They're using one of those new phones, the ones with GPS enabled. I got a laptop back here and I'm using it to track us to the location."

"Pretty cool, Lieutenant," said Robernaut.

"Ah," he said. "I got the idea from researching stalkers. Pretty easy thing to do."

"You'll have to show me," said Robernaut.

"Later," he said. "We're not far now. Make a left here. I think it's one of these houses along the lake."

Jackson turned, the car bumping across the uneven pavement.

"Slow down," said Bernard. The laptop was performing slowly, updating at the speed of a wireless modem connection. He grumbled.

Jackson slowed the car to a crawl. A curtain parted in a house at the end of a long driveway, a face staring through the glass at the slow moving vehicle. Police always draw the attention of people, no matter what they do. Jackson inched the car forward making careful observations of each house that they passed. Robernaut did the same on the passenger side of the car. Houses on his side bordered the lake. There was so much more to see in the lakeside properties.

"Stop here," Bernard suddenly said. "It's behind this house, I think." Jackson pulled over. The house was low lit, a driveway disappearing into darkness beside it. The gate was open. Even in the dark Robernaut noticed that the yard was unkempt and the hedges needed trimming. There was debris on the roof, leaves and pine needles that made patterns like the spots on a Dalmatian.

Bernard got out of the car and walked through the gate and down the driveway.

"Are we supposed to go with him?" asked Robernaut.

"I don't know," said Jackson.

Bernard scanned the house. The curtains were closed and he couldn't see any signs of activity. He followed the driveway into the darkness. He passed a side door to the house, probably leads to the attached garage he thought. He couldn't see much in the dark, his eyes were still adjusting after the glare of the computer screen. He took out his cell phone. Great devices these things. They have built in GPS. Maps and tracking applications. The web. It's what gave him the idea. Why bother with old fashioned maps when he could use technology to find her. He must be close. He dialed her number as he crept through the shadows along the side of the house.

He heard a phone ringing up ahead. The driveway continued behind the house into the back yard. He moved towards a flat building. Looked like a garage, big bay doors lined up like it was a jiffy lube. The phone got louder as he approached.

Six rings. He dialed it again and listened. The phone was definitely inside the flat building. He heard the sound through an open window beside a door. Bernard reached for the knob. A bright light flashed on his hand and he froze. He turned and looked.

It was Robernaut. He held a flashlight the size of a nightstick, a beam as bright as a flash bulb on wedding day.

"Thought you might need my help," he said.

"Thanks," said Matt. He touched the dial button on his phone. They heard the sound of the phone ringing again. Bernard nodded, made some gestures, silent language that all policemen understand. Robernaut nodded back, jerked his head towards the door twice. Bernard turned the knob and opened the door. Robernaut peered around the entrance, his gun drawn. He aimed with his flashlight, sweeping left and right. Bernard crouched low, moving in quickly and quietly behind him. They heard another ring in the back of the garage. Bernard jerked his head towards Robernaut and the big cop took off. Bernard headed straight towards the ring.

Robernaut went the other way, his flashlight scanning, his gun ready. He noticed it was a large garage, free standing, with a car next to the door they had entered. He checked out all sides of the car, glanced underneath. It was dark, and there was an oil pit under it. He moved around to the front of the car. Bernard was a short distance away, squatting near a pile of clothes by a sink. Robernaut lit the area up like the morning.

"Clear," he said.

"She was here," said Bernard. He couldn't help but notice all the blood. His stomach started dancing like he had swallowed a vibrating pager. "We found the phone, but no detective."

They heard a noise, muffled sounds of a struggle. Robernaut swung the flashlight around. "I think it's coming from over there."

They moved toward the wall. They heard the sounds of thuds and breaking glass. It was barely audible, sounding like a couple fighting in a hotel room next door. Robernaut dropped down. "I think it's coming from under the car. There's an oil pit down there." He shined the light under the car.

"You're right," said Bernard. He moved around the car and found the staircase going down. There were only a few steps going down and he squatted, moving in low and ready. Robernaut's beam rained from above, circling him in an unsteady light. It was creepy, messy, the walls spotted with oil and grime. He heard another thud and a scream. It came from behind a wall up ahead.

More sounds, thuds and screams, grunts. Furniture breaking. He pounded the wall. It sounded hollow behind. It moved when he touched it but something locked it in place. He felt around the edges, groping in the darkness for a knob or a trip or something. The sounds kept on. A fight, and then a grisly sound, something he never heard before. He dropped his shoulder, ramming against the wall. Robernaut was beside him and they slammed at it together. "Get a rhythm going," said Bernard. They hit it together, their combined force making the wall groan. Wood twisted, louder than the muffled sounds coming from behind it. The wall gave way and fell flat.

There was a smell, unmistakable, the odor of rotting flesh. Bernard and Robernaut fell forward, the flashlight dropping to the ground, a curtain of darkness falling around them like a net dropping over a school of trapped fish.

Chapter 50

Enough!

Couture held the knife out in front of him, his arm turning the blade. He thrust forward, jabbing at her.

Fu was in full control now. She stepped to the side, avoiding his moves. In her mind it was a dance. All fight scenes are choreographed, and nobody can dance like Fu Chan. She smiled and began to shimmy.

A belly dance move was the last thing he expected. It was not in Couture's book of hand to hand combat.

"What's the matter?" she said. "You did say you wanted me to dance for you." Her hands moved gracefully as she shimmied, following patterns taught to her long ago by her teacher Mellilah. Her hands fluttered and she gently dropped them to her side, two fingers held together in classic pose. Her eyes followed him, a smile disarming him with a look. He smiled back, looking confused. She turned, nodding her head as she executed a perfect hip down ronde-de-jambe, a move Harry the Marine might have called a foot sweep if he were in judo class.

Couture hit the floor but he was up quickly. The surgical knife was still in his hand. He threw it at her. She slid her head to the side, not even missing a beat to the music in her head. The knife whizzed by and stuck in the wall behind her. She turned, as if it were part of her dance routine, and she yanked the knife out of the wall. Now she had a weapon. She moved in front of him, gracefully going across from side to side, still two fingers together, the knife lined up against them. It was as if it were just a prop in her dance. She pretended to flick it at him, watching him flinch as she faked throwing it at him. She laughed.

There was fear in his eye. Dangerous fear. She could see it. He laughed too, a nervous laugh. She recognized humor as a mask for his fear. She was wearing him down.

She did a grapevine step, moving to the side, her feet gracefully avoiding the broken debris on the floor. She did a spin and broke loose in another shimmy, her hands going over her head.

Couture saw the remote control nearby. He lunged for it.

Fu saw what he was doing. She flipped up and forward, twisting sideways as she slid across the top of his desk. She bumped the control onto the floor and they both fell on top of each other. Couture balled his hand into a fist and beat at her. Fu ignored him and let him do his damage. She had the remote in her hands. She turned it over and opened the battery cover. There was a nine volt battery inside. She ripped it out, pulling the battery cap and some of the wiring with it. It would not be usable without some kind of repairs. She threw the battery in a corner and smashed the remote.

"No worry," he said. "The timer has been activated. We're on a countdown to your death," he said. He backed off, catching his breath. "I don't want to be near you when you go off."

She moved closer. "Why not? I thought you liked me." Her hips moved in figure eight, swiveling from side to side, her arms seemed to float like leaves in a breeze. So graceful. And her smile...

She shoulder shimmied, shaking her breasts in his face. He moved away. She moved forward, breasts pointed like loaded guns.

"You're as good as dead," he said.

There was a tremor in his voice. He was definitely lying.

"I could hasten it if I want. There are multiple controls and fail safes."

"You have nothing," she said. She reared back, smiling like Faten Salama, smiling with all the enjoyment life can offer. She framed her hips and snapped her fingers, wiggling in new patterns that beguiled her captor. She knew who was in control here.

"Are you sure?" he asked. "How do you know?" He moved towards her.

She stood and shimmied, inviting him closer. Fu Chan did not fear this monster. Who was it who said keep your enemy closer?

He took advantage, touching her at his will. "I have a secret detonator," he said. "Is it there?" He hit her on the hip. "Maybe it's there." He squeezed her breast.

He's just trying to throw my guard off, she thought. She was winning and he didn't want her to know. Time to use her wiles again.

"Why did you keep Dick's penis?" she asked. "I saw it labeled in a jar over there."

"Oh, so you noticed that?" he said. "I was going to use it again. Recycle it, just like the breast implants."

"You're sick," said Fu.

"And you're not?" he said. "Honey, you may think you're all woman, but you're still a man. You're living a lie."

"This is no lie, Carol," she said. "This is the authentic me. I am what I am. You're the lie. Where did you get your doctorate?"

"I am Doctor Couture. Everyone knows that."

"You're Carol Huntington," she said. "Everyone knows that. Now who's lying?"

"I'm your doctor. Look at what I did for you."

"You're no doctor," she said. "Doctors take an oath. Doctors don't kill."

"Stop being naive," he said. "Doctors kill every day."

"Don't twist my words," she said. "I can out think you Carol."

He moved close to her. His hand moved quickly, slapping the scalpel out of her hand. It fell into the corner in a pile of debris. His fists came up and he hit her.

She felt the blows on her face. Her cheek hurt and it began to swell.

"There's something I haven't told you yet," he said. "Aren't you curious?"

"You're full of lies, Carol," she said. "There's nothing you can say that will stop me."

He laughed as he stared at her crotch.

He was gloating now. Was he serious or just trying to distract her? What had he done?

"You're a true eunuch now, emasculated in a way you could never conceive."

What did he mean?

Behind them, in the display case Red was trembling. She was on her last breath. Her eyes bulged and her head shook up and down like some kind of mad jack in the box.

Fu saw a cable on the floor leading from the desk to the wall below the display case. She saw the scalpel on the floor. She squatted down, tumbling like a gymnast. When she rolled over she had the scalpel in her hand. She reached down with her hand and picked up the wire bundle, slicing the scalpel across them. The wires cut easily. There was a hiss in the display case and the corset loosened its grip. Red gasped for air and started choking.

Couture came at Fu, his fists pounding her. He knocked the scalpel out of her hand again.

She remembered something about his fighting style. The last time they had fought she had noticed a pattern. A few quick jabs with his left and then a long, straight right punch. It seemed to be his rhythm. To Fu, it was a musical beat that she could dance to.

Left, left, right. Left, left, right. On the next cycle she ducked when the right came forward. She grabbed his arm and fell backwards, her foot coming up into his stomach. He winced, her heel digging into his gut, but he had no choice. He fell over her and landed on his back.

Fu rolled, bouncing to her feet. "It's been a long time since I've done these cheerleader flips," she said. "It all comes back."

Couture rolled over. His eyes fluttered and he struggled to catch his breath.

"And I can balance in these heels now, thanks to you." She kicked them high, even though her sides ached. Fu Chan shows no fear.

There was a crash behind them. Rita had shaken the framework loose but still lay pinned in the corset. The bolts that secured it to the floor had finally broken. Splintered wood lay at her feet. She was exhausted and trapped but she knew she had just escaped certain death. The corset had loosened some but she was still choking. The smell was overpowering, not to mention the flies.

Couture turned and saw Rita. She was lying sideways on the floor. The storage bin had tipped over and the rotting piece of Dick Sooka had fallen out and had settled in front of her. She stared at the maggots everywhere, the air in the display case thick with agitated flies. Rita rolled on the floor, crushing insects under the weight of her body. She gagged and spat, her eyes rolling in her head. She kicked at the display window with her feet, trying to break the glass. There was a crack and the glass suddenly shattered. Big pieces fell outward, dropping to the floor of the office where they smashed into smaller pieces. Rita gasped as she fell forward towards the desk, broken glass shattered around her. Angry flies buzzed through the broken window and the smell of dead Sooka escaped with them.

While Couture was distracted, Fu made her move. She jumped, another cheerleader flip. She bounced off the floor and up in the air.

The scalpel was on the floor beside him. Couture picked it up and gripped it in his hand. He turned over, facing Fu as she came down on top of him. He stood up, his hand beginning to thrust towards her chest.

One last chance, she thought. She angled her foot precisely.

Couture looked up. Fear and adrenaline poured into his body but there was nothing he could do. Forces were set in motion, acceleration, momentum, gravity. They all focused on a single point in the air. The tip of Fu Chan's high heel. He tried to move out of the way and avoid it, but he had committed to an action he could not change.

The heel came down, right into Couture's eye. It pushed its way through the corner of the eye, through the sclera, the white piece next to the bridge of the nose. The eye popped to the side, making it bulge until it broke loose from the socket as the heel pushed further into his skull. The broken eye hung there by the optic nerve, dangling from a bundle of ganglia. The heel continued driving into the socket, guided like a bowling ball running down a gutter, it had no choice but to continue deep into his brain.

They fell to the floor together. Fu kicked but the head would not come off the heel. She shook her leg, beating at his head madly with her other foot, but the heel was stuck inside him. Blood and ichor began to ooze out the hole where his eye once was. Couture trembled for a moment then lay still. The other eye went cold and empty and a sigh escaped his mouth.

Harry would have screamed at the sight. Fu on the other hand stared in fascination.

Chapter 51

Rescue Party

There was a crash as the rescue party fell through the secret doorway. Bernard and Robernaut picked themselves up off the floor. It stank. The odor of rotting flesh was unmistakable. Bernard ripped off a piece of his shirt and tied it over his mouth. There were flies all around them, buzzing and lighting on their skin. As soon as he would swat them away, a dozen more would take their place.

They were in a short tunnel. It was dark but they could see a dim light ahead. They made their way through the darkness and into the next room.

It opened up into an office. The lights were low. There were signs of a struggle, the office was in disarray and there was debris scattered across the floor. It looked like a hurricane had ripped a hole in the wall and thrown everything around.

Bernard spotted a girl lying on the floor nearby. She looked like she needed some help. He moved closer, something familiar about her.

"Harry?" Bernard wasn't sure, she looked like Harry, then she didn't. He did a second glance to be sure. She was wearing a pink and black tutu like thing, he couldn't really describe it, definitely a one of a kind garment. Her breasts were pushing out and up and towards each other with cleavage that just kept coming. The outfit had an attached skirt with rows of black and pink lace ruffles that flounced at the hips, and...

Good lord, the woman had no genitals, just a patch of skin. Not even a sign that there ever was anything there. There was something creepy yet fascinating about it. No hair, no genitalia, just smooth skin.

She was lying on her back, twisted in a pile of broken stuff like so much garbage on the floor. A smashed treadmill, broken glass, rocks, an overturned potted plant, broken coffee table, magazines and paper all over the floor. She was cut in places, blood smeared on her arm and face and on her clothes. There were bruises and scratches.

Harry looked up through the haze. Fu Chan was still there, an accepted part of Harry's owned self, his authentic self. But he was still Harry. "It was Couture, Matt. He did this to me."

"It is you, Harry. By God. What did he do?"

Matt looked down Harry's leg, blood oozing out from long scratches in the pink stockings he was wearing. He followed it down further to his strappy sandals, stained with blood, the heel of the left one sticking into a reddened socket where Couture's eye once looked out on the world. It was raw, as if that heel had ground around and around in circles, churning Couture's brains like butter until it exploded out the hole in his skull.

"Help me, Matt," said Harry. "Get the bomb squad here. You may be at risk, too. He put exploding breast implants in me." Harry began to kick at Couture, hysterical for a moment, his heel hammering Couture's head like a tether ball.

"Calm down, Harry. Calm down," said Matt. He bent down and put his arm on his friend's shoulder and looked him in the eye. "It's okay. You hear me? It's gonna be okay."

Harry started to cry, twisting sideways in a fetal position. He looked like a helpless little girl. Bernard didn't know what to do. This was one for the shrinks. "Everything's gonna be okay," he said.

The high heels were locked onto Harry's feet. Bernard took a knife out of his pocket and cut the straps. The shoe fell away but the cuff remained. He did the same to the other foot. He pulled Harry's foot carefully away from Couture's still body and stood up. "Robernaut," he called.

The tall policeman had gone to the other side of the room. He found a woman trapped in a framework of wires, hoses, and fabric. She hung half out of a platform behind a desk, broken glass, wood, and twisted metal all around her. Slumped across a chair, she was trapped in some kind of bizarre apparatus. He saw a clamp on the side of the garment, the kind that you might use to secure a fire extinguisher to a wall. It was complicated but he managed to get it open. He found two more clamps and worked them open. The garment released her like a pearl from an oyster shell. He untangled her foot from some wiring. He lifted her free and laid her gently on her back on top of the desk. She was heavy but the Robernaut was strong. He checked her vitals. She had a pulse but didn't seem to be breathing. He checked the airway for obstructions, swept his finger through her mouth and found nothing. There was a box of tissues on the floor next to the desk. He wiped the vomit and spittle from around her face. He had a barrier in a pouch on his utility belt that he positioned over her mouth. He tilted her head back and delivered lifesaving breaths.

He was having trouble making a seal and his breaths were ineffective. He finally removed the barrier and threw it aside. He wiped her face with his shirt and made a better seal. He went back to the breaths. She started to choke, then cough. Robernaut pulled back, her red lipstick smeared across his lips from the mouth to mouth. She looked up at him, not knowing what to say, but glad to be alive.

"You okay?" he asked her. He was anxious, like a puppy dog waiting for his reward.

She laughed at the sight of him, then threw her arms around him. "My hero," she said.

He heard Bernard call him from the other side of the room. "Robernaut." So much for claiming his reward.

"You wait here," he said to Red. "I'll get you some help."

"I'm okay," she said. "I can breathe again. Thanks"

There was something about him she liked. Anyone watching the two would have seen it. They both had the same sparkle in their eyes, kindred souls of a sort.

Robernaut made his way to Bernard. "What's up, Lieutenant?" he asked.

"This is a crime scene," he said. "We need to seal it off."

Robernaut held his nose and waved at the flies circling him. "The sooner we get out of here the better," he said.

"Go then," said Bernard. "I'll stay here with the victims. Call for an ambulance, crime scene investigators, detective unit, and the bomb squad."

Robernaut stiffened at that one. "Bomb squad?"

"Yeah," said Bernard. "Bomb squad. I have a report that the perp rigged explosives on the scene."

"Holy crap," he said.

"Do it," he said. "Hurry back here. I need your help getting these people out of here."

"I'm on it," he said.

"Let me use your flashlight," said Bernard.

Robernaut passed him the light, then disappeared down the dark hallway that led to the garage and the outside world.

"Thanks for not saying anything," said Harry.

"About what?" asked Bernard.

"You know," said Harry. "The exploding breasts."

"I wasn't sure I heard you right," said Bernard. He laughed, and Harry joined him. "Crazy son of a bitch," said the Lieutenant. "Do you think he really did it?"

"Considering everything else he's done, I wouldn't put it past him," said Harry.

"How was he going to set them off?"

"You'll find a remote control over there somewhere. I smashed it in a fight with him."

Bernard looked down at Couture. "You did a lot better than the last time when you went up against him."

"I was lucky," said Harry.

"Lucky? How about this high heel in his eyeball? How'd that happen?" asked Bernard.

"Accident. We were fighting. I came at him with a flying kick. I didn't expect to hit him in the eye," said Harry.

They heard some coughing across the room. Harry recognized it. "Rita?" he called. "You okay?"

"Fine Harry," she said. She started to work her way over towards them.

"Sit tight," said Bernard. "You may have broken bones. Wait until the ambulance gets here."

"I feel okay," said Red. She continued to make her way over to Harry and Bernard. She stopped for a moment and started to scream, not in terror but with excitement. "The dress! The dress!" She was pointing to the wall. Bernard tracked her eyes with the flashlight, shining at the dress on the wall.

The golden fleece.

In this case, plain basic black. Simple. Except it had the Richard Sooka label.

Red hugged Harry, pointed to the wall again. "We're claiming the reward."

Bernard looked at more grisly items. He saw Dick Sooka's penis in a jar on a shelf nearby, as if it were pickled pigs feet in brine sitting behind a seedy bar. He looked at Harry and Red. They were both bleeding, Harry on the legs, Red all over. Then there was this grisly corpse in the corner.

"I'll need a statement from you both, but it looks like you did it," he said. "The dress is evidence for now, but I'll put you down as the ones who found it."

"Speaking of finding things, how did you locate me?"

"I just followed our plan, Rita," he said. "When I didn't hear from you I was worried. Then I remembered a report I read last year about how stalkers were tracking people using their cell phones. Thank goodness yours is one of the types that have a built in GPS."

"Where is my cell phone?" she asked.

"I heard it ringing upstairs when I called. It's still up there with all your clothes."

Red realized that she was naked. "Which way?"

Bernard pointed. "There's a sink up there against the back wall. Your stuff is in a pile next to it." He paused. "Wait. You're not going to just walk out of here, are you?"

"Why not?" she asked. "I can walk. I was thinking about cleaning up and changing clothes up there. I feel like crap."

Bernard didn't see any reason to stop her.

"Thanks for coming after us," she said. "You going to be all right, Harry?"

"I think so, Rita," he said. "I think so."

Halfway out she ran into the Robernaut. They bumped into each other in the darkness of the tunnel. He accidently rubbed up against her breasts.

"Sorry," said the tall policeman.

If there were enough light she could have seen him blush. "It's okay," she said. "You can touch them all you want. My hero." She planted another kiss on him.

"Meet you outside," he said. "I'm going to help the Lieutenant get your friend out of there."

She touched his cheek. "Slow down, big boy. Give a girl a moment to change clothes and clean up a bit."

Chapter 52

Diffusing a Bomb

Harry lay on the ground, Red close by. They had moved him outside and away from the rotting stench of Couture's lair. Red had found her clothes and gotten dressed. A paramedic insisted on examining her, told her she really should let them take her to the hospital.

"Who can afford that?" she asked.

"You can't put a price on health," he said.

"Yes you can," she said. "I just can't afford the pricetag."

She knew how to take care of herself. Years of cleaning up after barroom brawls and fights was part of the routine for her. These were just scratches and she had cleaned herself well, lowering the chance of infection.

"I'm going to get out of here," she told Harry. "I gave Bernard my statement and I just want to go home and go to bed."

"That sounds nice," said Harry. The drugs that Couture had been giving him were finally wearing off. He hurt all over.

Red gave him a kiss and took off. Harry closed his eyes and rested. He could hear sounds of activity all around him but it didn't matter. The ordeal was over.

He heard someone move beside him and touch the center of his chest. When he opened his eyes he was staring at an angel. The fantasy lasted about two seconds. Angels don't wear thick vests with Seattle Bomb Squad printed across the front in big white block letters.

"What are you doing here?" asked Harry. "Where's Hamilton?"

Jen Meyer looked down into Harry's eyes as she kneeled beside him. She was a tough police lady. Small but deadly. Rumor was she had a PhD but lied on her resume to get on the force. Dumbed herself down so she wouldn't intimidate the review panel. She never figured out why smart and pretty didn't go together for women, but she knew how to play the game. She liked the action. She was the best on the west coast, listed in who's who in bomb squads, and often on loan to DHS as a subject matter expert and part time consultant on terrorism. If anyone could diffuse a set of deadly breasts, she could. "I heard what he did to you Harry. I came as soon as I could."

"Why'd they send you?" he asked.

"I was briefed, Harry. They told me about your breasts. They thought a woman was needed for this job. Besides, Hamilton has a wife and three kids. I only have a cat."

Hamilton rushed up beside her, carrying a blast shield. "Somebody call me?" he said. He set the shield in place beside Harry. A crowd was gathering behind the bomb squad truck parked sideways a short distance away. Its thick walls would create a screen in event of an explosion. No one could come up with a good estimate for how big a blast zone the breasts would create. Couture never shared that information with Harry. It was anybody's WAG.

Hamilton moved to the other side of Harry, kneeling opposite Jen. He studied the garment, looking for clues. There was no sign of a detonator, no wires or circuit boards, timers or cell phones. No lumps. He lifted the frills.

"It's in the bra," said Jen. She had already spotted the electronics. She was the best. "Look, under this décolleté bow in the middle. There are two wires, one on each side. They follow the underwire of the cup, then turn back in, ending near the nipple." Jen studied the decorations. "Did the killer say anything about the construction of the bra? Any clues about how it detonates?" she asked Harry.

"There are supposed to be needles or some kind of injection thing. He said it would cause an explosion under my skin, in the implant. He said it would go off if I tried to remove it, or if he pushed the detonator button on the remote control."

"Must have a radio receiver somewhere," said Hamilton.

"That's what I was thinking," said Jen.

"He said he built an antenna into the corset stays," said Harry

"Ingenious," said Jen. She studied it, her eye scanning the garment like an electron microscope. She was also a fashion icon, sharp shopper, and had an eye for flaws in garments. "Look here." She pointed to a bulge in one of the stays, a small asymmetry that stood out ever so slight. Her finger traced it. She took out a pocket knife and started to cut something.

"Be careful you'll..."

She ripped open a seam before Hamilton could finish. "See, I was right. The antenna wire leads to this small decoration in the center of the bra, and there are wires under this ruffle that lead to the nipple of each breast."

"He said the detonation would be small, barely enough to singe flesh. But if it went off under my skin and inside the breast implants. Boom."

"So he's rigged some kind of blasting cap to set off the heavy stuff. What do you think he used?"

"I don't know. There's a shelf full of chemicals over in the garage. He had chloroform. Maybe you can tell what he made by looking at his ingredients.

"I'll check it out," said Jen. She put her hand on Harry's shoulder. "We're gonna get you out of this." She headed for the chemicals.

Hamilton tested the stability of the shield he set up. He laid some heavy weights across the legs of the shield, anchoring it to the ground. "We're clear," he yelled.

Bernard waved to the medial team. An ambulance had arrived, and a doctor shortly after. He and the two EMT's from the ambulance examined Harry while Hamilton took a small knife and began to cut more of the garment away. "Hold still, Harry," he said. He moved carefully, his knife razor sharp, his eyes narrowed and focused.

"I'm Doctor Litchfield and I'll be attending you here in the field. This is Sam and George. Sam is a PA and George is an EMT."

Harry nodded. "Nice to meet you. Thanks for coming."

"Who's your next of kin," asked the Doctor.

"I don't know," said Harry. "My ex-wife, I guess. Technically, we're still married."

"Do you have insurance?" asked the Doctor.

"No."

"Does your wife have insurance?"

"I don't know. Are these medical related questions?"

"It's complicated," said the Doctor. "That's why we have legal experts down at the hospital."

"Does it hurt here?" asked George, his hand gently resting on Harry's head. He cleaned around the open wounds on Harry's arms. He moved down Harry's body, stopping in shock as he saw Harry's crotch. "What the hell?"

"What is it?" asked Harry.

"You have no crotch," he said.

Sam spoke up. "That leg looks bad. Multiple lacerations, loss of blood, possible fracture."

George interrupted. "Leg! Hell, have you seen this crotch?"

The Doctor spoke up. "I see it. That's not why we're here. Our priority is to remove the explosives before we transport him. I will be performing a simple breast explant, followed by an implant."

"What are you saying?" asked Harry.

Doctor Litchfield ignored him and spoke to Sam. "I'll put him under, then I need you to monitor his vitals during the whole operation. The replacement shouldn't take more than five minutes for each breast."

"Replacement surgery?" asked Harry.

The Doctor continued to ignore the patient and spoke to Sam. "I want you to assist me," said the Doctor. "After the bomb squad removes the detonator and clears the area, we'll come in and get started. Our job will be to remove the explosives, implant the replacements, and prepare the patient for transport."

Jen came back. "Hard to tell what he made from the chemicals I saw, Harry. He has a pretty well stocked shelf. Could have been any number of compounds. It's anybody's guess what he put in those things in your chest."

"Jen, what are they planning?" he asked.

Jen spoke to the doctor. "Are you done with your preliminary?"

"Yes, but I really won't know until I have a chance to examine him without the clothes. Then I can tell you more."

"How long is the operation going to take?"

"Might take ten, maybe fifteen minutes," said the Doctor. "I'll need to establish a sterile field as much as possible, do my thing, then we'll truss the patient up for transport."

"Okay," said Jen. "Why don't you wait behind the truck in the safety zone. I'll call you when we're ready."

"Don't have to tell me twice," said the Doctor.

"Get Lieutenant Bernard for me," said Harry. The Doctor nodded and moved off.

"Okay, let's get ready do this thing," said Hamilton.

"Let me do it," said Jen.

"It's gonna take us both to do it," said Hamilton.

Bernard arrived. "What's up, Harry? Need me to hold your hand?" he asked.

"They're going to take these things out of me," said Harry.

"That's right," said Bernard. "Bomb squad's gonna dispose of them."

"Get the serial numbers off them first," said Harry.

"Serial numbers?" asked Bernard.

"Yeah," said Harry. "All implants have serial numbers. They're tracked. It's a Federal regulation. Get the numbers and match them up to the names of those women who got killed last year. I think we might have found the Greenlake Butcher."

Bernard smiled. Double bonus. "Good work, Harry," he said.

"Matt, you gotta do something for me."

"Whatever you want," he said. "Name it."

Harry stared into Bernard's eyes. "Look after Red for me."

"I ain't looking after her," said Bernard.

"Please Matt."

"I ain't looking after her because you're going to make it through this."

"What if I don't?"

"You will, Harry."

"Yeah, but…"

"Look, I already keep an eye on her. She's good people. Hell, I wouldn't have found you without her and the GPS in her phone. We had a plan. No, I ain't looking after her. You are. You're coming through this, Harry."

Harry nodded. "Matt, one more thing."

"What Harry?"

"They're putting breasts back in me?"

"Non-explosive ones. The experts advised them to. It's what they'd do for anyone who was in this situation."

"What situation? How many people have exploding breast implants they want replaced?"

"I'm not a medical expert," said Bernard. "Let the doctors do their job."

"Suppose I don't want them?"

"We have the best minds on this and they all agree this is the best course of action," said Bernard. "You're lucky we could find a surgeon who could pull this off. Litchfield is ex-Army, a former field surgeon in the war."

"What's a field surgeon doing practicing plastic surgery?"

"Don't know, Harry. Maybe he just wanted to put people back together right, do things he wished he could do for patients when he was treating them in the war," said Bernard. "Like I said, you're lucky we found him"

Harry nodded.

"Good luck," said Bernard. He moved back behind the thick, steel plated truck, "Seattle Bomb Squad" blazoned on the side. Anxious eyes wanted to watch, but Bernard warned them to be safe and look away.

"I trust you with my life any day of the week, Jen," said Harry.

"That's nice," she said. "Glad it's the weekend."

She was good at breaking the tension. Always a cool head. Small but steady hands. Good hands to be in. Harry felt safe. "What's the plan?"

She looked down at him. "Hamilton got most of the bra off of you. We traced the wires to spring loaded needles designed to penetrate your breasts. The minute they come away from your body, they're going to go off. If we stop them from penetrating your body, we stop the explosion."

"Okay," said Harry.

"Hamilton is going to yank the bra away while I press down on your chest," she said. "Hopefully the two will be far enough apart to keep the needles from setting off the explosion." She looked at him seriously. "Harry, I'm going to have to touch your breasts. Are you okay with that?"

"Do what you have to, Jen," he said.

"Are they tender?" she asked.

"They feel odd," he said. "Like they're not a part of me."

Hamilton spoke to Jen. "I think it would be better if you straddled his head," he said. "One knee by each shoulder. I'll get at his feet and pull the garment down and up as quick as I can."

Jen got into position. Hamilton squatted over his legs, his hands gripping the bra tightly. He was going to yank at the same time he stood, increasing his speed. He didn't know how fast the needles would move.

Jen reached under the cloth, resting her hands on Harry's breasts as best she could. "Am I hurting you?" she asked.

"Just get it over with," he said.

Jen nodded to Hamilton. "One... Two... Three.."

She spread her fingers as she pressed down on Harry's breasts. She tried to push her hands between him and the bra. She saw Harry wince. Wait until the doctor cuts you again, she thought. Hamilton was quick, she felt a tiny prick on the back of her left hand. The fabric whipped away from her in a blur. There was a pop and a fizzle behind Hamilton as he swung it backwards. The bra caught fire and he dropped it in an open area on the ground. A fireman ran out from behind the truck, an extinguisher in his hand, spraying a fog of white smoke and powder on the burning bra.

"Medical team, move!" shouted Bernard. The doctor was already on his way.

They rounded the truck, then stopped short.

Harry was lying naked on his back, Jen straddling his face. Her hands were on his breasts.

"Ohhh, that's hot," said George, the wise cracking EMT.

Harry looked at Jen who was laughing.

"Guess they'll really have something to talk about now down at the station," he said.

A flashbulb went off in the crowd.

Chapter 53

Minor Details

"Hold those tits," said Bernard.

Jen was taking them to be detonated. The Doctor had just removed them from Harry and given them to her for disposal.

"Bring them over here so I can take a few pictures. I need the numbers off them." He took out a small notebook from his pocket. Jen read the numbers while he scribbled them down. He took a camera out of the other pocket and snapped a few pictures. "Okay, get them out of here."

The EMTs had Harry on a stretcher. He was out cold but he looked okay.

"Take good care of him," said Bernard.

They loaded him in the back of the ambulance and pulled away. Emergency responders were everywhere, so many it looked like the set of a disaster movie.

Detective Sommers walked up to him. "I think we got this one wrapped up, Lieutenant," he said.

"What makes you say that?"

Sommers held up a cell phone, his hands clad in plastic gloves. "Sicko took pictures of his work. I got several shots of Crumstein going down." He punched a few buttons and showed Bernard. "Murder and arson," he said.

"What else you got?" asked Bernard.

"Rita said in her statement that the piece of stinking meat in there is what's left of Dick Sooka," he said. "A little DNA should support that."

"Yeah, what else?"

"There's the missing dress hanging on the wall," he said.

"Anything else?" asked Bernard.

"What else you need?" asked Sommers.

"I just want you to be sure the evidence is correct. I already have one detective that's convinced somebody else killed Sooka and Crumstein."

Sommers smiled. "I'm just getting started Lieutenant. Give me some time and I'll seal this case for good."

"Take the time you need and get it right," said Bernard. He looked off in the distance and smiled. "This is just going to ruin Van Dorn's day," he said.

Sommers laughed. "Not to mention the Mayor."

The emergency lights of the cars and trucks lit up the night. Bernard rubbed his eyes. It had been a long day and it was shaping up to be a long night. "Looks like you have things under control here, Jason."

"Yes, sir," he said.

"I'm going home."

Chapter 54

Recovery Room

"Why do I hurt so much?" asked Harry.

"You've been through a lot," said the nurse. "Doctors had you under for almost five hours of nonstop surgery. That's a long time. You've been sleeping for three days."

"Five hours?" asked Harry. "What did they do?"

The nurse checked his vitals. "Now, now. You just rest. I'll tell your doctor that you're awake and he'll come and talk to you."

"But I need to know..."

"Please, don't get agitated." She went to the intravenous pole and turned up the drug drip. Harry calmed down and drifted back into sleep. Deep restful sleep. His fears tried to resurface. Exploding breasts, missing crotch, stolen ribs, but it all merged into one big warm thing that felt like a lounge chair on the beach in the Caribbean. He closed his eyes and began to dream.

"Mr. Takanawa?"

It was the Doctor. "Can you hear me, Mr. Takanawa?"

Harry, still in his island dream, thought he heard the bartender or waiter coming to take his order.

"No. No. Virgin Coloda for me. Thanks."

"Harry?"

He opened his eyes. "I know where I am," he said. "Hospital."

"Sounded like you'd rather go back where you were," said the Doctor.

"St. Thomas, I think," said Harry. "I was about to go diving."

"Well, we'll let you get back there in a moment," he said. "You sound lucid, aware of your surroundings. Glad you're with us now. I was worried about you. Now that you're awake, I need to explain to you what we've done."

Harry noticed the man in the suit standing next to the wall behind the doctor. He was listening carefully while pretending not to listen. Just a casual guy in a suit hanging out while your doctor discusses intimate details.

"And you are?" Harry asked the suit.

"Ray Donaldson, Hospital Counsel," he said. "Please continue, Doctor."

"You were lucky, Mr. Takanawa. Except for some minor problems, you're going to be okay.

"Minor problems?" asked Harry. The devil was always in the details.

"You had a long list of problems when you came to us," said the Doctor. "Some were life threatening, some were not. We had to contact your next of kin, your ex-wife."

"She's not my ex-wife. We're still married."

"You may believe that, however, I met her, Mr. Takanawa," said the suit. "Whatever the truth may be, she prefers to be called your ex-wife. The fact remains; it was her insurance that covered your expenses. That, and some charitable donations."

Harry gulped. Why was his throat suddenly dry? He reached for the water cup on his nightstand and felt a spasm of pain in his chest. The Doctor eased him back against the pillows. He stepped out in the hall and stopped someone. "Nurse, this patient needs a glass of water," he said.

Harry stared at the water glass on his nightstand. The nurse came in, handed it to him, and quickly left the room.

The Doctor began again. "As I was saying, your ex-wife acted on your behalf and as your advocate."

The suit spoke again. "Let me say, your case was quite unique, Mr. Takanawa. Your ex-wife really took us to task on some interpretations of the law."

"She's a shark," said Harry. "Best divorce lawyer in Bellevue."

"I'm aware of her reputation. Anyway, as your advocate and next of kin, she authorized all your procedures. Now, you did say she is your wife?"

"Despite what she says," he said.

The doctor presented Harry with a clipboard full of forms. "Then sign here," he said. He put a pen in Harry's hand and pointed to a blank on the first page. Harry scribbled.

He flipped a page. "And here," he said, repeating the steps.

"And here." This went on several times before Harry asked. "What's this all about?"

"Almost done," said the Doctor. "Just two more." He sounded like a Pilates coach trying to get a student to go for one more squeeze of the thighs.

Harry signed, signed, and signed one more time. The doctor handed the forms to the suit who made them disappear like scarves in the hands of a cheap stage magician.

"So, give me the quick story, Doc. Did you fix my ribs?"

"Well, we didn't replace your ribs, your insurance said it was cosmetic. You can always do that at a later time. We have titanium ribs that we can implant..."

"Sounds expensive," said Harry.

"It can be," he said. "But we didn't do that. As I said, we mostly treated you for life threatening problems. The amateur surgeon who removed the ribs actually did a good job. He knew exactly where to cut. Took only the floating ribs. Minimally evasive. Very clean. We took x-rays and did MRI scans before we did any work and didn't really see the need to revisit your ribs."

"He did good work," said Harry.

"He knew exactly where to cut, even beveled the wounds for nominal impact."

"Probably why I don't hurt so much right now."

"Could be," said the Doctor. He was serious.

"Maybe if he were alive right now he could show you some technique," said Harry. "Maybe help you write a paper about rib extraction for the New England Journal of Medicine."

The doctor looked away.

Harry rolled around under the blanket. "What about my crotch?" he asked.

"Wait," said the Doctor. "Before you break something. Be patient, let's look together." He pulled back the covers.

Harry looked down at his body. "I have breasts," he said.

"Yes," said the doctor proudly. "We managed to salvage them for you."

The suit stepped forward. "Legally, we had an obligation to restore you to the same condition as when we found you. That meant breast implants. Your ex-wife was adamant about it."

"She's not my ex-wife," said Harry. "We're still married."

"Sorry," said the suit. "I know that's true. She knows it's true. She just prefers to be known as your ex-wife."

Harry looked down at the breasts.

"Doctor Litchfield did an incredible job in the field with you explant and implant. He was a field surgeon, you know, like at a MASH unit. Your breast pocket had already been modified by the other implants. To not replace them would have risked scarring and ultimately misshapen breasts. We agreed with Dr. Litchfield's assessment. He did the best thing for you and your wife agreed."

"Emergency breast implants? In the field?" Harry couldn't believe it. Even though it was once his fantasy to have breasts, it was now his nightmare. He really didn't want them, but what could he do now? "Where'd they come from?"

"Donated by the Bellevue Woman's League," said the doctor. "God those women are great. I don't know what the hospital would do without them."

"They donated breast implants?" asked Harry.

"God bless 'em," said the Doctor. "Don't worry," he said. "Millions of women get their implants replaced every year. Your operation was a complete success."

"But I'm not a woman," said Harry.

"Look. You had bigger problems down south." The doctor glanced at Harry's crotch. "Fortunately, the nut case that did this to you didn't do any permanent damage. Let's have a look."

He took a small scissors from his pocket and clipped some bandages around Harry's crotch. Harry watched, unable to hide his anticipation.

The doctor finished cutting, then pulled back the bandages. There was little Harry, all limp and wrinkly, but glad to be there.

"Seems this amateur doctor just slipped a catheter in the end of your penis and sewed it in place. A little tube ran to the back of your leg and was clamped at the end. That's how you were going to the bathroom. He then gathered up a clump of loose skin, mostly from your inner thigh, and pulled it up over the penis and sewed it place on the opposite side. Made it look like bare skin. He padded it with sterile sponges to smooth it out. Very bizarre, but very good work. We were able to recover everything."

Well, there's something to be happy about.

"Meanwhile, if you feel up to it, there have been some anxious people wanting to see you. I recommend a few days rest, but after that, would you like to receive visitors?"

"Yes," said Harry. "That would be nice." He looked down at his body. There would be some changes to get used to. All this can be fixed later if he really wanted. For now, go with the flow. Everything happens for a reason.

Chapter 55

Scars

Echoes of the past can sometimes take a long time to return. Something shouted at the top of your soul one day in your youth can return years later, well into middle age or adulthood. Then there are times it comes right back at you, bouncing off the walls of the shower like an off key song. Echoes. We hear our own voice call us, sometimes more than once. It has something to do with acoustics and large impervious layers of rock too thick to absorb anything.

Maybe that's why Harry needed quiet now. He had found the thick rock barriers deep in his soul, whether by echo location or by running headlong into them, he had no choice but to recognize their existence. Psychologists say we sometimes put these barriers up ourselves. Jersey Barricades that keep us on the narrow road of life, or at least within limits we define for ourselves.

Then, how do you figure someone like Couture into this? Someone who rips you out of your comfort zone. Someone who wields terror like a loaded gun in a bank. Give me all your money or the pregnant bitch gets it. Like taking away someone else's future will make your own any better.

Still, they leave behind scars. The brutals who share heart with Couture are good at this business.

Harry ran his finger across a jagged line near his crotch where Couture had sewn his skin together. He felt the bruises on his face, the swollen mound where he had been beaten.

These are the scars he could see.

The ones he couldn't see were just as real. They could easily be touched by a phrase of words from a stranger or an idle thought that wandered behind the barricades. A smell could bring them back, or a sound, or any number of somatic memories stored deep in his body.

The scars would be there for a while.

A social worker came to visit him. He couldn't remember what they talked about but he felt better afterwards. He did remember her saying it would take time.

The doctor said it was okay for him to have visitors now. Binky came to see him first. He had a newspaper in his hand and some flowers.

"These are for you," he said. "Get well soon."

"Thanks," said Harry. "Where's Farnsworth?"

"He's outside," said Binky. "I wanted to see you alone."

"What's up?"

Binky held up the newspaper. "You're a celebrity it seems." The headlines read "Detective Survives Booby Trap."

Harry laughed.

Binky handed him the newspaper. "You can read it later," he said.

"Thanks, old friend."

Binky smiled. "It's good to hear you say those words."

"In my darkest moment, I thought of you," he said. "I don't think I could have beaten him without you."

"What do you mean?" asked Binky.

"It wasn't me that killed the monster. It was Fu Chan."

"Fu Chan is back? Fu Chan?"

"She never left, Binky." Harry pointed to his head. "She was here all the time."

"I always liked Fu Chan. She's the smartest detective in the world," said Binky.

"Of course you like her. She was your invention," said Harry.

"You may think that, but it wasn't all me," said Binky. "You had a lot to do with her too. You made her real."

"I'll say one thing, I'm glad we practiced all those ninja cheerleader moves." Harry laughed for a minute, then his voice cracked and he started to cry. His breathing was terse, and he hid his head. "That high heel went right into his brain."

Binky was silent for a while. He put his hand on Harry's shoulder. "Rita told me that he made you walk in those heels on a treadmill," he said. "Seems like poetic justice to me."

Harry tried to wipe away the tears. His hands were trembling. "I don't think of myself as an instrument of justice."

Binky pulled a tissue from a box on the nightstand and handed it to Harry. "He had it coming, Harry. It was you or him. You're a hero."

"That's what they told me during the war. I thought I left those days behind."

"The world needs heroes," said Binky.

"At what price?"

Binky didn't have much to say after that. He knew Harry had enough for the day. He wished him well and told him not to worry. On his way out he stopped at the nurse's station and asked her to send in the social worker. The social worker wasn't available so they called the doctor. The doctor put Harry on a tranquilizer drip.

It was two more days before he had another visitor.

When he awoke he was surrounded with stuff. There were flowers and gifts everywhere. Lenny had sent him a boom box with a few cd's. Harry wondered who had sold him that. It wasn't in the best condition but it worked.

The biggest floral arrangement by far was sent by Carrie Rodriguez. "She delivered them personally," said one of the nurses. "She spoke with you for a long time but you weren't very coherent." She smiled. "Do you remember that?"

"No," Harry admitted.

"She also left you a complete set of DVDs for all the past seasons of Designer Derby."

The Bellevue Women's League sent him flowers and a gift card from Nordstrom's. There was a sweet note that began, "Dear Ms. Takanawa..." Poor ladies must still think he's a woman.

There were flowers and a card full of cash from his friends down at the police station. They had taken up a collection for him. He netted over two hundred dollars and a ticket to the policeman's ball.

There were pictures taped to the wall, drawn by the finest artists in Mrs. White's Second Grade class at Woodside Elementary School in Bothell. There was a picture of him in front of an American flag with the words "You're a hero," written at the bottom.

There was a Claxton fruit cake and also two fruit baskets.

There was a goldfish in a bowl with a card taped to it from an unknown admirer.

His wife had given him a new bra, the words, "You'll be needing this. Ha!" written inside and signed, "You can thank me later, your X."

There was even a small bouquet with a card made out to Fu Chan.

But in the midst of all this love and admiration Harry still felt bad. The Doctor came to see him that day and told him he was being released. He gave him a long list of things to do, recommended outpatient counseling, and follow up visits. He handed him a brochure titled "Recovering from your breast augmentation surgery" and left him alone.

Red came to pick him up. Bernard had arranged for the Volvo to be released from impound. Red had some trouble driving it at first. The car had its quirks.

An intern and a nurse both helped Red move everything. They loaded up two wheelchairs like shopping carts and a third that held Harry. A hospital volunteer carried the rest making it an odd parade from the hospital room to the far off parking garage where they loaded the car and drove off.

Harry was quiet. He sat and stared out the window. Seattle seemed so gray now, so empty. The drizzly rain was oppressive instead of nourishing. The trees and grass, normally flushed with shades of green, blended with the colors of the now drab buildings.

She kept asking him if he was okay.

"I'm sorry," he finally said. "I'm not very coherent. Not very good company."

"We went through a lot," she said.

"At least you're intact," he said. "I feel so... deformed."

"No, no," she said. "You're not deformed."

"There's something missing, something different," he said. "You know how you feel after having a tooth pulled? I can feel the empty hole with my tongue and it just doesn't feel right."

"You'll get used to it," she said.

"Used to what? These?" he stared down at his breasts. He no longer had the option of taking them off and storing them in a little suitcase in the corner of his closet. They were a permanent part of him.

"When we first met you were honest with me. You told me you wanted breasts."

"Not like this, Rita," he said.

"No," she said. "I remember you saying if you had the money you'd get breast implants."

"A childish wish," he said.

"Still, it's something you wished for. Why can't you accept that it's a wish come true."

Harry was silent.

Red put a hand on his shoulder. "I didn't get hurt like you did. He tried to kill me, but he didn't operate on me. He didn't have time to mess with my head."

"He didn't eat your fucking ribs!" said Harry.

"No, he didn't," she said. "But don't assume I came through this unscathed. He took my dignity, stole my freedom, and he beat me in a fist fight. That's the only thing I have to say about it. At least I gave it my best. I think in a fair fight I would have bested him. He's not the better man."

"Better man," Harry blurted. The Marine inside was crying for, what, lost manhood? He didn't really know. Confusing waves of emotion pounded against the shores of his sanity. He turned towards the window to hide the wetness in his eyes. His reflection did nothing to comfort him. The nurse had brushed his long hair and clipped it in back. Even without makeup his appearance had changed. The bruises stood out prominently and he looked like a battered woman. Fu Chan begged him to let her help but he had her zipped tight and back in her clamshell. The Jersey barriers were holding for now.

"Look, you can dwell on the past or you can face the future. Everything that has been done to you can be fixed. Maybe fixed is not the right word. 'Put back the way it was' might be a better description. You're in control again. The reward money is coming, plenty of it. You can do whatever you want with it, even take a vacation. But you have to move forward. It's the only direction to go."

He grunted.

Red decided to change the subject. She started with slow conversation but once she got going she talked the whole way home. Harry mostly sat and listened.

"I've been taking care of the office," she said. "I go in every day. There've been a lot of calls from all kinds of people. I have a list at the office. I refused all interviews and told them you were still recovering. Some got a little belligerent with me. Well, I didn't respond well and you might hear some things about me."

"Uh huh," said Harry. "Like what?"

"Just some things. You know how I get riled. People piss me off when they get pushy. They were just reporters." She paused. "Anyway, I don't think they'll be coming back. Not soon anyway." She paused again. "Not without their lawyers."

Harry tried to imagine the scene. In his mind she did him a favor. He didn't want to deal with the press.

"I collected money from Lenny and paid the office rent," she said. "At least Binky and that creep Farnsworth are off your back. And Lenny has more work for us. I got it all lined up, I just need you to show me what to do. You never did teach me how to do a skip trace. I was going to just ask Bernard but I wanted to wait for you. Lenny has been persistent and all you have to do is get me started."

He said nothing, just stared out the window. He was drifting like flotsam.

"Oh, yeah," said Red. "The web site is just about finished. Just need to show it to you before we go live with it. It's so cool, you can even register on line and join your fan club. My friend says you should cash in on your sudden popularity. He has an idea for some t-shirts he'd like to discuss with you. I think somebody beat him to it, though. I hear someone is selling shirts up on Broadway with your picture on them with the words 'Ultimate Designer Derby Challenger' on the front. The back is supposed to have Carol Huntington on it with 'Sore Loser' under it."

Harry remained quiet.

"Anyway, that's what I heard. I was going to try to track them down but I didn't have time. I've been busy, too. My boss at The Rose Hips wants me to stay. I'm not as popular as you but it's been good for business. Lots of people stop by to see me. I try not to get caught up in all this." She laughed. "My five minutes of fame."

Harry nodded and moaned.

Red tried something to get a rise out of him. "I met your ex-wife. She came by the hospital to visit you and sign some papers. She's really a nice lady. She says she really loves you but she just can't stand being around you. Something to do with the way you affect her. She says you're bad for each other. She says you're both better off without each other. Sorry that's just the way things are."

Harry nodded.

"Did I tell you about Van Dorn?" she asked. "No, I guess I didn't. He's not a detective anymore. He's been reassigned to some special cadre the Mayor's created. The word is his mother got him that job even though he embarrassed the Mayor completely. Van Dorn took the heat for him and made a public apology, but the worm still came out on top. Bernard's looking for a new acting chief detective."

Harry moaned again. He felt every bump in the road. He was dizzy and all he wanted to do was get home and go to bed. He was tired and sore and his new breasts ached. His mind had been wandering behind the barriers again.

He suddenly blurted out, "Why didn't I see it as a threat?" He started to lose it again.

"What?" asked Red.

"Marines are trained to treat everything as a threat. It was a war zone for God's sake." He was back in the war, manning his position as gunner and watching a team of men push a truck. He was sweating. "I never saw that truck as a threat. I just thought they were trying to get it started." He hid his head.

Red didn't know what to say.

"I'm so stupid," he said. "Too trusting. Even the killer was able to trap me."

When they got to Harry's apartment there was a warning notice taped the door explaining that the power will be disconnected in five days because of an unpaid bill. It was dated ten days after the first. Welcome home.

Red put the first load of stuff on the kitchen table. "I'll bring the rest of the things up from the car," she said. "You just relax. Take a shower or a hot bath if you want." She went downstairs and returned with another load. She refreshed the water in the flowers and put the perishable gifts away. She changed the water and fed the goldfish. On the third trip she noticed it was very quiet. She went in the bedroom and found Harry fully clothed and fast asleep in his bed. She pulled his shoes off covered him with a blanket from the closet.

She pulled the door shut, stopping to remove the notice from the door.

Chapter 56

Charity Begets Charity

Harry woke to exotic smells. Food and the smell of Sue Yen, both sweet in their own way.

She leaned over him. "Oh, good. You're awake." The sound of gentle frying in the background made her voice stand out even more. They came to him like a song, a rhythm and a melody. "How are you feeling?"

"A little disoriented," said Harry.

"It'll pass," she said. "I'm always like that in the morning. Until I've had my coffee. Do you like coffee?"

"Yeah," he said.

"Mom doesn't like coffee. She prefers tea. She's brewing some up for you now. Want me to go get you some?" She started to move away.

"No, no," said Harry. "Please stay here with me."

She sat down on the edge of the bed and smiled. "If that's what you want."

"Thanks," said Harry. "How'd you get in here?"

"Your front door was open. Do you always leave it open?"

"Not always," he said.

Her eyes moved to the corner of the room. He followed them. "I have a present for you," she said. She walked over to the chair in the corner and took a bag off the seat. She reached in and pulled out a pair of boots. Harry recognized them as the ones he had broken on the dock in the fight with Couture. She turned the bottoms up so he could see. The heel had been repaired and the boots shined like new.

He chuckled and she set them back in the chair. "Thank you," he said.

"They were too expensive to throw away," she said.

"Expensive to get fixed?" he asked.

"Not really," she said. "Mister Osaka down in the International District fixed them. I told him they were for me but he didn't believe me. He knows my feet aren't that big."

"Can't fool the old timers," he said. "They have kind of a quiet version of street smarts."

There was a pot of hot water, a dishrag, and liquid soap sitting on the floor next to the chair. "I have to clean you up. Mom wants to feed you and check your wounds. She thinks she's your doctor."

"She did a great job last time she was here," he started to shake and she reached for him. He flinched and she stopped, concern reflecting on her face. He took her hand. "Sorry," he said. The word 'Doctor' had triggered something behind the Jersey Barricades. "I've been seeing too many Doctors lately," he said.

She squeezed his hand and let go, sliding her fingers across his palm like an angel dancing across a cloud. She got the pot, dipped the washcloth in it and moved it next to the bed. "Let's see how you look."

Harry held the covers tight against his chest. He was embarrassed. He didn't know why, he just didn't want anyone to see him. Not like this, all mutilated and such.

"There's nothing to be ashamed of," she said. "I've seen it all before. Remember, I'm studying to be a nurse."

"You haven't seen anything like this," he said.

"Ok," she said, accepting his resistance for now. She tried another approach. She went to her purse on a chair in the corner of the room and took out a hairbrush. She cleaned it a bit then came back to the bed. "This is something that always made me feel better," she said. She gently reached behind him and propped him up. She began to brush his hair, slowly, gently. "Feels good, huh?" she asked. He nodded and she continued. "I like you with long hair," she said. "Looks good on you."

"Yeah?" he said.

She brushed the hair down his back, pulling it away from the surgical bra. He felt her hand on his back. She rubbed his shoulders a little, then went back to brushing his hair.

"What happened?" she asked. "Who beat you up this time?" She stopped brushing. "I'm sorry, if you don't want to talk about it..."

"It's okay," said Harry. "I should talk about it. The question is, do you want to hear about it?"

"Yes," she said. She started brushing again. "I'm curious. All I know is what I read in the papers."

The frying stopped. Mrs. Lee popped her head in the room. "Food almost ready," she said to Harry. She turned to Sue Yen. "You get busy," she said. Her voice had the twang of his old drill instructor. "I told you. Take all his clothes off and clean him up good. Now!"

"Yes, Ma'am," she said.

Momma went back in the kitchen. Sue looked at Harry. He lowered the blanket, realizing he had been holding it over his breasts like a girl.

She didn't stare. She approached it like a nurse, a true professional. She undid the surgical bra and put it aside. She cleaned his body. Harry told her bits and pieces and she listened. She never coaxed him and accepted it all at his pace. It all sounded too gruesome, too fantastic to be real, like some story a kid would make up to explain why he lost his homework assignment.

Mrs. Lee brought in soup, something made of fresh fried noodles with thin slabs of beef and vegetables and spices all in a nourishing broth. She gave the bowl to Sue Yen and told her to feed Harry while she looked him over.

"See what they've done to me?" said Harry.

"They do pretty good job for American doctors," said Mrs. Lee. "I have just the thing for these scars." She went to the kitchen.

She didn't bother to cover him again. No false modesty in her eye. Sue continued to feed him.

"What do you think?" asked Harry.

"About what?" she asked.

"These." He pointed his chest up.

"Nice," she said. "You know you'll have to wear a bra now."

"Figured that," he said.

"What made you decide to keep them?"

"Doctor's advice. My wife made the decision for me. I was incapacitated."

"She's your ex-wife, isn't she? What made her think you wanted breasts?"

"I think it's revenge for what I put her through. She had trouble with my cross dressing."

"What kind of trouble?"

"The usual," said Harry. "She thought because I had this thing for women's clothes that it was somehow all her doing, like she was somehow less of a woman. Really it had nothing to do with her. I was cross dressing before we ever got married."

"Did you tell her up front when you were dating?"

"Of course. She thought she could change me."

"All women think they can change their husband, after marriage, of course."

"I didn't cross dress for a long time after we were married. I really don't know how it got started again, but it did get in the way of our relationship."

"Kind of funky if you ask me," she said. "But what really matters is how you feel. Are you happy with the changes?"

"I'm not so sure," he said. "Used to be I wanted to look more like a woman. Now I want to look more like a man."

"That's going to be hard, but it's not impossible. You can always bind your breasts. And you can cut your hair, of course."

"I don't know what I'm going to do. The doctor recommended I recover from all my injuries before making any decisions. He said give it a year."

"A year?"

"That's what he said. The killer messed up my chest muscles when he operated. My insides need time to heal properly before they can take another operation. Did I tell you he cut out my lower ribs?"

She put her hand gently on the scars in his side. "Is that what this is?"

"Yeah," he said.

"Why did he do that?"

"He wanted to eat them," said Harry.

"Ewww," she said.

"He did eat them. At least I think he did. That's what he told me anyway. My sides hurt like crap. I didn't feel it while I was all drugged up but now I can hardly move."

She shook her head. "It sounds horrible," she said. "You're lucky to be alive."

Mrs. Lee came back in. She had a thick black salve with her that she began to smear on Harry's wounds. It was strong with the smell of herbs.

"You have to finish your soup," she said. "You need your strength."

"Yes, ma'am," said Harry.

"Later this week we come back. I fix you more kway teow."

He smiled. "Thank you. You don't have to."

"I want to," she said. "Selfish reasons, though. I never know when I may need you again." She finished applying the salve and barked some instructions to Sue Yen. "I have to go now," she said to Harry. "Sue Yen will finish dressing the wounds and clean up the kitchen. Also vacuum house and clean bathrooms. Get rid of germs. I leave you some tea. Please drink it all. I'll be back tomorrow."

"Thank you, Mrs. Lee," said Harry.

"You're a good boy," she said. "This also my way of saying thank you." She nodded to Sue and went to the kitchen to gather up some things. Harry heard her say goodbye and leave.

Sue went back to feeding him. "You'd better do what Mom says."

Harry went to take the bowl from her but she pulled it away. "Let me feed you. The less you use your chest muscles the better. Give it all time to heal."

He accepted her kindness. It would have been an insult otherwise, a sign of arrogance. Besides, he needed the help.

She vacuumed the house, cleaned the kitchen, cleaned the bathroom, even dumped the trash. The apartment reeked with the smell of pine disinfectant and floral fragrance.

"Hospital clean," she said.

She began to bathe him again. There were many spots she missed. "Momma told me to do a good job. You heard her."

"Do you always do what your momma tells you?" asked Harry

"Do you?"

"I try to," said Harry. "She usually has good advice."

"So does mine." Her hand moved across his chest, brushing against his breasts. She wiped the dirt and the pain away.

She washed his abdomen, steadily moving lower towards his legs.

"Oh look," she said, stopping at his penis. "At least he's fully functional."

"He's tired," said Harry.

"That's not what I'm seeing."

"That always happens in the morning," he said.

"Are you sure?" she asked.

"It will go away after I pee," he said.

"I know another way to make it go away."

Chapter 57

The Reward

"Rita, this is Bernard. I need to see you and Harry as soon as possible." The phone call was curt, businesslike.

"What's up?" she asked.

"Is Harry in?"

"No, he's still hiding in his apartment."

"It's important. It's about the reward. Bring him down here. In a wheel chair if you need to."

Rita coaxed him out of the apartment. She drove him downtown in the old Volvo. It was getting used to her. Harry wore a loose shirt, trying to hide what had happened to him, as if he could not accept it even now. He tied his hair back as Sue Yen had suggested. He wore one of his old sport coats, even though it didn't fit right.

"How you feeling, Harry," said Matt. Every eye in the office seemed to be on him.

"Okay," he said.

"And you, Rita?"

"I'm good."

"Come into my office." He pulled them along, refusing to say anything until the office door was closed. He sat behind his desk and they took up the chairs facing him.

"First a little business," he said. "I got a couple of statements for you to sign." He picked up a bundle of papers and spread it out before them. Red looked them over.

"Disclosure forms, statements of limited liability, services billed to the city, release of property, what is all this?" asked Rita

"Just the usual paperwork. Oh, and another thing. I got the paperwork for your license." He shuffled through the pile and showed her the certificate and binding conditions. She squealed. "Don't leave my office without signing the papers," he said.

Harry looked at the papers spread on the desk and started signing. If Matt needed his signature it was his.

Red signed where she needed, which was everywhere Bernard pointed.

Bernard held up a large manila envelope. It was a thick, padded, a shipping envelope with bubble wrap, thick with reward. He passed it to Rita and Harry.

Harry looked at Rita and she took it. Inside was a plaque and a letter. She read the letter.

Dear Mister Takanawa and Miss Rockwell:

Thank you so much for recovering the last dress designed by Richard Sooka himself. This garment has been valued at a minimum of seven hundred thousand dollars. Without your diligent effort, we would be missing the very centerpiece of our ball. The profits from the auction will benefit millions of individuals across the nation who depend on our charity.

Your generous donation was well received and our organization, The Seattle League of Retired Designers, a 501.3c charity, has included a receipt with this letter for your tax purposes. Please think of us often, now and in your will, as you will forever be in our thoughts. A copy of the enclosed plaque hangs in the hall of our offices, ascribed with your names, in commemoration of the noble deeds you have done.

Please accept this along with our fondest thank you, and best wishes for your future.

Sincerely,

Constance B. Wallington,
Chair and Senior Donations Coordinator
Seattle League of Retired Designers

She read it again then passed it to Harry, who read it himself. She looked at the plaque, an inscribed gold plated square of metal tacked to a piece of dark varnished wood. The logo of the League stood out prominently at the top, the gold plate filled with script writing. "For unsurpassed generosity and dedication to the Seattle League of Retired Designers, Lifetime Members." Almost as an afterthought, and if you looked very close in a different script, Harry and Rita's names were inscribed at the bottom. Beneath that in larger letters, the date and signature of Constance B. Wallington.

"This is it?" asked Rita.

"What did you expect?" asked Bernard.

"Money," she said.

Bernard laughed. "I thought you knew."

"Knew what?" she asked.

"Charity rewards always end up as donations. Like the annual motorcycle raffle the police have, or the fireman's raffle. The prize is usually donated back to the organization by the winner."

"I never heard that," said Rita.

"Shoot," said Bernard. "Nobody takes the prize. It's considered bad form."

"What am I going to do with a tax receipt for a seven hundred thousand dollar donation?"

"Claim it on your taxes," said Bernard.

"I don't even make enough to claim myself, let alone seven hundred thousand dollars."

Bernard didn't know what to say. "Sorry," he said. He turned to Harry. "How you feeling?"

"A little messed up, but other than that..."

"You back at work yet?"

"Taking it easy," he said. "One day at a time."

"Only way to take it," said Bernard. "We're pretty much done with the Sooka case. The papers you signed sealed all the holes. We found your ribs in the trash. His teeth marks were all over them."

Harry looked away.

"Thought you'd want to know," said Bernard. "You were right about the Greenlake Butcher. We found two more sets of implants when we searched his lair. Numbers on the implants matched up with the victims. Another case closed."

Rita was disgusted. A plaque, a letter, and a tax deduction. "Back to skip traces," she said.

"Huh?" said Bernard.

"Never mind," she said.

"So, who's the new acting lead detective?" asked Harry. "I heard something about Van Dorn transferring to the Mayor's special cadre."

Bernard laughed. "Yeah. I don't know what that cadre does, but he's in charge of it. How do you screw things up and get a promotion out of it?"

"Just ask his mother next time you see her," said Harry. "So, who has my old job?"

"I had to give it to someone. Jason Sommers is the new acting chief detective."

"So you accept the fact that I'm not coming back," he said.

"I think I accepted it a long time ago," said Matt. "I just couldn't follow through. Besides, like I told you, I like the new arrangement better. You're the one who said you can get things done that I can't. This case proves it. I got too many procedures and regulations to follow. You don't have these restrictions."

"True that," said Harry.

Bernard scooped up the papers on his desk, held them in both hands and clapped them on edge, organizing them into a neat pile. He went through them, checking for signatures and adding paper clips as he broke them into individual bundles. He picked up his phone and called for his administrative assistant Nan.

"Make a set of copies of these documents for me, then scan the originals for records retention."

"Yes, sir," she said. She stared at Harry but he avoided eye contact with her. She took the papers and left.

Bernard made small talk until Nan returned. "That will be all, Nan," he said. He opened several file folders on his desk and distributed the papers, moving them to folders on his desk. He took the copies and gave them to Harry. "For your files," he said. Harry folded them and stuffed them in the inside breast pocket of his sport coat.

Rita felt like throwing the plaque in the trash on her way out. "So, that's it?" she asked.

"Just about," said Bernard.

Harry went to get out of his seat.

"One more thing," said Bernard. He put the folders away, two in the credenza behind him and one in the desk drawer beside him. His desk was clean except for a white business envelope. He slid the envelope across the desk to Harry and smiled.

Harry opened it. There was a check for five thousand dollars and change in it. "What's this?"

"Your fee," he said. "Didn't you read the papers you signed?"

"I guess not," he said.

"One of them was a contract for services to the city. Remember me telling you about that?"

"I remember something."

"Well, look it up. Meanwhile, cash the check before the Mayor decides to earmark the money for his special cadre."

Bernard stood up and reached for Harry's hand. They shook, the way men do, firm and strong, just like their friendship had always been. You could see in Bernard's eye that he wanted to say more, that he would have liked to take all of Harry's pain away. An impossible thing to do, but sometimes a man can feel strong enough to do anything.

Harry finally felt fit enough to return to work.

Chapter 58

Now What?

"We have to go shopping for a bra," said Red. "Several."

"No way," said Harry.

"You can't put on the same one every day. And don't even wear that surgical bra anymore. It's tacky and it stinks."

"I can get away with it a few more weeks," he said.

"You need at least three more bras. One to wear, one in the drawer, and one in the laundry at any given time."

"I don't want to spend money on underwear," he said.

"Why?" asked Red. "The office is paid for. First and last month's rent plus a fat deposit. Same goes for your apartment."

"Yeah," said Harry. So this is what an entrepreneur was supposed to feel like. There were other rewards beside money. "And Binky is my friend again," said Harry.

"He always was," said Red. "He put us on this case and he fed us clues."

"He always wanted to be a detective. Maybe I should talk him into applying for my old job on the force."

"Ha," laughed Red. "I can see him working for Bernard." She sat down at her desk. "So what are we going to do now?"

"Start thinking about next month's rent," he said. "It's back to skip traces and surveillance."

"That doesn't sound very exciting," she said.

"But it pays the bills. We can't catch mass murderers every day, Rita. Big crimes don't always come our way."

"Why not?" asked Red.

The phone rang. Harry picked it up and answered. A familiar voice spoke at the other end.

"Harry? This is Bernard. I think you'd better get down here right away."

THE END

We hope you enjoyed reading *Case of the Missing Dick*. Harry Takanawa will be back in the sequel, *Dial M for Milkmaid*, due out in fall 2013. Look for it at amazon.com or check our website at halfabook.com.

Okay, so Harry won't be the only one back. So will Big Red and Bernard and Binky and Lenny and oh yeah Trish, Harry's ex who really isn't his ex, but she wants everyone to think she is, she'll be back. She even has a big part in the book. She turns up missing, disappears in a woman's dressing room, so Harry in his infinite wisdom decides to dress up in drag and go looking for her. Like that Hun guarding the dressing room entrance doesn't see through that disguise! Anyway, he finds her all right, gets thrown in a cell with her. How'd you like to be in lockdown with your ex? Talk about hell.

Okay, don't want to give away too much. Couture won't be back. Sorry, no trick villain popping up from the dead for one more terrorizing act. I know it happens all the time but not in this sequel. And no Son of Couture either. The new villain is Mr. Che and he is creepy in a whole new way. He gets his jollies making other people do bad things and he wants to build a six sigma corporation dedicated to crime. Of course, only one person can bring him down, and you know she'll be back.

Who? The only one I haven't mentioned yet: Fu Chan.